P9-BZI-114

Sofia

BY ANN CHAMBERLIN
FROM TOM DOHERTY ASSOCIATES

Sofia

Tamar

Sofia

ANN CHAMBERLIN

FORGE

A TOM DOHERTY ASSOCIATES BOOK

NEW YORK

FINKELSTEIN
MEMORIAL LIBRARY
SPRING VALLEY, N.Y.

00488 9712

This is a work of fiction. All the characters and events portrayed in this novel
are either fictitious or are used fictitiously.

SOFIA

Copyright © 1996 by Ann Chamberlin

All rights reserved, including the right to reproduce this book, or portions
thereof, in any form.

Map by Ellisa Mitchell

This book is printed on acid-free paper.

A Forge Book
Published by Tom Doherty Associates, Inc.
175 Fifth Avenue
New York, NY 10010

Forge® is a registered trademark of Tom Doherty Associates, Inc.

Library of Congress Cataloging-in-Publication Data

Chamberlin, Ann.
    Sofia / Ann Chamberlin.—1st ed.
      p.   cm.
    "A Tom Doherty Associates book."
    ISBN 0-312-86110-9 (alk. paper)
    I. Title.
PS3553.H2499S6 1996
813'.54—dc20   95-36251
                                                  CIP

First Edition: April 1996

Printed in the United States of America

0 9 8 7 6 5 4 3 2 1

This book is dedicated to
Debra Sandack
and the Book Club
who read it first.

ACKNOWLEDGMENTS

I'D LIKE TO thank first of all the Wasatch Mountain Fiction Writers Friday Morning Group for their support, patience, and friendship. Harriet Klausner and Betina Lindsey know the part they played. I'd like to thank Teddi Kachi, Judy Brunvand, Leonard Chiarelli, and the folks at the Marriott, Whitmore, and Holladay Libraries in Salt Lake City, especially Hermione Bayas in the Middle East section. My cousins Kourken Daglian and Ruth Mentley, my dear friend Alexis Bar-Lev, and Dr. James M. Kelly unstintingly shared their expertise with me.

I owe a great deal to the friendly people in Turkey, especially the guides at the Topkapi palace who hardly raised a brow as I went through the harem again and again. I'd like to thank my in-laws for their support and my husband and sons for their patience while my mind was elsewhere. And I'd like to thank the proprietors of Sofia's in New York City.

None of these people is to be blamed for the errors I've committed, only thanked for saving me from making more.

And finally, of course, there is Natalia Aponte, my editor, and Virginia Kidd, my agent, without whom *The Reign* would have existed, but never in the light of day.

Vienna

HUNGARY

ROMANIA

OTTOMAN

EMPIRE

Venice

ISTRIA

DALMATIA

Danube River

Adriatic

Italy

Sea

Rome

Edirne

Cons

GREECE

Helles

Sicily

Ionian Sea

Lepanto

Mara

Corfu

Gulf of Lepanto

the

Peloponnesus

Patmos

Malta

Crete

S

Mediterranean

North

○ Empire of Venice

▨ Ottoman Empire

Part I

Giorgio

I

OF ALL THE days in my long life, I remember the day I met Governor Baffo's daughter more than any other.

I, Giorgio Veniero, had climbed a convent wall.

This was no youthful Carnival prank, though it was both the year's season and mine. I'd been told I must do it. I must climb the convent wall to deliver a message. The message was unusual not because of what I must say—which was what the Doge of Venice would say to any young lady under the circumstances—but because of the lady herself. His Serenity's secretary had decided to humor this lady's own singular demands of secrecy.

My blossoming sense of romance and adventure had tingled to life from the first suggestion: I'd jumped at the chance.

I'd never seen a convent garden before, of course; I was no priest. I guess I'd envisioned it in the hull-splitting life of spring. But the naked branches of the plane tree—like hoary, shedding antlers—provided very little cover apart from their woolly winter tassels. Nor did the air—hard, cold, and clear as a diamond.

It was the bare-bone structure of a garden, odorous of moist loam and worms working. The beds were damp but barren, turned over for the season, and against anything but the sky I must stand out like a sapphire on sackcloth. Afraid this would happen, I'd climbed high in the tree. But I was going to be very dependent on the lady's skills of subterfuge, a position of helplessness for which I didn't care.

And my fingers were beginning to grow numb and clumsy with the chill.

She was in the company of her aunt when I saw her. The pair had appeared against the gray stone of the refectory at the far end of the garden. If I stood out like she did—a garnet on a weathered grave marker—I was in serious trouble.

The older woman was part of the stone—and she had her face to me.

My heart skipped a beat and my hands, grown stupid and senseless, slipped their hold. How careless of Madonna Baffo to bring her aunt out into the garden! Or, if this were a chaperon she could not avoid, to let the older woman look directly into my hiding spot—A young man hiding in the convent gardens! Whatever would the old woman say if she saw me?

The aunt's face was a crab apple at winter's end—chafing, red, soft, and wrinkled out of her wimple. It was full of bitterness, the bitterness of a fruit left neglected at the bottom of the bin, the bitterness of virginity consigned to a sisterhood, a sacrifice to the consolidation of the family fortune.

I dared no more than glance at this unhappy nun. If the girl were foolish, I would not add to her foolishness with a misuse of my eyes. And yet I had time to see, besides her features, that the older woman was enthralled in her companion. I can only think that Baffo's daughter knew she had control over her aunt and was playing with the danger as a tightrope walker may pretend to lose his balance for the thrill of having the audience gasp. And why, I ask myself, does the audience stay and watch, but for the thrill of gasping?

When next I dared to look, the older woman was gone—vanished, I knew not where—and she, the younger, was walking toward my hiding spot, whistling the popular tune by which I had been told I would know her. "Whistling girls and crowing hens are sure to come to some bad ends." I laid no particular store by this old wives' cant, only wondered how a patrician girl, raised in a convent, should have contrived to learn such a sure, brazen pipe.

She walked toward me in a manner that let me know I was not the first she had ever met there beneath the plane tree. Although slightly disappointed, I was not surprised. That she had so often managed that conjuring act with her aunt and that she was so young did surprise me, however.

I slid down the tree trunk quickly, hoping to impress with my rigging-learned grace.

Madonna Baffo was tall and womanly for a fourteen-year-old. But most of all, I was surprised by her beauty. Like demon-cold at midnight, she took my breath away.

Others have said it and I, who saw her in her youth before these eulogists were even born, will say it, too. When she walked, it was dancing. She came down the flagstone path with steps that swept like the galliard to the very tilt of her head. It was movement full of fascination to both viewer and executor, sensuous steps matching the popular and ribald tune she whistled. The tune was called, as I remember, "Come to the Budding Grove, My Love."

When she approached, I was compelled to sweep the cap off my head and brush its blue-tinted ostrich feather across the earth before me in a deep bow.

"Madonna Baffo," I said. "May I present myself? I am Giorgio Veniero, at your service, if you please."

"You're the Doge's man."

She stated rather than asked it and her business-like tone made me straighten up at once. But I gained no sobriety looking at her. Convent life was seen in the breach rather than in the compliance of her costume. The "brown" of her dress would really better be called the blush of sun-ripe oranges, and it was trimmed with peach and gold. Like a wanton giggling at her grille, the satin fabric flirted with the sheen of opulence quite naughtily.

Pleats, the depth of my thumbnail, crowded together four times the fabric more modest skirts would take to encircle that same slim waist. The confinement of a fashionably firm bodice was foreshortened and gave plenty of suggestion, through an almost sheer chemise, of the yielding reality beneath.

I thought there was a story in the great puffs of her sleeves: the stern old aunt had been cajoled to a limit of two yards a sleeve. But when her back was turned, the girl had snatched several fistfuls more; even made up, the fabric retained an avidity in the billows. So might Eve's stolen apple have looked in both appeal and wickedness.

"At your service," I repeated, conscious now of an uncomfortable and out-of-place tightness in my codpiece which before had seemed natural and pleasant, and which my foppish bow had aggravated.

I had dressed with care that morning. Knowing I would have walls to climb, I had refrained from my best, knee-length doublet of Turkish velvet, dark blue and shot with gold. That must remain for embassies of a more respectable sort. But I had not been disappointed in the effect of a sleek new pair of hose in varied green and blue, and a blue velvet doublet tucked and slashed to display a clean linen chemise beneath.

Life spent astride the rock and thrust of the sea had given me a fine, strong pair of legs, I knew, fine buttocks, and a fine, lean waist where the doublet pinched in tight and met the top of the hose with a gap for yet more chemise. For all the chill, I had not wanted to spoil the effect with overgarments, so I wore only the shortest of fighting capes. I was at the point of actual periodic shivering now from the long, inactive wait and from the feverish effect she had on me, but I tossed the cape behind my shoulders with a studied attempt at rakishness as I faced her and rubbed at my chin.

I had fussed more than usual with my beard—there wasn't much of it yet—combing and encouraging. In the end, I had shaved it off completely, hoping Madonna Baffo would like the clean-shaven look of the West better than the beard of the East I could not yet attain.

Now I doubted the wisdom of that decision—of anything I did—and it was not just that the only stubble I found on my chin after two hours was in my mind. At fifteen, I had already turned several more experienced hearts, but the self-confidence this had given me now wore thin.

Baffo's daughter fixed me with eyes as cool as brown autumn leaves. Her mouth, which I would later learn to know in its usual pout of delicious fullness, was set thin and firm for our interview. Her study of me was intense, minute, and not without desire. But it was not the complement of the desire which I had suffered as I watched her approach. That desperation so many other girls conceal so ill with blushes and fans was not even hinted at. If she pierced through my young nobleman's trappings, she sought not the flesh beneath, but something else.

I can give that elusive thing a name now, so many years later, whereas then I stood merely baffled and ashamed of what my own feelings were. That part of manhood she coveted of me—of every man she ever met—was power, even though in my case it was no more than the power to climb a convent wall.

Baffo's daughter danced when she moved, not like a courtesan but like a horse at the gate before a race. That afternoon when she was only fourteen years old, the passion that already burned in her was ambition.

"So state your message." She grew impatient with my confusion.

"I have been sent by the Doge with a secret message for you. . . ." I blustered, then faltered.

"It must be a full hour that you've been here." Her impatience exaggerated wildly. "And yet nothing you have said so far is news. I know you are the Doge's man, you know you are the Doge's man. Does every urchin in Venice know you are the Doge's man by now?"

I couldn't answer for watching how her flesh was pillowed against the opulence of her sleeves. She had beautifully sculptured shoulders, collarbones, and a long neck that vied with a string of pearls in whiteness. Her face was a fine oval like a Florentine alabaster egg with a pinch of chin and nose. Its shape was reflected in the heavy, teardrop pearls that hung from her ears, and her eyes were like almonds—that color, large and luscious.

"Come," she insisted, "what does His Serenity the Grand Doge of the Republic of Venice say to my suit? I, Sofia Baffo, daughter of the governor of the island of Corfu, have lately been ordered by my father to join him on that island in the middle of nowhere. It seems he has found a husband for me—some petty noble of the island—by which match he hopes to secure his position so as to govern with efficiency and as little bloodshed among the natives as possible."

Watching her as she spoke, I determined that the most remarkable thing about Baffo's daughter was her hair. Many Venetian ladies endured agonies with lemon and vinegar solutions only to have their hair bleach out to a harsh, lifeless, brittle shock of straw. Her blond, on the other hand, was real and full of life that could not be contained. Like polished gold filigree, it spilled from the somber white linen of her veil, a promiscuity of which, I decided, she was not totally innocent.

She was not innocent, but at the moment totally unaware of her effect. "I am to marry a Corfiot!" she despaired. "I who deserve—! God above, a peasant with dirt under his nails!"

Abashed, I shifted my cap and my hands behind my back, for I am always rather careless of my nails.

"I, Sofia Baffo! I, who should always be at the center of things. In the heart. That is all I ask. In the very heart!"

"Corfu is a lovely island." I tried to redeem myself with some display of my knowledge of the world. "I have weighed anchor in her lovely harbor four times. And I even met your father once. A striking gentleman. Much like his daughter." I nodded the compliment toward her and took her silence as permission to continue.

"And Corfu is not so far from the center of things as all that. She lies on the throat of our trade routes to the East, at the very mouth of the Adriatic Sea. A secure Corfu is very important to Venice."

"Fool!" she exploded. "You think I don't know that? My father writes very pretty letters, yes. But what is Corfu . . . ? What is any place on earth compared to Venice? Here in the Piazza of St. Mark, here where the Doge sits and governs, here in the Great Basin where every merchant ship must finally dock from every corner of the world. *Here* is where I intend to stay—here, whence things are truly controlled."

I found it curious that she imagined the world in this guise—and that she felt such feelings so keenly here in the peace of the convent.

"So tell me," she continued. "What does the Doge say? Has he not found some husband for me a little better than a Corfiot peasant?"

"The man is not a peasant." How anxious it made me to be speaking another's suit! I couldn't make it sound honest to save my soul. "His family's name is listed in the Golden Book." *So is mine, so is mine!* my heart, if not my tone, kept saying. And I am the only male left of our branch, and so allowed—obliged, *dying*—to marry. "The name must be in the

Book, or a marriage to a noble Baffo would be unthinkable."

Baffo's daughter brushed my words away with a wave of her hand. Just so easily could she brush away the Golden Book as well. "There is the Doge's nephew, I hear. A fine young man, unmarried. . . ."

Now it was my turn to be impatient, for I knew the nephew to be a fool though he was twice her age, hardly a match for this creature before me. "Yes, the Doge's nephew. You did have the audacity to make that very suggestion in your letter to His Serenity, didn't you?"

"Well, why not? I am a Baffo, after all, and though my father may have belittled our name by taking that governorship, I will not be as he. I will speak as I see fit to any man on earth. To the Doge, to the Pope, if I care to. No, I would not hesitate to speak my mind to Saint Mark himself, and if he doesn't listen to me, then it will be his own fault if he passes by an excellent opportunity."

"Saint Mark is hardly one to be in need of opportunities for self-aggrandizement," I said, having felt a shudder at the blasphemy—in a convent garden, no less. "And a young woman should not go about arranging her own marriage. Even widows are rarely given that privilege. Young women. . . ."

"Women, fie! A flock of silly geese. I have to live among them; you do not. Well, I never intend to behave like one, for they are all too whiny and ridiculous. Tell me, what does the Doge say? Am I to marry his nephew or not?"

"I think not," I replied.

"No? Well, who shall it be, then? One of the house of Barbarigo? Andrea Barbarigo would not be a bad match, for all that he's young."

Ready for action, the blood surged to my heart at the familiarity with which she mentioned that young nobleman's name. But what action? I only managed to shift on the gravel beneath my feet, and it made a sound that accented my awkwardness.

She ignored me and forged ahead. "A Priuli, perhaps? A Barbaro?"

She did not mention Veniero. Ours was a house as favored as any she had mentioned—once. Our fortunes, however, were on the wane. I grew more determined than ever to repair these fortunes personally.

"Well, what is the Doge's message, then?" she demanded. "Since he has sent you at the appointed time and the appointed place, he must have something to say to me."

By now I was angry, as much at myself as at her. "His Serenity the Doge says you are to get on the ship bound for Corfu and do exactly as your father bids you or he will personally turn you over his knee and thrash you as he would his own daughter."

"What sort of message is that to a daughter of Baffo? I shall have you pilloried in the Piazza, you scoundrel, for speaking to a gentlewoman so."

"Forgive me, Madonna, but those were his words exactly. If you wish to confirm them, come with me to the Palace, and we will stand before the Doge together."

It was not quite the truth I told. I had never actually been in the presence of His Serenity at all, but only in that of a lowly secretary whose task it was to answer routine letters. But I was not going to let this girl have the power of that knowledge over me. Governor Baffo was, after all, one of the citizens responsible for the Doge's election. A petty secretary knew how Governor Baffo must be obeyed, even if his own daughter did not.

Baffo's daughter believed my little lie that was almost the truth with a wash of angry pallor. "Very well. Good day to you, Signore."

"Veniero." I repeated my name for her. If she could not grant me noble status as I had done with the title "Madonna," she could at least get the cognomen right—and know it was as noble as hers.

"And if you are considering writing any notes directly to the Barbarigo"—jealousy put a sharpness in my voice—"you may erase it from your mind. You might as well know that I will be sailing on the same ship as you. The great galley *Santa Lucia*—I am her first mate."

"The first mate!" she exclaimed with scorn. "Now I know you are full of lies. You are much too young to be the first mate of a fishing boat, let alone a galley."

Although this time I had spoken the truth, her scorn cut as deeply as if I had been caught in an abominably proud boast.

"My uncle is her captain," I insisted. "I have been at sea with him since I was eight and he does indeed charge me with such responsibility. As a matter of fact," and now I sought to get back at her, "I have been personally charged with the safe conduct of both yourself and your holy chaperon." I nodded in the direction of the aunt's convent. "Good day, Madonna Baffo. I will see you on the dock at the rising of the tide on Saint Sebastian's Day."

The girl sucked her breath at this and then let it out in a little squeal of anger. She stooped down and grabbed a handful of pebbles from the path which she flung at me. I scrambled up the wall in a moment—it was easy for one used to the rigging of ships—and sat perched on the top, out of her range.

I tipped my hat once more and bade Governor Baffo's fair daughter a fond "Until Saint Sebastian's Day."

Then I dropped over the wall, pursued by her curses to the end of the lane and the canal.

II

"A WILLFUL AND headstrong girl," my uncle Jacopo said with a disbelieving shake of his head as I finished telling him my afternoon's adventure.

His voice gave me a moment's chill, coming as it did from behind the mask he was trying on before a small mirror in our room. The black mask's beetling brows that made the eyes empty pits and the grotesque nose that gave a sepulchral hiss to his words had me convinced for a moment that my uncle spoke to me from beyond the grave.

Uncle Jacopo swept the mask off his face. It was of a piece with the tall, conical white hat, so that he now stood revealed as the man I'd always known and loved, who'd taken me in when my own parents and his wife had died in the same epidemic. Life fairly burst from his dark eyes, the flash around them heavily crinkled from much gazing across a sunburned sea. The gray on his wavy hair was no more than the white-caps formed before a warm, gentle south wind that made for good sailing and a quick homeward journey.

"Why don't you wear this mask tonight?" he asked, handing me the now-limp disguise.

"Me, Uncle?"

"Oh, I masked my share in my day, I can tell you. Used it to cover youth and folly and more indiscretion than I can remember."

"You, Uncle?" I teased. "My pious, God-fearing uncle? I won't believe it!"

"You don't believe it because I was always careful to wear a mask when I did it," he replied with a conspiratorial wink. He rested a hand on my shoulder, which was now almost level with his. "The time comes to pass everything on to younger blood, those with the stamina to take it. Accept the mask as the first of everything I shall leave you."

"Uncle, I expect to be best man at your remarriage any day now, and then what follows—"

"No, Giorgio. I won't remarry. I couldn't get a son if I did. Too many whores in too many ports. The pox they carry— I won't put another decent woman through what I put my Isabella in her honest attempts to get an heir. It's up to you. The continuation of our line, the charge from God in the Garden to multiply and replenish, it's all on your shoulders now. See that you don't fail that responsibility as I have done."

"I shall not," I answered my uncle's sudden and unaccustomed sobriety with what I hoped would match it. "But let's not think of that now, not tonight, not at Carnival."

The mood would not leave my uncle yet, though he pushed at it with sarcasm and a flourish. "I bequeath to you the grand old mask of the Veniero revelers."

"Thank you, most gracious uncle. I accept." When he phrased it like that, I could hardly refuse. "But you will wear my visor. For Carnival."

Uncle Jacopo took my simple black satin band and fingered it as he turned to look more out the window than at what he held in his hand. We were on the third story; the more prosperous branches of the family claimed the lower floors but allowed us these small rooms whenever the sea brought us home. Our long months abroad, after all, paid for their tapestries, their Persian rugs, their silverplate, their long winter evenings by the fireside. Our labor paid for their glass windows, a luxury we rarely saw elsewhere, but which were common here, even on third floors, like the one my uncle gazed through now.

The window was made of twenty or more separate little panes, their round bull's-eyes leaded together in a pattern of alternating red, green, and clear. All I could see from where I stood was the occasional dart of a sea gull through the clear circles. I supposed my uncle could see more.

"Ah, Venice." He sighed, laboring under his mood of dark premonition. " 'If the Earthly Paradise where Adam dwelt with Eve were like Venice, Eve would have had a difficult time tempting him away from it with a mere fig.' "

He was quoting Pietro Aretino, the famous satirist who was then but six years in his grave. I knew my uncle meant merely to comment on the fact that in none of her colonies, where we spent most of our time, was the tradition of masks at Carnival allowed. But I could not help recalling the image Baffo's daughter evoked for me in another garden that afternoon. Signorina Baffo was a subject I felt we had left too soon, but I didn't know how to bring my uncle around to it again, especially with this mood on him.

I had gone so far as to admit aloud, "I shall never lose the taste for talk of her."

At this my uncle had laughed and joked about my "growing lad's appetite." Then he'd gone on to say, "I wonder about Governor Baffo's willingness to entrust his daughter to the year's first sail. What is she, that the marrying of her cannot wait for more settled weather?"

"The governor must be acquainted with your skills, Uncle. He trusts you to find the harbors in the worst storm and bring her safe if any can."

"Let us pray to Saint Elmo it may be so." My uncle let me know by his tone that my sense of immortality was a youthful rashness. With a sigh, he'd gone on, "I, for one, am ready to be off. Enough of this anchored life, this tedium! This constant sense our land-locked cousins give me that I cannot swim in this little drop of theirs. Pray, Giorgio, for good weather on the twentieth, lest the Council rescind its leniency, fear more losses of the Republic's profits, and shove the day of first sail on into Lent once more."

To distract myself as much as anything, I fit the mask on my head and over my face. I breathed the sour, slightly salty smell of my uncle as if the black leather over my nose were his own flayed skin. But what a transformation I discovered in the mirror Uncle Jacopo had propped up in the niche along with the guardian statue of the Virgin!

The anxious hunger for more about Sofia Baffo that twitched my cheeks was wiped clean like a slate of chalk marks. Such cleansing power is in the mystery of the mask, the total evaporation right before the eyes of all individuality, of joy and sorrow, of good and evil, of youth and old age. Even male and female, the very first attribute with which a midwife burdens a babe, even that could vanish behind a mask and one could be at once unborn, as yet only hoped for. I had heard stories of it happening.

When the world sees us as individuals, it robs us. "So much may you do," it says, "but no more. No more as an untried youth, the lesser son of a lesser son. Or as a woman." But take all of that from a man's face—what freedom is there! And power.

I felt a thrill and turned to my uncle for his approval, the first time since I'd climbed the plane tree that other things besides "Saint Sebastian's Day" set my heart to skipping.

Even as he frowned the lips below his simple black band in a thoughtful nod at my sudden erasure, the bells of Venice began to ring all about us. The bird flight across the clear glass panes darted faster now, as if the gulls and pigeons were evensong made corporeal.

"There. It is time we were going," my uncle said. He took our two evening capes up off the bed and tossed me mine.

We stopped by briefly to beg, unsuccessfully, that Husayn in the next room should join us. He was such a good old friend of the family that we could never see him put up with the rest of his kind under the watchful eye of Messer Marc Antonio Barbaro. But it was wiser for us to ignore a Carnival recklessness, as Husayn always managed to do, and to remember that he was a Muslim passing as a Christian. He was good at his cover, but every time church bells rang, you could see he was hearing the muezzin's call. His face betrayed a certain longing that might be called homesickness, or merely an ache in the knee joints to sink onto a carpet facing Mecca once more. The less Venice saw of that, the more serene the Republic could remain.

So we left Husayn with his ledgers and went on our way, stopping only once more to pick up our black Piero from the servants' quarters. We would need him to bear the torch on our return.

We began to wish Piero had taken a torch from the bracket at home. Dark came early these winter evenings. A storm was blowing in off the lagoon and it began to drizzle, extinguishing all but the most stalwart of the shrine votives. Venice's alleyways were usually quite well illuminated by these public displays of piety. Now we passed only a few ghostly Madonnas, shivering before the blast.

The very stones of Venice seemed to be weeping, the wood loosed the smell of damp rot. The canals pockmarked in the twilight, the stairs on the bridges over them grew slick. The low arches we passed under were some cover, but ghostly light thrown up from the water danced on the corbels of their roofs. It was a night for the closed cab of a gondola, but as a mariner, my uncle took hard ground when he could get it, even when it meant, as it did that night, going the long way round.

"Though I am hard pressed to call Venice *terra firma* under any circumstances," he quipped. In several places, the dark water had begun to lap its way up into flagstone yards and piazzas.

We came at last to the palace of my dead mother's kin, the Foscari. I did not know this center of wealth and power well, these four stories of imposing red brick. The Foscari lords hoped that an occasional invitation to such events would be enough to discharge their familial obligations to us. And if we were at sea when the summons came, all the better for them, pity for me.

The manservant in brilliant scarlet livery who opened the door failed at first to recognize my name. My uncle exchanged a glance with me. Even masked, that glance urged long suffering. I silently swore, as I had done so many times, that some day with heaven's help I would put the Foscari in their place and make them recognize me.

"No wonder Venice is so full of public demands of heaven, lining their alleys with votives." This murmur into my uncle's ear was as close as I could come to long suffering when at last the door closed at our backs and we were relieved of our wet wraps. "Perhaps I should buy a candle and make such a compact with heaven tomorrow. Do you think that would help them remember my name?"

Uncle Jacopo smiled and gestured for restraint as we entered the Foscari lobby, rich with paintings by Bellini and Titian at which it would not be good manners to gawk as closely as I wanted to. I did fully intend to make such a vow. But that is one more youthful resolution I never got around to doing.

My Foscari uncles had footed a play in their own private theater that night, something to give Carnival a shove off its moorings of Christmas and Epiphany. The prologue had already begun as Uncle Jacopo and I slipped into our seats on the left-hand side of a tiered arrangement that bracketed the stage on three sides. We might have received scowls for our tardiness, except for the fact that this was Venice and many others were even later. In our masks, we might have been the Doge and his nephew for all the others knew.

And this thought set my mind stirring in its old direction again. "Do you think, Uncle—?" I sued into his ear. "Do you think there's a chance Baffo's daughter might—?"

"We must think of her as any other package of goods we are hired to carry," he replied firmly.

No one scowled at our talk, for no one in the audience kept quiet if it didn't suit them. In general, they carried on a lively chatter among themselves, slapped down tin playing cards, ventured at dice, and even brawled. And scarlet-liveried servants mingled, offering drinks, antipasti, and tasseled cushions to keep the feet off the cold marble floor. The production on stage was, in fact, hardly more than the background, like a group of instrumentalists set up on a balcony over the conviviality in a sitting room.

It was a new play. I've forgotten the author if, indeed, it had one and was not a joint effort of the cast. I didn't take long to get the gist of the plot. The characters were those familiar to us from *commedia dell'arte*. Their relationships were the same, as it must be with any set of caricatures. Only their surroundings were novel, and the smell of fresh scenery paint made me worry for the actor's costumes any time they passed too close to the rear flats.

My uncle read my thoughts through the mask at the first entrance of our young female lead, Columbine. "We must give our cargo the care of uncut jewels," he counseled, "but ignore her like salted fish."

Our sweet maid Columbine did not undergo her perils in Italy as usual. She had been kidnapped from the bosom of her family and spirited away to the harem of the Turkish Sultan, a part Pantalone took on himself in a leering mask, familiar for all its darkness and token turban. And of course it was up to Harlequin, the blustering Captain, and their friends to save her with lots of slapstick, pies in the face, and tying the Pantalone-Sultan up in his own turban "for Saint Mark and for Venice!" No matter how distracted the audience was with themselves, the expression of these sentiments never failed to elicit applause and a cheer, so it was repeated, frequently and loudly from the stage.

"I am glad Husayn stayed home," I told Uncle Jacopo.

I was struck at once by the strange fascination the transport of familiar characters to this exotic setting had on my fellow countrymen. The Sultan was an adversary at whose discomfort any Venetian could cheer. But the spectacle of scores of beautiful, nubile, totally dependent, submissive young women bored to voraciousness answered some deeper fantasy. *This says more about what we wish for our womenfolk,* I thought, *than about the barbarousness of our enemy.*

And presented by the illusion of harem walls on stage, the afternoon's scene in the convent garden wouldn't leave me.

"Corfu is not such a long journey," Uncle Jacopo said in sympathy.

Having established the plot so it no longer required my undivided attention, I remarked how odd it was that actors in masks should be playing for an audience equally, if not more heavily, masked. Who had the greater persona to create? The most to hide? I remembered the surge of power I'd felt when I'd first let the mask obliterate my features. The power an actor has to commit gross fooleries on stage and yet risk no censure when he returns to normal life.

Even more than the actors' power, however, was the power to see without being seen, the power of an omniscient audience who knew that Harlequin was concealed behind that screen, when the Sultan did not.

The fact that our familiar Columbine added to her lacy pink mask the effigy of a Turkish lady's veils made me take one more leap of association. What if the harem was not at all how we wished it could be for our lecherous old Pantalones?

"What do Turkish women feel when they drape their faces beyond the profane gaze and escaped the trap of individuality?" I asked.

My uncle laughed out loud, but only shrugged. "Your afternoon has turned your head. You can never know what any woman is thinking. Turkish women might not exist for all we may fathom them. And for your information, the same holds true for Baffo's daughter."

I had been with my uncle to the lands of the infidel. I liked our friend Husayn, knew him to be no barbarian. But it occurred to me that my mind brought nothing—nothing at all beyond these same lecherous imaginings that were the product of my culture, not theirs—when I tried to conjure with the words "women of the Ottomans." The women I knew in Constantinople were all Europeans—wives of colleagues. And the whores my uncle frequented, who gave him his disease. Women who'd found their profession too congested here and sought advancement on foreign shores.

They were never spoken of, Turkish women, certainly not paraded on stage like this. I'd never seen a Turkish woman that I could recall. Perhaps they all had two heads and that monstrosity was what the flitting grilles and passing sedans camouflaged. Perhaps it was some other secret. Great, unearthly beauty my countrymen liked to believe. What about influence? Power?

The Turks did have shadow puppets. I remembered seeing a shadow play in a public square in Constantinople once. The characters seemed to be the same stock figures we knew in Venice. There had been women—shrewish old ones; fair, sweet young ones. That was all they were—figures in a shadow play. But suppose that is what I was to them? All men were to them, seen through their screens? And who was pulling the strings?

The rows of candlelight in Venice's alleys told me that— for all their bruit, their annual presumption to take the Adriatic as a bride, their masks and lavish spectacles—even the Foscari, the greatest of my countrymen, were never fully confident they ruled the world.

I remembered the feeling of power hiding my face had given me—continued to give me as I looked brazenly about that evening's assembly. I let my eyes rove where they would, on bosom or codpiece, on pompous righteousness or untrammeled debauchery, never bothering to censor my thoughts lest they register in my face. Suppose Turkish women had that same freedom not just on Carnival nights but all day, every day, from birth—

God above! What was I thinking? The last thing on earth I wanted to be was a woman!

"Still to understand them—" I tried to tempt my uncle.

Action on the stage distracted my musings at this point. No piece of brilliantly rehearsed staging, but an unforeseen blunder produced the sudden general guffaw. It caught everyone off guard and prohibited further advancement of the plot while even the actors struggled with tears of mirth under their visors.

Our Columbine was guarded by a great buffoon of a eunuch. I knew the man playing the part. No amount of makeup or yards of silk costuming could hide his bulk. He was my maternal uncles' gondolier, called in to play this bit part for which physique and a gregarious personality if not his booming bass recommended him. Had I come upon him out of context, I might not have recognized the face, but the gondolier's girdle of muscle added to the girth around his hips would have betrayed his occupation anywhere. And I had seen him often enough bellowing out his soulful lyrics as he poled the gold-trimmed launch with the Foscari crest about the Serene City. The Council had spent a lot of time ruing the extravagance of our nobility's gondolas, but at this date they had not yet brought themselves to condemn us all by edict to a uniform and somber black.

I knew the poleman easily now as he took the brunt of a tightly rehearsed dialogue focusing on the words "capon" and "pruned" and "gelded," as all the while he lamented his state in the face of our beauteous Columbine. I squirmed in my seat at the very thought of such a handicap.

I was not the only one who recognized the gondolier-eunuch. A two-year-old hovering beyond the lamp glow did as well, escaped his keepers and toddled up onto stage, chirping "Papa! Papa!" as tickled as could be.

Once the illusion was broken this far, everyone suddenly remembered that this man was the father not only of a two-year-old, but of ten others.

"His wife," I overheard from neighbors, "prays daily for Santa Monica to spare her that gondolier's virile embrace."

When he could no longer ignore the tugging on his robe, the great man bent down and acknowledged his offspring, swept him up into his arms and accepted the "Papa!" adulation until the child's mother, visibly expectant yet once again, struggled up to reclaim her child, a peck on the cheek from her husband and the bawdy cheers of the audience.

Eventually, the scene crumbled to a conclusion. So enthralling had the whole comedy been for some minutes that it took me quite by surprise to return to myself and discover a hand on my knee. It was slowly working its way higher.

III

FLESH SHOWED ABOVE the black of my uncle's mask as he raised his brows in a quizzical expression. He, too, was conscious of the liberties being taken upon my person by the unknown masked figure that had appeared suddenly in the seat on my other side. If my uncle did not complain, how could I?

She was a tall, slender vision in burgundy velvet with quantities of jewels, beyond price but unmatched, on her hands, neck, and waist. Her wide square décolleté was filled with the finest lace worked in gold thread, her black hair draped in cutwork, but her face was a mystery, hidden behind a moiré burgundy mask trimmed in the same gold lace. In this she was perfectly Venetian: the laws of our city forbid any noblewoman to appear in more than one color, exempting gold or silver used as trim. To my mind, this law enforced good taste, which might otherwise have descended to a Harlequin patchwork of gaud.

Her first words to me were, "I'll wager you wouldn't have the difficulty of that poor cropped Turk. I'll wager you could give a lady the pleasures of her life."

Her accompanying laugh was loud and shrill. With my mind still dipping into my afternoon from time to time, it had occurred to me at first that this might be Baffo's daughter taking on the freedom of a mask to escape from the convent by night. I had been hoping for such a meeting to the degree that I fully expected it, and at the most unexpected times. The laugh convinced me this was not she; the girl of my dreams did not laugh like this crackle of lightning but like the soft breezes of a spring garden. And yet, the figure, at first glance, was similar. The storm was here, now, with a most sultry presence and, force of nature that it was, I could hardly resist it.

My biggest concern became how to join in her laughter without letting my vocal chords betray me into registers higher than hers.

"I just adore the *intermedi,*" my new companion declared, easing her ministrations when the strains of an instrumental group warming up announced a lull in the action onstage. Singers and dancers would now give pause to the actors who'd been on a merry chase from dungeon to the highest tower in the Sultan's palace.

A tapestry dropped over the minarets of Constantinople. It announced "pastoral" and gave me another mental brush with the convent garden in the afternoon. These fanciful trees were in full leaf, the illusion of a million tiny stitches taken by a dozen seamstress's hands; real leaves and flowers were difficult to come by even for the very wealthy at this season of the year.

The scene devised to play in front of this drop caused something of a jolt, however. It featured Phlegyas, the boatman from Dante's *Inferno,* who appeared naked, but flickering with red gauze flame at the vital parts. This apparition quite took my masked companion's breath away. At least, she had none to spare for me.

Phlegyas steadied his boat to receive the Damned, who represented a wild confusion of theologies: fauns and satyrs along with Adam and a buxom Eve, more recent heretics of note, traitors to the Serene Republic and the particular enemies of the Foscari. The Turkish Sultan himself brought up the rear, a stretched attempt to make the *intermedio* have something to do with the play it interspersed. It gave the pious illusion that the eternal was in some way watching over the fooleries of the mundane.

The Damned sang a dirge as they approached in a solemn grapevine. Phlegyas shook his chains to mark the rhythm, and imps sounded suitably woeful chords on trombones and bass viols which an ingenious costumer had disguised as instruments of torture.

"And the music *is* an instrument of torture," I commented lightly to my companion.

To my confusion, she did not share my opinion of the entertainment. With rapt attention and even the glint of a tear of remorse through the moiré slits, she counted up her life's sins and contemplated her own fate at the crack of doom.

So much for my evening, I thought.

Looking idly about for some other distraction, I noticed the tardy arrival of a pair of gentlemen who attracted my attention because they could well be my uncle and I: an older man and a younger. The similarity was further exaggerated by the fact that the younger's black mask and white cone hat were the very image of mine. No mask, however, could conceal the graying, chest-length whiskers of the older man. All Venice knew them as sprouting from the chin of Agostino Barbarigo, head of the great Barbarigo family, one of the dreaded Council of Ten, in line for the post of Provenditor.

This identification saw through all attempts by the younger for anonymity. He must be the Barbarigo's heir, Andrea. And as soon as the name Andrea Barbarigo passed through my mind, I recalled the last time I'd heard it pronounced, on the pouting lips of Sofia Baffo. My hand went automatically to my left hip. I must duel this man to the death, was my reflexive thought.

Young Barbarigo was looking anxiously about the audience as well. When his gaze met mine, like a mirror, he paused.

It was as if the very same thoughts of blood coursed through his mind, too. With a mask, however, it was impossible to tell. Presently he only gave me a stiff nod of acknowledgment, which such a lingering stare required even if we weren't acquainted. I returned the nod, equally stiff. His eyes moved on.

By this time, our lovers were back on stage, romping through the seraglio with fantastic impunity once more. My companion in gold lace had forgotten all about hellfire in the time it takes to raise a tapestry forest. Or at least she'd decided to transfer perdition to play upon my person in a dozen places instead. It did in fact seem that her attentions were what drew Barbarigo's elsewhere, convinced him that I was no threat. They certainly distracted me.

Nothing less than a servant's tap on my shoulder brought more than my codpiece upright again, and made me straighten my mask. The servant, like everybody else, was masked and identified by no more than the scarlet Foscari livery. Wordlessly, he pressed a tightly folded piece of paper in my hand and, with a conspiratorial nod, vanished among the milling numbers of his species.

My companion in the moiré mask had still not righted herself from her attempt to make a bed of our stiff and high-backed chairs. She'd worked my chemise out of its tuck between hose and doublet and was tickling my bare skin with pricks of gold lace.

"Perhaps we need to go find out if this palace has a room that is not quite so crowded," she murmured.

Her languid "Hmm?" might indeed have made me pocket the note to read later, but my first inquisitive unfolding had revealed a signature. It was a single feminine *S* elaborated with curlicues and flounces. Now the note burned in my hand more than the chafe of any gold lace.

Ignoring the gold lace mask, I opened the note, caught it

in the glow of the nearest torch, and strained against darkness to read:

My love— Second intermedio. *In the lobby as planned.*

And then, that far more communicative *S.*

"My love," the moiré mask cooed in my ear. "What is it?"

I snatched the note away from her groping fingers, realizing now, as I hadn't when they were on my codpiece, how aged they were, and spotted. I realized, too, how, for all the gems she did wear, one jewel was conspicuously absent, one on her left hand that now exposed a telltale band of white.

"My love—?"

Her use of those words irritated me. "Business," I replied brusquely.

I looked to my uncle for confirmation as I did reflexively whenever "business" was mentioned. My uncle's eyebrows were even higher than before. In retrospect, I have to admire his restraint. In spite of all the inept fumbling with gold lace going on in the seat next to him, he'd managed no comment. Or at least he'd managed to match his guffaws to the general rise and fall following Columbine and her Harlequin.

"Oh, business. Yes!" He started as if with sudden memory.

And then, off the silken hose of his knee, he pointed a finger to the opposite arm of the audience. My friend in moiré did not see this signal, but I followed the line of Uncle Jacopo's fingers across the room, realizing that he knew whence the note came.

They were late arrivals I hadn't noticed until this moment, seated in a far section of the audience reserved for women who wanted to keep to the convention of separation that was usually the rule. They were almost alone there, masks and Carnival erasing the lines between courtesan and honest woman that were otherwise observed.

Blinking against the dim light, I recognized the chap-faced nun first. She looked angry to be the only unmasked face on three tiers, uncomfortable with the worldliness about her and the bawdiness on stage. Although both young ladies with her were identically masked, it didn't take me a moment to reject the nun's right-hand charge as too giggly, and lay claim to the taller one on her left.

It was exactly the conclusion the very form of the *S* and my mind's constant echo had set me to from the start. She seemed to steal torchlight from the stage. And her intense gaze coming back to me left no doubt whatsoever. Oh, how long could these buffoons on stage keep it up? How long till *intermedio*?

"Say you mustn't go. Can't we escape together for a few moments? Can't the business wait?"

I brushed at the sting of gold lace as at a bothersome mosquito and tried to clear my head enough to think straight. But all I could do was to wallow in the wonder of it. I lost all consciousness of the stage. *Me? Baffo's daughter calls me "her love"!*

The refrain of my thoughts began to have musical accompaniment. The tapestry had dropped again and the rewards of the Blessed were now revealed in song and dance. Seraphim were joined by a celestial nonet of Muses on lutes, double harps, bowed rebecs, recorders, transverse flutes, one straight and one curved cornet. The continuo sneaked on stage as a harpsichord within a gauzy cloud.

No host of heaven could compete with what was ringing through my mind. Or rather, the stage was my mind's perfect, if less extravagant, complement. I got ready to excuse myself.

And then, the host and their clouds parted to reveal divinity. No patriarchal Jove, but an Apollo in golden armor and corona was flown in on ropes you could see only if you were spoiling for them. The continuo hit two crashing chords to bring him in, and Apollo opened his mouth to address us.

The sound that flung itself suddenly to the furthest corners of the theater was beyond belief. It riveted me to my chair and washed my mind blank to any other thought. At first I raked the stage with my eyes, looking for the full woman's chorus that must be concealed somewhere to make the noise Apollo's lips only pretended to. Then I was beaten back to the realization that this torrent of sound was a full octave above the normal range of women. The notes were brilliant, painfully so, showering like slivers of shattered crystal on the ear. They sparkled and ran glancingly through the most breakneck cadenzas as if they required no effort at all. That it was this fine figure of an Apollo who tossed his golden locks with every breath was impossible. Absurd. My first reaction was to laugh out loud as no harem escapade had induced me to till then.

But this was hardly the reaction in the rest of the audience, so I had to stifle mine. My companion in moiré leaned forward, transfixed as if it were indeed divinity she heard.

"It is!" she exclaimed in her rapture. "It is!"

"It is what?" I demanded.

She said a name I cannot now remember, but definitely a man's name, then added: "Messer Foscari promised me he would lure this singer out of his church in Florence and onto our stage. He has done it. And oh, isn't the voice just as divine as reported?"

I struggled with this definition of divinity and its music for a while. Even so, all I could find to say was: "But how——?"

"He's a castrato. A childhood injury, poor man," my companion enlightened me.

Mariners miss a lot at sea, I realized. And then, since the host of heaven had decided to render their lord praise in their common, mundane voices for a time, she continued.

"At least, that's what they say. But I have it on good authority that he was a choirboy in Florence and his family was too desperately poor to let him grow out of a good thing. There are physicians, I understand——"

"I won't believe it. That a family would do this to their heir?"

"Oh, you must believe it. And you must tell me, honestly. What else is to be done? The Apostle tells us 'Let women be silent in Church.' But it is the soaring, high voices that draw our thoughts most nearly to God. Boys' voices are soft and clear, but boys will be boys"—she gave me a nudge—"hard to discipline, and impossible to keep in the required range long enough to gain much proficiency. I understand His Holiness the Pope has heard this man sing—and is looking for his like for his own choir. His Holiness grows weary of the strained notes of these Spanish falsettists which have otherwise been so popular. And, if His Holiness approves—"

"But that's—that's unnatural!" I exclaimed.

My companion shrugged her shoulders up into the gold lace about her throat so that their lack of youthful firmness was evident.

"Society puts unnatural claims on us all," she said simply. "We find ways around them. Then who is to say what is natural and what is not? You are but young yet, or you would know."

Thoughtfully she rubbed the blatant, naked finger on her left hand.

The continuo struck two more warning, introductory chords and then fell silent, unshackling Apollo from all ties to the ground. And he soared, skipping notes from cloud to cloud like the lightest of sparrow flocks catching the setting sun on their wings.

The music affected me deeply, but I cannot say that I was struck with open-mouthed awe like the rest of my company in that theater that night. From my present perspective, I am tempted to suggest that the sparrow-flight of notes hung in the air over my head like some grave consequence, as yet unborn, as yet even undreamed.

At the time, the juxtaposition of a creature the butt of

cruel jokes one moment, the same creature adored for his unnatural, otherworldly nature the next—I found it too perverse. God that this Apollo was, he was limited. There would endlessly never be any two-year-old for him to father. What kind of god was this, who knew limitations? Like many another contradiction many another fifteen-year-old has perceived in his surroundings, it niggled me with fear. And to escape fear—to which age soon grows blind—I turned it quickly on its head as scorn.

Desperately, I looked across the hall, hoping youth, even in another sex, would have sympathy with what I felt. Then through all the wild ether of sound came the hard bass of realization in my heart: Sofia Baffo was no longer cloistered at her aunt's side.

"Business!" I exclaimed, as much to convince myself as my companions.

I jumped to my feet. It was, I suddenly remembered, the second *intermedio*.

IV

A MAN IN scarlet livery directed me through the lobby, disappointingly empty save for glowering Foscari portraits and the Titians, to a chamber on the left. "Gentlemen retire this direction," he said.

"Gentlemen" were not at all what I was about, but I didn't know how to contradict him. And since the man himself—or his twin—had given me the message with the eloquent *S* in the first place, I decided to take this advice as well.

I found myself in a lavishly wood-paneled hall illuminated by low-burning beeswax candles, even more alone than in the foyer. The most art-dreading of gentlemen was not going to miss the spectacle of a castrato. The paradox of high notes pushed by a man's lungs forced its way into this room as well. How clever of Madonna Baffo to plan our meeting for this time! But, then, where was she?

A curtain concealed a balcony where a man could add his water to the Grand Canal. To ease my nervousness, I used it, thinking how fresh the air smelled in the dark for the night's rain. This action restored my equilibrium somewhat. Odd that the organ we are always at such pains to conceal from the world should be so much a part of connecting with it. As my water joined that of the Grand Canal, so I felt myself joined once again to the human race, male as well as female. The disturbing world of castrati and harem attendants vanished behind flats and scrims like a conjuror's illusion. I felt ready for reality again.

And that reality would tonight contain Sofia Baffo! Sofia Baffo, who only waited for me to find her.

Back from the balcony, I followed the stretch of a sideboard, heavy with food and drink. Oddly, the usual scents of such a board failed to reach my nostrils. The entire spread all seemed untouched, as if more than just the goblets were encrusted with gold. Whole birds glistened in their juices like brass. The burnished pears, the coppery figs, the oranges, the pyramids of nuts, even the intervening bunches of bay and sage had a high, della Robbia gloss to them. In the guttering light, they feasted the eye more than the belly—

decorative, opulent, but unnourishing, hard, and unnatural.

I noticed briefly how the room's floor was made of four colors of marble, inlaid in such a way that the darkest gray seemed to retreat and the lightest gold to leap forward. It fooled my eye into believing I was walking on cubes.

And as I walked, I heard the click of rapid footsteps echoing off that floor. I turned, looked up and then adjusted my hat and mask carefully as I found myself in the presence of an unknown youth. The youth wore a parti-colored Harlequin mask and a large, droopy sack of a hat. Of course, this was the salon for gentlemen, but the sound of those footsteps had at first made me think—

And then I saw the boy move and I knew it was no boy. The galliard and "Come to the Budding Grove" were no less incongruous in a hose and doublet than in the convent garden.

"Madonna?" I stammered.

"You didn't recognize me? Then I shall easily fool them all."

I wasn't hearing very clearly. When I saw what the hose revealed, I understood why women's legs are customarily draped in fabric, the more yards the better.

"In any case, you've come. And about time!" The words burst from her. "A brilliant decoy, that trollop who was all over you in the theater when I came in.

"The clothes—see!" She spun on the illusionary floor. "They're a perfect fit."

They were an awkward fit, actually, cut for a larger, male figure that went in where hers went out. The foppish hat disguised the most glorious of her features—her hair—and the padded codpiece was truly ridiculous, slipping from side to side as it did. But I couldn't criticize anything into which she chose to put that body.

"Madonna—" was all I could think of to say. Perhaps I was calling on heaven.

"Just a minute. I must have a look at how the other half lives now, as this brief masquerade allows."

She swept past me and I followed, enraptured by her dance.

"Hmm, the food's much the same," she declared, giving it only a passing glance. "Although you do have better drink. And we have daintily painted little pots behind our curtain. I suppose I should have a difficult time hitting the Grand Canal from here——" She mused, peering over the stonework railing into the night with an unnerving display of hips and thighs below the doublet.

"Well, come, my love," she concluded.

She dropped the curtain before the balcony again and danced back to me, sweeping a fig from the sideboard as she passed. She presented the fruit to me with a bat of eyelashes in the holes of her mask and then she slipped her arm through mine.

I had known the scrub of gold lace. The touch of Sofia's bare skin was molten.

"Come, Andrea. Don't keep me guessing any longer. How are we to make our escape?"

And just in the moment when I realized she was mistaking me for someone else, that someone else joined us in the room.

"Sofia!"

The arm resting on mine grew rigid and cold.

Andrea Barbarigo threw off the mask and conical hat that so closely resembled mine. "You found the clothes in the lobby all right, I see," he said stiffly.

"I—I did," Baffo's daughter replied.

"And they suit you?"

"They—they'll do just fine for the purpose. But—but you didn't get my note?"

"Note? What note?"

47

Her hand vacated mine altogether and through Harlequin's parti-panes her eyes flashed with anger like sequins.

"Come, Sofia. The gondola waits at the rear entrance. We haven't a moment to lose to make good our escape. As I live, you shall not marry that Corfiot. Or anyone else"—there was a sharp glance in my direction—"but me."

"Yes, Andrea. I belong only to you."

Her hand touched his arm with her uncommon desire for possession and in that moment Andrea Barbarigo burned to life. I knew the feeling. *Duel him, duel him!* came to my mind, but the necessary words of challenge got lost in my confusion, my hurt, and the accompanying feelings of worthlessness.

The fire remained with my opponent and he shot these words at me with a look that cut through the black of his mask. "You breathe a word about this to anyone, and I will personally see that your name finds its way into a lion's mouth."

A lion's mouth! Now unabashed terror was added to my confusion and hurt. Lions' mouths were dark shadows to the votives in Venice's alleyways. I had not looked at them on our walk that evening because they were hidden by shadows, but also because I knew they were likely to induce nightmares. Hollow-eyed carvings with open mouths discretely placed throughout the city, the lions' mouths invited anonymous naming of enemies to the Republic. The furtively slipped accusations went to the secret Councils of the Ten, who investigated each with the full gravity of bell, book, and candle: the serenity of the Republic was not to be trifled with. A man might never even know of what he was accused before he vanished—like a slip of parchment into the mouth of a lion in a dark, damp alley. Why, the elder Barbarigo was one of the Ten. His son might only drop a quiet word over dinner—

Two pairs of rapid clicks fell into step with one another across the floor of marble illusion. Thunderous applause to an Apollo encore covered the sound to all but my ears.

The instant Sofia Baffo was out of my sight, my head cleared as if I'd been doused with cold water. Andrea Barbarigo wasn't going to drop my name to his father over dinner. He was eloping with Governor Baffo's daughter. He'd be fortunate if his father ever allowed him in his sight again. As for the lion's mouth—I was in a mask. Barbarigo wouldn't recognize me on the torturer's rack. He didn't even know my name. And what is more, Baffo's daughter didn't either. There was no indication that she equated me with the messenger in the convent garden that afternoon.

"Ways around society's constraints." The words came so strongly to my lips I thought I must be recalling some old sailor's saw. It took me a moment to remember my companion of earlier that evening in gold lace and moiré.

What else could I do? What any opium eater would do who saw the source of his drug drying up. I ran to the lobby, to the first man in livery I found, tugged on his scarlet sleeve and pointed to the escaping pair, muttering a few choice words about "elopement" and "dishonor on the Foscari household."

Suddenly, there was scarlet livery everywhere, like the plague of blood in ancient Egypt. The theater emptied like Goshen, only with less unified direction. Perhaps they were the plague of hopping frogs instead.

The nun shrieked in a poor mimicry of the castrato and had to be given smelling salts. Old Barbarigo fluffed up behind his beard like a thunderstorm. I caught a glimpse of burgundy and wanted to learn something more from the moiré mask about "society's constraints." But gold lace slinked away under the confusion into the dark night as if I'd betrayed her as well.

The young lovers were bundled off quickly in separate gondolas. Baffo's daughter dissolved into tears and her streaked, alabaster face seemed so young and naked in the glare of torchlight with her mask removed.

Andrea Barbarigo tried to send a glare of revenge in my direction, the challenge of a duel, but Sofia Baffo was out of his view now and the words failed him as they had me earlier. And old Barbarigo jerked his son around by the collar to march him to the door and gave him no chance.

This was fortunate because tears stung my own eyes as I watched Baffo's daughter exit. Even a mask did not seem disguise enough for me at this point.

So the seraglio was wiped from everybody's mind like sewage from the canals in a high tide. Columbine, for once, did not make good her escape. For all that, my Foscari kin came up to thank me afterward and declared that, the honor of their house intact, we could all live happily ever after.

I had made the great lords of Venice take notice of me. Why was I then so miserable?

"Business," I shrugged at Uncle Jacopo's congratulations as we followed old Piero's bouncing torchlight home.

Would that those congratulations were as easy to shrug off as the continuing rain. My uncle sensed my mood and was careful to say no more.

Halfway home, I discovered I still held the fig. It had lost its brass-plated appearance and grown close to mush with the heat and pressure of my hand during the evening's conclusion. On the off chance that the sickness in my stomach might be hunger, and to empty my hand, I ate it. I remembered only after the fact how the crunch of that fruit's seeds always set my teeth on edge. The fig turned my stomach sticky and spread the ache to my hands and face besides.

"Saint Sebastian's Day," my uncle murmured. "It won't be our easiest sailing."

The ache spread across my shoulders with the comradely fling of his arm.

"Well, she is a willful and headstrong girl," he murmured.

As if that were any consolation.

V

"A WILLFUL AND headstrong girl."

I murmured the words aloud as I stood on the deck of the anchored *Santa Lucia*. I gazed pensively over the Venetian Basin with the spur of Santa Elena to starboard. The gray-green hills around Mestre draped the forward horizon and the city's bustle. The colors everywhere were bleached, pastel, like scraps of life, lost at sea and drifted to shore. The day was so clear that even the foothills of the Dolomite Alps were visible. My eyes teared at the sight, for they were the source of the stiff, cold wind that numbed the nose to Venice's usual slightly foul smell of swamp and sea. The wind set Saint Mark's ubiquitous banners popping. Just like fireworks, I thought, were the explosions of the banners' red and gold against the mountains' blue haze.

The wind brought no ice; there would be good sailing this Saint Sebastian's Day.

Off port was the island of my namesake, San Giorgio. There was talk of building a grand, new church for the holy monks sequestered there. I remembered the chill, the thrill of processions toward the old church: every tiny boat in the Republic lit with lamps that bounced off the black of Christmas Eve waters. As a child, I had thought the holy season some how special for me alone because San Giorgio was *my* saint. I still got the feeling, looking toward the island, of heaven's special favor.

I blushed at the rapid beating of my own heart. "A willful and headstrong girl."

A high, piercing laugh jarred the thoughts I'd imagined I was keeping to myself. "Oh, I see."

"I'm sorry, Husayn." I did not see what the man who'd just joined me did.

"The sea," he replied. "*She* is a willful and headstrong girl. I misunderstood for a moment because in my language 'sea' is a he. We Arabs see him sometimes as a little boy, playing, sometimes as a sleeping giant, sometimes as a youth, pining for love. Sometimes, Allah have mercy, the sea is a madman in his fury. I was just thinking how like the coils of a serpent the waters of the Basin look today, shimmering beneath us as the tide slithers landward to its height. So you see, I would not understand at once when you likened 'him' to a willful, headstrong girl."

He continued: "But now I comprehend your comparison, and it is a beautiful one, my friend. I can see your girl, too, shimmering in silks and jewels and—rather brazen, no? Were I her father, I would pack her into the harem at once. Who knows? Perhaps this serpent I see slithering over the Basin is a she-serpent, painted and shameless, a temptress."

I joined Husayn's smile and, because I enjoyed the poetry of his voice so much, I did not bother to correct him in the object of it. Husayn had been a friend of our family since before my father died. I remember bouncing on his knee and rejoicing in the lumps of Turkish sugar wrapped up in multicolored squares of silk he used to bring me when I was but a child. If my uncle had become a father to me since I'd been orphaned, Husayn had moved into the position of godparent, an interesting role for an infidel.

But of course it was not the sea that had caught my interest at all, and the distraction irritated me. The sea had always been like a mother's arms to me, surely Husayn realized that. I trusted it implicitly, even when it was rough.

It was Baffo's daughter I did not trust.

My uncle had made Madonna Baffo my particular charge. I had been watching for her since dawn—and all the previous afternoon while I saw to the boarding of an infinite number of trunks and crates labeled BAFFO—CORFU. Crate after crate pulleyed up over the low center of the *Santa Lucia* that balanced between the sharp, high sweep of prow and the broad elevation of the stern. Here, when fully laden, the deck was almost sea level.

No matter how many times I told myself that to my mind such crates must only contain salted fish, my heart skipped a beat every time I read the stencil. They certainly didn't give off the odor of fish. Every once in a while, I'd catch the fragrance of lavender or cloves from between the slats. And the crew had an easier time hoisting this lighter burden from the tenders over the sides of the ship and into the hold than they ever would have had with fish.

Still, the planks of a ship were not like a convent garden, not like noble drawing rooms where I felt young and awkward. I was first mate here; I was at home, and the accustomed work, the rapid obedience by the crew of every order I gave, made me remember my betrayal in the halls of the Foscari in a different light. Here, I knew what was expected of me and did it. I did it well. That put the weight of all of Venetian society on my side. A disobedient young girl had no hope of having her way against such a weight. I had no need to be unnerved by her like a landlubber in his first storm.

"Now that is one thing I have always liked about Turkish," Husayn interrupted my thoughts with his again. "They are not so particular as either Italian or Arabic about the gender of things, so similes can be many things at once."

"Come, my friend," I said, elbowing him more impatiently than was necessary toward the spot where he could better oversee the stowing of his cargo. "You must be careful how you speak of your native tongue. One of my oarsmen might have heard you just now, Husayn, and no one must know you are not what you seem."

"Surely you are afraid of pirates, my friend?" Husayn smiled.

"Turkish corsairs? Not with you on board."

"I had in mind more certain *Christian* crusaders."

"You mean, perhaps, the Knights of Malta?"

"Truly no better than pirates."

"All right, no better." I agreed with him to hasten our exchange along.

"They don't want anyone going to Constantinople. They are opposed to all trade and free enterprise."

"It's not the trading they oppose."

"The idea of material gain offends their spirituality."

"The material gain of *Christians* presents no problem."

"That of Muslims, on the other hand—"

"I apologize for my co-religionists," I said.

"As I apologize for mine."

"My point is, Husayn, you are a Syrian, a subject of the Turks."

"You find fault with my Venetian?"

"Your Venetian is nearly perfect—as is your Turkish and your Arabic and your Genoese and your French. Being plump and rather fair-skinned, you need only a change of costume to make a proper merchant of the Republic out of you."

Husayn laughed at my appraisal of him and shifted the taut waist of his gold-worked doublet with vanity so the hem of it reached properly below his knees again.

"Granted, you love the clink of ducats more than the niceties of religion. You think nothing of drinking wine, eating pork sausage, crossing yourself, or even saying a 'Hail Mary' or two when the need arises. Still, when a longing for home hits you, I can detect the Muslim beneath the gloss."

Husayn thoughtfully smoothed his moustache into his beard.

"I didn't give it a second thought when Uncle Jacopo agreed to transport you, seventy bolts of textiles, and four dozen carefully straw-packed crates of glassware to Constantinople on this voyage. I only rejoiced, thinking of the company."

"My friend, I thank you." Husayn's exaggerated graciousness was not devoid of sarcasm, but good-natured enough. "You and your uncle will always display the most lavish gratitude for my business."

"I would like to keep this company."

"And the business. As I appreciate the season's earliest possible return to trade and escape from this land of ignorance."

"My uncle knows you are harmless, I know you are harmless."

"Now, is that a compliment or not?"

"You are only trading in the finished product, after all, not in the technical secrets that made Venetian glass the wonder of the world."

"Secrets for which men have lost their lives in your serene Republic."

"All I'm saying is that with self-righteous pirates on the

seas, it is prudent not to burden any more souls than necessary with your true identity."

Husayn flashed me one of his guileless smiles, sparked with the vanity of gold teeth, and said, "Very well, my friend. No more Arabic or Turkish lessons on this voyage."

"Thank you, Husayn."

"But then you must stop calling me Husayn."

I blanched at my slip. "Enrico," I stammered. "Enrico."

Husayn smiled. "You are but young in this sort of business, my friend, to be lecturing me of pirates and disguise. But you will do well in time. Enrico is my name, if you please. Enrico Battista. Until we reach Constantinople. Then I may well call you Abdullah, the servant of Allah—"

He suddenly cut short what had all the makings of another long discourse to scurry across the deck like a well-fed rat and yell at the careless seaman he'd caught manhandling his crates. "Ho! You clumsy oaf! Watch how you toss that glassware around!"

Curses are the first thing a trader learns in any tongue and my friend acquitted himself flawlessly, progressing from "Son of a cow!" to "The Madonna of your quarter is a whore! Not worth two tapers!" and "Your saint couldn't work a miracle to save his life!" Had anyone guessed he was a Muslim, the entire town would have been up in arms. But such blasphemy was taken lightly enough between Christians and, since things soon settled back to business on deck, I felt my earlier fears unfounded.

"And now shall we see if we can tame this sultry, watery mistress of ours?" Husayn said with a wink when his attention returned to me.

"Aye, aye, Uncle Enrico, sir."

I joined in Husayn's laughter and he clipped me heartily on the back as he set off about his business and left me to mine.

VI

I'M AFRAID MY activity consisted of entirely too much leaning against the landward bulwarks; I draped myself like the rigging there. Mist and rain had risen that morning for the first time in days, revealing Venice as I shall always remember her. The city grew straight out of the water. Over-sized chimney pots jumbled on the sky line with the city's banners. The Piazzetta opening onto the Basin rose like bread in baker's pans up to the domes of the Doge's Palace and the tower of the Basilica of San Marco.

And all around as far as the eye could see was the life this parton saint engendered, life as I imagined it would always be. Nurses strolled across the square with their young charges, past the gibbet on which a pair of malefactors had hung since dawn. A midwife scurried around the families of beggars. And the beggars sat comfortably displaying their dead in hopes of garnering alms enough to bury them, one corpse forced to perform the service until the stench kept even the most charitable away.

Seaward, merchantmen like us dominated the view, load-ing and unloading goods from a thousand ports. A spice trader with an exquisitely carved prow and a hull of the newer, swifter, stabler cog-shape rocked off to our port. She was close enough that the scents of cumin, cinnamon, and pepper wafted over us in succession.

Amongst the bigger, ocean-going vessels were the hum-bler, but no less vital, local ships. Flat barges hauled crops of winter root vegetables with the fragrance of Brenta earth still clinging to them. The fishers bounced from swell to swell along with the day's catch and a powerful smell of calamari.

The scream of gulls intermingled with the shouts of straining seamen. Between the steady marking of the hours from every church tower was the ring for the dead in one parish, a wedding in another.

Dominating all this mixture of human and animal, life and death, land and sea, was the hiss of waves and creak of hulls on the ear, as the reflection of water and sky colored everything that met the eye. It was the combination of so many ingredients, like the baker's loaf, that blended into one, daily, nourishing unity. The smells, sights, and sounds, some obnoxious on their own, when part of the whole, seemed as wholesome as new-baked bread, browned on top to a crisp crust, dipped into one large bowl of January-cooled milk that was the Basin.

But that day was different from any other time I'd seen the same scene.

" 'O Titian, where are you? And why aren't you here to capture this scene?' " Uncle Jacopo had quoted his favorite Aretino to me in one of his quick passes as he, about his business, was urging me to mine.

Our proximity to the spice ship made me think of more than the daily staff of life. A special holiday loaf, laced with cinnamon, currants, and the subtle sweetness of honey, made me linger with anticipation longer than I should have over the panorama of sights and sounds.

It was Saint Sebastian's Day, the incoming of the tide. It was also a Sunday, but the sea and the year's first voyage could not wait for Sabbaths.

All Saturday I had wondered if I wouldn't have to return

to shore and lend the old aunt a hand in dragging the girl bodily from the convent. But I had seen the two women arrive on the Piazzetta in good time that morning with servants and parasols, lap dogs and canaries—a walking market of possessions. It was not the convent, of course, that Madonna Baffo was loathe to leave. It was only now, in the public of the Piazzetta, that her machinations began in earnest.

What whining, pleading, and sobbing went on, I could only guess, being too far away for sound to carry. But in the bright pink gown she wore, it was impossible to miss her antics. Indeed, the girl drew a crowd to her as if she were an actress or a dancing bear. Some were sympathetic and cheered her on. Others thought her wicked and told her so with wagging fingers and gestures of appeal toward the higher authority of either the Doge or heaven itself.

Baffo's daughter fainted. Baffo's daughter threw fits. Baffo's daughter ran away and had to be chased and dragged back by the members of the crew who were trying to coax her into the tender. She flirted with the crew. She showed them her ankle. She shifted her bodice lower. Her eyes toyed with them over her fan. She blew them kisses, paid them bribes of gold ducats, and even fell to her knees in tears before them. When all this failed, she "accidentally" let her puppies and canaries loose and would not set foot in the tender until they had all been recaptured.

It could not last forever, neither my distraction nor its cause, and finally my uncle ordered, "Call them out, Giorgio. They've wasted enough time kissing their tarts good-bye. We must sail before the next bell or wait for another tide."

I flagged to our men on shore and then watched with full attention to see what would happen next.

For the canaries, it was hopeless. People would be seeing their flashes of yellow and hearing their songs over Venice's canals for weeks. But every dog, the old aunt, and the servants were all in the tender now in various states of ill ease. I saw the spot of bright pink being handed down off the wharf and into the small launch.

"Very well—"

I barely had time to form the words under my breath when, suddenly, Sofia Baffo shot up like a belch of cannon fire. She ran straight for the center of the Piazzetta where the two great, red-granite pillars of Venice stood, dispensing their firm justice. The bright blur of pink leaped up onto the gallows, grabbed a spare rope, and proceeded to hang herself next to that morning's executions.

The aunt fainted dead away. The crowd gasped, shrieked for the guards, or stood as still as statuary about this bizarre sort of Calvary. Husayn, watching beside me, slipped into Arabic to murmur a charm against the evil of disbelief. The rope was about her neck, fit in between the strands of daintier stuff—the pearls, emeralds, and gold. She was a tall girl, as I had already noticed. She did not have to stand on tiptoe to fill the space of a condemned man.

With a kick, she sent the little stood off the scaffold and fell—into the great black arms of my uncle's man Piero. I had charged him with her safe arrival on board our ship and I knew he would not fail me, but even I let out a sigh of relief at his near miss. Then I laughed heartily with all the rest, both on board and on shore, as old Piero sat down on the stool beneath one of the dead men, turned Baffo's daughter over his knee, and gave her the spanking she deserved right there upon the gibbet with all Venice to cheer him on.

I shall never forget the picture they made, the great black man and the flailing pink arms and legs. The contrast of colors pleased me so well that I resolved to buy my uncle's man a bit of coral for his ear when we should reach Constantinople. With this thought, I returned to my work with a single mind. Madonna Baffo would not waste any more time in coming on board.

The public taming of the signorina gave me confidence that I could be master of myself as well. I had watched her antics all that morning with the detachment of an audience, of a harem woman behind her grille. I felt the power of that. From the distance of the middle of the Basin, her physical beauty had no effect on me. All her machinations had come to naught. They seemed foolish and juvenile. I need have no fear of her. With the slap and surge of the sea under her, Sofia Baffo would be humble.

A brisk wind was behind us, filling the wedge of our lateen sail and sending our ship singing over the billows like the strings of a zither. The sailors were fresh and exuberant, and by evening the peninsula of Istria was already a low, gray mass along the port side. The lowering sun hit the coast with such brilliance that any detail was impossible to make out. But the winds carried the smell of oak forests upon our ship, the source of the ribs, keel, and planking that rocked beneath us. The vivid colors of the sunset, like a noblewoman's silks, gave promise of good sailing on the morrow. The evening star was a diamond in milady's ear, the whip of Saint Mark's banner over our heads the whispering of her words of love. Dolphins leapt for joy before the bow.

I had my work to do, ordering the sails to the proper tack with the evening rise of winds, fine-tuning with the oars when needed to pass a particularly difficult channel. When I was obliged to use them, the rowers flashed water rainbows from the sweep of their oars as if showing pleasure in the activity.

Truth to tell, I had quite forgotten about our willful passenger until then. She had been very quiet.

But, "when the children are quiet," my old nurse used to say, "I know they're up to mischief."

VII

My uncle brought the old nun to me. "This is my nephew Giorgio, the ship's first mate," he said. "He will see to your difficulty." A roll of his eyes as he left told me privately that he did not have time for the foolishness of the problem.

The nun's face was tear-stained and already a little green from the movement of the ship. She faced me with courage, however, clutching her beads for support, and defied me to resist the divinity contained in them.

"Holy Sister?"

"Young Signor Veniero." She heaved an ample bosom in my direction with anything but eroticism. "Signor Veniero, I demand that you discipline your man."

"My man?"

"That monster of a blackamoor, Signore."

"Piero? Why? What's he done?"

Once or twice she opened her mouth like a fish gasping in air, but she could not bring herself to speak the name of the atrocity. She had to take me across the deck, through all the benches of heaving rowers, and show me. Our progress halted on a stretch of forecastle where we could see the spray mowed before us in golden sheaves and the twilight sky above caught in a web of rigging.

There was my uncle's man, in the place I expected him. Legs crossed in his long, exotic white cotton trousers, he was dutifully mending ropes in the day's last light. But beside him, perched on a great coil, was Governor Baffo's daughter.

She had changed her costume. It was plum velvet now, flashy with gold chains and rings. But the pink silk was still with her. She had spent the afternoon, it seemed, ripping and cutting up the skirt and now, armed with needle and thread, she was in the process of making it up into a shirt for old Piero. After a morning spent playing mad on the quayside and swinging on the gibbet, there was little use in her trying to salvage it for another display of fashion. Nevertheless, how well the color suited my uncle's man had not been lost on Baffo's daughter, either.

She hadn't progressed far with the project—firstly, because she was not a very good seamstress. Her second difficulty was that she was maintaining an extremely active interest in Piero's work to the neglect of her own. She watched his fingers, commented on their agility, asked any question that came to her head as if she would be required to mend ropes herself the very next day.

While I stood and watched with the aunt, I saw Baffo's daughter bend over the slave twice, once dropping her thimble in among the coils, which he gallantly retrieved. As this produced no more result than that, she bent a second time with feigned interest in the ropemaking that served to reveal more of her cleavage than of his hemp. It seemed very clear that Madonna Baffo had decided to begin her flirtations with, of all the men on the ship, her rescuer of that morning, our black slave.

I had to laugh out loud.

"Signore!" the aunt said, appalled. "This is not a joking matter."

"No, Sister, certainly not," I said. "But I don't know what you expect poor Piero to—" I clamped my mouth hard upon the thought and tried to suck the bitterness of the nun's face into mine to keep the corners of my mouth turned down. "Send your niece to me in our cabin. I will speak to her."

"My niece!" the nun said. "I most certainly will not. It's your man that needs curbing, not Sofia. And I certainly will not allow her to enter a strange man's cabin. Alone? Unchaperoned? God have mercy on me."

"As you wish, Holy Sister. But our man is not very bright. He will stand right in front of you and nod at every word you say, but turn around and do exactly what you asked him not to do the next minute."

"Signor Veniero, I am not talking about a simple scolding. I want your brazen man punished—whipped, scourged—whatever is customary here at sea."

"Even that, Holy Sister, rarely has any effect. He is as big as an ox, twice as tough, and three times as dull-witted." I had to direct the nun's attention elsewhere to keep her from seeing the broad winks with which Piero was greeting my attempts to get him out of his fix. "Just look at the scars across his back and shoulders there: beatings that would have killed an ordinary man. But they made no impression on him. He is quite incorrigible, I'm afraid."

"Then I wonder that your uncle keeps him," the aunt replied with a tight breath of air.

"What we could get for him would not be worth the trouble."

I lied, of course. Piero was more than our slave. He was part of the family and clever enough to cover for me if ever I were kept from my mate's duties. But the nun, being the simple, sheltered soul she was, believed me at once.

"Very well," she said. "I will do as you ask. But I will stand outside your door and hear your every word. If my niece should but draw her breath. . . . Besides," she muttered as she tripped over the ropes to where the unlikely pair sat, "I don't know what you can say to correct her that I haven't already tried. Sweet Jesus, if we can only get to my brother safe and alive. . . ."

And with the girl's virtue intact, I silently read the end of the sentence in the old nun's face.

"COME IN, MADONNA Baffo," I said to the knock on my door. "Come in," I said again as she entered and closed the door behind her. Sitting in my uncle's great armchair, I thought, gave my voice strength and authority.

"Have a seat," I invited her.

She sat.

"Have some wine?" I offered, pouring. "It's very good. Last year's vintage from Cyprus."

She looked at me warily, but she took the dare and the goblet. I raised my own drink to her, but she did not return the toast. She quickly put the wine to her lips and drank. She was not used to drinking on board, however, and a sudden swell sent the strong liquid up the back of her throat and into her nose. She choked and sputtered. The aunt burst into the room at the sound.

"Auntie, it's nothing," the girl insisted, trying to conceal the breathlessness that still lingered in her throat. I knew she was humiliated, and I smiled quietly at this first triumph as the aunt grudgingly left the room again.

To make up for her original defeat, Baffo's daughter turned to me now with a haughty fire in her eyes and a rigid perfection in her limbs. I had to fight the disability the sight of her gave me. She *was* perfection. The plum color, I thought, suited her best of all. And the velvet was as soft as night. Her face was like a clear, pale, cold moon in that night. It could easily turn a man mad. I was in grave danger of losing my advantage.

"Madonna Baffo," I said. "It seems you have—er, fallen in love, shall we say?"

"What business is that of yours? You have got me on the ship, and that is all your duty."

"It is no business of mine," I agreed, "except that it is our man you have dropped your kerchief for." I took a sip of wine and looked at her askance. "Truly, Madonna Baffo. A lovely young lady such as yourself. A ship full of healthy young sailors. And a black slave is the best you can do? By San Marco! You're much too intelligent a young woman to feel you must reward a man simply because he saves your life. And of course, you must know I paid Piero to watch out for you and promised him a coral earring for his trouble. He has been recompensed. If anyone is your creditor, then I would say it is myself."

I could see by her eyes that she did not like being in my debt. I counted it as another point in my favor.

"Well, lest I bring your auntie in here for my presumption, let me immediately say that I quit you of all repayment. I need no reward. It was my duty to see you safe on board. It was business. No—more than that. It was a pleasure."

Baffo's daughter sniffed her skepticism.

"However, on one point I am still unsatisfied."

Baffo's daughter stirred in her seat.

"I cannot understand why—why Piero, of all the sailors . . . ?"

The girl leaned toward me, showing off the white softness of her cleavage again, which the cabin's lamp highlighted and shadowed far better than the light on deck.

"Guess," she said, and took a sip of wine.

"Very well." I thought for a moment. "You want to make your aunt jealous."

She giggled. "No."

"You want to hurt me. Get at me for some offense committed"—I blushed as I thought of the offense she could hold against me, of the burn of her arm on mine in Foscari's hall, then struggled to recover myself—"committed unwittingly, I vow—and so you pursue my man."

"You flatter yourself, Signor Veniero."

A point for her. "Very well. Someone else on board?"

She shook her head.

"It's not anyone on board. But it is someone. You do want to hurt someone. Who is it?"

"My father."

"Your father?"

"Of course. And that stupid peasant I'm supposed to marry. Signor Veniero, you are a simpleton."

"But I don't understand. How can your dalliance on board ship affect someone who is not even here to see it?"

"Easily." She sat back in the chair with a self-assured look that told me she expected to win the game with what she would say next. "I expect your dear Piero to give me a child. What fun I shall have when I present my husband with his heir—a little blackamoor."

She began to laugh heartily at the joke and its doubtless effect on the listener outside the door. But she stopped short when I joined her mirth. I roared helplessly until the tears rolled down my cheeks. She sat glaring at me with her fist clenched angrily about the stem of her goblet. What finally stopped my laughter in a series of heavy gasps was that very look. By God, she was lovely with that mixture of scorn yet puzzlement in her eyes! Though I was certain now I would win our little contest, I somehow felt myself in serious jeopardy. I was sobered, but fortunately still in a sporting humor.

"Come here, Madonna. I want to show you something."

From the lap desk on my bunk I took out a fresh piece of paper, dipped my pen in ink and wrote:

Madonna, can you read this?

With a wicked glance toward the door that would keep our writing in confidence, she snatched the pen from me and scribbled, *Yes.*

There was silence in the cabin save for the creaking of the hull beneath us and the scratching of the pen in my hand as I wrote, *Madonna. My uncle's man cannot make you pregnant. He is a eunuch.*

"What's that?" she snapped aloud.

I resisted another laugh and replaced it by a smile of fatherly indulgence at her innocence. *A eunuch*, I wrote, *is like the castrato who sang at the Foscaris' last Saturday night. Or were you too busy running off with Andrea Barbarigo to notice? A eunuch is a man who has had his male parts cut off so as to make him impotent. Among the Turks, where my uncle bought his man, it is a common practice. To get slaves they can trust with their women, the slavers in Turkey. . . .*

I stopped writing, for no more was necessary. It was a lie. I was sorry to have to defame Piero twice in as many minutes, first to say he was a simpleton and now this. A big, healthy eunuch such as our Piero would make—if the operation didn't kill him—was worth too much money on the international market for poor mariners such as ourselves to own. He was, alas, as virile as anybody else.

Nevertheless, my bluff, inspired by the memory of those piercing, unearthly notes that had underscored our last meeting, worked. If I, the foolish first mate of a small galley bound for Corfu, knew about her failed attempt at freedom, how much further up the heap of Venetian society had it gone? The young woman hung limp with humiliation in her chair.

I smiled gently again, but her eyes refused to meet mine.

"Come now," I teased, almost sorry to see her humbled so. "Drink up your wine before you go. It will help you not to die of a broken heart."

In a fury that spilled every drop, she slammed down her goblet and fled from the room. She made no reply to her aunt's eager inquiries outside, but vanished down the deck in the direction of their cabin.

I gently closed the door behind her and sat and finished my wine, bemused into dreams by my brief treatise on the sexless ones, headed by her little scribble, *Yes*. The Venetian *Sì*: its capital *S* was the same as had undersigned the note that began *My love*, which I still kept close in the bosom of my doublet. I folded this correspondence, too, and stored it in the same safe place.

❧

I SAW NO sign of either aunt or niece all the next morning. Only in the heat of the afternoon did the aunt have to come on deck to relieve herself of the sickness. I went over to offer her my condolences and what help one born to the sea can give without seeming to mock. She looked up at me with more gratitude than I would have thought possible from one in such distress.

"Bless you, Signore," she said, then struggled to say more. "I don't know what it was you showed my niece in your cabin last night, but whatever it was, it worked wonders. She hasn't stirred from her bed since then."

"I pray heaven she is not sick, too."

"Oh, no, not she. She has a stomach of iron and veins of ice. Only—what shall I say? Soundly subdued. Yes, that's the only word for it. Subdued. Subdued at last. Pray God it may last to Corfu."

VIII

THE YEAR OF our Lord, 1562. The end of January. Under the winter sky, the Dalmatian coast seemed more stark than usual, the fir trees like last defenders holding out upon the fortress of white granite cliffs. We had put in at Ragusa for supplies and to avoid a storm, but the storm was past now and another two days, three at the most, would see us in Corfu.

It was hard to believe that any voyage could be so uneventful. But for one that carried that she-demon Baffo, it nothing short of unnerved me. Certainly I saw her again. She spent no more than a day locked up in her cabin before the moans and smells of her aunt's sickness drove her to seek fresh air and diversion outside. But somehow she always contrived to be at the other end of the ship from me. If I were helping the men drag in fish on the starboard side, she would be interested in the coasts off the port. If I went port thinking to point out the landmarks we passed, she would find the sunset more attractive. If I had conversation with the pilot in the stern, she would be at the very point of the prow, leaning forward like a figurehead, as if she couldn't wait to be in Corfu. And if I went forward, she hung over the stern longing for the places we had already been.

She also avoided poor Piero as if he had the plague and never did make him his pink silk shirt. I did see her in conversation with my friend Husayn several times. At first I assumed she was trying to make me jealous and so I studiously

ignored it. Then I thought perhaps it was my duty to write
her a little treatise on why young Christian maids should not
consort with Muslims lest they find themselves in the dark
harems of the East. Perhaps the notion of such a treatise ap-
pealed to me because I relished the idea of having her alone
in my cabin again, rich purple and gold in the swaying lamplight, nursing another goblet of my uncle's best wine.

Fortunately, before I made such a fool and traitor of myself, Husayn assured me that she spoke with him because, besides my uncle and myself, he was the only person of her class
on board who was not sick. My uncle was a man of business
and "had no time for children" as he put it. As for myself, as
far as I could tell, she never even let her eyes stray in my direction.

I suppose I should have been grateful for the peace and
quiet. But I was young and could not escape the haunting feeling that if Baffo's daughter arrived uneventfully in her father's
arms within the next three days, she was not the only one
who would have lost the only opportunity for true adventure
and power that life would ever offer her.

I'm not sure what part of my musings I first spoke aloud
to Husayn, but I remember his answer given with a sparkle
in his eyes, caught from the gold of his smiling mouth. "Just
as I thought," he said.

"What do you think?" I asked.

"You are in love, my friend."

"Nonsense."

"Very well. Have it your way. You are not in love."
Husayn gave a shrug. Then he stood staring over the black
night water with a teasing grin.

"All right!" I exclaimed at last in exasperation. "You win.
But is it so obvious?"

"About as obvious as are her feelings for you."

I felt myself burn with humiliation like a child caught at

some prank. "Yes, I know she loathes the very sight of me."

"Oh, I don't know," Husayn said, trying to cover his grin in a thoughtful purse of lips. "But if so, then that loathing is twin sister to your love."

"Did she tell you this?" I asked, violent with jealousy at their confidences shared on the other side of the ship.

"No, no, my young friend. We only speak of the weather and of Venice, nothing more. But I can tell, as I can tell with you."

"My friend,"—I laughed and brushed all his comments away with a wave of my hand—"you come from a land where no self-respecting woman ever shows her face in public. You can't read women's thoughts; you have no practice. If you had been paying any attention at all, you would have seen how studiously she's been avoiding me the past week. I'll bet you a solid-gold ducat that even now she's over there, hanging over the port side for no other reason than that I am over here on the starboard."

"Keep your ducat, my friend," Husayn said. "I am sure you are right. She does avoid you like the plague."

I was glad for his refusal, for a quick perusal of the figures across the oarsmen from us revealed only men lounging there. She must have gone to her cabin early tonight, I thought, convinced I had spent so much time watching her figure from afar that I could recognize it even in the weakening light. I said nothing, but let Husayn continue.

"You two are like a pair of cats which must hiss and scratch and yowl before you mate," he said. "Personally, I prefer a business match. The father gives you his daughter in exchange for trading privileges. Much easier on the purse and on the heart. One lives longer."

"And you, Husayn, have as many wives as you have trading connections. One in Aleppo, one in Constantinople, one in Venice. . . ."

"Praised be the Prophet who allows me such blessings. Even with twenty wives, I would outlive you, my friend, with your scratch-and-bite romance."

"What do you propose I do, Husayn? Present myself to Governor Baffo? 'At your service, sir. Do not marry your daughter to your Corfiot nobleman. Why should you want to stabilize factions on this island when you can have me for a son-in-law? I—a shiftless sailor. Of a good Venetian family, perhaps, but one that has seen better days. A godless man who drinks and swears, a man who will be gone nine months out of ten, leaving your daughter alone in Venice. . . .'"

"Venice is where she wants to be," Husayn counseled.

"By God, I wouldn't leave that girl untended in Venice with money and freedom to spend it if it were the last place on earth."

"No, that would be rather unwise," my friend agreed, visions of the lattices of his harem before his eyes.

"And how could I, Giorgio Veniero, settle down to life in Venice as a stodgy old merchant with nothing to do all day but sit in my warehouse and count ducats? I am married to the sea."

"And she is a harsh mistress," Husayn said with a smile.

"Husayn, my friend. I think I prefer you Arabs' image of the sea as a man."

"A master lets you go home at the end of the day. A mistress is more jealous and greets you at the door with your slippers—and more demands."

"What should I do, Husayn?"

"That is one matter in which—for all my costumes and my perfect Italian—I shall never be a Venetian. You like our images of the sea. Perhaps other images will serve you as well. You Venetians always wonder, 'What should I do, what should I do?' As if there were power in your hands to change the world. Nay, as if the whole responsibility for worldwide good rested on your vain but nonetheless narrow shoulders. My friend, it is in Allah's hands, for all that we little ants can do. '*Inshallah,*' we Muslims say. 'May it be as Allah wills.' "

A sudden noise startled us from our philosophy. A stack of wood just on our left tumbled to the deck with a clatter. As my companion and I turned toward the sound, we saw a figure fleeing from it, a figure whose full satin skirts catching on a splinter had been the cause of the misshap.

"Who was that?" I gasped.

"You need to ask, my friend?" Husayn said.

"My God! Baffo's daughter. I wonder how much she heard."

"Everything," Husayn said, and gave me a smile that was curiously somber and fate-resigned.

The humility of what I immediately saw as the girl's first real triumph over me sat like bad food in my stomach. I rehearsed the conversation over and over in my head, but there was no escape. She had come over to *my* side of the ship one single time—to hear me confess my love for her. There could be no denying that this is what she had heard. The thought of her gloating, laughing, counting the stones of ammunition she now had with which to attack—it was unbearable. I thought of a thousand defenses, but they were all lame. I was stuck with the overwhelming handicap of a weak and simpering confession.

The more I thought of it, however, the more certain I was that Husayn had extracted that confession from me with his teasing smile. Like a testimony given under torture, one could not believe it. I certainly did not believe I loved the girl. She was a child, after all. A mere child, a naughty child with more spunk than wit, more ambition than either affection or sensuality. I satisfied myself I could and would be in control of the situation—firmly, violently if necessary—but it took me all night to struggle to that assurance. And when, before dawn, I was called on deck, I was haggard and raw-nerved from lack of sleep. I never stopped to think that in all she'd overheard, there was something far more dangerous than just a profession of love.

IX

"SHIP HO!" WAS the cry that brought me and my uncle out, and I immediately found cause to be short-tempered with the lookout. Because of the darkness of the night, he had thought the approaching lantern was only a star and ignored it. But by dawn they were close enough that we could see the device on their flag. It was a jagged white Maltese cross on a black ground—the Knights of Saint John of Jerusalem.

"Thank God," the nun said with a clasp of hands and a glance heavenward. "I was so afraid they might be pirates."

I suppose my my nod and grunt of reply were full of wariness, for she caught the skepticism there.

"But surely they are friends," she exclaimed. "They fly the banner of Christ."

"They will want to board us anyway," I replied. "They will search the ship."

"Whatever for?"

"They are looking for Turks." I gave the door to the hold an angry kick as I passed it.

"Well, that's all right, then. We have no blasphemous Turks here. Have we?" She looked at me.

"Of course not," I said quickly. "But it will slow us up considerably. It may take us another two days to get to Corfu now."

When the ship—a small carrack in high disrepair but armed to the teeth—came alongside to board, the nun had her niece and all their party out on deck, on their knees praying furiously. Had I been a Knight of Saint John, this display would have seemed too pious to be real and I would have smelled Turk at once. But perhaps the old woman's simplicity was too great to possibly be feigned, for they were soon passed by. Then again, perhaps it was the unfeigned gold of the signorina's hair that convinced them. I saw their captain finger it longingly, but there was no way in heaven he could find Turkish property there, much as he would have liked to. I burned with anger, not so much at that caress, but at the fluttering eyes and coy little smile with which the girl answered it.

The captain of the Knights was a thin, knobby man with rat-brown, chest-length hair as limp as wet linen. He was the only one of his crew who wore even the surcoat of the once-proud knightly uniform and, instead of the traditional broadsword, he had armed himself with a pair of fierce silver pistols. Hand-to-hand or even with swords, I was certain I could have beaten him easily. God had blessed him with neither wit nor brawn. But with those pistols (probably stolen), heaven was turned quite unnaturally in his favor and we had to cower before him like sheep before a wolf.

After a morning's search, however, the Knights turned up nothing suspicious and had to be appeased by an invitation to join us for dinner. The cook served up salt pork with fried apples and biscuit, which we washed down with quantities of wine. All on board partook—the nun more piously than was good for her sea-sickened stomach and Husayn as non-chalantly as any Christian weaned to the stuff.

I could relax somewhat and joined in the toasts to a sea "free of Turks." I put my feet up against the mast, leaned back against the hatch, and felt a surge of well-being that erased the effects of a night awake with a cankered spirit. The food and wine were good, the sun was warm, but tempered by a freshening breeze. The sky was a perfect blue and the sea reflected it like a polished mirror. Among the empty rigging, gulls were preening themselves, making themselves at home.

Alas, the unction was as short-lived as it was blessed. It was interrupted by a stare as sensible as a slap on the back of my neck. I turned and saw her eyes, jealous of my ease. *Now we shall see*, those sultry brown eyes said, closing to an intense squint. Those words were as clear to me as if they had been spoken aloud. Her eyes dropped as soon as I met them, but there was plenty of time for the message to be passed. She thought, I suppose, that it was only fair to give me warning of what she was about to do. Either that, or she was so certain of victory that she took no care to have it be an ambush.

When Baffo's daughter was assured she had my attention, she got up from her place and moved to the one her aunt had vacated to go and rid herself of salt pork. The place just happened to be at the elbow of the Knights' lanky captain.

"Venerable Knight," the girl began tentatively.

"Yes, Madonna?" The Knight sat up to attention and blushed to be so addressed.

Madonna Baffo herself remained as white and cool as cucumber flesh. She continued, "Venerable Knight, why do you search Christian vessels for Turks? Surely good Christians have no commerce with the heathen?"

"You'd be surprised, Madonna. They're like rats, and no ship on the sea is free of them."

Madonna Baffo was shocked and amazed—at least, she

pretended to be so. "But what sort of Christian would allow such a thing?"

"It's not always easy to tell a traitor from the outside. But I will tell you this, Madonna. Your Venetians are the worst offenders. Worse than the Spanish, worse than the French!"

"I can't believe it!"

"As God is my witness, it's true."

"But why?"

"Because they love money more than Christ Jesus. Because they've been on the Turks' side since we took Jerusalem. As the Lord said, 'they are whited sepulchers, full of death and corruption within.' "

"I cannot believe it," she said again. "*I* am Venetian."

"Ah, but you are pure and innocent, Madonna. Innocent of the ways of the world. It gives a man pleasure to protect such innocence. It makes me feel that the job I do is worthwhile."

"I thank you for it," she told him. "And may sweet Mary and the angels bless you."

She was playing stupid for him. For this man she had to play very stupid indeed, and I knew it was a dangerous game she was playing, even had their talk been of other matters. I got slowly to my feet and walked with feigned nonchalance to the dying fire on which our quiet ride at anchor had allowed the cook to heat his pork. There I furtively picked up a glowing coal in a pair of gunner's tongs. Pretending absentmindedness, I continued to listen intently to their talk.

"But how should I know these corrupted men when I meet them, Messer Knight, if you are not about? You have assured me greatly that this ship is clean. And yet, how should I have known otherwise? I might have thought that there were Turks aboard. How should I know our captain, Signor Veniero, for example, from a friend of the Turks? He seems harmless enough, but. . ."

"How has Captain Veniero raised your suspicions, Madonna?"

"Well, it's foolish of me, of course. . . ."

"Perhaps not," the Knight said, intensely interested. "You can never tell. What has the captain done?"

"Nothing, really. But there is his great black slave. He got him in Constantinople, they say. A Turk and a heathen, I am almost certain of it. He frightens me senseless. See how I shiver, just thinking of him." And she tugged up her sleeve to the elbow to show the gooseflesh and, incidentally, a fine white arm.

"He is a terror to look at, that black man, yes. Certainly to one of your delicate sensibilities. But he is—forgive me, Madonna—a eunuch and a slave besides."

Over the couple's heads, I caught Piero's eye as he stood testing the foot-ropes along the withdrawn sheeting so as to be ready to unfurl the instant we were allowed. I shot him a look of congratulations: he *had* been playing his part well. Then I shifted the tongs carefully in my hand so they remained behind my back as I continued to work my way around the deck.

The Knight pursued his topic: "You have nothing to fear from him. I trust your captain has had him baptized a proper Christian name and has actually done much to save the poor devil's soul by bringing him here to these waters."

Baffo's daughter could not hide her disappointment that she was not to see Piero, her first disgracer, shot full of the Knight's lead. But when she had recovered from that, she began at once to seek other satisfaction.

"I'm certain you are right about Captain Veniero," she said. "You have so much more experience than I in such things, and I trust your judgment implicitly."

The Knight reeled with flattery; he was ready for the strike.

"And yet, there is his nephew, the young Signor Veniero, the first mate. I just happened to overhear such a curious conversation of his last night."

"What conversation was that?" the Knight asked.

"Well, he was speaking to Messer Battista, the merchant on board."

"Yes?"

"Only, instead of calling him Enrico, he called him Husayn."

"Husayn?"

"Well, it sounded something like that, anyway. It was certainly no name I'd ever heard before. And we all know that Messer Battista's Christian name is Enrico. Isn't that strange?"

"Yes, it is," said the Knight, but without her notes of puzzlement.

"But it wasn't. . . ."

"Madonna Baffo," I said. I said it quickly, but with enough force that she could not ignore me. "Don't say another word, Madonna, or I shall have to do something we may all regret."

The Knight, the young lady, indeed, everyone on board turned in my direction. They saw me with my live coal only a hair away from our cannon's fuse, and the cannon was trained dead center on the Knights' carrack. At that range, the charge would easily split the little ship in two.

The Knights' captain went for his pistols, but, "Throw them to the ground," I told him. "And that goes for all your men, too."

They did so.

"Now," I continued, "very quietly and calmly, I would like you all to go back to your ship, cast off, and allow us to go peacefully on our way to Corfu."

My uncle was by my side now. He did not physically try to stop me—I don't think there was any way he could have done that. But he did speak in that very soft tone of his which could easily have stilled many another mutiny. "Giorgio," he said. "What do you mean? Putting so many lives—Christian lives—in jeopardy? For what? For a single Turk and his few bolts of cloth?"

I have said, my uncle was the father of my material needs, but Husayn had provided the spirit. "Yes, for Husayn I will do this. But I will also make certain that this accursed daughter of Baffo gets where she belongs—in her father's care on the island of Corfu. And I hope the peasant she marries has two wooden legs and a hunchback."

At this Madonna Baffo burst out, "By Jesù, I *will* tell them what I heard last night, and you, Veniero, damn you, you will not stop me."

"Madonna Baffo, I warned you. . . ."

"They talked about Messer Battista having three or four wives. They talked about Messer Battista's Turkish language. And then Messer Battista swore by his demon god. 'By Allah,' he swore, and the sea seemed to lurch with demons beneath me."

She stood there on the hatch, her fists clenched and her eyes spitting fire. Her golden curls were spilling unchecked from the confines of her coif and her breast heaved with passion. It never occurred to me that my mere threat was already all the proof the Knights needed. I was too angry to think beyond a lunatic desire to teach that girl a lesson.

Before there was time to think, I touched the ember to the wick. At the same instant, or perhaps a moment earlier, the girl jumped down, picked up one of the Knight's discarded pistols and, shouting his name like a war-cry, tossed it to him. He shot. My uncle took the bullet meant for me full in the chest and crumpled in agony at my feet.

The cannon went off with a roar. Concerned about my uncle, I took no precautions to cover my ears and the sound splintered my head and left me witless for several seconds. When I came to myself again, water was already rushing into the carrack's gaping hole.

Now the Knights lost no time at all. Quickly they retrieved all their guns and complete control of our ship. They bound my friend Husayn and threw him onto the deck of the sinking carrack. My uncle, because he soon died in my arms, they threw onto the doomed ship, too. Then they cut the carrack loose and hoisted up our sails to flee the scene with all possible haste.

As for myself, I was bound in chains and thrown in the hold. They meant, I soon learned, to bring me to trial for murder and mutiny at the next Venetian port. Instruments of torture would be more sophisticated on land. But I suffered torture enough in that dark hold from the echo of my dear uncle's last words.

"Son of my brother," he said. "What have you done? You will be the last Veniero ever to sail the sea. And this will be the last voyage you ever take."

X

IN THE DARKNESS of the hold, days passed of which I was ignorant, punctuated only by waves of agony threatening to drown me in grief over the loss of my uncle, my only close kin, and our friend Husayn. I could see some light through the boards of the deck and I knew night because the darkness was then as complete as that within my soul.

We ran into a storm of physical dimensions on the second day, however. I cannot say how long we tossed mercilessly about and seawater poured down on me through the holes in the deck I could no longer see. I suppose I should have been grateful the Knights did not set me among the rowers, for those poor men stood it out with only canvas awnings for shelter and few of them had even a change of shirt when they got soaked to the skin.

In the darkness I shared with rats and the stuffy cargo of fabric and glass crates, I got terribly seasick. Usually a brisk walk around the deck, a silent communion with the waves, and a few deep breaths of fresh air were enough to cure me of any symptoms, but I was allowed none of these. The food Piero was given to bring me was lousy, and lying there in my own mess did not help matters.

I might have felt more compassion for the nun and the others who must have been suffering, too, if every thought in that direction did not make me burn with regret over my dead friends and fury over Sofia Baffo's betrayal. I had been a fool to stop her elopement from the Foscaris' hall. If I'd kept my mouth shut, she would now be the Barbarigos' curse instead of the Venieros'. After all those thoughts, I was much too busy feeling sorry for myself, captive and without a friend in the world, and feeling the chafe of iron about my ankles and wrists with every lurch of the vessel to feel sorry for anybody else.

Though I did not know how many days had passed, I knew we had left the Adriatic, turned around the heel of Italy and were now on the open sea. I could tell by the size and sound of the swells even when the calm returned. So we were not to go to Corfu after all.

Piero brought me confirming word: "The Knights have decided not to risk it."

"Yes. The heroism they profess might too easily be discovered to be the piracy it really is on Corfu."

"The young signorina—"

"I'll wager she had something to do with this decision."

I couldn't see Piero's dark head there in the hold but I knew he was nodding.

"If she can't return to Venice, Malta will do—for a while at least. It is certainly better than Corfu and the match her father has in mind."

"The young signorina is"—Piero tried to break it gently—"the center of the Knights' attention."

"No need to be gentle with me, Piero."

I did feel my punishment to be harsher—though no less deserved—than the many times that same dutiful slave had been told to take me out and thrash me with a birch cane for some youthful indiscretion. I remembered fondly how I'd plead for mercy, and Piero always gave it. He was incapable of giving it now.

I sighed. "Yes, I'm certain the blushing, lanky captain cannot do enough to show his dotage. More than once I've heard the strains of a dance played on the panpipes above. I've heard a lady's light step match paces with the pirate's boots."

"And I have heard the Knights' captain curse heaven," Piero said slyly, "that he took his holy vows before he met this daughter of Baffo."

"And so it is to Malta, the Knights' lair, that we are headed. Malta is their great beachhead against the heathen threat of North Africa."

Did I mean to comfort Piero with this resort to the plain, hard facts of the case? It certainly didn't comfort me.

Sofia

❧

AFTER PERHAPS A week at sea, when we were just recovering the distance lost in the storm, the usual deck activity above suddenly became more animated. "Ship ho! Off the port side!" The lookout's report was repeated to all corners. In a moment, I heard the oarsmen pushed to double time, and then even faster. We were making a rapid retreat toward the starboard.

"Good God! Three of them!" I heard a Knight overhead exclaim. "We're done for now."

"Pirates! Turks! Pirates!" The cry rang out. "Man the gun for Christ and for Saint John!"

I struggled with my chains and tried to get some view of what was going on, but it was in vain. As far as I could gather, our three pursuers were such small craft that they could not be seen for perhaps ten knots after they had sighted much larger ships such as ours. This characteristic allowed them to slip in and among the islands like serpents, swoop down upon their prey and get away almost before it was known what had struck. Their small size also allowed them to overtake heavier ships in a very short time. So, though our rowers bent to with all their might, standing up on the footrails Venetian fashion for the sprint, the Turks were very soon within firing range.

The Knights sent off the first volley, but for such small ships, the Turks certainly had plenty of guns. By sound alone I distinguished five cannon to our one. Our single gun, too, was only able to defend to the forward, of no use as long as we were fleeing. With three ships able to scud across the water like the wind, the Turks very soon had us surrounded.

The Knights fought long and bravely in spite of such odds, and their fabled courage suffered our galley to take many heavy blows. As each charge made the timbers of our hold quiver like autumn leaves in the wind, I was convinced it was the last we could stand. All the tales I'd ever heard of shipwrecks came flooding into my mind like nightmares. I remembered most the helpless, horrible deaths of men in chains: in the hold like myself or chained to their benches at the oars. Some, rather than drown, hacked off their own limbs to escape the shackles, but such men eventually bled to death among the flotsam of the wreckage or attracted sharks to all their shipmates as well as themselves. Compared to that, drowning was an enviable end.

The hardest thing to bear was my helplessness. Had I had a pistol in my hand, I don't think I should have minded this fate so much. Even being blown into the sea by a cannonball as I fought would have come easily because my mind and body would have had occupation other than this already black semi-death.

One sound from the deck gave me some measure of consolation, however. Hardhearted as it may seem, it was the shrieks and moaned prayers of the women on board. Unarmed, still they had to be where they could see the carnage in all its gore, and their cries portrayed the horror clearly to me who could not see. At least, I thought to myself as another ball shook our ship, I shall go down with the knowledge that Baffo's daughter is punished for her willfulness. How she must long for the peaceful sight of Corfu harbor now!

The battle raged throughout the afternoon. Terror and hunger were muddling my wits, but when one blast took away a corner of the hull above my head, I was able to see the sun sinking and, every once in a while, the prow of one of the little attacking ships. Swift and light, its sails bound up for the engagement but with banners fluttering fiercely over the rower's heads, this bark circled closer and closer, shark-like. The banners proclaimed the attackers' nationality if I'd had any doubt before: they were the white crescent voraciously champing for a star on the scarlet flag of the Ottomans, the green of Islam.

By nightfall we were boarded and the battle continued hand-to-hand by torchlight. I followed its slow but irresistible progress by sound and smell only now: the surge of battlecries, the screams of the wounded, the gurgle of rowers crushed at their oarbanks, the pound of feet, the swish of blades, all encloaked with the thick brimstone of fired powder.

Then, as he was taking a final stand against the main mast, the Knights' captain ran out of powder for his silver pistols and, helpless now as a ten-year-old lad, he cried for quarter. The Turks pretended not to understand and cut him down where he stood with their wild Damascus blades.

The stillness that followed the final knowledge of defeat overwhelmed the ship for several moments and seemed about to sink her of its own oppressive weight, sorely battered as she was. I heard the Turks round up their booty—that with legs first, as it was most likely to jump overboard and escape.

Then, endlessly later, the hatch was thrown open so that the nonliving merchandise could be inspected.

A blazing torch was thrust down into the hold and I was blinded by the light. The torchbearer, too, must not have seen clearly, for he called out, "I say, my young friend? Are you in there?"

The words were Venetian, but it was Venetian with an accent, however faint, that I could not fail to recognize.

"Husayn, old man. What the devil are you doing here?"

XI

I WAS BROUGHT up, cleaned off, and allowed a change of clothes and some warm food. We had chicken, fresh-killed from the galley's coops, for the Turks had thrown the salt pork overboard as offensive to their taste. I got no wine, either, for all the kegs had turned the sea purple and the fish drunk in our wake. But I soon felt much better than I had ever hoped to again. It was a feeling heightened by contrast to what had gone before, and I sat down with my friend to try and sort out what toss of heaven's dice had brought us together once more.

"I really thought I'd be joining you in Neptune's kingdom before this day was out," I said. "By God, how is it that you are even alive?"

"Thanks to Allah, this small fleet of Believers sighted the Knights' carrack before she sank. Rescuing me and finding me to be one of their own, they determined upon immediate revenge. It was Allah's will, however, to send that storm, during which we had to seek shelter in a cove near the Italian Gallipoli, and subsequently lost you for several days. Late yesterday we finally sighted you again, and so it was."

My friend was much changed since I'd seen him last. His Venetian merchant's clothes he had traded for the long, full robes and turban of the man he really was. He was, no doubt at the core, still the same person, but I could not help but be struck by a seeming change in character that he had put on as easily as new clothes. The heavy blue velvet of his robes seemed to soften him considerably. He seemed tender and compassionate in a way that might have appeared effeminate to others, but which to me seemed easy, natural, and at the same time almost saintly. The color became him, but emphasized the gray in his beard and made him seem older than I remembered. His turban, neat and somber, gave him a look of great and hoary wisdom, while the wide bands of flowered silk sash tight about his midriff made him seem stouter.

Although his sash was stuck now with a silver-hilted dagger and a pistol which was probably still warm, it gave him a look of well-fed bourgeois comfort that put me at ease. I remembered the day I'd first met him in our orchards on the Brenta River. I remembered how his brown eyes had sparkled with mirth and kindness under thick brows that grew together in the middle. I remembered his square-cut beard, grayer now than then, under a broad, slightly hooked nose. And those gold teeth when he laughed—that was something to hold a child's fascination!

I remembered what a day it was, a beautiful summer's day in the luminous Paduan sunshine, and we'd known at once we would be friends. He had sung me songs from his boyhood, songs I did not understand, but I had not hesitated to leave the nurse and take his hand to hear more. With a sort of sixth sense like an inward suntan, that glow returned to me now, though it was night and the Brentan land had long ago gone to pay debts. The feeling came to me that it was the Syrian part of Husayn I liked best. The Venetian man spoke my language, but I never could quite trust him in the same way, perhaps because he did not quite trust himself— or trust his God to be with him—in such a guise.

Some of the same feeling, I think, touched Husayn, too, that night. I heard it in his voice as he spoke his thanks to me for risking my life in his defense. His words were rather stilted and formalized—how else does one pay such thanks, especially one who feels debt like a physical stamp upon his soul?—but I heard the feeling nonetheless. Perhaps there were lines of those old songs in it.

"It was nothing, my friend," I said, and "You would have done the same for me."

"No," Husayn said. "I cannot say that I would have. To tell the truth, I thought you were out of your mind. Extremely foolish, at any rate. What was the purpose in such rashness?"

"Had I not sunk the carrack, the Knights would have blown your brains out instead of thinking they had a ready-made coffin to tie you to."

"What Allah might have willed to happen, we cannot say. But even you, my friend—with all your self-confidence—even you, I cannot think, were able to second-guess Him quite so well. No, from the human perspective, I still say you were all but mad. Ha! I can see you now, standing there with the smoldering coal between your tongs, daring the whole mob of pirates to move. Would to Allah I might always have such a defender!"

"Truth to tell, Husayn," I said, sobering, "yours is not the only skin I have on my soul. There is Uncle Jacopo besides. Dear God, I shall pray the rest of my life and never forgive myself for that."

"It was Allah's will," Husayn comforted me. "And you mustn't blame yourself. The Knights would have shot him anyway for harboring me."

We spoke of my uncle for a while, remembering his goodness. Then I cried out helplessly, "That girl had me at my wit's end!"

Husayn nodded thoughtfully. "So tell me, how do you feel

about the girl after a week in the hold? Can you think soberly of her now?"

I had no answer to that.

"The reason I ask," Husayn said, "is that our commander is anxious to make a division of the spoils."

"Spoils?"

"Of course. Slaves and ducats and jewels and such. We have taken quite a rich booty with this galley."

"You mean you're taking us as booty?"

"My friend, it was a fair battle, you must confess, and we are the victors."

"But . . . but the Republic of Venice is friends with the Porte—we have a treaty signed."

"And you are friends with the Knights."

"They are our co-religionists."

"People who walk along the blade of a scimitar must take a fall every now and again. Come, now, don't put on such a face. You, of course, will go free. I have spoken for you and told them you are like my son. Any man, our commander decided, whom the Knights of Saint John keep in the hold cannot be such a blasphemous nonbeliever as all that. I have my goods returned to me, so that is fine. The rest, however, will be divided according to our ancient laws of booty, instituted by the Prophet, blessed be he, nearly a thousand years ago. This I cannot plead against."

"The people, too?"

"Of course, the people. Our ships need oarsmen, our cities need slaves. It is only fair, my friend."

"Fair!"

"Well, then, let us call it Allah's will and accept it at that," Husayn said. "We did find five Muslims among your oarsmen and, having liberated them, we will need replacements."

XII

"COME, COME. I am being harsh with you, but it is only so you will understand how things stand. Our commander has a merciful heart and he has opened up these options. We may sail now toward Corfu and offer the governor there the chance to ransom as many souls on board as he will. Or, in gratitude for saving my life, our commander will give you the girl to have for your own and you may both go free when we reach Tripoli. That is more than just. That is very magnanimous. And I wish you much joy in her, my friend."

I struggled in silence against the feeling of easy comfort I had so shortly before enjoyed in Husayn's presence. He was an infidel, after all.

"You seem indecisive, my friend. Come, I will take you to her and then we shall see what you say about our commander's generosity."

As Husayn led me across the deck, I saw a sash of pink silk around one Turk and a teardrop pearl in the ear of another. I realized at once why they were so familiar. The female prisoners, Madonna Baffo, her aunt, and their two maids, had been allowed to remain in their cabins but their trunks had been rifled.

When the guard opened the door for us, we found the nun suffering from a nervous fit. The two maids were applying cold compresses to her forehead and had had to remove her wimple to give her air. The close-cropped hair—dull, pale, and sticking out all over like the pinfeathers of a plucked goose—seemed more obscene than had we found her totally naked. I turned away, hardly noticing that the niece was not present. I did not ask why.

Husayn asked the question instead, demanding it of the guard in harsh tones and in Turkish. The fellow's reply was equally impassioned. Though I did not understand him, it seemed he pleaded helplessness and asked for mercy. The girl's disappearance should not be laid to his head. He had done his best to remain at his post and he flung a wild arm off in the direction she must have gone.

Husayn shook his head as we hastened to follow that arm and muttered something about the wrath of the commander and the foolishness of Venetian girls. Seeing his concern beneath that wise turban made me worry, too. Baffo's daughter, I thought, is a captive—no, now a slave—and these lecherous Turks have been away from their harems for God knows how long. How could I in reason expect them to ignore her beautiful face, her young, lithe body? Why had I let myself be lulled in good humor so long? It was the days in the hold; they had muddled my senses and made me place too much value on food and cleanliness. While I had been made comfortable, a pack of circumcised scoundrels had dragged her off—onto one of the little Turkish ships, it seemed, sailing tight on our flanks, where her screams and struggles could not be heard from the galley.

Now, as we dropped over the port side of the larger ship and rowed to the companion vessel, what screams there may have been had faded to quiet moans. And perhaps those were only the animal sounds of satisfied men. Perhaps she had already passed from this life in grief and shame and pain. . . .

The first thing I saw in the Turkish ship was a great, black figure that made my heart stop. A second look assured me it was only Piero. He was holding up a torch that glowed on his skin as if he were a lump of coal, and he moved gingerly among rows of prostrate bodies. These were the battle's wounded: men shot in the arm, in the leg, slashed by a wicked blade across the face or burned by exploding powder. Men of both sides were here and many would not live through the night. It was all a horrible, blow by blow account of the fierce battle I had been spared during the day.

Among this human butcher shop, leading Piero and his light, moved a tall, slim figure in pale gold. She had been stripped of all her jewels, but to me she seemed more divine than ever. She knelt beside one body in Venetian blue, braced herself by forming a cross upon her breast, and then pronounced, "This man is dead."

Two shadowy sailors came to throw their companion overboard with quick and simple rites.

Next I saw her stoop beside a Turk. She inspected his wound, then called for a bucket. The bucket contained a portion of salvaged wine which she was using to cleanse the wounds. Though our hull was full of fine linen and wool, she was allowed none of that. When she needed dressings she turned aside and, I saw, tore off portions of her chemise that now barely covered her hips. When, thus armed, she moved toward the wounded man, he shoved her away in terror. She tried again, speaking soothing words, and this time his attempt to escape was so violent that blood spurted anew from the gash in his side. He was, I believe, more afraid of her witchcraft than of bleeding to death.

Baffo's daughter got to her feet with a sigh and moved on, giving him the benediction, "Bloody stupid Turk," in tones of such exhaustion that he could never guess their meaning.

"You must stop her," Husayn said to me, "before our commander. . . ."

But he spoke too late. The commander had appeared at the galley's near railing. He was a fierce-looking man with heavy black moustaches that hung from his upper lip to below his chin like a pair of pistols. The rest of his face he shaved, but either he had not had time for a razor in the last week or the beard grew with such vigor (I suspected the latter) that it was now in dark shadow as well. His great arms and chest were as if bearded also, and he stood, arms akimbo, on the deck and bellowed with such force that he could have filled the sails.

Husayn replied to the fury in words that seemed to begin every sentence, "With most humble respect, my lord. . . ."

Though I saw no way on earth humility could make any headway against such violence, that single bow of deference before each phrase did seem to entrench my friend in a position beyond defeat. The commander got in the final words, shot between his moustaches like lead before a wad of powder, but when Husayn turned to me after his final bows his little smile told me we were far from being lost.

I found this difficult to believe when two burly Turks came and bodily snatched Madonna Baffo away from her work. She fought them so fiercely, I feared other wounded would soon replace those that had died, but they were firm and dragged her, kicking and swearing, back to the galley's cabin. I was determined to jump to her rescue, whatever the odds, but Husayn stopped me with a touch on my arm. I still trusted him and was content to follow quietly.

A new, sterner guard had replaced the old one at the galley's cabin door. There was a look in his dark eyes as if he had been told he would lose them to a red-hot poker if he were as negligent as his predecessor had been. On the other side of the door he guarded, Baffo's daughter was pounding and screaming such abuse that, had the night not been perfectly clear, I would have feared the wrath of God upon us in the form of a thunderbolt. That, too, would make one cautious to open the door, and Husayn had to cajole the guard for quite some time before we were allowed even a crack.

It was only my friend's frequent gestures in my direction that finally seemed to win him.

"I told him you were her brother," he said to me later.

Madonna Baffo fell back when she saw us, silent with hate and accusations of treachery, and this encouraged the guard to let us go in all the way. He did, however, take the precaution of locking the door behind us.

Husayn and I took a seat on an empty trunk by the door while all four women cowered on the nun's sickbed at the other end of the room. Madonna Baffo took her aunt's frail hand in hers and whispered private words of comfort, but this seemed to me to be only an act. To her, a woman's sickness, gotten from nerves and a weak heart, were not worth the attention of men's ills caught in the face of guns and swords. Women's lives, this contrast told me, were to Baffo's daughter dispensable because women were soft and weak. This impression was so strong that, where I'd found her beautiful among the wounded soldiers, the ugly smears of dirt and blood, the torn dress, and uncombed hair now made me look away with loathing.

The women sat occupied with their patient, Husayn and I sat staring nowhere but at our own hands, until I brought myself to whisper, "Come, my friend. Let's go."

"You will not have her?" Husayn asked once the door and the stern guard had come between the women and ourselves.

"You should know me better than that by now, Husayn," I said. "I cannot take a woman like that, like a slave, like booty, as you Turks can. Especially not this woman. If I am to have her, I must win her, heart and hands, fair and square."

"It may not be Allah's will ever to offer her to you again."

"Let that be between me and God," I said, as a man goes to what may be his death.

Husayn nodded. "Very well. But I do not understand why you men of Venice enjoy making things ten times more difficult for yourselves than they ever have to be. And, I must say, you make it hard for my commander."

"Oh, yes," I said with bitter sarcasm. "Now your commander must force himself to enjoy her favors all alone."

"My friend," Husayn sounded hurt. "He wanted to give her to you. He wanted rid of the responsibility. This girl, he knows, will be difficult to keep virtuous."

"I can see your commander's lust even now tottering on the edge."

"You sully the commander, Veniero, and I cannot allow it. Uluj Ali is on commission from the Sublime Porte itself and sails under the Kapudan Pasha. Uluj Ali is known throughout the Middle Sea as one I would trust my own harem to. He respects his women captives as if they were his own sisters."

I knew I had to believe the earnestness in my friend's voice. I also had to let some bitterness out. "He will keep them locked up like his own harem, though."

"For their own protection, yes."

"Madonna Baffo was tending the sick, not playing with broadswords."

"Many of our men have been assigned to the boat where the sick are, and they were uneasy to carry out their duties with her there. Men should tend the male sick. Women have their own to comfort."

"But what harm could she find among wounded men?"

"We cannot say, my friend. It is best not to tempt Allah."

"But most of those men were Christians. She needn't fear among Christians."

"Needn't she?" Husayn asked. "Our experience with the Knights of Malta and other of your Crusaders has been different. Our women in Algiers, for example, have learned that it is better to fall upon their husbands' swords than to fall into the 'mercy' of those demon Christians' hands. No, my friend. If you will not take my commander's mercy when it is offered, you must not balk to submit to his law afterward."

"Tell your commander to sail for Corfu," I said. "Let it be so."

XIII

FOR TWO DAYS we sat with the island of Corfu visible on the horizon. Flying the white flag, the Turkish commander tried to bargain with Governor Baffo for the release of the hostages he held. The tender he sent in never returned. The message was as clear as if we had been there in Corfu's public square to watch the execution of the messengers ourselves: "Damn you, Turk. We will send you to hell before we pay your godlessness a single ducat." The Governor's daughter, I saw, came by her pride and stubbornness legitimately.

On the third day, every ship in Corfu harbor (there were four) came out toward us in a bristling fleet.

"The Governor's a fool," Husayn muttered to me. "And a barbarian besides. What sort of man would attack a ship that carries his own daughter and his sister?"

Uluj Ali, in Husayn's eyes, showed such more mercy. He turned our ships and fled rather than throw lives away in battle. The great galley slowed us down. The hole in her hull, in spite of some attempts at patching, was taking in a lot of water. But the Turks were prepared for this. They had herded us all onto their little craft and filled them with as much of the galley's cargo as they could. I was given another choice—would I stay with the galley and return to my compatriots or would I sail with the Turks?

Since my uncle's death, I had no kin and hence no sure future in Italy. Husayn was the dearest friend I had, and yet it was no easy choice to decide purposely never to see Venice again. Madonna Baffo must have overheard the offer, for her eyes shouted me a dare as I considered: "You are a coward, Veniero. I hope my father cuts you to ribbons for being a traitor."

My fate was sealed with a glance of those eyes. I climbed down the ladder into the Turkish ship and, with that move, bade farewell forever to the Great Basin of Venice.

When the Corfiot ships began to gain on us, the Turks cut the galley free. While Governor Baffo paused to board and secure her, we caught a fine southerly wind, and by sunset we were safe in the open sea without a sail of pursuit in sight.

"Now where do we go, my friend?" I asked.

"Constantinople," Husayn replied with a golden smile. On his tongue, the word was like pure honey—too sweet to be eaten straight, but tempting nonetheless.

Two days after this, the nun was released from this life into the hands of her merciful God. A week later, after a longer but, in the end, no less futile struggle, one of the two maidservants died as well. It was a fever, and it also carried off more than a few of the wound-weakened men and old black Piero besides. But I had seen death at sea before and I managed to keep my spirits high. The more time I spent with Husayn, the more I enjoyed his company. The songs and tales with which he regaled me were new ones suited to my age, and I wondered how I had ever thought the childish ones fascinating when these were yet to come.

I also began to learn a little more of his language. Actually, it was not "his language." The language he had grown up with was Arabic, but the politics of the Islamic world now required one to speak Turkish, so Husayn had sympathy with my struggles. I had known words for "hello" and how to bargain somewhat from traveling with my uncle, but now my knowledge became more than just phrases with which to humor the native. It was a whole different language, neither more nor less than Venetian, and, most important, it expressed a whole new world I had never imagined to exist. Though I had been to both Antioch and Constantinople several times before, life there had always seemed like puppetry to me, a show put on for our visit that couldn't possibly have reality once the audience had gone.

Now I saw that it did. Not only reality, but a depth and life that sometimes made me doubt the reality of the life I had left behind. I listened to these men as they sat about on the deck in the evenings talking of their homes as sailors all over the world do, and I found my view of life to be doubling in size.

My first attempts to join in this talk were met with hearty laughter. It was not, I soon learned, a mockery of my clumsy speech, but rather a true delight to have one more added to their numbers. Half a dozen or so of my countrymen, realizing that the alternative was an early death at the Turkish oars, soon professed Islam and joined with us as well. I did not scorn them for their apostasy. How could I, seeing that only a statement of ten words or so stood between our two virtues? Soon we were a very merry company indeed.

One thing only I felt was missing. Saracens, you must know, never speak of their women. They are quite particular about this; it is a tenet of religion with them. Even Husayn the Syrian was different from Enrico the Venetian I had jested with earlier on the *Santa Lucia* in this respect. When one of the converts sought to entertain us with a tale of his adventures in an Algerian brothel, he received such a look from my friend that he let the subject fall as decidedly bad taste. From then on, we might have been a ship of monks.

Madonna Baffo and the single female companion left to her remained guarded and separate, even though this called for the construction of a sort of screen about one end of the small ship because there were no cabins. Makeshift as the bits of canvas and broken crating were, they were effective, and so, besides being unspoken of, the women were also unseen and it was possible to ignore them altogether.

For others it was possible, but not for me. One day as I happened to pass near their corner of the ship, the guard motioned to me. I remembered him as the fellow who thought Madonna Baffo was my sister. I approached and saw through a flap in the canvas that the Governor's daughter had been trying to ask something of her captors, but without success.

Smiling more at the guard than I dared to at the girl, I asked, "What is the matter?"

"I only wanted to know," Madonna Baffo said with extreme and sudden coldness, "where they are taking us."

"Constantinople," I said, full of glad tidings.

"Constantinople. I see. Thank you, Signor Veniero," and the canvas dropped behind her.

I explained the exchange to the guard as best I could. He nodded, and we shared a good laugh over something that, without direct reference to them, might well be translated as "the simplicity of women."

Later, however, I thought the matter over and was deeply moved to pity. There those two women had been for over a week now without any knowledge of what their future might be. What dreadful fancies must have stirred their imaginations! Now that they knew the truth, surely their fancies could be no less oppressive. Madonna Baffo had been in sight of her father's ships and his safe harbor, but had been violently torn away. If Corfu seemed a nowhere place, then Constantinople was the end of the world, a land of barbarians and infidels.

I thought perhaps I might go and lighten her heart somewhat with assurances that it was really a grand and civilized place, actually larger than any city in Christendom, more decently policed, and wealthier, even, than Venice. But that would be telling her fairy tales she would never experience in true life. If it was the galleys and the mines for the men, it was slavery in the harems for the women. Ah, there was a thought, the pain of which I had gladly and purposely avoided until that brief interview brought it home. And when it hit, the pain was great indeed.

Still, I could not share my pain with anyone. It would not be seemly to speak of women so to the Turks—and besides, these were less than women; they were slaves; it was Allah's will. Now I knew some of the stifle the young women suffered. It turned the pain inward, made it fester and turn to gangrene. At least they had one another to cling to. Their talk could serve as a surgeon's lance to let infection out. I had no one. I could not even speak to Husayn, my dear and closest friend. No, I had made my choice and, like a Turk now, I must learn to be satisfied.

For days on end the doubts and fears ran like a drunken brawl through my mind. Sometimes it grew so fierce that I could no longer bear to sit among the quiet, pleasant company of sailors and I had to seek out a lonely spot to suffer it alone. The spot I found was behind some boxes and barrels of provisions.

Turks are mistrustful of the loner. For them, even the

most stifling company is preferable to the terrors of solitude. That comes, Husayn once told me, from the old days in the desert when loneliness was a constant curse for which there was only rarely ease. But they were considerate of a Christian's idiosyncrasies and the cook learned to come and make his rummage through the stores with respect, even if he couldn't do it completely free of all suspicion as to what a mind alone might be hatching.

It just so happened that this little corner was bordered on one side by the space set aside for the women. I would have found this a thing to try to escape in my state of mind, but it was a portion of their compound the women avoided, being exposed to gales and spray. Even the legend on the broken crating between us, BAFFO—CORFU, was a liability until I learned to avoid its sight and look only at the ever-changing, yet ever-calming, mind-wiping monotony of the sea.

One day, however, I suffered an intrusion. We'd hit a calm; the oars clashed rhythmically, loose in their leather slings. It was shortly after we had caught a glimpse of Patmos off starboard. I remember this detail because that island is everywhere revered as the home of Saint John, and what happened to me there had the quality of revelation about it.

Between the slats of a rifled crate, Sofia Baffo appeared to me in a vision. She walked slowly, tenderly cradling a bundle in her arms. I remembered our first meetings to which this was a sharp contrast. Music again accompanied her steps, but the tune she hummed was a dirge and her steps the measured ones of a funeral march.

Yet, I thought as I watched her approach, she would be no easier to catch in this guise than she had been when she was lively in the convent garden. A log is no easier to pick up when it is flaming than when burned to a white ash. Such a cold, burned-out log did Madonna Baffo seem to be now.

She is like Phaethon of old, I thought. As the sparks of his fall were strewn across the sky to become the Milky Way, so the fire of her last journey must be making an eternal trail of golden bits across the blue Mediterranean. And by the time we reached Constantinople, there would be nothing left at all of the blaze that had once been.

I almost thought I could see through her. She wore the light gold angel's dress she had worn since her capture and her figure had grown markedly thinner. Even her hair lacked luster and remained, for the most part, trapped beneath her plain square kerchief. Certain that the merest puff of air would disintegrate her, I did not dare breathe as she came near.

No more than three paces away, Baffo's daughter caught sight of me and started. If possible, she grew paler and thinner still, then quickly turned on her heels and made to go back the way she had come.

"No—no, don't go," I said in hardly more than a whisper. She stopped. She turned. These were two definite movements separated by a long pause of thought and a deliberate tightening of the shoulders. She took a step or two toward me, but still I could tell that she trusted me no more than had I been a spirit myself.

"What do you want?" she asked. She said it quietly, not so much from a fear of being overheard as from listlessness that could not find the exertion of full voice worth the trouble.

"How . . . how are you?" I asked, tentatively cheerful.

Her look told me at once how stupid and tasteless my question was. How should she be under such conditions? It did not deserve an answer.

"I'm sorry," I stammered, then tried brightness on a different tack. "What have you got there in your arms?"

She looked hard at me, then came deliberately up to the partition. She whipped the corner of the cloth away from her bundle. My heart skipped a beat and my eyes looked down in confusion. In her arms she held the little corpse of her favorite lapdog. Of aunt and maid, canaries and dogs, this was the last, and now he, too, was gone. His little needlelike canine teeth showed in a mouth half-opened in a sort of bizarre grimace.

I did not know what to say and finally came out with a clumsy, "I'm sorry."

I'll bet you are, her stare told me. She then covered the little creature up once more, carried him to the rail, and silently let him drop into the sea.

A long time passed in silence before she turned to me again. Her eyes, I saw, were dry, as dry as chalk, so it must hurt the lids to close over them.

"His name was Cosi-cosi." She fixed me with a look whose aridity seemed to drain the moisture from all it touched. "Cosi-cosi. Because he was half brown and half white. I had him for five years, ever since he was a pup." Her final statement that was worth an hour's storytelling: "He was a gift from my father before he sailed for Corfu."

"I'm sorry," I said again.

"I wanted to say good-bye to him alone. I wanted to be alone. But you are here."

"I'm sorry," I said for the third time. "I'll go." And I scrambled to my feet.

"Just a minute," she called. I saw she had come to the partition and was thoughtfully picking at the splintered wood where the Turks' axes had broken into her possessions.

"Yes?" I asked.

"I have been alone much lately," she said, "and I have done much thinking."

"About what?" I asked. She was making my own thoughts verbal.

"Well, I have been wondering."

"Yes?"

"I have been wondering if you meant what you said to your friend that night before the Knights boarded us."

"Of course Husayn is a Turk. That must be plain by now."

"No. I meant . . . I meant what you said about me. About you . . . and me. . . ."

"Oh." I blushed. "That." She had heard it all.

"You didn't mean it." She nodded slowly and began to turn away.

"No! No!" I blurted. "I mean. . . ."

From this stuttering and looking at the ground I was suddenly drawn up into the hollows of her eyes and found myself speaking poetry. Though I had the impression that the whirlpool I felt was caused by her eyes, she, too, seemed caught up in it. We spun thus in a wild, inescapable swirl where time and the world about us meant nothing. We communicated at such a pace that words were rendered obsolete and eyes, gestures, and soon the touch of hands through the partition were called on to second them. It was only common lovers' talk, the calloused may say. Yet I am constrained from exposing it to paper and possibly their profane eyes much as the Revelator himself was:

And when the seven thunders had uttered their voices,
I was about to write, and I heard a voice from heaven
saying unto me, "Seal up those things which the seven
thunders uttered, and write them not."

At length—a time that seemed a thousand years in but a minute—we slowly extracted ourselves from the violence of that thundering whirlpool. Being mortal, we had to return to breathe our mortality or die. But I found earth's air rare and I panted over her hand as I bade it farewell, planting heavy-breathed kisses on its white knuckles, palm, and wrist.

"Be true, my love," she said.

"My love," I vowed, "I shall find a way to free you and for us to come together in the end. By my life, I shall."

XIV

WE SAILED AROUND the rugged sentinels of Lesbos and Limnos, their tops helmeted in rock and plumed with fleecy clouds. The western sun poured on our track, gilded with glory the hither projections of the armor of these Greek watchers and filled the great gorges beyond with dark purple shadows.

Oblivious of natural beauty, my sole purpose was to seek out other times to meet with Sofia and whisper to her through the ax-holes in the crating. The all-consuming passion we had experienced the first time never repeated itself. It returned only like sparks in an all-but-dead fire to light our dialogues. And our dialogues were otherwise composed of little but sighs and long pauses of dark despair between statements which all began with "Oh, if only . . . !" or "How I wish . . . !"

Still, there was more than enough kindled between us to drive me to attempt to achieve satisfaction no matter how desperate the chances. I determined to approach Husayn. I did not mean to betray our love, but only to sound the waters of the Turks' mercy as with a plumb line.

However, I got no further than to say "Husayn, my friend, I was wondering . . ." before he stopped as with a heavy hand upon my shoulder.

"My young friend," he said, "do not even ask. Such choices were offered at the first, but now it is too late. Tripoli, where you might have gained your freedom, is now a harbor left long ago in our wake. Constantinople will be reached shortly and Uluj Ali is determined upon his course. Throw your lot in with Allah. Trust to Him, and we shall see what He may do for you in the days to come."

I said no more, for the hand upon my shoulder was a silent warning. I thought I had been so cautious in my courting, but now it was clear that any more boldness could very well put not only our happiness but our very lives in jeopardy. Fortunately, my inactive wait was not very long. That evening, the Turks prostrated in a slightly different direction for their prayers, for we had entered the Dardanelles and changed our all-important orientation to the Holy City of Mecca. By morning light the other city, Constantinople on the Golden Horn, could be seen, rising from the mist in brilliance like a second sun.

In the confusion of throwing anchor and then unloading, I ventured one last interview with my love. The *Santa Lucia*'s banners of Saint Mark, her crucifixes, and her images of the Virgin were hung upside down along the gunwale. Any boat that was close enough and idlers on the shore saluted this announcement of the Turks' victory. The Sultan's customary fifth of the spoils disembarked first and was tendered directly to the daunting seaside walls of the Sarai by wharfage collectors.

I found Madonna Baffo standing at the rail, in the exact spot where she had buried her little dog, watching all of this. I hoped the blasphemy to our icons did not distress her too much. I would tell her heaven could hear and answer the prayers of the righteous even upside down.

I spoke her name and she acknowledged my presence but she did not turn. Indeed, she never let her eyes leave their bewondered study of the scene before them: the myriad boats, tiny fishers and great galleys, bustling on the water like crowds in Venice's market. The activity on the ridge before the great seawalls and, finally, the city itself rose as a backdrop with minarets and domes, great palaces and the stuffing of teeming slums in between. She was oblivious of insult.

"This is Constantinople?" she asked.

"Yes," I replied, trying to draw her attention to me by a display of worldly knowledge. But to say, "Yes, this is Constantinople" could have been done by a fool. It was obvious; there was no greater city in the world.

So I began to point out the sights to her. "The Turks like to call it Islambul, which means 'Islam-abundant.' That great dome is the Saint Sophia. Named, as your own sweet self, for holy wisdom, it was once the greatest monument of Christian faith in the world. These last hundred years, however, stripped of all but the shell of former glory, she has served the Turks in their heathen worship. There, beneath her great domes, are the lesser domes of Saint Irene and the columns of the . . ."

But she was not interested in my services as a guide. In a tone that indicated she would become angry if I disturbed her meditations further, she exclaimed, "By God! It is magnificent!"

XV

HUSAYN HAD PATIENCE with me and was content to linger
in the square just inside the seawall after we had disembarked. Here I hoped to try and catch a glimpse of Sofia and
see where she might be taken. The landings of Constantinople are a hurly-burly compared to which those of Venice are
as regimented as if marching in review beneath the Doge's
balcony. In Constantinople, it is as if an anthill—nay, three
or four anthills each with ants of a different size and species—
were all kicked together. The collisions, fights, and aimless
running to and fro I witnessed were remarkable. Only as a
second thought, it seemed, were goods, like bundled ant
eggs, being salvaged and transported to safety. Even then,
only one move out of twenty seemed to be the right bundle
to the right human or animal back headed in the right direction.

It was as if the many decks of cards of all the peoples of
the world were shuffled into one by a child who had
no knowledge of the rules of any game, but only liked
to shuffle. This led to some very curious combinations: a
great black African guarding a shipment of dainty Chinese
boxes rich with ivory inlay and carving; a tiny Chinaman,
stripped—ribs starting—to a thin waist, strained under a
heavy, vicious-looking load of elephant and rhinoceros
tusks. Cool Indians, slippery like snakeskin, bargained with
fat, basted-duck Italians in God-knows-what language for incense from Arabia, while the Arabians, secret, silent, ghostly

men, more white robes and headdresses than flesh and blood, eyed sacks of grain as if they were filled with precious myrrh.

And everywhere were the Turks, Turks of all shapes and sizes. There were rich Turks and beggar Turks, Turkish fishermen, merchants, porters, pashas, soldiers, admirals, pickpockets, and customs officials. A Turk in a foreign land is immediately picked out for what he is, but here in their own land, one would be hard pressed to name a single trait that all of them shared. It was the Venetians that seemed more a caricature of nationality here.

I was glad to be able to step out of this mêlée and view it objectively. I knew from experience how easy it was to become part of such a crowd, taking communion of its madness. I knew how easily that madness could become my own catechism, and I could find myself weeping tears of faith for its litany. And besides, after more than a month at sea, every step I took jarred my frame most painfully. I was obliged to sit upon a great bale of imported woolens so all my attention could be relieved of discomfort and concentrated on my vigil.

Of all the brands of humanity present on the landing, one was conspicuously absent. That was the women, of any race or color whatsoever. Even the painted whores that flounce the docks of Venice were gone. This was the topic of desperate conversation passed between two sailors who had just been released from three months at sea, but they would have to go elsewhere and be much more private to make their talk material. I was certain that Sofia Baffo would stand out here in this male crowd like a circle among squares.

It was Husayn, however, who saw her first. He had had the wisdom to look not for her tall, slender figure, or light-gold gown, but for the short, greasy slave merchant who had spent the morning haggling with Uluj Ali.

Baffo's daughter and her maid were brought from the ship swathed in veils, looking more like passing shadows than human beings. I could only tell which one she was—even after Husayn pointed them out—by the fact that she was uncommonly tall and because she kept fidgeting with the wrap in order to get a better view of the wonders about her. The slaver tried to correct her of this fault, for, if it gave her a better view of those about her, it also gave them a view of her, his prized merchandise, which he was not prepared to put on display there on the landing like nothing better than a waterlogged bundle of silks. Fortunately, the man had a covered sedan chair waiting, into which Sofia and her maid were rapidly loaded. Heaved to the shoulders of eight monstrous porters, they were carried out of sight with giant strides. Even had the condition of my legs allowed pursuit, Husayn's heavy hand wisely counseled against it.

Husayn took me then to his home, where I was welcomed with hospitality that could not have been greater had I been indeed his son. Having visited him once before on my last trip to Constantinople, I knew it was not actually his home, but that of his father-in-law. As a native of Antioch, Husayn had found it business-wise to contract a marriage with a young lady of Constantinople, the only child of her wealthy merchant father.

The house, though in town, was located near the Langa Bostani Park and fronted on the Sea of Marmara itself. It sat behind high walls in a small but delightful park of its own, the focal point of which was a large fig tree with the buds just swelling. A confusion of lesser oranges and lemons still in fruit were propped up by rose and mimosa bushes, which, in months to come, would fill the garden with color and scent. Jasmine, protected in a pot, was already in bloom and almost overpowered the garden from corner to corner, like the perfume of some aging courtesan.

The house was not one of those glaring things of Constantinople's new rich but, being made mostly of wood, it had weathered into its surroundings as if the product of nature. I think it may have predated the Conquest: the pillars that framed the entrance, at least, were of Greek workmanship. Lattices had, however, long stood guardians over the windows on the second floor where the harem was. I saw no more of the inside during my stay than the three reception rooms of the *selamlik*, or men's quarters, where the fresh whitewash was pleasantly softened by rugs and cushions. One room in particular enjoyed a view of the sea and its flocks of ships, great and small, from a divan that ran along two full walls.

I never saw the wife, of course, but a small son was sent out of the *haremlik* to greet the father he couldn't remember and who frightened him with his loud greeting and flash of golden teeth. The little fellow cried, staining the red silk of his new little shirt, and had to be quickly removed. It was the reverend old gentleman Husayn had married, after all, and the two met anew with tender affection and respect such as I have seen between few husbands and wives.

The house had a private bath and the first order of business for these fastidious Turks was to use it. Husayn and his father-in-law invited me to join them in a communal wash, but I declined, enduring the time alone with my thoughts as best I could. Then they retreated together to evening prayers and left me to make my ablutions alone.

The small room had an awful lot of water in it, in basins and tubs, all uncomfortably hot. I took off my doublet and chemise, poured a bowl of water over my head and rubbed it into my scalp to rid my hair of the salt spray's stiffness. I sloshed a little up under each armpit. Then I noticed a stack of clean Turkish garments on a low stool: a pair of *shalvar*, shirt, vest, sash, and the long-sleeved jacket to go on top. I refused their lure and put on my own clothes, stiff with my own smell and sweat again. I would not be made an effeminate Turk so easily.

Husayn and his father-in-law exchanged glances when I rejoined them. I guess I did smell a bit. But, swimming in politeness, they said nothing, and turned to their conversation once more.

My two hosts conversed easily and at length and, in true Turkish fashion, were in no hurry to come to any topic in particular. It was nighttime, long after supper and the rest of the house was still, before my friend even began to recite the adventures of our voyage. (What had they been discussing all the time before then?) And, anxious as I was to come to the subject of slaves and slave-taking, I nodded off while Husayn was still tied on the Knights' sinking carrack to the singsong of his father-in-law's exclamations, "Allah preserve you!" and "Allah give only your enemies such a fate!"

I AWOKE WHILE it was yet night, but I found myself alone in the guestroom and the lamps dowsed. The chilling moisture of a winter wind blowing steadily off the Black Sea had found its way even in here.

Husayn, I supposed, had gone at last to beget another son if Allah willed, and the old man had his own room, too. Without the lullaby of voices about me, my mind and nerves grew taut with tension and sleep could not return to such a hard bed. Rather than sit in the dark, I began to fumble about for a lamp, but without luck.

Suddenly I heard a sound in the room at no great distance from where I was crouching. Rats, was my first thought. Having a sailor's natural aversion to those rope- and store-destroying creatures, I froze lest I inadvertently touch one.

I hoped they would find the crumbs they sought apace and then leave.

But presently, to my wonder, I saw a lamp kindled and knew rats light no fires. Imagine my surprise to find first the hands, then the face, then the entire figure of an attractive young black girl illuminated by that light.

"Good evening, master," she said, bowing with her hands crossed on her breast, and she smiled. Her teeth were perfect and her eyes like the flames of her lamp, yet kinder.

"Good evening," I replied.

She wore nothing but a chemise, although the room was anything but warm. Beneath the sheer fabrics her flesh was like well-salted black olives in color and texture and, before I could stop it, an image of biting into it with great appetite flashed across my mind.

It was clear why she was there. It was a supreme act of hospitality on the part of my hosts. And she did not seem to mind being presented thus, like the numerous plates of dainty cakes and pastries that had preceded her in that same service that evening. It was easy to see why. She was a nubile young woman in a house where the mistress had first claim upon the often-absent young master and the old master was gray beyond lust. Of course she shared the ambition of all slave girls to get a son of a free male, for then her child must be freeborn, and no freeman, grown of age, will long see his mother a slave.

Before I had quite sorted out all of her motives, these motives had already brought her to my side where she began to croon and then to fondle me. I thank heaven for my codpiece, a mystery she had never seen before, else I might have been lost at once.

Of course my true love, which had become something akin to instinct by that time, refused to let me spend my virginity thus. I began to try and explain this state of affairs to the girl, but alas, each of us came to Turkish from a different direction; we never quite met. My speech was further hampered by the fact that I had never heard the language used to speak to women before and it does make quite a difference. Those of my phrases the girl did understand only made her tumble into fits of giggles because they were said in merchants' and sea captains' speech. To speak thus to a slave girl was to attribute a power to her that was truly ridiculous. The girl could not help but think that I was toying with her as lovers sometimes do, and she did not take me in earnest even when I pushed her physically away. I actually had to slap her—quite hard—across the face before the lights in her eyes were flooded out by tears.

"No!" I said. "No!"

The girl crept off to a corner of the rooms shaking with sobs that my offer of a blanket could not still. I did not try to hush her more than that, for the sound of a slave girl weeping in the night was the perfect pathetic accompaniment to my thoughts, which would have kept me awake anyway. The girl wept and wept, fearing the wrath of her master in the morning because she had not made a satisfactory gift.

I was somewhat encouraged by this gesture of sympathy. Husayn had not forgotten my plight in the joy of his homecoming, after all. He had sent this girl hoping to divert me from my true love. Well, her tears in the morning would assure him that I remained unmoved.

XVI

MY GUESS CONCERNING Husayn's motives proved correct. When he came from his prayers to rouse me that morning, he brought the glad news that between the two of them, he and his father-in-law had decided they could put up fifty *ghrush* toward the purchase of Sofia Baffo from the slave merchants.

A trip across the Golden Horn that morning won promissory notes for another hundred and fifty *ghrush*. Here in the suburb of Galata, where merchants of my homeland lived in a tight little colony, the Venetian ambassador and other kind-hearted souls who knew either Governor Baffo or my family were glad to help out.

From previous experience with my uncle, I knew that anybody's coins were legal tender in Constantinople: the familiar Venetian zecchino, Dutch ducats, German groschen. Even Turks tended to favor these European mints to their own because the many sites throughout the vast empire where coins were struck did not maintain much unity among themselves as to weight and alloy.

Also, according to Muslim religious prejudice against drawing figures, the Sultan Suleiman would only distinguish his coinage in Arabic script. Besides being difficult for most Europeans to decipher, it was much simpler to alter a few tendrils of script than it was to deface the entire figure of Saint Mark blessing the standard of Venice. I knew the dealer among the Turks must be constantly on guard not to accept as legal tender disks of base metal stamped in back alleys with meaningless curlicues and crosshatches. But this was easier said than done for one who didn't read Arabic.

Every transaction, therefore, demanded a separate adjustment. The transaction depended on the known variations in the different currencies one happened to have in his pocket at the moment. It depended on each individual's judgment as to how many times a curl of silver had been shaved off the edge of each individual coin. It also depended on whether the partners in this present deal would decide to line their own pockets with this roundabout way of charging usury in a land that otherwise forbade it. I realized the details would have to be haggled out with the slaver when the time came.

At the moment, I was content to know that we had a sizable purse full of zecchini, ducats, and groschen that could be figured roughly and generally as two hundred Turkish *ghrush*. Uncle Jacopo had always told me to equate *ghrush* with *grosso*—"those big silver coins"—to distinguish them from plain "silvers," the little aspers, of which there were one hundred twenty in a *ghrush*. I knew that the chief cook at the Sultan's palace, with fifty cooks under him, could brag that he earned forty aspers a day. It would take him three days to earn one *ghrush,* nearly two years with very few holidays to earn what we had in that purse. How much more could a slave possibly cost? A master had to feed and clothe his purchase after all, all those things, Husayn reminded me, a poor orphaned sailor would be hard pressed to provide for a wife like Sofia Baffo.

Husayn advised that we should wait a day or two for other men to consolidate their funds and raise perhaps another fifty *ghrush* or so, but I could not wait. The figuring of such a sum could only fill me with confidence.

A second night with the black slave girl passed much as the

Sofia

first—only just fast enough to keep my impatience from turning to distraction—then, armed with the two hundred *ghrush,* I made Husayn take me to the slave market the very next day. We were there when the great wooden doors opened.

There are several places one can go in Constantinople to look for slaves. Rowers change masters on the quayside so they are never free from the sound and smell of the sea. If one is looking for a good strong Ethiopian to be his man-of-all-work or a docile Sudanese woman to help in the kitchen, one goes to a tumble of buildings a stone's throw from the Haseki caravanserai.

Husayn took me, however, to the exclusive courtyard no great distance from the Sublime Porte itself. We had to pass through a district of pearl merchants to reach it. Such an array of gems of every hue and size, displayed in so many shop-windows on velvet cushions that set off their luster, served perhaps as a probation. If the sight were too rich, one was warned away from the treasures that lay in the courtyard of the slaves beyond.

Rugs, low tables, and smoking braziers were set beneath high, mosaicked colonnades. Here narghiles and sherbets were served with compliments to the prospective buyers who might linger all day over their purchase as if at a party. The merchandise itself seemed the least important thing in the market. It sat discreetly to one side of each shop door-way, warmed by the sun of an early spring morning.

Impatience, I knew, was one sure way to drive the price up, but I would not let Husayn make even the briefest show of leisure. I drove him up and down the colonnade until I spied a familiar face—Sofia Baffo's maidservant. The woman sat with a pair of young Circassian children in one particu-larly fine shop. She had been given a needle and thread and was supposed to be demonstrating her fine stitchery. Unfortunately, tears so shook her form that she found work impossible.

"Foolish woman," Husayn said with a shake of his head. "She should appear cheerful even if she is not. The sort of master she will find with a face like that will assure her misery for the rest of her days."

My friend sat down at the table beneath this arcade and waited for sherbet, but I could not constrain myself. I ran to the maidservant immediately.

"Maria, Maria!" I said. "Where is your mistress?"

The woman was startled from her grief and could not speak for a moment or two. This allowed the young salesman to see my interest and to come to my side.

"You are interested in such a slave woman, my friend?" he asked. "You have good taste, indeed. You could not have made a better selection had you spent days combing all of Constantinople—no, not months going throughout all the lands of Islam. She is a bit thin from the long sea voyage, but a few weeks in your generous kitchen, sir, will see her fat and fit. She is skilled. She will work and do your bidding. She is eager to learn any task. She is not yet thirty-five years old and, though married once, it was to some body-hating Christian who gave her but a single child. The child died of the damp climate of her homeland. But you will see that here in our climate, with her health and vigor, she may yet bear you a pair of sons and prove an excellent, loving mother to them. Three or four sons, perhaps, if it is Allah's will and your major interest, my honored sir. In any respect, she will pay you back the price within the year, I can assure you."

I wasn't well enough acquainted with Maria to know if a third of what he said was the truth, nor, if it were, how he had possibly come to know it. My speaking knowledge of Turkish stopped me at, "I was looking for. . . ."

Fortunately, Husayn saw my difficulty and came to my aid.

"Actually," he said, "we were on the ship that brought this woman here and—"

"Praised be Allah! What a happy coincidence!"

"And we were wondering about another woman—one younger than this—with golden hair. We are interested in her."

The young man pressed his lips together and nodded thoughtfully. Then "Excuse me," he said and disappeared into the shop. Shortly he returned proceeded by the short, greasy merchant I recognized from the quay. The young man bent his head and spoke in an agitated stream into his elder's ear.

"I am Kemal Abu Isa," the older man introduced himself graciously, "and this is my son. Please, you are welcome here."

Husayn returned the greeting and introduction with profuse confessions of the honor it was for us to be in that shop. They made my flesh creep.

XVII

"PLEASE BE SEATED," the merchant said. "My son will bring you a smoke, a tray of sweets."

This rigid politeness continued for what seemed like another century. The merchant stroked his greasy chin, Husayn stoically sampled a tray of preserves and made up more pleasantries than I imagined existed in any language. I passed the time bouncing my knees nervously under the low table.

At long last the merchant broached the subject. "My son tells me you are interested in a particularly fine young slave I have recently acquired. Is this slave for yourselves, or are you merely acting as agents for another?"

"We are not agents," Husayn said.

"Forgive me for being so frank," the old man said, "but this is business, is it not? A man must make a living, with the help of Allah. So tell me, just how much were you gentlemen expecting to pay?"

Husayn hummed a little note of indecision, but I blurted out, "I have two hundred *ghrush.*"

"Two hundred *ghrush,*" the merchant repeated. "Again, forgive my frankness. But for such a prize as that fair-haired one—a prize I shall not see again if Allah wills me a hundred years—I expect to get three hundred, maybe more. No, do not try to bargain me down, my friends. I told you this in frankness. If I expected you to bargain, I would have started out at half again so much. I mean no offense, but such a prize—a jewel—is not for common merchants like you and me. Indeed, I am charging a quarter of your price in earnest money of any client I will even allow to see her.

"Now, for two hundred *ghrush,* I would be glad to sell you her companion here. She in also of European origin and equally fair-skinned. No, for you, my friends—one hundred and fifty. No? You are not interested? Come, do not take offense, my friends. I am a man, after all. A man who must, with the help of Allah, make a living. The golden-haired one is a virgin, my friends. I had the midwives certify. I shall not see another such prize—no, as Allah is my witness, not in a hundred years."

I was ready to bolt to my feet and grab the old man by his greasy neck, but Husayn constrained me.

"Your concern is most understandable, sir," Husayn said. "She is a prize indeed. But tell me, would you allow us just to see her?"

"Fifty *ghrush*," the merchant said, stroking his chin. "That is my price. And usually I bring such merchandise to the privacy of your own house. This is most irregular."

Irregular or not, Husayn had now found something he could bargain on. I balked at spending a quarter of our money that must somehow grow to four hundred *ghrush* in the next few days on nothing but an interview. But I underestimated the power of my friend's golden smile. He persisted and, finally, with a double lie that first, we had no real interest in her purchase, and second, that I was the young lady's brother and it would be an act of charity sure to bring heaven's blessings, he got us in for nothing.

"Very well. For you. Because you are my friends," the merchant concluded the deal.

The merchant led us back through a small shop room which seemed to be used for nothing besides the mixing of sherbert and the storage of a pair of narghiles. On the back wall of this room was a bell which the merchant rang loudly and then waited for a few minutes to give any woman in the rooms beyond time to disappear before we entered. When at last he threw back a curtain, we found ourselves in a long, deserted passageway lined with heavy doors, many of which were bolted. Those that were ajar led into small but, I had to admit, not uncomfortable cells. Those that were closed but not locked hid, I supposed, the man's womenfolk and their work and sitting rooms.

A door at the very end of the passage was still locked. This the merchant opened with a key worn round his neck and then he stepped aside to allow us to enter first.

We found ourselves in a large room, wanting in neither air nor light, for it enjoyed a row of windows near the ceiling. The windows, I noticed, were large enough for a man to crawl through, and the gentle sounds of women about their daily tasks came in through them. The room was appointed as pleasantly as any Turkish sitting room I had ever seen. The rugs and cushions on the divan were of bright, tasteful design and perhaps more luxurious than those in Husayn's house.

It was upon these cushions that I saw her. Baffo's daughter had thrown herself across the divan in an attitude—belly down, legs swung up in the air behind her—one often associates with sobbing fits. But she was not crying. She had before her a silver tray of dainties and was enjoying the luxury of a late breakfast.

She did not start and cower at the sound of the opening door as one would who was used to the visits of a cruel master. She continued with the business of breakfast and only stirred when she saw for certain that it was Husayn and I. Then she made the effort to roll on one side the better to regard us. She propped her head on one arm and let the other rest upon her hip, from which that hand dangled idly. The straight line of that arm accented the curves of a small waist and firm, round hips. I felt that I should be reduced to tears if she continued to show no overwhelming relief to see me. And she did not—anything but.

"Why, Veniero!" she said—not "Giorgio", not "my love"—and her tone was light and easy as if I were a casual, everyday visitor. "How nice of you to come today."

My earnest questions, "How are you? How are you treated?" fell somehow short of the long distance that had to be maintained between us with the merchant on guard.

"Just fine," she answered easily. "Just couldn't be better."

The awkward void that followed left me speechless, but Baffo's daughter was induced to fill it with anything that came to hand.

"Look!" she exclaimed. "Just look at what they have given me to wear!" And she jumped to her feet to give us a better view.

The major portion of her costume consisted of a jacket made of red and orange patterned velvet with trapunto work in gold thread. Its sleeves were wrist-length and ended in stylish points. The waist cinched in skintight, closing with a row of tiny pearls before it flared out to the ground. Above the waist fastening, the jacket was cut away, allowing for the natural swelling of the breasts which were covered by only an underbodice of the lightest gauze.

Conscious of this detail, Sofia shifted the bodice and giggled. "I used to be grateful I was not so big so I wouldn't have to suffer the agonies other women went through to appear chestless as Venetian fashion prescribes. Now I have to pray I may yet grow a little."

A shift in light allowed us to see that the gauze was translucent and I blushed with heartache as her nipples appeared through it like a pair of round, sugared comfits.

"And look!" she cried with sheer delight, the bodice and its lack of modesty quite forgotten now. "Just look! Pants! Pants like a man's!"

The over-jacket split at the center to reveal a pair of red silk trousers. For all that they were luxuriously full, caught tightly at her small ankles and with a crotch no higher than her knees, when she kicked her legs up in them they seemed very immodest to me.

"*Shalvar,* they call them," she explained and looked to the merchant for a confirmation of her pronunciation.

The old man nodded and smiled with pure pleasure at his merchandise's performance. He couldn't have whipped better from her. A pair of crimson slippers and a jaunty little round cap fitted with a veil completed the costume.

"And just look what I am given to eat!" Sofia said next, returning to the tray on the divan. "Such dainties! Here's a sort of compote made with quince and honey and yogurt. Here are dates stuffed with almonds, this sort of cheese with a strong, salty flavor. And such curious flat pancakes for bread, sprinkled with fennel and caraway seeds! But these here are my favorites—these little pastries. What are they called?" she looked to her master.

"*Taratir at-turkman.*" He smiled.

"And that means 'little bonnets of the Turks.' His wife makes them, deep-fried and I dip them in clotted cream— oh, they are really too heavenly. Here, Veniero. Won't you try one?"

But I declined and soon made excuse to leave. I hardly had patience to bid the slave merchant a decent farewell, wanting only to escape that place.

"From the palace," Husayn mused as soon as we were out of earshot.

"What?" I asked.

"That eunuch is from the Sultan's palace," he elaborated. "You can tell by the tall white hat and the fur-trimmed robes."

"Which eunuch is this?" I asked, for there was more than one for sale in that exclusive bazaar.

"The one sitting now at Abu Isa's table. Didn't you see him? We walked right by him on our way out. Abu Isa's son has brought him out a narghile and he is smoking."

I confessed my mind had been elsewhere. I turned now to take a look and found nothing much to be impressed by. Beneath the towering white hat was a man with skin that seemed as white and pasty as unbaked bread dough set to rise by the heat of his narghile. It looked as if one careless touch could deflate him.

Of what interest is an old eunuch to me? I thought as I hurried my friend along.

XVIII

"THE YOUNG LADY is clearly content with her new life," Husayn insisted to me.

"It was a show she put on so her master wouldn't beat her."

"Abu Isa is one of the most exclusive slave dealers in all the lands of Islam. He is not such a fool as to go about injuring his merchandise."

Husayn had paused in our progress away from the slave market in a small public square with a fountain. The square sat awkwardly on a slope and the stones paving it were so uneven that they must have been laid in the days of the Roman emperors and had no attention since.

Besides the water-bearing slaves, sweetmeat sellers, and tumbles of rowdy boys such places attract the world over, there was also a gypsy with his bear on a chain. The animal seemed a thin, torpid creature, his pelt yellow and mangy, probably whip-driven out of his natural hibernation to this spot where he blinked at the world of men in a stupefied haze. The gypsy managed—by his own strength, not the bear's— to get the brute to sit up. But that appeared to be the only trick they knew, and for the bear this was a signal to start licking his own lurid pink genitals in a most embarrassing manner. This attracted the shrieks and hollers of the watching boys but no gain to the gypsy's cup.

I suspect Husayn lingered so long before the spectacle hoping it would distract me. It did nothing of the sort, only increased my agitation and impatience. When my friend finally turned to lead us elsewhere and stopped to donate the first coin of the day, I slapped back his hand.

"Please," I said, apologizing for the roughness of my action but not for the action itself. "Don't squander a single asper of the purse that must double in size before tomorrow."

Husayn opened his mouth to speak, but what he meant to say I never heard. Instead I saw a little brown hand slip back around the smooth cordon of his waistband, the cut strings of my friend's purse clutched in its knobby, thin fingers.

"Stop! Thief!" I cried.

And then I had the presence of mind to remember the Turkish word for "cutpurse" and I hollered that, too. This word stuck in my mind because Husayn had told me it was one of the worst names you could call a man. It was saved for only the nastiest of altercations, even when one's opponent had never intended a robbery.

Cupid made fleet my heels and strong my arms. So would some lyric poet describe what happened when I saw half of Madonna Baffo's worth—the only half we had in hand—vanishing across the dirty square. I did manage to jostle Husayn out of the way, kick the naked brown feet out from under the little thief and recover the purse not an asper lighter in less time than it takes to tell about it. But the poet would not reckon on the consequence my shout of "cutpurse" had had on a square of half-formed Turks just looking for an excuse to punish the gypsy for bringing his obscenity into their midst.

The youths had swarmed together to effectively cut off the little fellow's escape before I ever got to him. After I returned triumphant to Husayn, they closed ranks about the cutpurse and took care of the rest of justice. So potent was the sentence that the boy's own father—I knew they were father and son by the identical gypsy wildness in their black eyes—did not stop to help him. The man slunk from the square as fast as his chain could drag the bear, which was not very fast at all. The bear, the only creature around the fountain that had not understood my "cutpurse" cry, was much too fascinated by his sitting posture to collect his feet again.

Husayn discovered something lyrical in my actions, however, for after he'd thanked me with such Turkish profusion that it cramped his Venetian, he stood considering the purse with its frayed strings for quite some time in silence.

He smoothed the corners of his moustache down into his beard and then at last he said, "You are convinced that purchasing the young lady's freedom is the thing worth most to you?"

"The most important thing in the world." I panted the words, not because I was still winded by the rescue—though I wouldn't mind if that's what he thought—but in an attempt to bridle my impatience. This short, round, domesticated Syrian could not catch the desperation of the case!

"There is a way we might——" he mused.

"Well, why for the love of Saint Mark do you hesitate?"

Saint Mark made no impression on the smoothness of his moustache. "A way I could get quite a lot of money."

"Two hundred *ghrush*?"

"Maybe more. Maybe quite a bit more."

"Quickly?"

"Perhaps, if it's Allah's will, before evening."

"Then we must do it at once. By God, we have no time to lose."

Husayn dropped his hand from his moustache and nodded with sudden decision. He collared one of the smaller boys dancing excitedly but ineffectively on the outskirts of the little gypsy's beating. He gave him a few quick directions and one of the smaller coins—one of those crude angularities of ill-stamped metal, as flexible as ribbon, that are the bread and butter of Turkish exchange—from his rescued purse. The boy was off like a shot and, while I nearly gasped at the disappearance of one of our precious coppers, I suppressed it, believing with desperation that Husayn could realize his plot.

"Come." He took my elbow. "Let's be off."

I was only too glad to leave that nasty little square, but still I had to ask: "Where are we going?"

"The baths."

"The baths? You have a private bath at home."

"We do, and I have already washed the sea from me in it. But the bath at home is not a public bath."

"So much the better, I should think. We have two hundred *ghrush* to gain and you plan to sink yourself in the indolence of a Turkish bath?"

"You may be surprised," Husayn said, smoothing my rudeness. "Many business deals are made in the baths. You Venetians are forever complaining that the Turks are a closed society and have unfair advantage because we will not let you in on our trade secrets. Perhaps if you'd clean yourselves up once in a while, they would not be such secrets."

He lead me up the great, broad thoroughfare that served in Constantinople much as the Grand Canal does in Venice, providing a viewing ground for the height of local culture. Awnings of the most exclusive coffee shops, catering to the latest fashion, and numerous elegant mosques in tree-planted squares lined our path.

The paving stones were kept meticulously clean by a full-time army of sweepers. When I compared this to the rat-filled heaps of rubbish in every corner of Venice, I saw briefly the image of a garden that hasn't been dunged in years. How could anything grow here? But fertilizer was clearly no problem as every step brought some new face of the throng to my view. Now it was a face from one corner of the world or the other, now the face of some local Turk or Greek animated with purpose so that even if happiness could not be read there, of life there was no doubt.

Facades of palaces provided a calming respite to the bustle of our path. These facades were, however, mostly left from before the Muslim Conquest, and whether they actually announced the homes of the wealthy or served as an anthill for the hovels of the poor was difficult for the stranger to tell. A wealthy Turk was more likely to situate at the end of some narrow back alley. In this paradoxical world, seclusion, when you managed to see it, was a sign of ostentation.

Never was a town more harnessed for commerce than Constantinople. Under every spare arch huddled some entrepreneur at the city's expense and halfway up the boulevard, we passed the covered Grand Bazaar. Here, behind its eight iron gates and under its acres of miniature domes, a man could buy anything from chickpeas to gold nuggets by the sackful as well as raise the capital to do so in the Turk's roundabout manner. For the mercantile arrangements were also remnants of the previous occupants.

I had experience of such matters through Uncle Jacopo and knew that Islam's Prophet forbad the taking of interest. But even that couldn't stop commerce in this metropolis. In order to raise the means to cover the risk of any venture, it was customary to make two transactions. The first was the straight loan of interest-free funds. The second, on the side, was the exchange of some item of value, a house, a horse—even a shoe would sometimes serve. The item was sold first to the man interested in the loan and then immediately sold back to his creditor at the agreed percentage of interest higher.

The Grand Bazaar in whose nooks and crannies such metaphysics took place in a score of different currencies seemed the best place for us to go for our purpose. But no. In the Turk's roundabout way, we went on up the avenue.

We arrived in a square, untidy with tombs and trees and bounded on the north by walls. The walls were impossible to see beyond but, by the red-robed janissaries passing in review before them, I knew they must enclose part of the imperial household. The Grand Signor was promiscuous enough in his habits to fill any number of palaces, scattered about the empire, with his cast-off concubines and bastards.

Such images of venery held no fascination for Husayn. He was more taken by the mosque on our right. We were just in time for the midday call to prayers from the pair of wide-spaced minarets that cluttered the skyline along with numerous domes.

"Built by the architect, Yakup Shah" Husayn told me, for our great Sultan Bayazid, two—three generations ago."

I hadn't the slightest interest in the history of the place, and was quite annoyed when Husayn felt he had to join everybody else in answering the rather mournful yet insistent demand for compliant and immediate devotion.

"We haven't a moment to lose!" I insisted.

"Moments with Allah are not lost," he replied gently. "Besides, who is there to do business with when the whole world has turned toward Mecca?"

"I guess I hear the bells of Venice instead."

So I stayed out in the square, the chaos of the place doing little to ease the chaos of my soul.

Over against the palace wall, the janissaries now on guard, I noted, were excused from prayer to maintain their vigilance. The sun had just turned on its minaret pivot and filled the space before the mosque with pale early March light, every gloss of warmth still encasing an inner core of cold.

Flocks of pigeons, however, seemed to find this rarified light the perfect mating medium. By some birdish alchemy, they had divvied up their usual anonymous masses into perfect pairs, though there was as yet no breeding going on. Each darker, generally more purple male pursued with incessant coos and low, scraping bows, oblivious to anything in the world but his chosen one. This groveling courtship also included dragging the tails along the flagstones until I wondered that the feathers weren't worn away, whether the poor besotted fellows would ever manage to fly again. I came to recognize the scraping. I would turn at the sound—and never fail to find yet another poor sap cooing deep in his throat and bobbing up and down convulsively along the peaked rib of a tomb or up and over the cramped roots of a tree.

All the while the females couldn't care less. They avoided the males all together, intent on their customary waddle from crumb to crumb. Whenever possible, they flew off, only to be pursued relentlessly from tomb to fountain and back again by the fruitless, tedious—even I could see it was tedious—bowing and scraping. I was unnerved to find myself divided from all other males except these featherheads by the rise and fall, the droning surf of recited Arabic ebbing between the mosque's arches.

But before I had time to embrace the ramifications of this thought, prayers were over. The mosque disgorged. Husayn rejoined me and led me to the western side of the square, where the baths were.

"Also built by Sinan and Bayazid," he told me.

"But on Christian backs."

Accusingly I thrust a palm in the direction of the pillars that flanked the bath's entrance. They were carved with repeating curves and ovals representing peacock-feather eyes, obviously reused, and obviously of Byzantine origin.

Husayn forgave my tone with a *"Mashallah."*

It—even the fall of Constantinople into infidel hands— was God's will. I might have been more agreeable to the sentiment had it not been said exactly the way Uncle Jacopo used to say *Che sarà sarà* when considering the limits God had placed on his life. I remembered the final limit, and grieved, refusing to accept.

"Remember, too," Husayn said, "that the Christian Romans rifled many of Constantinople's treasures off conquered pagan temples first."

My friend then proceeded to give more of our precious aspers to the bath attendant.

XIX

THE FIRST OBSTACLE to overcome in our visit to Sultan Bayazid's gift to clean posterity was a continuous stream of slaves bent under the weight of the wood required to stoke the bath's furnace. A single furnace served both sides of the establishment, both the men's and the women's around the far end of the building of which I had caught no glimpse. This efficiency did little to ease the straining of these men, some of whom were past their prime.

I grimaced. What similar heavy labors would Sofia Baffo's young, lithe body be forced to undertake if Husayn's vague plan did not work out? It hardly bore thinking of, but I couldn't help myself.

Husayn read my thoughts and steered me deeper into the edifice with an arm meant for comfort about my shoulders.

"Trust me, trust Allah," he said. "And trust Abu Isa. Abu Isa will not do anything to damage his own goods."

The first room into which he ushered me was divided into many small cubicles. Marble—water-stained, mildewed in the pores, dilapidated with age—covered the low dividing walls. Clearly it, too, had served in previous buildings.

We each laid claim to an empty cubicle as Husayn tried more diversion. "I must say, my friend, you have a very curious notion of slavery. You seem to think it some great moral wrong, while all the time you Venetians are among the greatest slavers on the seas."

More male slaves, bare-chested, with only red-and-white-striped towels about their loins, paraded here and there between the cubicles with stacks of other towels on their heads. One remarkably tall African—who could see over the division of my cubicle with no difficulty—shoved one of his stack at me. It was of a very thick fabric, cotton made plush by leaving the loops of the pile uncut. Stringy fringe as long as my hand trimmed the raw edges to prevent unraveling.

Husayn continued chatting over the partition. "Your uncle, mercy on his soul, kept old black Piero."

My exploration of the towel—indeed, everything about his station, not just me—seemed to entertain the towering African. His full purplish lips were set in something of a smirk. I understood that I was to strip down until my costume matched his. I didn't know if I was prepared to do this among strangers, infidel strangers at that. All these men in the neighboring cubicles, I realized, would be circumcised, as the Turks' barbarous custom was. Probably even the African had undergone the rite. This realization made me very uneasy: I shrank perceptibly under the weight of my codpiece.

I must say modesty prevailed throughout the bathing ordinance, even in the case of the African, who could have looked over the partition but, after one final smirk, did not. Modesty is, Husayn informed me, a tenant of religion with Muslims, even among the same sex and in the bath. But I could hardly keep from recoiling at the thought of identical mutilation under identical towels and irrationally feared that if I took the towel, I might likewise lose what was under it. This made me very slow to carry through what was expected.

All the while, Husayn kept encouraging, not in so many words, but with his continuous prattle. This was meant to assure me that he was not far away, but it only served to make me realize that he, too, was alien.

"I know your father had four or five purchased servants in his household while he yet lived."

Husayn was right, but I wouldn't admit it. "It is different when it is someone you know."

"As I recall, your nursemaid—the very woman who suckled you—she was not a freeborn woman, was she? Yet you do not love her any less for that."

I could avoid the inevitable no longer. I presented myself outside the cubicle; the safety of my clothes remained behind. The sight of Husayn exposed in near nakedness quite startled me. His flesh was fish-pale, hairless as a woman's, with woman-like breasts and an ample belly. Most startling of all was his head. I'd never seen him without either a Venetian cap or Turkish turban. The entire dome of his cranium save a single knot at the top was shaved as naked as a boccie ball. This was a ball that had seen hard use in the alleys, however, for the bumps and seams of a human head are as graceless as most bodies are unrobed.

The intimidating African reappeared to provide each of us with a pair of pattens for our feet. These shoes were inlaid with mother-of-pearl on the in-step straps. The delicacy of the work belied the clomping weight that suddenly overcame the foot once it slipped into the clog. Each sole was elevated off the floor by chunks of wood as large as the blocks on the *Santa Lucia*'s banner pulley. I felt like a courtesan crossing the Piazza in her chopines.

"They keep your feet up off the cold marble, the spills of dirty water on the floor. They prevent slips and falls," Husayn assured me.

Husayn gave a tightening tug, meaning to be helpful, on the clumsy knot of my towel. Besides almost unfooting me as I tried to get the knack of the shoes, he otherwise gave no sign that I looked as out of place as I felt other than to amend his assurances to "These pattens do take some getting used to."

He must not have found my appearance as distasteful as I found his—or that of most of the other men in the room.

Of course his lack of criticism might be due to the fact that my host was occupied at the moment. A slave from Husayn's house had just arrived, no doubt at the bidding of the urchin paid off earlier. The menial brought a small crate with him, and I was distracted from my awkwardness to recognize it as a straw-packed crate of Venetian glass the *Santa Lucia* had taken into her hold over a month ago.

"I suppose you mean to find a buyer for that here in the baths?" I asked.

Husayn smiled but didn't exactly commit himself one way or another. He told the slave to set the crate down in his cubicle and then to join us. The baths would certainly be the strangest of bazaars if haggling was to go on dressed the way we were. A haggler needs to hide much of his intent in order to be successful; layers of clothing can only help in his efforts.

Still, I appreciated the fact that Husayn might be willing to put up his profits from such a sale toward my cause. The costliest goblet would, with luck, bring perhaps only half of the price we were looking at, but I couldn't ignore the gesture. I determined to be more gracious to my generous host.

As we waited for his man to join us, Husayn chatted on.

"The life of a galley slave is not so enviable, granted."

"Or one of those out in the forecourt hauling wood."

"Those are free Turks we saw out in the forecourt hauling wood. Wood-haulers' guild."

"I see. But why were they so—so—"

"Desperate?"

"Yes, desperate."

"A free man is not assured food for his family at night. The slave is—unless his master is bent on ruining his patrimony. The free man works against hunger, the hunger of his children, the illness of his parents, old age, the crippling effects of his work. The slave doesn't have these at his back."

I happened to catch another glimpse of the tall African. He was swinging his way through the room as if to some heavy African rhythm only he could hear. He still smirked superiorly and I realized the small heap of towels he wore like a janissary headdress was not calculated either to wear him out or make his master rich. I had a flash of the shrine to Saint Gummarus in Venice, always full, rich with offerings. Saint Gummarus was the patron of ruptures, much frequented by the porter's guild, the *zannis* we called them, when a life of desperate freedom had come to the end of its usefulness—

"But yes, I will agree. To be but a nameless body in a nameless mass of power-production—like one stick in the baker's fire—that is no life for a man, black or white, Muslim or Christian. Slave or free, I may add. Therefore I approve of using only criminals in the galleys—men who for some act against society have forfeited their right to be counted in that society. The same does not apply to domestic slaves, who are always taken into the master's home and treated with dignity."

The household slave did appear now and I gave Husayn, at least, credit for practicing what he preached as we went on to the bath's next phase, all three together.

The next room, like the first, smelled of dominant male. A dome pierced by numerous star-shaped windows sieved down drifting sunbeams. Four fountains of cold water tumbled out of lions' mouths—these must have been of Byzantine origin as well—into marble basins before running off in little channels set into the floor. A slave attendant was fast asleep on a pile of more red and white in a corner, giving some credence to Husayn's words. These words, along with every clomp of clog or touch of mussel shell to marble, echoed achingly off wall and crisp water.

"It is quite common, my friend, for poor families in the wild hills of Caucasia for example to sell their sons and especially their daughters to Constantinople-bound merchants. Not only do they need the money, poor souls, but most importantly, they know their children will eat more, dress better, and have a better chance of advancement here than in their poor land where a decent living cannot be eked out."

In this room, Husayn had his slave plaster him with a caustic, whitish putty concocted of lime and water with a touch of arsenic. I did not need the warning to be careful how I touched it to my lips or my eyes. No amount of coaxing could get me to undergo the treatment which, after about a quarter of an hour, the slave skillfully scraped off with a mussel shell. This was how Husayn maintained his unnatural hairlessness, which fashion he was obliged to rescind every time business brought him to the west.

"You know, Suleiman the Lawgiver—our present ruler, may Allah find favor with him—he is a very strange case for a sultan. He married the mother of his sons. Usually the women of a sultan's harem are purchased—every one of them—and what an advancement for a girl! To rise from poverty so desperate that she must run barefoot through deep snow, to become Valide Sultan—the highest post any woman can reach in our empire—a post only slightly less powerful than that held by the Sultan himself. What is to be pitied there? All our sultans, you see, are the products of slave women."

Husayn recited this while he deftly shifted his red-and-white toweling this way and that so the slave could even attack his genitals. I certainly would never allow that, no matter how much time I was forced to spend among the Turks. Perhaps it was an accident with just such a purple mussel shell that had first set the absurd fashion of circumcision into play.

I did allow myself to be scrubbed by a bathhouse slave. After slathering me with suds from a bowl filled to the brim with musk-scented soap, he encased his hand in a sleeve of nubby toweling. This he adroitly alternated with horsehair cloth and the dried skeleton of a gourd named from the Arabic luffa. The only thing he didn't use on me was wire gauze, but all of his implements felt like it, abrading and tingling the flesh. I had been afraid to loose more vital parts to a mussel shell. This treatment cost me a good deal of skin. I think, in fact, that my attendant commented with a gap-toothed grin something to the effect that he had never found so much filth to flay on a client.

It was quite touching to watch, at another basin, a young man about my age giving the same treatment to his enfeebled grandfather. All together, soap and skin was flushed from us down the marble channels with bowls full of tap water.

"Slavery is not so hopeless nor as powerless as you imagine," Husayn gurgled between dousings. "Especially not for a young woman with the looks and talents of your signorina.

"And you must admit she was quite content when we left her," he reiterated. "Do you think, my friend, that, having tasted those dainties she breakfasted on today, she could ever be satisfied with what you could provide her? Forgive me, my friend, but she is a vain and frivolous young woman. She has expensive tastes and I despair for you if you should try and meet them, an orphan as you are now and a sailor.

"Come, come, be merry. Let me send the little black girl to you again tonight and this time do not shove her away. Enjoy her. Her life will be improved if you do. And so, Allah willing, will be yours. Lose yourself in her and see if the memory of Sofia Baffo is not gently coaxed away. Madonna Baffo is content with the fate Allah has willed for her. My friend, be you content as well."

With a violent hand to my head, I signaled I could never be content as we went on to the bath's third room.

XX

THE CEILING OF this third room was held up over its central pool by four columns whose elaborately foliate capitals were of obvious Byzantine provenance as well. More architectural details, however, escaped me as the room's main feature—its heat—grabbed me by the throat.

Heat rose up off the pool's surface as from a pot shortly before the cook tosses in the pasta. Heat throbbed up from the floor. Heat shot out in sulfuric jets within alcoves spaced around the perimeter of the pool. Heat glowed from the skins of two score Turks lounging about in attitudes of the most grotesque indolence. Shapes floated toward me through mists of steam. In slow motion, they revolved and vanished like wraiths. Form blurred at the pressure of heat in the corners of my eyes.

In short, nothing on earth has ever so closely re-created one of the lower cauldrons of Dante's *Inferno* as a Turkish bath. The self-indulgent denizens of Sybaris and the cardinally slothful are condemned to a fantastic parody of their sins. The Foscari stage came nowhere near this apparition of strigils and luffas as whips and scourges, the masseurs as torturing demons.

"Take me out of here!" I begged of Husayn, struggling for breath in the dense atmosphere.

But all comprehension of Venetian had steamed out of Husayn's mind. My words were lost in the murmuring undercurrent of sound made by subdued laughter and whispered conversations—or the awe we all felt to find ourselves the objects of eternal damnation.

I had no choice but to follow my host down two steps into the cloudy, neck-high depths of the pool. We kept our red-and-white knee-length skirts about us as we did so and the cloth floated up to the surface about our waists until the water saturated it.

This pool is hot enough to boil an egg, I thought, but couldn't say it aloud. My voice box seemed hardened already beyond any vibration. The heat cut the tendons in my joints and flattened me, like the water itself, against the marble at a level.

It was quite remarkable that in this place of everlasting torture I caught my first good glimpse of a Turkish woman. She was upon us before I knew it, skirting the poolside with rapid steps as she took the shortest route from door to door.

I never actually saw her face, as she held both hands before it and glimpsed the world—at least so she wouldn't tumble into the pool and join us—through the narrowest of spaces between her fingers. But that she was a woman left no doubt, and had there been any blood left that wasn't already on the surface of my skin, I would have blushed.

A number of men were watching the woman's progress with interest, and Husayn felt obliged to offer some apology. "She is accused of adultery," he said, proving that he hadn't lost all use of Venetian after all. "She runs this gauntlet to prove her innocence, her husband and brother observe. She wears no *shalvar* and, if she is guilty, her skirts will blow up over her head."

"If they do—?" I gasped. I was more concerned for my own temperature, and relieved to find voice, than for the woman.

"If this happens, her husband has the right to kill her, same as a wronged husband would in Venice. This gauntlet is an old custom, existing, like the capitals of these pillars, from the time of the Greeks."

"She is innocent," I judged, as did husband and brother.

"Of course," said Husayn, looking away from the spectacle with disinterest.

"Why do you say 'of course'?"

"Because if she has the courage to do this, she mustn't have a guilty hair on her head. I can only think it will make her look at her husband differently from now on. She will have learned he is not the only creature Allah made so, and that He, all praise to Him, made many much better. I'd say any man is a fool who demands this of his wife in the first place."

With this dismissal, Husayn returned to his soaking and I must confess that my own discomfort soon numbed me to anyone else's.

I was aware of the curious and rather unpleasant sensation

of other men's naked, parboiled flesh against mine under the water, but again, I was too numb to think much about it. I didn't think of it, in fact, until Husayn suddenly leapt up out of the water, steam curling from his skin, and began a most shocking tirade. I thought for a moment that it was aimed against me, and that he'd forgotten once again that he needed to go easy on the Turkish for me.

"A curse on your religion!" This harangue started where the Venetian began and progressed from there to "May Satan stick his finger up your ass!" and "They found your grandfather's shoes under your mother's bed, you know that?"

I recoiled from the horrible blackness of such thoughts as from a physical blow. He was better in this language than he was in Venetian, I had to grant him that. Cursing is the first thing a traveler becomes fluent in, I reminded myself, and, if I couldn't comprehend the reason for the abuse, I could at least learn the flair.

But presently the realization sank through the heat-fog in my brain that the object of his abuse was not me. It was the creature who'd been pressing so restlessly up against my opposite side.

I blinked against the steam as the figure retreated before Husayn's barrage and then vanished at Hades' rim. The steps were more exaggeratedly feminine, I thought, than those of the accused adulteress. It was only then that I realized what neither Husayn nor I could express in each other's tongue. I'd been picked out by a sodomite as a likely candidate to share his vice by my shoulder-length locks, my hairless chin, and the air of not quite belonging, all of which matched his.

I couldn't even meet Husayn's eyes to give him thanks for my deliverance. My shame was too great—the helpless, polluted guilt of a victim. I hadn't the strength to shove the blame off where it belonged—on the aggressor. Where was the gauntlet I could run to prove my innocence in this case?

Husayn offered none, but ushered me quickly back to the room where we'd begun our ceremony. Here our clothes still waited in their little cubicles and the cooler air seemed to fist space for breath in our lungs once again.

But there was to be no safety in clothes yet. The smirking African quickly replaced my dripping, loin-clinging towel with a dry one. He then threw another over my shoulders, a third over my head. I tried to smile some gratitude back at him and I saw the smirk lose its edge.

At this point, Husayn brought a Turk across the room for me to meet. The stranger was towel-draped like everyone else. Why my host should pick this Turk and not any of the identical others escaped me, and I have no recollection of his features beyond the fact that he was over fifty.

I assumed at first that this introduction was to distract me from my recent shame by presenting decent examples of the race for me to know. Acquaintance was bound to be minimal. The stranger knew no Venetian at all and the sickness in the pit of my stomach kept me still preferring the African's softened smile.

Still, Husayn persisted in making the introductions. He gave a name I've now forgotten and modified it with "From Iznik, where he is head of the tile works there. His kilns are famous. No one else in the world knows the secret he keeps of firing that brilliant cobalt blue that is so valued. He is the man I brought you here hoping to find."

When I made no reply, the man salaamed, a gesture of graciousness as it is incumbent on the younger to bow first. I tried to imitate the gesture, unsuccessfully on the platforms of my pattens. After that, there was very little else to do but stand and grin awkwardly at each other until by mutual though nonverbal consent we retired to our cubicles. I went to one, Husayn and the tilemaker together to the one next door.

The African, now sharing some of his hidden rhythm with me under his breath, saw me couched on a pile of pillows and rugs within the cubicle. He swaddled me as any infant in yet more towels, these holding the delicious warmth of sitting by the furnace still in their tiny pockets of nap. He then proceeded to wick the wet from my body by pressing his long, black, pink-tipped fingers gently up and down the toweling.

I found the sensation quite pleasant but had no desire to be handled in any way by any man, I didn't care whose chore it was. I gestured him away, refusing likewise the signs I took to mean "Massage?" and "Narghile?" I did take the offer of "Coffee," a word novel to Turkish that I did understand.

Two similar thimbles full of the sweet, thick, frothy, muddy Arabic stuff went next door as well. And I supposed it was the tilemaker who was smoking that medicinal, relaxing weed first discovered by the savages in the New World but lately cultivated in the lands around the Black Sea. The warm, dark, tangy balsamic odor filled the air, one of the first times I ever smelled burning tobacco. Such was the latest fashion in that drain of all the world's indulgences, Constantinople.

I've heard it said the seduction of tobacco can also affect others in the room besides the smoker. Certainly combined with the purgative of heat and water, the sweetness of the coffee, and the emotional storms I'd been through that day, it had its consequences. I found I could no longer stave off a gradually enveloping and voluptuous drowsiness. I suppose I did doze, and perhaps for quite some time as the interminable and soporific asking after health and welfare droned on in the next cubicle.

I could not at first determine what it was that brought me awake until I heard it again. I heard the slats of a packing crate creaking open, the nestle of straw. Even more to the point were the words I heard. In sharp relief, as foreign words always are when they tumble into the otherwise smooth stream of native speech, I heard Husayn pronounce the names of Filippo and Bernardo Serena.

Venetians. Not just any Venetians, either. These were two brothers, now deceased and succeeded by their sons. Close to thirty years ago the Serena brothers had patented the almost magical process by which canes of opaque glass—usually white but sometimes the very skillful managed blue as well—could be imbedded in otherwise clear crystal. The masterpieces the Serena factory had been turning out—goblets, jugs, plates—continued to amaze the world. And shortly it was not just Serena but the entire glass-making lair of Murano that worked the magic. Venice set little store by patents when there was citywide profit to be made.

Letting the profits go beyond the Republic, however, was a different matter all together.

I had imagined there might be a few of these pieces among Husayn's imports. It was only natural, as there was never enough supply to fill the Turks' luxuriant demand. My suspicions were confirmed when I heard the tilemaker's husky exclamation as the straw parted to reveal its contents followed by Husayn's pronunciation of the Italian term for the technique, "*vetro a filigrana.*"

So Husayn has found a buyer. That is well, I thought as I drifted back toward oblivion. Just at the edge, however, I suddenly burst into wakefulness.

This was not just any wealthy buyer. This was a man who had a certain technical skill, a certain vested interest. This was a man who could turn a little knowledge into a going concern. He would not just buy a vase, and he would pay much, much better than vase price. He would buy an industry—and undermine the wealth-producing monopoly of another.

Somehow, somewhere, Husayn in the guise of a Venetian merchant must have learned the secret of *vetro a filigrana* and was about to sell it. Venice was ruined.

I was up off the stupefying rugs in a moment, finding that without pattens the marble under my feet shot cold up into the cocoon of my swaddling along my staggering legs. Towels dropped from me like puddles of water as I groped for at least the dignity of my chemise. My skin that had been scrubbed down to the shine shrank from the dirty linen and my own smell crinkled my nose as it had never offended before. The shirt was stiff and rank with sweat and salt. I gritted my teeth and ignored the sensation. Indeed, I felt that with the shirt, I was reclaiming the birthright that had been scrubbed from me.

Still struggling with the points of my hose, I burst into the neighboring cubicle.

I knew I was not mistaken in my appraisal of the situation when I saw Husayn look up at my arrival. His hands were frozen in the act of describing the glassblowers' mold and showing how the opaque canes alternated with the clear ones in lining that mold—more than even I knew of the secret process before that moment. I didn't need Turkish to understand.

And neither did the tilemaker.

The tilemaker had risen out of his cocoon of towels with the excitement of what he was learning. In his hands he held the archetype of all his future profits: an exquisite *tazza* spun with sugarlike decoration from the heart of the deep-petaled lobes around its bowl to the foot of its finger-thin pedestal.

I said something. I'm not certain what it was—doubtless the blackest curse I could bring to my lips—but the roar of anger in my head made me deaf to the rationality of any language. In one moment, I whipped the doublet off my shoulder and through the tilemaker's hands, bringing the *tazza* with it. The glass shattered into a million slivers on the mottled marble of the floor, likewise rifled from another empire.

And with the glass shattered the world.

Pushing Turks aside, I made my way alone to the open chaos of Bayazid Square and its hopelessly unsatisfied pigeons.

XXI

I FLED DOWN the street I'd climbed in Husayn's company earlier that day, hoping the late afternoon surge of traffic would cover me.

He would come after me, of that I was certain. I was so certain that even an hour later, with the setting sun melting Aya Sofia into pure gold, I was still taking my steps at a lope, trying to look all ways at once like a hunted rabbit. I actually thought I caught a glimpse of the bounce of his turban, there in the square before the greatest of all Constantinople's holy places. Husayn was answering yet another call to prayer.

At this sight, real or imagined, my exhausted feet found one more burst of strength which carried me around the huge heap of the mosque to the left. There, off in a corner, I saw a dark doorway that seemed deserted enough. I claimed it.

A single torch left by workmen and reaching the end of its life illuminated thirty or so well-worn stone steps that sank downward. I followed them cautiously. The earth closed over me, shutting out all sound, all threat of the strange city in which I was alone and a foreigner.

As I descended, I began to hear water, lots of water, below and, off, beyond sight, a metallic drip, drip, drip. Frail but precise notes sounded as if the strings of a lute were being methodically touched. The failing torchlight revealed a great underground cistern in yellowed highlights, with enough water to provide an imperial city for the duration of the longest siege—or to keep the gardens of an extravagant palace green for several peaceful stints from May until October. I could not, in fact, see the end of either water nor the columns that held the arched roof over it. The columns, too, were rifled Byzantine, I noticed bitterly.

I bent and, with a cupped hand, tasted my discovery. It was dullingly cold but sweet. With quick scoops I replaced all that the baths had sweated from me.

Thus refreshed, I discovered that the notion of siege held my mind. Here, in this underground fountain, was water, safety, a deserted and secure hiding place.

When at last I emerged from the reservoir—when both torch and sun had finally burned out and all the world was dissolving down to a uniform sludge of twilight—the inkling of a new plan had formed in my mind. The top of the cistern's stairs stank of cats, wiping the fresh, clean smell of the water below from my nostrils but not from my mind.

The thing to do now was to try to find the slave market. The slave market and Sofia Baffo.

⁂

THE STREETS OF Constantinople were silent and grave, cold with the disappearance of the sun. The public world of men, I saw, was but the vain, garish illusion of the day. It was the private life of the harems that was real, and to that reality all mortals retreated at night.

Like the blooms of some gigantic morning glory, the shops and houses had folded in upon themselves. But everywhere, I could feel the tight tendrils of the plant that remained after the blooms had faded. At first I feared my feet might become entangled in this unseen growth as I made my way through the streets alone. Then I assured myself that they were but the invisible connections between houses made by the women, women invisible themselves in veils or closed sedans. Yet by exchanging gossip, comfort, lore, and measures of flour, they made bonds that were strong enough to be sensed even in the dark.

I myself felt attached to such a tendril. It led me unfailingly to the great wooden gate of the slave market, but of course that gate was heavily bolted. It had been so since noon, for it was unmeet to expose either merchandise or buyers, all of the highest quality, to the heat of the day even in March.

Finding the rear of the establishment was not quite as instinctive. I had to calculate footsteps and try to work them through the domestic solids with a complicated sort of geometry. At last a strong tug on my invisible tendril assured me that I had the right alleyway. I climbed up a wall, over a roof of crumbling tile, and finally dropped into what, if one can recognize by sight what one hears by sound, was the very courtyard I had heard through Sofia's windows that morning.

Yes, there were the windows, high up in one wall, still large enough for a man to crawl through. The only trouble was that they were shuttered. The shutters were flimsy with lattice so that the cool of a summer night's air would not be lost. But now they were adjusted for the winter weather and might effectively keep out any thief such as myself. Determination must supply where inexperience failed.

The slave shop and its courtyard had been designed with security in mind, but long, uneventful years must have made the occupants careless. The produce and shade of a grape arbor had come to outweigh the danger of placing it right against the wall. It was a fragile ladder and it swayed ominously as I went at the shutter with an adze I had found leaning against an outbuilding. Between silence, security, and haste, no straight line could be drawn, but in spurts and starts I pursued my task.

The hinges began to give.

I am no theologian, yet I am persuaded that God has a special place in His heart for the insurgency of youth. Often He does no more than wink at what, if dared by an older man, would immediately bring down wrathful punishment. Up to this point, fantastic as it may seem, I am certain I had His approval—or, at least, not His strong disapproval.

Or perhaps it was not God but something more magical— perhaps a kiss planted on my infant forehead by my mother as a talisman when she knew she would soon die and leave me without her kind protection. I do not remember such a kiss, but I did feel some power watching over me that night and I am certain that, had I backed down any time before those hinges came loose, I could have made it back to the guest room in Husayn's house with no punishment at all.

Indeed, my immunity may have extended beyond that point. I have rehearsed these events over in my mind a thousand times every day since that night, searching for the precise step I took that was one step too far. At one exact moment, I believe, I gave up the freedom to act of my own will, to retreat, to retrace my steps, to have my life tumble on in a different, happier vein. Where was that moment when my will abandoned me, when a fate was kicked loose to tumble down upon me in a landslide that cannot be stopped and still dumps its debris on me even now? I have been unable to answer this satisfactorily. Husayn, I know, thinks it was the very moment I left his care. But I am convinced I could have gone even further than the removal of that shutter with no permanent damage done.

Madonna Baffo, as it happened, slept alone in that great room that night. She had heard me scrambling about in the dry grapevines and was awake and aware of who I was even before moonlight poured through the open window into her room. She did not, therefore, scream to betray me. She stood waiting, looking in the brazier-smoked moonlight like a costly icon in a wash of exotic incense. She gave me a hand as I let myself down through the window and smiled with pleasure as she greeted me in a whisper.

"How nice to see you, Signor Veniero."

I did not take time to plead with her that she call me Giorgio. I had greater demands of her. "I have come to rescue you," I said.

To my surprise, she turned and walked a few steps away, toying with me.

"But . . . but this is impossible," she said.

"It's not. I've found the perfect place for us to hide. An old cistern quite near here where you can wait—"

"I've no desire to be damp and cold in a cistern."

"It'll be just for a short while, just until I manage to get across to Pera and get one of our countrymen to bring a boat and—"

"But Signor Veniero, I can't. I can't climb walls like you can—like a fly. Like you have been doing, so it seems, since the very first day I met you."

To be likened to a fly was not what praise I had expected for my feat, but I ignored it.

"You can," I insisted. I was offering her what she had most

coveted of me at our first meeting, after all. "I will help you. You can do it. You must do it."

"I don't know." she said. Not that she was afraid, not that she mistrusted me—simply that she did not know.

I did know. I grabbed her quickly and firmly about the waist—(that waist, my God! the touch of it made my arms fall into weak spasms)—and carried her to the window.

Sofia gave a little squeal—of delight? of fear? of protest?— and fought against my arms until I was forced to set her down lest someone overhear us.

"Signor Veniero," she said, having come, it seemed, to a sudden decision. "First sit down and let me tell you something. Let me tell you what happened to me today."

"Tell me later." I was pleading, not ordering. "When you are safe and there is time."

"Oh, no, please." Her decision gained momentum and insistence in response to my weakness. "I simply must tell you. I've been bursting with it all day and I've had no one to tell. I wanted to tell my maid Maria, but it seems they've already sold her."

"They've sold Maria?" I asked, and a curious premonition passed over me. *You should have bought that woman Maria while you had the chance,* it seemed to say. *Such a chance will never come again.* Perhaps this was a warning that the point of no return was rapidly approaching, but I refused to understand it. "Where have they sold her?"

"Oh, I don't know," Sofia said. "To some old man who wanted kitchen help. I don't know. I can't understand a word of what they say. I do think it was rather inconsiderate of them to leave me without a confidante on this, of all days. When I have seen—oh, such wonders! Please, please sit down and let me tell you before I burst."

There. This is the point where my fate was decided. I think I even felt it. As Baffo's daughter spoke her last request, her beauty and her presence got the better of me. I felt the energy that had spurred me forth all night drain and leave me weak, clumsy, and stupid. Perhaps it was indeed the departure of God's pleasure or the charm of a mother's kiss. My knees gave way and I had to sit, lulled by the spell of her voice and the wonders she described with it as if it were a powerful Anatolian leach.

"This morning, just shortly after you left, they put me in a closed sedan chair and carried me off—nay, I know not where. All I can say is, there is no place like it in all the earth. I am almost constrained to say that it was not earth at all, but that those porters were angels and I was carried for some few hours into heaven itself.

"At first I felt and heard the crowds pressing all about and I did not dare to peek out, for I knew that would displease the master. Besides, I was somewhat afraid, for the crowds seemed loud and rough. But soon I was aware that they were thinning and those people whom I heard seemed ever more sober and respectful, as if it were some great shrine we were approaching. Now I dared to pull back the curtain just a bit and to have a look around me.

"I saw that we were passing through a great and wonderful garden. Tall cypress tress stood as sentinels in perfect straight lines along the numerous and delightful pathways. Beneath each tree, in rows as regimented as if they had been planted there, a gardener in a red headdress was at work.

"And, oh, what exotics grew beneath their hands! The lawn was as plush and uniform as a rug, as if every blade were hand-knotted into place. And as if deep borders on every side were set in out beds of flowers. Is it not still Lent? Have we not still a week or two till Easter? And yet I saw them: rank upon rank of brilliant pink, red, and white blooms like an infinite army mustered for review. The flowers resembled the Turkish army, I vow, for they were just like so many turbaned soldiers standing up oh so straight! I have never seen anything of the kind before."

Tülbend, those flowers must have been, I thought. That is a Turkish word for "turban," which Europeans mispronounce as "tulip." Mispronunciation does not keep occidentals from coveting these wonders for their own gardens. And, though the Turks guarded the secret of the flowers' cultivation carefully, I had heard a rumor that some Dutchman had recently contrived to smuggle the mysterious means of their propagation to his homeland.

Still, I did not hope to see them soon in Venice, never in such profusion as Sofia now described. Indeed, I did not know any place in all the parks of Constantinople where they were so abundant nor so well tended. Surely she was exaggerating, for only the Sultan could afford such luxury.

The Sultan . . . , I repeated to myself. Was it possible that Madonna Baffo had actually been taken within the Grand Serai? God forbid! I listened on.

"Presently we came to a great gate at which point the bearers of my sedan were obliged to halt. Even my master was allowed no further and, wrapping me closely in veils as I descended, he entrusted me to the care of a large white man who had come with us from the shop. This man wore a heavy green robe trimmed with rabbit fur and on his head was a tall white hat shaped like a cone of sugar."

I recognized this description as that of the eunuch Husayn had called my attention to earlier that day. "From the palace," my friend had said. So it was true. And it was more than just the palace, the Sublime Porte where any beggar might go to seek justice. It was into the harem itself that she had gone, the very heart of the heart, where no man had ever set foot save only the Sultan himself. I listened on.

"This man led me through the door. Then—oh! how can I explain to you how I felt? I felt as if I'd been swallowed by a great, ravenous beast, a beast whose insides were cool marble. I grew afraid. Yet, do not look like that, Veniero. It was a fear that sent a shivering thrill down my spine. What a wondrous beast! I thought. What a great, powerful, wondrous beast who turns and the earth shakes, who winks an eye and the world is in darkness or in light. Oh, that I could become part of this beast, I thought, even if it meant being swallowed whole and never seeing the light of day again.

"We walked down the long, marble corridors of the beast's insides. They were deserted, save for several black men in turbans and fur-trimmed robes something like my guide's. They stood guard at the various portals we passed through as we were swallowed deeper and deeper inside. Then, just when I thought we must have reached a dead end, a door opened and I found myself dazzled by light and sound.

"The light was reflected innumerable times by an absolute riot of mirrors, giltwork, jewels, satin, and polished faïence tile painted and carved in all the colors and detail of a garden in bloom. These surfaces had the same effect on sound. There were caged birds in the room and a company of female musicians, but mostly it was the chatter and laughter of a crowd of women—oh, twenty at least—the most beautiful women I have ever seen.

"All different kinds of women: black and white and brown and yellow, some with blue eyes, some with eyes like pitch. Red hair, brown hair, black hair like ravens. They were all dressed in unspeakable elegance, so weighted with jewels and silks and cloth-of-gold and velvet that I can't imagine how they managed to walk about. And yet their discourse was animated and happy as they sat on soft cushions and rugs and partook of pastries, sweets, and rosewater.

"My guide directed me to bow and I did as he told me, falling to the ground as low as any tortoise. I tell you, it was no small feat, all swathed in veils as I was. But I might have bowed anyway, without being told, solely at the opulence I saw, pulsating there at the Beast's heart. It quite overwhelmed me.

"Well, soon enough I saw a little yellow calfskin slipper there before my nose and one of the women was helping me to my feet. Then she reached for my veils and, with a grand flourish, removed them. The room full of women, which had fallen silent on my entrance, gasped. Then they began to chatter all the more excitedly. Some of them, I could tell by the sudden pallor of their faces, were quite jealous. I can tell you, it was very gratifying, especially in such company.

"One woman in particular seemed pleased with me. I, at least, was impressed by her. It was not that her clothes and ornaments outshone all the rest—they did, indeed, but to describe her dress would not tell you what impressed me most. Neither was she the most beautiful woman there, being past her prime. She must once have had remarkable features but she is now nearly forty—at least old enough to be my mother. Still, her skin was flawless, as cool and white as ivory and, if she dyed her hair to cover gray, she used some magical formula I know not of that lets a natural sheen come through. She wore it swept up and back to display her high forehead and fine cheekbones to the best effect.

"And yet, for all of that, it was her eyes that were most remarkable. She plucked her brows into narrow crescents. And under them, wore copious amounts of black kohl around the lashes, as is popular among these Turks—my master made me put on all too much before we left. But those black eyes cut through any amount of antimony and pierced the heart. The kohl is, perhaps, a sheath, for otherwise those eyes would be like a dagger pushed up against the ribs, demanding obedience or instant death.

"And they did obey her—instantly—all of them. The girl who had uncovered me was now instructed to make me turn, walk, and then move toward the mistress, which she did immediately. The girl did not play tired or coy for her mistress, as Maria might have done to vex me. I might have had to ask again, raise my voice, or even stamp my foot to get such a response from some of our Venetian domestics. But the woman did it all with a glance, or at most, a word in undertone.

"Even the huge man in the white hat. He could have snapped that woman's neck with his two hands, but he scraped the floor with his hand when he bowed to her and, had he had a tail, it would have wagged with delight when she complimented him on his taste. If she can rule such a mountain of a man, I would not be surprised to learn that she is mistress of the world."

I did not venture to explain to Baffo's daughter that eunuchs could be white as well as black and that her admiration of the man was again misplaced. She was enjoying her recitation far too much to be served such disappointment.

"With a flick of the bangles on her wrist, this incredible woman at last bade me approach her cushions. She felt my limbs, examined my teeth, my ears, my neck. Finally, she had me remove my jacket and shirt so she could satisfy herself concerning my. . . . Well, Signor Veniero. I felt no shame in front of her, even with that big man present, but in front of you—you must just imagine how I was examined further. Rest assured that no horseflesh ever received closer scrutiny before a purchase. One would think she was buying me for her own pleasure."

I did not tell Madonna Baffo the tales I had heard of the Sultan's harem, which would not put that purpose beyond possibility. I sat in glum silence which Sofia remarked and scolded.

"No, Signor Veniero. I must tell you I was flattered. To be considered by such a woman! That she did not ignore me all together or dismiss me to the gutter with just a flick of her wrist. . . . !"

And now her voice swelled to ecstasy as she swore, "By Saint Mark and by the Blood of God as well, I tell you I have no greater ambition in this life than to belong to that woman! Such discrimination! Such power I have never seen in any woman! No, not in any man, either. I would be content to mend her clothes and wash her linen just to be near her, just to stand an outside chance that some of that power might filter down to me.

"I pray I do not scare away good fortune by speaking it aloud, but I think she may take me. She took my hand in hers before I was led away. She took my hand, patted it and smiled, saying something as she did which, had it been in Venetian, might well have been, 'We shall be great friends, my dear, you and I.' "

XXII

SOME SOUND OTHER than Madonna Baffo's voice had made its way inside my head halfway through her last burst of eloquence, but I had pushed it impatiently aside. It came again now, louder and much clearer, and could not be ignored. Someone was coming down the hall toward the room where we sat and now they were at the door.

"By God!" Baffo's daughter exclaimed. "If they find you here. . . ."

In her confusion, she did not stop to think that even a whisper would confirm their suspicions. And in my confusion, I did not think to try to save her. But it was no use trying to save even myself. I caught the window ledge in a bound, but one leg still dangled into the room. It was grasped about the ankle and wrestled to the floor.

My fall knocked all the wind from me. I cannot have been senseless for more than two beats of the heart, but the next thing I knew, I was lying flat on my back. On top of me sat the weight of the young slave merchant and in his hands was a heavy blade, aimed straight for my heart.

"Isa! Isa! Wait!" I heard the older man shout. "It is the young Christian who visited us today."

"I shall cut his heart out first and circumcise him later." Somehow I was getting the gist of this conversation. Profanity, as I have already noted, comes easiest.

"But wait. He may have important friends. We do not know. It may go ill for us to have his blood upon our hands. The girl is unharmed, and that is most important. If we spill blood or demand vengeance according to the law, the affair may come to the notice of the Sublime Porte. Fearing their merchandise damaged, they may refuse to go through with the deal."

The young man submitted to his father with an angry grunt. The tension in his arms had to thrust the sword somewhere, so he throw it with violence against the wall.

Without ceremony I was immediately dragged from the room. The last thing I saw of Baffo's daughter, she was sitting calmly on her divan, straightening her bodice as if nothing had happened at all. I spent the rest of that night locked up in one of the merchant's spare cells, fearing the worst.

In the morning, however, I got the impression that my

captors' lust for personal vengeance had faded somewhat. They turned me over to the custody of a man who owned one of the other shops in the colonnade.

Salah ad-Din, in spite of his heavy flowing robes, was one of the thinnest men I had ever seen. At the same time he was quite tall, and the combined effect was bizarre. It seemed clear that poverty was not the cause of his want of weight and still I could not credit nature to condone such freakishness.

This man held his hands constantly before himself, studying the long, bony fingers with the same narcissistic delight as he also constantly fondled his heavy growth of black moustache. It seemed that both were attributes which he cultivated and which gave his great pride. Perhaps a streak of miserliness made him feel that money spent on food was money wasted when it could be better invested in merchandise. I had the strange feeling, however, that he cultivated these things—thinness and a moustache—because persons of his acquaintance, for some defect in their persons, could not do so. I knew of no slave trader, however, who could not grow as heavy a beard as he wished, and there was more glory in flaunting the rich foods one could afford than in keeping trim.

"Call me Francesco," Salah ad-Din said in Italian as he extended his hand.

I learned, then, to my surprise, that this man was a native-born Genoese. Giving up his Christianity had allowed him to start a very lucrative business here in Constantinople as a slave trader. I wondered not so much at this as at the fact that he should choose for his Muslim name that of the great defeater of Christians and the scourge of the Crusade.

"Ah, I still miss Italy," Salah ad-Din divulged to me. "And I always enjoy talking to a fellow countryman."

I returned this compliment by confessing something of my

own origins, too—that I was orphaned and how my guardian uncle had died at sea.

"By the roasting flesh of San Lorenzo, that is a pity," he said with a piety both rough and, at the same time, a little studied.

"A great pity," he repeated. "You must allow me to offer you breakfast."

A silent slave brought breakfast—yogurt, olives, dried prunes, and flat bread—to the back room of Salah ad-Din's shop. In spite of all I had been through—or perhaps because of it—I ate with good appetite. Salah ad-Din did not join me but watched as a customer may watch with fascination the jeweler at his work. I got the impression that he restrained himself because he felt himself above the animal lusts to which I was a slave.

In the middle of my meal, a colleague of Salah ad-Din called him to the door for consultation and, though they spoke in Turkish and though I missed most of what they said, I got the impression it was some piece of slave flesh they were considering.

"He is too old," the colleague said.

"There is no beard."

"After twelve or thirteen success is but limited. Death is more than likely."

"Yet such skin, such a figure, and that hair," Salah ad-Din argued. "How dare we pass it by?"

My breakfast finished, I now rose to take my leave. "I think I must return to my friend Husayn," I told the Genoese. "He has betrayed me and Venice—and you may gloat at that as much as I mourn. But I have no other friend in this town. And I know he must be very anxious for my well-being."

To my surprise I was detained.

They had not known I could understand a little Turkish, else they would have left the room.

I was the piece of slave's flesh they were discussing.

My struggles and protests availed nothing. If anything, they made Salah ad-Din determined to hasten the process.

Before noon, I was ferried across the Golden Horn and beyond the walls of Pera to a small house in the countryside.

What was done there is against Islamic law. It had to be done beyond city limits and by those whose Islam was a will-o'-the-wisp thing.

THE VERY SAME day that I went beyond Pera, Abu Isa got four hundred *ghrush*—more than his wildest dreams—for the blond-haired slave girl from the corsair's ship. Toward evening, the closed sedan chair again made its way from the shop to the palace.

But this time it returned empty.

Part II

Safiye

XXIII

WITHIN THE BELLY, as she called it, of the marble beast, Sofia did not find herself back in the glittering presence of the woman with the dark, piercing eyes. The eunuch showed her, instead, to a narrow string bed at the far end of a dark, dank dormitory two flights up. A thin mattress covered the bedstrings and, when she sat upon it to get her bearings, it jolted her hard, for it was crushed by much use.

Nine forlorn, dusty-looking girls stared back at her from their own hard pallets. A few chirps of greeting revealed a multitude of foreign tongues among which she could not exchange a single word.

Only the eunuch had something to say. On his way out he stopped to verbally lash one of the girls, for what offense it was impossible to say. The girl, a mousy little thing, didn't reply, even if she was able. The eunuch then grabbed her thin arm with one meatlike hand. She gasped and then shrieked, pain mixed with terror, as the eunuch shoved her out of the room in front of him. Sofia saw the girl pause and scratch something into the wood of the door frame against which his first bad aim flung her.

Later, when the girl's shrieks had been swallowed in the marble bowels of the place like heartburn chased by the parsley of gathering night, Sofia got up and went to look at the door frame. Ostensibly she went to help herself to the saucer of oil and a floating wick which was the cheap source of the room's only illumination. She needed it to ensure that her bed was free of the worst sorts of vermin.

But she did not fail to take the opportunity to investigate the doorpost. She saw a scratch of shallow, raw wood. It seemed unlikely that the girl could have made such a mark in such hard wood without drawing her own blood or at least breaking a nail. But all Sofia could make out was the shape of a cross, a desperate but silent sign to say: "I was here. The world does not heed my short and miserable passing. But, witness God, I was here."

Sofia turned back to the others in the room to tell them— To tell them what? Those who had not already buried their faces in a pretense of sleep did so now. No words had place in this oblivion.

More than once Sofia felt inclined to join those girls who dissolved to tears when the light went out and safe anonymity came. Tears, at least, were universal communication. But somehow she refrained, telling herself all the while, "Be strong. Be patient. Come morning, things will be better. Prove to that great woman that you are worthy of her." Somehow she had gotten the notion that that woman, like God, would have those piercing eyes on her even in the dark. Lulled by such thoughts, she managed to sleep.

Come morning, however, Sofia woke to find herself lying in a pool of blood.

"Oh, God's wounds!" she blurted out. "Not the curse!"

Her words drew the attention of the others in the room, just waking, and attention was the last thing she wanted. Sofia pulled the quilt over her head and wished she could vanish off the face of the earth.

Why does this have to happen to me? she moaned to the dark quilt. "Be strong. Be patient," seemed absurd advice when utter weakness had her in its grip. Her hopes were dashed. The wonderful woman who had so admired her the day before would want nothing to do with her now, messy as she was. For surely the woman herself never succumbed to such weakness. Never. She was too controlled, too beautiful and gracious, too powerful, one might almost say *too male* to ever, ever be so burdened.

And there was that between us which let her know I was not such a silly female, either. But the continuing warmth between her legs told Sofia all control had vanished.

Sofia had never quite believed Saint Mark truly reposed in the golden reliquary her aunt made her go up and kiss on high holy days. What did it matter that the heist of the body, hidden in a barrel of pickled pork, from the indolent and heretical Alexandrians was well documented: in glimmering frescoes to either side of the chapel, in the preserved and sanctified slats of barrel displayed nearby?

Sofia had seen—and smelled—enough week-old corpses displayed by beggars in the Piazza to have her doubts. If that lumber pile encased in gold really was the reverend limbs of the Apostle, she couldn't help suspecting that, beyond pickle brine, somebody was helping heaven along with a little coating of "incorruptible" arsenic and wax. And if heaven really was working a miracle of preservation here, she would never believe beyond that. This deity's conjuring trick could never have any efficacy for anyone else. Not for the distasteful bulk of the blind and lame and palsied who had contaminated the reliquary with their lips before her. And certainly not for Sofia Baffo who actually, most days of the month, scorned the idea that heaven could do anything she couldn't do very well by herself, thank you.

Similarly, against all evidence, Governor Baffo's daughter continued to refuse to believe in her menses. If some mistake—like getting overheated and catching a cold when all the nuns did, too—had made it happen once, her greater sense would prohibit it happening again. And when it came a second time, she would surely not let it happen a third.

How long had it been now? This was not something with which she liked to clutter her head. Only when *it* rudely imposed *it*self on her being did she think about *it*. Now was one of those inescapable times. A year. Maybe more. To the best of her calculation. Every month, as regular as a full moon. As regular as fish on Friday—which she hated.

Sometimes she had thought *it,* like so many other unpleasant, stifling things, was a consequence of convent life. If she once escaped her aunt's scrutiny . . . the long arm of her father's law. . . . But now it was clear *it* had pursued her even beyond Christendom. *It* was with her to stay, no failure of circumstance or of those fools she was forced to suffer around her, but an integral part of her own being. A curse indeed.

Part of her ability to deny this unpleasant state of affairs was due to the fact that always when she had bled before, her aunt had taken responsibility. The first time *it* came, unannounced, unprepared, the very scriptural thief in the night, Sofia had taken to her bed, convinced she was going to die from this terrible and unnatural thing her body was doing to her. After two days and no sign of returning health, she had finally confided to the chap-faced nun, for whom two days missing matins was cause for third degrees of inquisition. Sofia had used her most contrite voice to speak the dreadful words, steeling herself for the barriers they would make her jump before they'd let her get to heaven.

Her aunt had slapped her across the face. Well, what else had Sofia expected to the confession of "blood" and "down there"? It was the sermon that came afterward that had taken her by surprise.

"Where is your head, wicked girl, whenever Genesis is read? Have you never heard of Eve's wickedness? The curse, girl. The curse upon all daughters of Eve for our Mother's sinfulness. Every moon, we are thus reminded of our fallen state and must pray to all-merciful God to release us from it quickly by His Grace."

Sofia had only ever heard "in pain shalt thou bear" and "thy desire toward thy husband," both clauses which she was determined *she* at least could thwart heaven and avoid. She had heard nothing about *this*. But of course she had only ever believed in a paradisiacal Eden about as much as she believed in Saint Mark: for people who needed that pabulum, not for her.

So every month thereafter she'd endured the slap and the sermon. It was the bleeding, in fact, that had started the flurry of letters between Venice and her father in Corfu that had eventually culminated in his ultimatum of marriage. And every month, as soon as they got up off their knees after asking forgiveness, Sofia gave the responsibility for her state up to her aunt in every way possible in such an intimate matter. Her aunt provided the clean linen rags, took the soiled ones away so her niece didn't even have the bother of looking at them. Well, the nun enjoyed feeling sinful. Let her have her fill.

Sofia could see now that her long denial had left her singularly unprepared now that her aunt was gone. She was more helpless even than the curse gave cause to be, but there was nothing she could do about it but lie there in that strange bed and bleed.

The foreign smell of the inside of a rusting, copper kettle left carelessly damp swept up her body to her nostrils, violating her. There was pressure on her bladder and in her bowels. These comforts she had strength to deny and forestall, but not the orifice between. She had faced pirates and Turks, slavers and eunuchs, but before none of these had she felt dirtier, more a victim, more shamed, exposed, invalid, impotent, violated—and alone.

And she felt even more so with every drop that trickled uncontrollably down to ruin her *shalvar*—the beautiful silk *shalvar* she had loved so much because they made her feel so masculine. She could see now there was a reason why women wore skirts with nothing in between the legs. Her memory that the *shalvar* were red provided little comfort.

Turkish women must not be subject to the curse of Eve, she decided, if this is what they were allowed to wear. If this was so, she envied them all the more but was certain now she could never attain to their power.

In spite of herself, the poet might have said, she began to weep. But Sofia felt she had precious little self left at this point to spite. Anything that might have been self was slowly but surely bleeding from her. But weep, indeed, she did, hot, silent, choking tears in rhythm to her flow.

So Baffo's daughter lay as the others in the room got up, got dressed and answered the call to prayer. So she lay as the palace around her roused, shook itself and took on its great, world-commanding business. So she lay, alone indeed, and hoping for death.

XXIV

PRESENTLY, SOMEONE ENTERED the room. Sofia wanted to remain alone, for that at least was similar to death. But she could not prevent them. Yes, "them," for there were at least two people. Women. She could hear them talking together, quick, playful banter of which she could not comprehend a word.

One of the voices stopped and called. Sofia knew the call was meant for her, but she couldn't answer. Concentrating on bringing her sobs under control, she thought that if she could just lie as still as death now, they would not see she was there until death should come to hide her shame.

Hard-soled slippers clicked quick steps across the bare wooden floor. A hand touched her. It touched her again, shaking her. The voices exchanged quizzical comments. A firmer shaking. And then the quilt was yanked from her hands and off her face.

Sofia sat upright instantly, blinking against the morning sunlight that streaked across the room. Of the two faces peering down at her, one was familiar, the one in front, the one in charge. It was not, however, the woman with the piercing eyes as she had hoped—or feared with her worst fear. Instead, it was the woman that the piercing-eyed one had ordered to examine her the day before. A midwife, Sofia might call her, or granny woman.

As she swung her legs to the floor, Sofia immediately recalled her state. She could hardly ignore it. Activity pressed even more blood from her, like wringing did from a damp cloth. *You've done it now,* she told herself and then, more hopefully, *If you're careful and don't move any more, they'll never see. Don't stand up—they can't make you, two middle-aged women like this—and they'll never know.*

The midwife gave a brusque greeting and a rather sour smile. Sofia nodded and then repeated as best she could the two syllables the woman enunciated while patting her own chest. Baffo's daughter took those syllables to be the woman's name. It was a nickname actually, Ayva, which Sofia would learn meant "the Quince." It was the only name necessary to distinguish the midwife in an inner palace full of women whose health and physical well-being, including and especially their most intimate parts, were in her knotted hands.

That bitter fruit, the Quince, suited the woman better than even the most heartless of mothers would have thought to name a daughter at birth. There was, in fact, something of Sofia's old aunt about the woman, the aunt having had the aspect of a crab apple, and this one the greener but no less astringent cast of quince. But her aunt's true nature had been so compressed by the wimple and enforced maidenhood it was hard to tell what she might have been if left to herself. With the Quince, there was no guessing. She was just the way God made her—and she had probably overruled Him on any count that mattered.

Very little gray showed under the woman's plain, no-nonsense caplet that was tied to her head at an angle more careless than rakish with a silk scarf. The silk was the green of olives. Anyone with any care for appearances would have told her that even a border of gold sequins could not keep this color from accentuating the similar sallow green of her own complexion.

Still, the black of the Quince's hair declared her to be younger than the acidity in her eyes at first betrayed. No honey of social grace could mask the bite of those eyes. Had she thought about it, Sofia might have realized that such un-relieved tartness came from much unromantic staring death in the face. Death—and life as well, for who was to say which could disabuse a woman sooner?

The Quince smelled of her namesake as well: the vague scent of linens packed for the winter among lavender, cloves, wormwood, and ripening fruit. Her black hair continued down into her face: not only upper lip and chin were covered by a decided brush, but the quince-fuzz made ingress to the cheeks as well.

There were many reasons for harem nicknames. Why should it be not so when each one had been winnowed by a hundred female tongues? But this Sofia had no way of knowing yet, and was not likely to learn as long as the wall of language stood between them.

To the end of breaching that wall, the Quince pushed the second woman forward. Without the push, it was clear, she never would have come forward on her own. The reason for such reticence was evident at first glance. At some point in her early life, this second woman had contracted smallpox. She had survived the disease, making her one of the lucky ones, although the ruin it had made of her face might give her cause to doubt that fortune. The pustules had littered her cheeks with craters, swelled one side grotesquely and eaten up half her nose and as well as every hint of eyelash.

Pits on her hands indicated that the rest of her body was equally ravaged and a roughness on the pitting spoke of the ongoing abuse of hot, sudsy water. The world was generally relieved of the sight of this poor face because it was kept down on its work of scrubbing floors. Indeed, a patch of damp over the woman's belly and on each knee confirmed that she had already been about that task this morning and was called away unexpectedly.

The ravaged face grew uglier still with the confusion the woman was presently suffering: the peculiarily acute confusion the very ugly feel in the presence of the very beautiful.

Sofia had enjoyed the advantage of that confusion all her life. In the normal course of things, she wouldn't have given that face a second glance. She couldn't bear ugliness, had no patience with it, beyond knowing she could rule it absolutely. Besides, she almost believed it was catching. Reason did tell her she was more likely to catch the pox from the Quince, who showed no sign of ever having contacted the disease, than from the mopper of floors who plainly had. Reason assured her that one who had survived the ordeal was henceforth immune. Reason had very little to do with aesthetics, however.

But then, just as Sofia was on the verge of rejecting that pitted face all together, what should she hear from those sadly pitted lips but a soft, shy whisper. *"Buon giorno, Madonna."* And she knew that, besides a roaring case of smallpox, the woman had also, at some point in her life, managed to catch a little Italian as well.

The seraglio had need of many languages and, considering the widely varied origins of its inmates, was usually able to provide. Italy was not one of the more common sources. This gave Sofia a sense of the relative power of her homeland, pride that not all His Serenity's posturing, calls for arms, and a greater defense budget were in vain.

Of course, this was the purpose behind calling the charwoman up off her knees. It was a strange Italian, southern—Naples, or perhaps even Sicily—and now heavily troweled with Turkish. But Italian nonetheless. There were words here, not just jumbled sound.

Sofia leaned forward, eager to hear more, as she hadn't heard an intelligible word since—well, since that young Veniero. A sweet enough lad, but of no consequence after all.

The Quince, too, awaited the next Italian phrase with impatience. When it was not immediately forthcoming—the uneven lips trembled in pursuit of speech—the Quince joggled the charwoman with her elbow and repeated the phrases she wanted to convey.

Following a deep breath, the poxed lips firmed and spoke. Sofia strained—and heard the same phrase repeated slowly, deliberately, syllable for syllable—in Turkish once more.

The Quince's meaning was more plain. "Idiot!" Anyone in the world could have understood the sense of her outburst. "You're speaking Turkish. You're just repeating the same words I said, only slowly, like baby talk. Come on, woman. Italian. You're from Italy. Remember the Italian!"

After another great strain, exaggerated by the fluster the scolding set her to, the charwoman finally dredged up something more. Sofia clung to every stammered gasp.

"Good day. I am—"

Distress overwhelmed the woman once again as she couldn't remember the name that went along with the language. A Christian name—the groping for it tortured her already tortured face. But there was no hope for it. The name was too far gone.

"I am Faridah," she finally settled for, "and this is the Quince. She is our woman—our woman with the babies." She struggled for meaning, the precise term beyond her. But Sofia had already guessed "midwife."

"A pleasure. I'm Sofia."

Sofia didn't want to delay the communication any longer than the agony of the present pace. Hoping to push things along with the immediacy of a hug, she got to her feet—and uncovered the large red stain on the blue-and-white ticking of the mattress beneath her.

XXV

AFTER THE MORTIFICATION, the tears, and the apologies, the Quince took matters firmly in hand. She enlisted the charwoman's strong arms, but Sofia had to bear her end of the bloody clothes and bedding, too.

In this way, the harem's newest slave was introduced to the laundry, where teams of two dozen women steamed and sweated at once. She learned her way to the fresh bedding stocked along the walls in every room where sleeping was done, the wardrobe where linen, cotton, and woolen garments were issued, more mundane than brocade and cloth-of-gold, but clean and eminently serviceable.

"Until you get clothes of your own," the Quince explained tantalizingly.

The Quince showed her the latrines, one large room containing five separate closets and space for ablutions. A flush of cleansing water harnessed on its wash from mountains to sea perpetually sounded in the bottom of the dark holes.

Hard by, in a little cubicle, a girl of eight or ten was occupied full time cleaning and carding the soft absorbent wool required by over five hundred women. Concealment of the offending fluids of one's body would not be possible here. In fact, Sofia mused, the entire palace probably knows a woman is pregnant before she knows herself. But then, she carried the thought further, perhaps it was only trying to shuffle their lives into life paced by men that made women's concealment necessary.

"But don't toss all of it with the wool down the latrine hole," the Quince said, handing her a palm-sized earthenware pot with a rough cork stopper.

It took Sofia some time to understand what the midwife was asking her to do with this pot because she could not believe that what the charwoman translated could possibly be true. But eventually, by question and gesture, she confirmed the sense.

"As long as you remain a maid, save as much of your flow as you can. I can get a good price for it. Why, don't you know? The monthly blood of a virgin, either taken internally or used as an ointment, is the best cure known for the scourge of leprosy."

Sofia was so impressed by this value placed on what she was accustomed to considering the vilest of things that she didn't think to ask if she could profit herself from the project until it was too late to do so with any tact. They left the little jar on a shelf in the latrine until her next visit and went on.

After that, the Quince introduced her to the kitchens. Her time of month, it seemed, was Sofia's introduction to the whole complex, as if the buildings were actually clustered according to her need. Her condition was the key to their layout, not whatever it was that dictated dwellings where men were lords.

The three women could actually only peer at the kitchens—ten double domes all smoking at once—across a broad courtyard. Every one of the cooks, not even considering the hewers of wood and drawers of water needed for such a vast operation, were men.

"Usually food is brought over at mealtime by the halberdiers," the Quince explained. "Such a man you see across the courtyard now. When he comes here to the harem, he will drop the two long side tresses of his wig-hat down before his face so he can look neither to the right nor to the left and thus invade our privacy. Periodically, the halberdiers also bring us a supply of wood for our braziers.

"At mealtime, a bell will ring, and you must make yourself scarce from this entry hall until the halberdiers have set the platters down, exited, and the eunuch rings the bell a second time. Then you know it is safe to come into the hall and—if it is your duty—retrieve the platters from these banks of marble. You see the counters are so contrived that hot dishes remain hot and cold dishes cold. The accepted order among us is to serve and enjoy one dish at a time, and that is how they must be served. You will eat with the rest of the girls in your mess. I will introduce you to one or two of them shortly and they'll help you find your way.

"As you've already missed your breakfast today, I will have a eunuch run across the way and bring you something. Something special for your time of month. Yes, special orders are always possible. Salt and pickles are not good. Nor meat, not during your menses. But we will send for hot water for some tea. I will provide my usual preparation for this time of the month from my dispensary: angelica with a touch of myrrh and lots of cream and honey. Yogurt is good. Parsley, chickpeas, pomegranate, if we haven't seen the last of them this year. A cucumber, but, alas, they're out of season. Some fresh hot bread and—"

"And *taratir at-turkman?*" Sofia asked.

The Quince smiled at something that needed no translation. "Yes, one or two of those won't hurt. The cook in the Crown Prince's kitchen makes the best pastries. I will be certain you get some of his."

The warm tea and good food amazed Sofia with its ability to perceptibly ease the tension in the heart of her pelvis. She tried to thank the midwife for what seemed little short of a miracle with as much grace as the clumsiness of translation would allow.

The Quince answered the thanks with a snort and looked away. Sofia couldn't tell whether that snort meant, "I'm only doing what any fool should have known to do for herself," or "Don't mention it. I'm only doing my job."

Faridah gave no translation for the snort. The midwife took the gratitude as an invitation to say more which, in any case, she needed no encouragement to do. If the little charwoman could hardly keep up with the transfer of words, that didn't matter, either. Over many years, Sofia would come to have the Quince's lectures memorized. Health was a subject the harem never tired of and the midwife never tired of exhorting in that direction, even when her hands were not needed.

"It's good to have new blood," the Quince began. "We are always looking for new blood. You don't know how difficult it is to provide the masters with bed partners sometimes, as no matter what schedule she's on when she enters our realm, it doesn't take too long before any girl's cycle is drawn to coincide with that of our Valide Sultan."

"Valide Sultan." Sofia tried the word on her own tongue and found it as sweet as the honey in her tea. "Who is that?"

"Who is that? Only the most powerful woman in the empire. The most powerful woman in the world. The mother of the Sultan."

"And who is that?"

"Technically, there is no Valide Sultan at present. Our master Suleiman the Lawgiver—Allah save him—he lost his mother long ago. Since the death of his beloved wife and the mother of his heir, Khurrem Sultan—Allah have mercy on her soul—the household has been divided. The Shadow of Allah's daughter Mihrimah Sultan takes care of our lord's most immediate needs. For the rest, we have only the mother of the son of the heir to be our head."

"And who is that?"

"The woman whose four hundred *ghrush* bought you— Nur Banu Kadin."

Sofia knew without being told that this was the name of the wonderful woman with the piercing eyes. Baffo's daughter also looked carefully beyond the translator to the face of the midwife as she replied. *The Quince doesn't like the marvelous woman.* The thought surprised the harem's newest slave; she would not have thought it was possible to be in the presence of those eyes and not be impressed. Then she remembered how the midwife's tongue had caressed the syllables "Khurrem Sultan" and decided maybe it was only a matter of missing a dead woman and the difficulties of accepting anyone else in her place. Still, the caution with which the charwoman hedged her translation spoke of looking to her own neck.

This was all very interesting, Sofia thought, and useful information to have from the very start. There was something more, something she couldn't quite put words to. It had to do with the Quince. She didn't have to listen to the midwife long to realize the midwife loved women and their bodies almost to distraction. To her, they were divine, perhaps the only sort of true divinity in creation. There was something, too, in the way the Quince had handled Sofia from the very start, that very first inspection in Nur Banu's presence. Gentleness, reverence were sensations that came to mind. Sofia had sometimes felt the same from men, even from their eyes alone. From the best sort of men, the men she knew would be the easiest to manipulate although manipulation seemed absurd with this strong and self-possessed woman.

Whatever it was, Sofia would gladly hear treatises on women's health all day long to glean such tidbits.

"Sometimes we're even obliged to send some girls to

other palaces," the Quince continued. "To the New Palace just outside the city walls or even farther afield, to the summer palace in Edirne—just to get them on a different schedule so they can serve the master when everyone else cannot. The birth of a baby gives one the strength to set her own rhythm for a while. Change of life, a girl just starting out, these, too, can cause oddities. We did have such a struggle getting the young Princess Esmikhan Sultan on a regular schedule. Exposure to the full moon helped. Now she cycles with her mother to the day.

"A woman at her time is at the height of her powers." Did the Quince even blush and turn away under what she thought was the cover of Faridah's translation? "You don't need to worry about this yet, but that is why she should not be with a man until she has visited the baths and washed holiness from herself afterward."

An incomprehensible argument ensued between the two women at this point. The charwoman translated something about "gross impurity" and "the curse of Mother Hawa— Mother Eve" by which Sofia understood that not everyone in the East believed what the midwife's study had led her to. Probably very few in fact did, else the timid charwoman would never have dared to contradict so. Clearly, if she'd a mind to feel sinful, Sofia would feel right at home here in the land of the Grand Turk. She wasn't sure she wanted to go as far as the Quince finally got their go-between to urge her, either.

"This is your Sabbath, as men have imposed one holy day on us once a week according to their schedules, Friday in Islam, Saturday among the Jews, Sunday where you come from. You should not waste this holy time on everyday tasks, nor should you allow your attention to be broken by male concerns. You should experience all of your being exactly as it is, and concentrate on its messages. This is the way to health, in the body, in the mind, and in the world at large."

Sofia decided that, with the Quince's aid toward ignoring what she couldn't change about her physical being, she at least wouldn't let her curse time distract her again. She would hold as tight a rein as ever woman held upon the maverick of her body. No guilt or any other further discomfort would mar her concentration on her goals. She did intend, in any case, to let no one draw her to their cycle, not even Nur Banu Kadin with the piercing eyes.

"BUT NOW, AS midday prayers will soon be upon us, we must hurry and finish the business for which Nur Banu Kadin sent me to you in the first place," the Quince said. "We must perform an engrafting, child."

The charwoman had no idea how to translate the word into Italian. She interpreted the word with long, detailed explanations and gestures. She even brought Sofia to a grilled window on the second floor. Here they watched a number of gardeners, recognizable by their tall cylindrical hats of red felt, busy in a potting section of the grounds. Among heaps of manure and cabbage seedlings, the gardeners moved with stubby, curved blades and balls of string along a row of saplings. All Sofia could learn was that they managed to put new twigs into young trunks where there were none before.

"This is engrafting," the charwoman said.

"But surely you don't mean to put a—a new limb on me!" Sofia exclaimed.

Everyone laughed at the preposterousness of the idea, Sofia a little more hesitant than the other two. Who knew what the Turks had in mind to do to her? They were barbarians, after all. She was in their power; her search for power had brought her to this and there was no doubt power could be dangerous as well as attractive.

"Let me try another tack." The charwoman gestured to the Quince and then turned to speak her own words to Sofia, for the first time that day and with an earnestness Baffo's daughter could not ignore.

XXVI

"WHEN I WAS a child," the charwoman began, "a long, long time ago, I lived, like you, among an ignorant people."

Sofia did not believe the Serene Republic to be a den of ignorance and the thought must have registered in her face, for Faridah's earnestness increased until it brought tears to her eyes.

"No, no. They were ignorant. Ignorant of a great means of health that merciful Allah has vouchsafed to the people who worship Him. If this were not true, would I wear the scars of ignorance in my face?"

"Smallpox?"

"Yes. I had it as a child. Most of my family died of it and I was left, left like this. Ruined."

"I'm sorry." Sofia didn't know what else to say to such intensity and pain.

"You have never had smallpox."

"No, thank San Rocco."

"Thank Allah, not a saint. It reads in your beautiful face."

"I have been lucky."

"Allah has preserved you. Until you could come to know the Quince. The Quince, in her wisdom, will engraft a bit of smallpox into you."

"What? You mean give me smallpox?"

"Yes."

"Make me sick?"

"Yes, a little."

"No!"

Sofia looked to the hairy, slightly greenish face with horror. She saw her world on its shaky pillars of good luck crumbling around her into unredeemable ugliness and along with it, powerlessness.

"I've no desire to come anywhere near that plague," she reiterated when she could find more words.

What were these people, jealous? Did they crush any threat to them with such ferocity? Is this how they ruled the world?

"I have been fortunate enough to avoid smallpox until now." Sofia took a few steps backwards. "I intend to do everything in my power to avoid it in the future."

"The Quince will make you sick, but only a little sick. After that, you will be immune. Like me."

"But my face—"

"Yes, some pustules may grow on your face, but they will scab and then fall off without scars. The Quince does this to preserve your health and your beauty, Madonna. Trust her. You don't want to run any risk of ending up like me. Such beauty is too great a gift of Allah not to put it under His protection. The girls we get, from all over the world. Who knows where they come from, what diseases they bring? All are engrafted when they first arrive, even—no, especially those who are destined for the honor of the Sultan's presence. They are engrafted to prevent what could only be the worst of disasters among these, the most beautiful women in the world, living so on top of one another and confined as we do."

Sofia looked from the charwoman to the midwife now in wonder. The Quince had been listening to this tirade of words she couldn't understand with complacency, her hands folded quietly across the girdle at her waist.

"You—she can do this?" Sofia asked, her voice echoing with awe.

"She can," Faridah said.

The Quince nodded after her with the same quiet confidence.

"Nur Banu Kadin wants me to have it done?"

"Yes. Please, you must undergo it."

"I suppose you would force me if I disagreed."

"We would, but it needn't be that way. Please. Do not be afraid. For your beauty's sake."

"Very well. Very well, I will undergo the—the engrafting."

"*Mashallah!* That's good, Safiye." The charwoman couldn't contain herself and reached out to press Sofia's arm.

"Sofia," Baffo's daughter said. "My name's Sofia. With an 'o.' "

"No. Safiye," the charwoman insisted with all the intensity of which her already intense face was capable. "Safiye. It means 'the fair one.' And fair you will stay. I promise you, as Allah is Merciful."

"Come then, to my infirmary," the midwife said.

She led the way down a hall of a dozen doorways that must all be opened at once to catch a glimpse of trees in their first green haze of spring at the end. Under the trees, as the women made a right turn at the end of the hall, Sofia caught a brief look at the freshly shooting perennials in a carefully tended and well-stocked herb garden.

The bellies of row upon row of Chinese porcelain, japanware, and blue Persian jars leaned in upon the patient from the walls of the narrow infirmary. On a matchingly narrow table were stacks of books, mortars and pestles in three sizes, scales, a filigree stand to hold a small glass bowl over a lamp's flame.

Sofia couldn't tell Turkish labeling from the elaborate tendrils that twined about the pharmacopeia, but her nose was assailed by the smells of their contents. Sweet cloves and cinnamon, sharp garlic and bitter gentian. There were the darker odors of moss, clay, and virgins' blood, as if she'd walked into the very heart of her own pelvis. Animal parts preserved in brine—all slaked with a wash of alcohol. For ever after, the sharp, clean odor of alcohol would return the scene to Sofia's mind, the scene and the pervading sense of power.

She had seen apothecaries before, of course. There was even a sister in the convent. The Quince's domain differed on two counts. The first was that any Venetian herbalist, when he wanted to praise a remedy as the best, most powerful of its kind, most failproof, even bordering on black magic, would never hesitate to dress it up in adjectives indicating "secret of the East," "the Muslim's cure," "ripe with the wisdom of the most wise Avicenna." Turks, from Avicenna down, were known to be the most skilled physicians in the world. The wealthiest Western noblemen hired them when they could, and here she was, Sofia Baffo, in the presence of one who treated Eastern nobility. The Quince had no need to point elsewhere for her justification.

The second impressive point was that this was a woman. The best medicine in Venice came from men, for women were never allowed in medical universities, in Padua or

Seville. The convent herbalist made it clear—and Father Confessor behind her made it clear as well—that she was only good for the day-to-day comfort of women. Serious ills required male power and a man would certainly be called when they occurred.

There was none of this in the Quince's air. She was the best money could buy and she knew it. Ironically, a great deal of her confidence came from the harem walls and the close society they created. Here, plainly, even if more serious disease did crop up, a man could never be resorted to.

And now this woman was going to work a miracle and make Sofia impervious to smallpox.

Ever after, when she'd smell alcohol, Sofia would remember the sense of power in that room. A shiver would run down her spine every time she thought of it, remembering having to strip naked in that unheated room. Remembering the Quince's scrutiny of her. And remembering all that power focused on her unprotected skin. This, for once in her life, was not power she could aspire to. A power of life and death, a power to thwart even the almighty will of God. She shivered again for neither cold nor nakedness.

But she could aspire to make such power subservient to her own.

"Engraft away!" she ordered.

"We usually do this in the fall," the Quince described as she made her preparations.

Sofia sat and waited with a quilt about her shoulders on a small cot with Faridah translating beside her.

"After the hot weather is past is the best time, but Nur Banu Kadin agreed with me that we were early enough in the season that there will be no complications."

"Inshallah," Faridah added.

"And that your beauty was too precious a thing to trust to the tender mercies of a summer."

The Quince went on. "All those to be engrafted—children around seven or eight are our prime subjects, but all the new girls, too. All these we usually take on something of an outing to the Sweet Waters of Europe. It is a diversion. Women ask their friends, 'Shall we take the children to get smallpox next week?' much as they may ask them to come for sherbet."

"I can hardly believe such a thing," Sofia said, fishing for assurances.

"Well, you wouldn't. Men don't know the secret, actually. No male physician could engraft you. The secret is kept among women, and mothers get their sons protected before they leave the harem, before they can remember just what happened to them."

The Quince had availed herself of a large, sharp needle which she heated over her lamp. In her left hand, she held a walnut shell filled with a yellow, pus-like matter.

"The best smallpox," the midwife described it. "Sometimes we have to send for it from quite a distance, although the foreign communities in Constantinople are usually able to provide. Sealing it in a shell keeps it from drying out before it is needed. There is cowpox here, too, taken from the udders of cows. It was the observation that maids who milked cows with the pox were immune to the pox themselves that first taught my teachers this method.

"Now, the Greek Christians," she went on, "when they perform this engrafting, believe one should mark each arm, the breast and the middle of the forehead as a sign of their cross. But as each place I touch with this needle will leave a scar, I prefer to let the forehead alone. And the breast where a lover may rest his head. Let the Christians have their superstition. I will mark four spots instead, one on each hip and on each arm. Believe me, if the master gets so far with you, he will not contain himself for a little dimple in each of these places."

The Quince eased down the quilt and made a quick jab at Sofia's right arm. The newest slave flinched, but it was no more painful than a scratch. Then the midwife gathered up as much of the pus as would fit on the end of the needle and smeared it into the blood beading at the wound. The application was a little cold, but it didn't sting. Faridah helped to cup the place with another walnut half which she bound on with linen strips. They repeated the process on each limb and then Sofia was allowed to get dressed.

"That's it."

"That's it?"

The Quince nodded. "Now we would just let the children romp about if we were on an outing, feed them sweets, weave garlands for their hair. I'm sorry I can't pamper you with that diversion today. I don't suppose you're quite as frisky as an eight-year-old, either, but you are free to go. Your time is your own—and that of the moon—until the mistress comes for your religious instruction."

XXVII

"RELIGIOUS INSTRUCTION" SMACKED much the same as it had in the convent. Prayers and scriptures memorized in Arabic were not much different from prayers and scriptures in Latin, although they presented themselves much deeper in the throat. The postures and prostrations had parallels, too. Sofia concerned herself with the meaning to the same degree.

The main difference—and benefit—she found in Islam was that in a harem, unlike the theoretically feminine world of a convent, no bishop or priest would ever come to catechize her. The religious instructress certainly took her duty just as seriously as Sister Seraphina had, but she was much more content with a mindless mimicry. Greek and Armenian girls balked at declaring God to be One and Muhammed his Prophet. They, who clung to their native beliefs with tearful fervor and cared to argue Trinity and Transubstantiation, took much more of that woman's attention than Sofia, who held her tongue. Of course one recalcitrant girl in the whole convent declaring when pressed (and there was a lot of pressure) that it was all a waste of time did not present quite the challenge of a shipment of a dozen new girls a week from as many different lands and creeds.

Reprieve also came with the fact that, on account of her menses, Sofia was barred from the harem mosque for the whole first week of her stay, for all that it was a shrine exclusively for women to begin with. She was expected to pray on her own, which she never did unless someone was watching, not till the end of her life.

By the time she was required to take her place in the ranks of new girls, her personality, bleeding or no, had made its mark. Everyone had already forgotten that she was a novice and that all eyes should scrutinize her every move. Since prayer and recitation were always performed in groups, Sofia perfected the skill the convent had first taught her of keeping no more than one syllable or posture behind the leader. In this fashion, her dissent—if passive lack of care deserves the name—was never remarked.

But with the end of her period and the dropping of the walnut shells from her limbs of their own accord, Sofia began to feel the limits of her new station. She had impressed everyone there was to impress among the charwomen and frightened new girls who shared her quarters. Already she was their undoubted leader, even over the language barrier. The religious instruction turned quickly into reading and writing at which she studiously remained no more clever than was necessary. Here, too, nothing taxed either mind or soul. But she had yet to see the wonderful Nur Banu Kadin again. Or anyone else of more than menial or spiritual account—which meant no account at all.

Sofia grew restless.

The Italian word *seraglio* is actually derived from the phrase meaning a cage for wild beasts and, like a beast, Sofia began to pace the halls of the warren in which she found herself. Her steps measured the hallways from one dour guardian eunuch to another until she thought she would roar with tedium. And this was only after a week!

One evening of particular restlessness, she found herself unwatched in the dim corridor she recognized from her first visit to the palace. Here was the door which had taken her into the presence of those dark, piercing eyes. She measured the shadows of the hall in front of it for several minutes. No one came. The door remained shut. At length, Sofia could contain herself no longer. She dared to let herself into that room once more.

To her dismay and confusion Sofia found the room dark and deserted. Had what she'd seen that first day been only a reflection in a mirror, it could not have vanished more quickly and without a trace. Not only was the room deserted of people, but it was also in the process of being stripped of most of the furnishings that had made it so elegant as well.

Rugs and mattresses lay stacked in coils against the wall. Fine sweetmeat services and copperware peeped out of their shipping crates. Chests of silk and damask sat open and half full, while other garments in neatly folded stacks and heaps of jewelry, all like so much dross without people to animate them, waited nearby.

Nur Banu was clearly deserting the place—harem walls could never be a barrier to such a powerful woman. Nur Banu and all her glittering, lively suite—

And Sofia Baffo would be left alone in this—this prison. The thought overwhelmed her, flooded her with heat and fear. Her knees grew heavy, her head light, and she sank to the empty, echoing floor with a gasp.

Later Sofia had only a vague memory of how the great white eunuch came and quietly led her away, closing and locking the door behind him. She remembered how, when she couldn't walk, he picked her up in his arms like a child and carried her up to her narrow bed on the third floor.

At some point, through a haze, his face took on the aspect of someone she knew. Yes, that young Veniero from the convent garden, from the ship. Inexplicable guilt overwhelmed her at the recognition, coming in tangible waves and roughness. Veniero—Giorgio—come to save her once again, but this time . . . this time she would take him at his word.

No. This was a eunuch. She remembered the paper in the lurching candlelight of a ship's cabin. No children . . . no virile young Venetian sailor. . . .

Later she recognized it all as delirium.

"Smallpox." The word entered her fevered brain. The pustules on her face had the telltale indentation in their centers. Her face reflected that of the ugly little charwoman. Her face, her life, it was all over, worthless.

"No, no." Sofia heard the Quince's calming voice and its little Faridah echo. "The wounds—where I engrafted the venom—they remain open, weeping. See? It will be necessary to keep them clean, but that is the way the poison leaves the body, so it never becomes acute. I haven't lost a patient yet. Believe me."

"Inshallah," Faridah added.

Sofia became aware of time again two days later, which finally convinced her of the Quince's power. Victims of real smallpox, even if they were destined to live, could not hope to be over the fever and delirium in less than a week. Nonetheless, she was left feeling like the burned-out hull of a ship, as empty as a marble hall with the rugs packed away, tile and mirrors reflecting only emptiness, tired and listless.

"It is something else that ails her," the Quince said firmly, "not my medicine. See? The scabs have sloughed off as clean as you can wish. Only the entry cuts remain and they will heal. Because she is full-grown, not an eight-year-old, they will not expand as she grows, but remain as they are, no bigger than a fingernail. No, it's something else—"

After Sofia's second week in the harem, the Quince pronounced her fit to travel and vowed she wouldn't come to visit any more.

"And no, I will not believe it's witchcraft until I have much more proof than this, you superstitious chit," were her parting words to Faridah. "Depression. All too common a condition in here, and I won't prescribe drugs for a case as minor as hers. Travel is the best therapy. The new girl is fit to travel, and travel I order her to do."

Faridah wept as if losing her only friend in the world.

Fit to travel didn't mean willing to travel. Sofia's listlessness lingered on to the next morning when eunuchs with whom she couldn't communicate, and wasn't expected to, once again swathed her in veils. Where they led her she was too hollow to care, but it turned out to be through the gardens by another route until she reached the water's edge. As passive as a doll, she was put in a boat and ferried across the Bosphorus until she arrived at the dock at Scutari on the Asian side.

Once more she was loaded in a sedan chair, but this time the journey did not end until nightfall. And, come morning, it began again. And all the next day and the next. Sofia soon realized that the wonderful city of Constantinople, harem or otherwise, was not to be her home after all.

Sometimes her chair halted for an hour or two in a bit of afternoon shade. Sofia would find herself in the middle of a muddy field with muddy peasants tending muddy crops and she would despair. She might have married the Corfiot after all. At least she understood what that play for power was all about. Here was no one to tell her where she was going or why. Even had the porters been able to understand her questions they dared not respond under the careful eye of the great white eunuch.

The journey lasted a full week.

FORTUNATELY, ON THE third day, Sofia's single sedan overcame a much larger company and joined it. She had closed her curtain tightly against the dreariness of the countryside, and when she first heard the noise of these new companions, she thought it was only another crowd of peasants on their way to market. She imagined them with scabby donkeys loaded to breaking with wives, children, hens, and cabbages, and she closed the shutters even tighter against their noise and dust.

When they halted at noon and the noise persisted, she refused to come out, even to stretch her legs or relieve herself, though she needed to do both quite badly.

Presently, however, the shutters were thrown open from the outside, and a heavily veiled face, startlingly spectral, peered in at her. A hand to her mouth betrayed Sofia's uneasiness to which the other face replied by removing a corner of its veil.

Sofia recognized the revealed eyes at once and gave a squeal of delight. All lingering exhaustion left her. She and the wonderful woman were traveling companions after all!

"We stopped to visit friends along the way. To give you time to recover from the pox."

So much she understood of Nur Banu's greetings, but it didn't matter. It didn't matter, either, where Sofia was carried, even to the end of the earth, as long as that woman came along. That the woman's wagon had room for one more added to the new slave's delight. Needless to say, at the end of two weeks, Sofia's command of Turkish had grown by leaps and bounds.

Kutahiya was the name of their final destination, not that it mattered much to Sofia. It was Nur Banu's destination, that was enough for her to know.

It was a small town: if every soul there had been taxed half a *ghrush,* they would not yet have the price to pay for a Sofia Baffo. Nearly as large as the area covered by the tile-roofed houses of the natives was a sprawling citadel that crowned the hill. An ancient building, its foundations and cellars predated Islam; only repairs had been made in current memory. Here the governor of the neighborhood lived with his family.

Sofia was installed in the harem of this citadel.

XXVIII

"KUTAHIYA IS A terribly tedious place to have to spend one's days," Nur Banu Kadin said.

Nur Banu, Sofia soon learned, meant "woman of splendor," and she continued to think that no woman had been more aptly named.

"The winters are undoubtedly the worst, damp and cold. Can you blame me if I use every ruse to be able to spend them in the Grand Serai? Unfortunately, the complaints that work for winter do not serve for summer, for Constantinople is far more humid and full of fevers than than this place in the mountains."

To be given such confidences turned Sofia's disappointment at the smallness of the place into the same sort of abiding patience her mistress showed.

"We must simply be content and wait our time. The old man cannot live forever, Allah have mercy on him."

Sofia put a fervent hope in these words of the older woman, though at first she had no idea who "the old man" might be.

"Let me tell you, my little cloud from a foreign land, who we are, and how it is we came to Kutahiya, for it will help you to know your new master and how we live, even if you do not yet understand every word I say."

Sofia nodded her willingness to hear the tale, which promised to be of some length. Such attention flattered her. To be reminded of her "new master" was not irksome. She had not even seen a man since her arrival except for the great hulk and several others of his kind whom she now knew were eunuchs. Rather than prison keepers, she grew to understand that they were her guardians. When she should come to need such services, they would act as emissaries between herself and the outside world. At the moment, she learned only to trust the constant gaze of their eyes and to call them, not a name that referred to their less-than-whole status, but either *khadim,* "servant," or *ustadh,* "teacher."

And Sofia had ceased to mind references to her "master" altogether when she learned that Nur Banu was also a slave to the same master.

"I was taken from my poor parents at the age of four. I have never really known any other life than that of service to the whims of a great man. Of course, my position is somewhat augmented by fate, which had made me the mother of that man's oldest son."

"Are you married to the Sultan's heir, then?" Sofia asked in awe.

Nur Banu sighed. "No, I must give up on that. It is not Allah's will that Selim will marry me as his father married his favorite, Khurrem Sultan."

"So then you are a slave—like me."

"Yes. Though on the books I will never be anything other than a slave, there is a very good chance, if Allah is favorable, if He wills I live long enough, that I will find myself in the position of Valide Sultan."

"Mother of the Sultan." Sofia tasted the word again and found it as delicious as ever. "Few men can entertain such high ambitions."

She learns quickly, this one. Sofia could read the thought in Nur Banu's eyes and felt proud.

Certainly nothing but pride sounded in the older woman's voice as she continued, "My master is Selim, the eldest of four children born to the great Sultan of all the Muslims, Suleiman—may he reign forever—and his only legal wife, the beloved Khurrem Sultan—may Allah have mercy on her soul. Their third son, Djahangir, was always a weak boy and crippled—may Allah spare you from such offspring—and he died many years ago. The only daughter, Mihrimah, Suleiman gave to his Grand Vizier, Rustem Pasha, who has died this last year. Though Mihrimah Sultan suffers his loss greatly, poor thing, he left her an incredibly wealthy woman. I hope she may be well enough to make your acquaintance when next we are in Constantinople."

"Mihrimah keeps her father the Sultan's private household, doesn't she?"

"That is true."

"And as such she is a detriment to your power."

"Who told you so?"

"The Quince."

"The midwife, eh?"

"On my first day."

Perhaps my lack of skill in Turkish made the statement too blunt, Sofia thought, reading the older woman's face carefully. *Perhaps it were better to keep such observations to myself.*

Nur Banu did take some time to regain the composure in her flashing eyes before she continued, changing the subject. "Between my master Selim and his younger brother, Bayazid, there has always been fierce competition. My master is the elder, but their mother favored Bayazid. Indeed, it is said she never would have killed Mustafa for Selim, but only for Bayazid."

"Killed—? Who was poor Mustafa?" Sofia asked.

"He was Suleiman's first-born son, only by a concubine. Though his mother soon lost out to Khurrem in Suleiman's affections, Mustafa was much more tenacious. Khurrem Sultan had to have him strangled."

"Strangled?" Sofia repeated, unfamiliar with the word. Though many other words she did not know were allowed to pass by, she had to know what this one meant.

"Strangled," Nur Banu said again. "With the oiled, silken bowstring. Silk is reserved for the members of the royal house. And the bowstring—it is a sin to shed royal blood. That is how it's always done."

"It is done?" Sofia asked.

"Strangled, so!" And Nur Banu suddenly stood up and gave a violent demonstration of the act upon the defenseless air, her fierce eyes flashing.

"The great lady Khurrem Sultan did this?" Sofia asked.

"Oh, no!" Nur Banu said. "Such is not a thing for ladies. Actually, I must give her credit. The old woman had such a way with Suleiman. She filled his ears with lies, and he was like potter's clay in her hands."

"The Sultan killed his own son?" Sofia asked.

"Not with his own hands, either, of course. He had three of his men's ears punctured and their tongues cut out so they could tell no tales after they'd received the orders. It happened in the Sultan's own tent when he had invited the unsuspecting Mustafa to dine. Suleiman himself sat but on the other side of the curtain in his harem and saw it all. Then he pretended not to know what had happened and he returned to Constantinople. There the news was brought to him, written on black paper in white ink, as the custom is. Only then did he join his people in a public show of grief. She was something, Khurrem Sultan was," and Sofia nodded in joint wonder at the slave girl who had had her way over the son of the world's greatest emperor.

"As for his remaining two sons," Nur Banu continued, "—my master and his brother—the Sultan thought it wise to get them out of Constantinople, where they might fall victim to similar plots. He gave them each a *sandjak*—Selim in Magnesia and Bayazid in Konya."

"What is a *sandjak*?" Sofia asked.

"A fief, a province they must govern and tax, sending the revenues to the capital and keeping for themselves only enough to live on. You must know that Magnesia is the traditional *sandjak* of the heir to the throne and, though she tried, even Khurrem Sultan could not move my master Selim from this place. Oh, how I loved Magnesia! Perhaps I loved it so because that is where my son was born and we were very happy together when he was small and could still play at my feet in the harem. From Magnesia, we could often take jaunts to the sea coast and that was pleasant—Ah, but one must not weep over what it is not Allah's will to have endure forever.

"Four years ago, Khurrem Sultan took mortally ill. Suleiman was mad with grief and decided to fulfill her last request. She had not asked that her favorite Bayazid be moved to Magnesia, only that Selim be moved elsewhere. The rest, she supposed would follow, for she had great faith, not unwarranted, in Bayazid's ambition.

"But even grief could not blur Suleiman's eyes to the needs of the Empire altogether. Under the wise counsel of the vizier Rustem Pasha, he decided to move my master here to Kutahiya, which does have the advantage of being much closer to Constantinople. In case of emergency, my master can reach the Sublime Porte in five days of hard riding. Bayazid, on the other hand, was not moved to Magnesia as Khurrem Sultan had desired, but to Amasia in the Pontic Mountains. Because of bad roads and the greater distance, he could not hope to reach Constantinople in anything less than two weeks. In case something, Allah forbid, should happen to the Sultan, Selim would have that much advantage to carry the day. This fact was not lost on Bayazid.

"We were not overjoyed to move to Kutahiya. It was not

our beloved Magnesia, after all, and the climate is abominable. But we always made haste to fulfill our sovereign lord's desire, and when we were told to leave Magnesia, we did. Not so Bayazid. He refused to go to Amasia. Have I told you? No. I guess not. Amasia had been poor Mustafa's *sandjak.*

" 'I will not go,' Bayazid said, 'for it puts me in mind of my poor dead brother, and how can I rule with such grief on my shoulders?'

"In fact he was thinking, 'If Magnesia is the place where princes go to grow into sultans, Amasia is where they go to die.'

"Well, still muttering such things, Bayazid finally did go. And he discovered that in that eastern land of Kurds and wild Turks one need only say the name 'Mustafa' to conjure up an army, for they all loved Suleiman's eldest son dearly. In their ignorance they began to say that Bayazid was a resurrection of the strangled Mustafa.

"Soon, entrenching himself with arms and men, Bayazid stood in Amasia in open rebellion against his father. Perhaps it was his mother Khurrem Sultan who encouraged this in him before she died, hinting that his father was old and weak and that a show of force would finish him. Still, Allah was with the right and did not support such blasphemies against the man girded with Othman's sword. My master joined his armies to those of his father and, loathe as he was to fight against his own brother, defeated him on the fields of Konya.

"Bayazid fled first to Amasia and thence to the court of the Persian Shah, where he remains today. That is where our master Selim is, where he has been since the snows cleared this spring, menacing on the borders of Persia and warning the Shah that Suleiman means business. The Shah for his part has made a solemn vow that he will not give up Bayazid nor his four little sons to Turkish heretics while he yet has breath.

So the matter stands. Allah alone knows how it may all turn out, but I pray daily that He may favor our master and bring this to a speedy, victorious end."

Sofia nodded her amen to this prayer and her appreciation for the confidences. She thought of them often in the days that followed. More memorable than the words, which she still could understand but imperfectly, was the action she had witnessed. Cool, sedate Nur Banu had risen to her feet and "strangled" the air with a flick of her white, bangled wrists and a twist of her painted red fingertips. There was power indeed, and more than in all those bungling princes and their armies.

XXIX

SPRING GAVE WAY to summer there at the edge of the Phrygian highlands. The fields of thistle whitened and dust, once raised, took all afternoon to settle.

Sofia learned Turkish. She also learned the ways of the harem. She learned to groom herself with the help of the lesser slaves and she learned what fabrics and colors were most becoming according to Turkish tastes. She learned to dance. She learned the communal dances when lines of women holding one another's belts followed the small, bouncing steps of a leader. And she learned the more strenuous individual dances, where one accompanied a lot of movement from hip to navel with the clicking of wooden spoons. At this latter pastime, with her long, graceful limbs, Sofia soon excelled.

She learned to sing, to adjust some of her Venetian songs to Nur Banu's aesthetics while at the same time giving them an exotic flavor all her own that delighted her audiences. She also learned to play a little on the *oud* and to accompany others when they performed, but at this she had less patience and so made less progress. She enjoyed being the center of attention too much herself.

But Sofia did try hard to make friends and was extremely good at that. Soon no gathering in the harem could pass without loud applause and the cry of her name. Turkish tongues from the little charwoman on turned "Sofia" into "Safiye," meaning "the fair one," a name that suited Baffo's daughter as well as it suited those who gave it to her. Soon she had almost forgotten she had ever been called anything else.

Toward the middle of summer, there was great rejoicing, for the master returned victorious and tales of the Shah's capitulation and Bayazid's ignominious death were circled in the harem versions with great relish.

Still, Sofia—or Safiye, rather—was not quite as content as such news should have made her. Even though she had never seen the master, now a war hero, of one thing she was certain: he was a man of appetite. Besides the boys it was rumored he liked, every evening he would send word into the harem via the great white eunuch. Nur Banu would then deliberate and choose three or four of the prettiest girls to send out for his perusal. One or the other would be chosen, or perhaps a favorite would be called for again, and she would be the one honored to spend the night with the master.

Safiye watched this process closely. She came first of all to admire the incredible power Nur Banu wielded by it. The master himself, though he craved women more than food, had very little notion what went on in his own harem. He did not even know precisely how many souls it contained. "Twenty or thirty" he might say if someone had the rudeness to ask, but most had manners to avoid such topics.

Though the numbers varied, Nur Banu could have told at any moment exactly how many there were, and that it was closer to fifty. In these matters, which concerned a full half of his household, Selim was totally at the mercy of Nur Banu and what she chose to tell him. Though she herself would never share his bed again, she had perfect control over who could.

If one girl won her disfavor, she had only to send word, "Rejoice, my master, for she is with child." When favor returned, she could just as easily say, "Alas, my master, for the girl has recently miscarried and is much desirous of your company to comfort her."

And Selim, who included any precise notion of where babies came from among his ignorances, had to believe her.

Safiye was quick to learn that if she were to satisfy her ambition, there was no other way than through these channels. She could be the darling of the harem, but that meant nothing if she had no ties to the public world of men. Only if some daring girl could win the favor of one of the eunuchs behind her mistress' back was there any hope of her voice being heard on the outside world without Nur Banu's consent. And Nur Banu kept very tight reins on all the *khuddam* of her harem.

Safiye watched the other girls return in the mornings to gloat or show off little presents the master had given them if he'd been particularly pleased. A much rarer, but much more important event occurred when a girl found herself with child. Allah willing, it would be a son, and then her power in the outside world would be limited only by the power of that son and the devotion she could command in him. Fortunately for Nur Banu, though, there were many daughters born and her Murad had only four competitors for princehood, for all Selim's lust.

Safiye was a quick and willing student of this system, its petty jealousies and little triumphs. Every evening when the eunuch would repeat the master's desires in an undertone to Nur Banu, she would become instantly alert. When Nur Banu would turn slowly and survey the girls before her, Safiye would try to sit up straight, smooth her bodice, flutter her eyes, fold her hands gracefully in her lap—whatever that day's musings determined had been missing from her appearance the day before.

But never once in many months was her name among those the mistress quietly murmured when her decision was reached. Never once was she among the girls who jumped instantly to their feet to scurry off to the baths with high color and high hopes to prepare themselves for the master.

At first Safiye felt it must be her newness, her ignorance, her stumbling with the Turkish tongue or with their manners. This spurred her on to evermore concentrated study. But soon she began to suspect that none of these was the cause at all. Sometimes she would catch Nur Banu's eyes upon her as she played with the other girls.

She watches me as my father used to watch young colts frolic in the fields in springtime, Safiye thought. *Satisfied, proud, as if she had created me herself. I see no disappointment in her at all. I am clearly her favorite. When she does not wish to eat with the rest, she never fails to call me to join her alone in her room. She often draws me aside for private talks, and she laughs with delight at nearly everything I say. She gave me first choice of the new cloth we got last week—even before she took the blue silk for herself. And yet she doesn't choose me! Why? Oh, why?*

Such thoughts came to haunt Safiye more and more frequently as the everyday chatter of the harem grew more and more common to her ears, until she knew no great secrets were being told and that she could second-guess nearly everything that was said. She began to feel, for the first time since just after her arrival in the East, that she was a prisoner and a slave indeed. She managed to hide it well, but she even had bouts of homesickness.

The feeling of being trapped was not so easy for her to conceal. It often made her mind wander so she answered stupidly when addressed or sometimes didn't answer at all. Then her feet began to follow the wanderings of her mind, and she found herself pacing once more, back and forth like a caged lioness. This was not an image she wanted to portray to Nur Banu, that woman who was the constant epitome of control, but some days she simply couldn't help herself.

One such day came in the heat at the end of summer. All the other women had sought shelter in the baths or with fans and sherbets in the central marble hall. But Safiye wandered out past the untrimmed roses, the dried hulls of earlier lily bloom—these were too depressing in any case—to the very end of the harem garden. There, clinging to the iron bars, she stared through the narrow window in the wall to the furthest distance her eyes could reach. The white thistle fields and the grain golden stretched far below and seemed to taunt her with their free swaying in the puffs of breeze.

Most frustrating of all were the hawks.

"Ah, to be a hawk—!" Safiye sighed. "Their haunt, the sky, has no walls at all from Turkey clear back to the Piazza San Marco in Venice."

"I thought I might find you here." A voice interrupted her dreams.

"Lady!" Safiye exclaimed as she turned quickly around to find Nur Banu just behind her, accompanied in the garden by a little black slave and a sunshade.

Safiye knew Nur Banu did not trust a girl who liked to be alone, just as, in her interior decorating, she could not bear to have blank space for anything, but must have pattern upon pattern to feel comfortable. Safiye covered the window with her back as if the view were an extra pastry she had wickedly stolen and with which Nur Banu must not catch her.

But a window cannot be hidden as easily as a pastry.

"What is it you see outside that is so fascinating?" Nur Banu asked, gently pushing the younger woman aside. "I see only sky and fields, the same today as they were yesterday."

"You are right, lady," Safiye confessed with a self-critical giggle. "There is nothing to be seen. I have learned that for myself and intend never to look out that window again."

"And yet you were here yesterday and the day before. There must be something."

Safiye hung her head, caught in her little lie.

"It will spoil your lovely white skin," Nur Banu said, "to be so much in the sun."

"Of what use to me is lovely white skin if I am never to. . . ." Safiye burst before she could stop herself.

Nur Banu smiled and nodded gently, forgiving the outburst even though she could only guess the end of the sentence. "Come here, Safiye. Come under my sunshade and let us talk."

Safiye did as she was bidden and, though she was defensive and cold, the older woman slipped an arm about her waist with affection. They walked thus for some few minutes until Safiye felt she would soon be driven to make apologies and flee to the baths to join the other girls. Even that would be preferable to this silence.

"Safiye," Nur Banu began at last. "Aren't you happy here?"

"Yes, of course! I'm very happy," Safiye replied with too much energy rather than too little.

"Yes, you are happy," Nur Banu repeated. "Except that you are frustrated. I know. I can see it in you."

"I am sorry, lady," was all Safiye could think to say.

"So am I," Nur Banu said. "So am I."

After they had walked a few more moments in silence, the older woman began again. "Have I ever told you about my son?"

"If you did, lady, it was before I could understand what you were saying. I knew you had one, of course, because you are the master's first lady and the head of the harem. But more you haven't said. If he is at all like you, lady, I am sure he must be a very bright little boy, and fair to look upon, may Allah shield him."

" 'A little boy!' " Nur Banu repeated with a laugh. "Oh, that he were, that I might still have the pleasure of his company day in and day out! No, my son is now a man, full-grown and more like himself than he is like any other. Allah give him many more years: he is eighteen."

"Eighteen!" Safiye exclaimed. "Lady, I assure you I never guessed!"

"Yes, it was eighteen years ago that Murad gave me all that pain and grief. Ah, but it was worth it. I'll tell you, my dear, no one is more surprised than I am that time has gone so rapidly."

"Lady, Allah shield you, but I never would have guessed you had a son so old. You are still young yourself—no evil eye upon you, if Allah please."

Nur Banu smiled at these flatteries and at the superstitious cautions that accompanied them. Perhaps she remembered when she had first learned to squelch her own religion and call on Islam's god. Then she began to speak again. "My Murad is as fine a son as any mother could wish. I have concern for him, however, and it is very great. He has for this past year or two—almost since we first came to Kutahiya, in fact—become heavily addicted to his water pipes.

"Opium is not such an awful vice. I myself put a little in the narghile or indulge in a *beng* confection from time to time. But in one so young and to such excess—! He takes pleasure, I am told, in no other pastimes. He refused to accompany our master to the Persian border, and his place as counselor and friend in time of war was taken by a captive janissary.

"He neither hunts nor attends his father's government sessions nor practices with arms nor improves his mind with reading and scholarly discourse with the ulema. Even poetry and music he enjoys only as an accompaniment to his trances. Should the music become too lively or the epic too enthralling, he will send the performer away so as not to interrupt his dreams. For companions too, he will have none but those weak, pale-faced youths who will join him in his habit.

"Perhaps I shouldn't worry quite so much. He is young still. But I am his mother. And, though far be it from me to presume to second-guess Allah, it is very likely that upon the death of first his grandfather and then his father—Allah forbid them both—he will become Sultan of all the Faithful. What sort of occupation is the pipe for one who must lead armies with the sword? Worse than keeping him from his duties, it may well open him up to manipulation by ministers and counselors who would like nothing better than to see his overthrow. Even now, some slippery fellow has but to say that the opium he has in his pouch from such and such an exotic field is more pleasurable than any in this world and my son will give the rings off his fingers and sacks of *ghrush* besides to have it. If he is like this now, before he is twenty—Allah stay me!—what will he be like when he is forty?"

Here Nur Banu sighed and shook her head. Then she continued, "As Allah is my witness, I have done all a mother can do to divert him. I nag and cajole, but too much of that, I know, and he will never come to see me again—no, not even on holidays. I make his fine clothes. With my own hands I bake him special dainties which I know he loves. But what is the use? He can always escape into the world beyond my reach. At first, of course, I thought he was simply a young man, bored here in this small town and, when his father would not get him a girl (Selim likes them all for himself), I did. You know Aziza?"

"Yes," Safiye replied. She knew the girl.

"Well, she lasted less than a week. Then I got him Belqis. Her, too, you know."

"Yes," Safiye said again.

"Do you know what he said to me after Belqis? 'Mother,' he said, 'No more of your silly girls. They are such a bother! They waste my time.' My own son! Now a man who will not even bother to get children, what sort of man is that? He should not be a Sultan, for who would reign after him? He owes it to his people, at least, to preserve them from civil wars of succession and give them an honest heir. No, he should not be a Sultan. He should not even be a eunuch!

"Now, my dear," Nur Banu suddenly turned from her passion to address Safiye directly. "Now do you know why I bought you and brought you here?"

"Indeed, lady, I do not," Safiye confessed. Then she added that she was startled and puzzled by the question in such a context.

"Because," Nur Banu announced, "because you are the one, my dear, who must draw my son away from his drug."

XXX

SAFIYE STOPPED IN her tracks and the little black girl, carrying the sunshade behind her and hastening to keep up so she would not miss a word, ran into her. When apologies and blessings had been given all around, Nur Banu began again.

" 'It might well be a girl my Murad needs,' I thought to myself. 'But Murad is no ordinary young man. He needs a girl above the ordinary.' "

"Belqis and Aziza are not ugly girls," Safiye protested.

"Oh, no, but girls like that can always be found in the market. Slavic girls from the Sultan's campaigns—I can get two of them for what I paid for you—maybe three, if I bargain well. 'No, no.' I said to myself. 'My son needs something extraordinary.'

"So I was content to bide my time, to pretend to heed his warning, 'No more of your girls, Mother.' But all the while, I had the Kislar Aga, my head eunuch, watching the slave markets carefully. Many girls, many, he found and brought to me. But none of them was quite right. Then, early last spring—just before we were scheduled to leave Constantinople for Kutahiya once again—he brought me you.

" 'This,' I said to myself, 'this is the girl for my son.' "

Nur Banu's arm squeezed Safiye's waist in both affection and ambitious possession. Safiye murmured something in reply about how unworthy she was of such an honor.

"But my dear, you are most worthy! Do you never look in the mirror? Your hair, that is the most remarkable thing.

You will win him with your hair. And your face— Yet it is something besides your outward features. I sensed it from the moment I saw you. 'Such a girl,' I said to myself, 'should never belong to Suleiman.' For you might as well know that had I not seen you first and bid higher, that is exactly where you would be now, in Suleiman's harem in Constantinople. You were so much more important to me than to him, you see, that I bid so much higher.

"You think you would like that, eh? Being Suleiman's odalisque? Think again, my little mountain spring. He is an old man, beyond the getting of children. If he has girls, it is only to keep his bed warm, like King David of old. If you ever got to sleep with him—I say if, for the chances are, in that mob of odalisques, that even you would not—you would never get a child. And then, in three or four years, however long it may be (Allah grant it may be a hundred), when Suleiman dies—that would be it. The end, no more. Because you had once belonged to him, by a glance of his eyes if nothing else, you could never belong to anyone else. You would be shipped off to the cold, dark harem in Edirne to rot away until Allah was merciful and granted you death. No children, no diversions, no fine clothes, no jewels, nothing. That is not a life for you. I knew it the moment I saw you. 'If anyone can make a Sultan of my son,' I said, 'it's this one here.'

"Now, my dear. You see? In three days we will celebrate Id ad-Adha, a festival in honor of the pilgrims in the Holy City of Mecca. My son has agreed to share the sacrifice with me, a mundane duty for him, but for me—I mean to give you to him on this holy day. Tell me. What do you think? Do you think you can do it?"

"Yes," Safiye replied with such confidence that she almost forgot to add, as she had been taught one must always add when speaking of things yet to happen, "if Allah wills it."

She set her mouth in a firm line as she said the words. So

might a young recruit do when he is given orders full of danger and responsibility. She knew if she succeeded there would be glory indeed. But if she failed, only death could save her from the ignominy. She thought of Aziza and Belqis, girls who never received the call to go and wait on the master Selim either, though they were fair and pleasant tempered. Once rejected by Murad, their lives now offered no glimmer of a future at all.

The two women continued to walk in the gardens arm in arm, talking and planning, until the shadows grew long and tangled among the swelling rose hips.

Just before they turned to re-enter and join the other harem inmates, Safiye spoke, "Lady, there is one thing I must request before I go to your son."

"Yes, my dear. What is it? You know you may have anything I can give you, clothes, jewels. . . ."

"You have the means, have you not, by which one can keep from getting a child?"

"Yes. Yes, there are some potions I know of. But—"

"Please, provide me with some before I go to your son."

"What? What talk is this?" Nur Banu exclaimed, dropping her arm from about Safiye's waist in her horror. "Are you as perverse as he is, that you do not care for children? What kind of woman are you, who cares so little for her own future that she will throw away any chance to get a son?"

"Lady, forgive me," Safiye said. "I would heartily love to have a son—and give you a grandson. If Allah is merciful I may yet be granted this blessing. But the first thing to be done is to get Murad away from his water pipe. Who can say how long that may take? Surely I can trust neither Allah nor what poor charms He may have given me to assure victory in the month or two that may pass before I become pregnant. Then, if I become sick or bloated and ugly, I will be beyond any hope of diverting your son, and we may lose him for good. By your leave, lady, give me your remedies that I may use them until victory is assured."

Nur Banu nodded, slowly at first, for she was a woman who was always loath to credit any mind other than her own with good ideas. But Safiye knew she could not help but see the wisdom in this plan. Safiye would get what she wanted.

AS THEY PARTED within the *haremlik,* the older woman stood behind and watched the younger go, that tall, graceful frame that seemed to dance as she moved.

Yes, she congratulated herself. *I have chosen well. Very well.*

But a little gnawing voice came right afterwards. *Perhaps too well?*

XXXI

SAFIYE OPENED HER eyes at midmorning. The harem had spent a late night and she would have enjoyed the luxury of sleeping past noon, but she remembered what day it was. That evening would mark the Great Feast, Id al-Adha.

"For me, it shall be a sort of birth as well," she murmured to herself.

She stirred and found herself covered with rose petals. She remembered how delightfully cool they had felt on her naked skin when they'd first been showered on her, but the warmth of her sleep had wilted them and now her every move bruised their narcotic fragrance into her skin.

Safiye lifted her hands to her eyes to rub the sleep away, but she found her lower arms swathed in white and yellow silk. Now she remembered that she must not use her hands for anything.

The previous evening flooded back to her in vivid detail. Physically helpless, her mind grew active, fed by the night's dreams. Once again she saw how the lamps of perforated brass swung star-shaped blotches of golden light down on the entire harem. The assembly of women sat packed knee to knee on the divans and on rugs on the floor; the lamps raised a slick of sweat on every curve of skin.

Into their midst, Nur Banu brought a silk square full of old, dried leaves to which she gave the name henna. Safiye had heard this identical word before in Venice, usually hissed behind critical hands when some woman beginning to go gray suddenly appeared with her hair the lurid color of flame. Here among the Turks, she had seen women dip their fingers in a henna pot after their baths to stain the nails and tips the hue of overripe apricots.

Now Nur Banu worked these leaves into a fresh paste moistened with rose water. When it was done, the paste was an unpleasant dark greenish-gray and smelled like a horse stall as well.

Unpleasant though it was, the pot was placed at her knee and Safiye gave her right hand over to Esmikhan Sultan. With the thinnest of sticks, this girl began to paint the paste onto the hand in an intricate design. Excited chatter and the comments and encouragement of the rest of the room barely concealed the fact that over an hour had passed before the artist had completed one hand.

When it was finished, Nur Banu held the hand over a dish of glowing coals. Then the older woman placed a gold coin in the palm and wrapped it with linen strips, finally covering the whole with a silken bag. Then the process began all over again with the left hand.

Safiye liked being the center of all this attention, of course, but her body throbbed with the effort of holding still. Her throat ached with thirst, her stomach with hunger, her bladder with its burden she wasn't allowed to release. Her head reeled.

Ribald jokes passed among the older women about how men had to assert their dominance and women had to pretend to go along. *Is this active forcing of passivity to teach me this?* Safiye wondered. *No. Alluring as is this safe, enclosing feeling of all these women about me, I will not succumb to it. I have strength enough to go through passivity to even greater power.*

"I am not as skilled at this as our Lady Nur Banu is," Esmikhan apologized. Her hand was soft with plumpness, white, warm, and pressing Safiye's with the strain of her concentration.

"Nonsense." Nur Banu watched the work with close scrutiny in spite of her words. "Besides, a girl about to lose her virginity—Allah willing—must count it auspicious to have those who've never known a man among her attendants."

Esmikhan and Fatima Sultan, her younger sister who sat nearby, blushed deeply at their stepmother's words. They were both close to Safiye's own age and also both Selim's daughters, princesses of the royal Ottoman blood. This fact was betrayed by the "khan" suffix on the name of the eldest. Safiye spent much time studying both girls' plump, happy faces and full red lips that always wore smiles under the yellow light. Since they were Murad's half-sisters, she might discover some resemblance.

"Don't bother." Esmikhan divined Safiye's thoughts and bent over the hand she was painting to warn her in a whisper. "I am nothing like my brother at all."

The older women passed another joke, putting verbal shackles on a man who wasn't present to defend himself and was shackled by his male nature in any case.

This did not keep Safiye from wondering all the same.

After both hands and the painted soles of both of Safiye's feet were bandaged, she was finally allowed to use the latrine, which she couldn't do without assistance, and then offered food and drink. Meanwhile, the rest of the harem had availed themselves of the remaining henna.

And then, at long last, came the dancing while the low-burning lamps scalded down. Safiye could hardly contain herself. The thunk, thunk-a-thunk of drums and the squeal of shawms fairly tickled her feet and her hands, which she was forbidden, forbidden, forbidden to scratch. There was nothing for it: she must leave the dancing to those whose allotment of henna had not been so incapacitating.

A harem is nothing like a convent, Safiye mused in her inactivity. She wondered what her aunt would have said to the gyrations now executed in the tight space of floor in front of her.

It was one thing to perform the dances as she was taught them, feel the rightness of the roll and thrust as her body reached for the tugging rhythm of the music. It was another thing altogether to watch Esmikhan work out the tense burden of a long time at delicate work, to watch the exquisite release and expect none of her own, no, not even from clapping.

Is this what henna night is all about? Safiye felt the tension of her shoulders and arms slipping down to the glowing heart of her pelvis. She must no more release that than she must scratch her hands and feet.

Esmikhan and Fatima Sultan began the dance by trying to outdo one another with mimicries of their brother. *They are not very respectful,* Safiye thought. *Can you imagine if the nuns had taken it in their heads to characterize Father Confessor so?* Father Confessor had not been a young man like the dance portrayed: sometimes swaggering, full of himself, sometimes reeling from his opium, sometimes broiling with rage. But the priest had had equal foibles at which Safiye might have enjoyed poking fun.

Do they mean to turn my thoughts from Murad altogether? If I am to love this man, revere him as a master, why do they portray him to me thus, now? Is this sisters' tease to answer the hunger I feel?

But then Safiye realized that the sisters danced by way of promise. They offered her the power of objectivity, of refusing to take the outside world of men too seriously. Whatever should come of her dance with Murad, whatever needs he might not fulfill, or however brief his infatuation, there was, they promised, nothing like other women for understanding and compassion.

The lamps swayed and burned like kettles over a fire. The music rose to match their glowing heat and the Sultan's daughters, exhausted with their efforts and with laughter, gave way to other dancers. Other arms and legs delineated other fantasies with the shimmer of bangles and the float of gauze. No convent girl could imagine what Safiye saw in the dancing that night, what she learned. But then other things are expected of convent girls when they come to their marriage beds than are expected of odalisques when they come to the heir of the Sultan.

Last of all, way was given to Belqis and Aziza. Safiye

thought she could see Murad in their dance as well, but it was a different picture of the young prince they painted altogether. The two young slaves reeled and arched, the clicks of their wooden spoons pulsing faster and faster. The sway of their sash ends plunged and rose; the metallic cicles of their waists throbbed in the lamplight like arterial blood.

Safiye's throat grew dry and her breast constricted with sympathetic desire which no amount of Esmikhan's proffered pomegranate juice could quench. Climax neared, wriggled tantalizingly away, neared, escaped, until at long last the two odalisques collapsed, moaning in each other's arms.

Safiye caught her echoing moan in her teeth and closed her eyes. As the music faded, she yearned for the release of sleep to bridge the time to the festival as quickly as possible.

XXXII

So Safiye opened her eyes on the day that would consummate in Id al-Adha. The henna paste, which had gone on cold, seemed—unlike the rose petals—incapable of absorbing her body's heat. Even in the half-dreams before full waking, she felt the pattern of tendrils laid like a network of cold lead on her hands and feet. She wanted to peek under the bandages to watch the magic happening there, but she knew she must not or the effect would spoil.

She wanted other things, too. She wanted, oh, so much to know what—! But everything, even desire, must not be peeked at yet. Not yet. Come evening. . . .

Safiye must have been unconsciously avoiding the use of her hands even in sleep, for an uncomfortable stiffness pressed her shoulders back among the cushions where she'd slept with the rest of the harem for company in the big main sitting room.

Now I am helpless, Safiye thought. *I shall have to lie here forever.*

But even as she thought it, Esmikhan and Fatima Sultan saw that she was awake and picked their way to her side with giggles that would not cease and baskets full of more rose petals. With her silk-mittened hands, Safiye found it impossible to fend them off and so had to submit—and enjoy— another cool, scented shower followed by the warm hugs and kisses of the two girls. Other women entered then with breakfast on a tray which consisted mostly of Safiye's favorite "little Turkish bonnets."

"No, no!" Esmikhan cried. "You must not use your hands."

And she and Fatima Sultan proceeded to feed their charge with tidbits until Safiye pleaded vehemently: "If I eat any more, I'll burst!"

"There is so much to be done today," Nur Banu hurried them. She betrayed her own nervousness by not eating at all. "Time cannot be taken for another meal. You must avoid meat, onions, leeks, and heavy spices in any case. Women who eat such things are bound to lose their attractiveness."

Throughout the day, however, Safiye found that sweet-smelling fruits and pastries were never far from her, and should she so much as look in the direction of the tray, there was always someone ready to pop another bit in her mouth.

So her attendants got her out of bed and, the whole harem following with more rose petals, laughter, and song, they led her to the citadel's bath. Safiye had grown used to the ritual of steam and water. She had even grown to like it. Like any self-respecting Muslim woman, she, too, now felt the dirt if she failed to participate at least twice a week, particularly during the summer's hottest days and after her bleeding time.

"A bride is bathed the day before her wedding, hennaed after." While they progressed, Nur Banu explained this for Esmikhan and Fatima Sultan—girls who would be lawful brides—more for than Safiye. "But then a bride's day is filled with the rites that make her consummation legal in the sight of the world. A slave's purchase is the legality in this case. So we all bathe now for the feast to come while outside the men are busy with their prayers.

"First we had better see to those hands," Nur Banu directed, interrupting the usual flow of the bath ritual when they had all undressed and reached the second room. "Should the stain remain too long, it will turn black and that would be a bad omen."

So with great solemnity and flourish, Esmikhan unwound the bandages from first one hand and then the other. The gold coins dropped from Safiye's palms into her lap.

"Keep them," Nur Banu said. "They're yours."

The first that is really my own—in my life. Safiye pulled them as close as she could with neither hands nor feet to work for her. *The first of so much more. If this is slavery, the institution has been greatly maligned.*

Safiye forgot the good thoughts as she reacted at first with horror to what a quick flush of warm water discovered. The dried-on henna paste sloshed down the water channels about her pattened feet. Her hands were revealed, as veined and splotched as an old woman's. Closer inspection, however, revealed the color was not brown but a brilliant, warm, rich orange, like sun-ripened fruit. The color formed a delicate pattern of tulips, dots, and tinted nails that Safiye joined all the others in admiring. When she moved her hands, Safiye noticed the butterfly-like flittings the design helped them to make. Her hands were the one part of her anatomy that might be exposed, even in a bazaar. But henna plunged those hands and all they touched into the perpetual mystery and allure of half-seen forms behind a lattice.

What might they so flittingly touch, come evening?

Her bathers made some attempt to avoid her hands and feet as they worked, but no matter what they did, the stain would remain vivid for a week or more. On every other part of her body, the scrubbing Safiye got was so vigorous that she feared she would be left quite raw. She discovered, however, that the skin she had left when they were finished was softer than a baby's and glowed a delicate pink.

Then, from that tender skin, every vestige of hair had to be removed. A pair of women, expert at the task, cooked up the depilatory favored for brides because of its sweetness and because it tore the hair out below the skin. Made of two parts beet sugar to one of lemon, it was stirred constantly over a flame until a drop crystallized in water, then spread on the offending areas. When their experience judged the time was right, the women removed the hardened candy in quick, sharp yanks. Safiye's underarms, legs, as well as her pubes were soon cleaner than a five-year-old child's.

A beauty pack followed to ease the sore skin. It was made of oil and rice flour mixed with honey and various sweet-smelling spices. In the heat of the steamy baths Safiye began to feel herself to be a living pastry, baking for the festive day.

Another bath followed with more lathering and scrubbing to remove the pack save for the scent and smoothness it gave Safiye's skin. As they scrubbed her down, Esmikhan and Fatima Sultan repeated the word *Mashallah!* over and over as a crooning song. It was an invocation to their God to keep the evil spirits that might covet such a beauty from casting a spell on her while she was naked and helpless.

The sun was now past its zenith and came in, in long beams made tangible by the steam, at the high west-side windows. Safiye's hair was washed with water in which roses and heliotrope had been allowed to steep. Then, stretched out naked on a bed of snow-white cushions and towels, she submitted herself to the hands of the harem masseuse from the time the sun was dappling the water in the pool until it was reflected off the smooth tile wall at shoulder-height.

Now is the pastry kneaded, she thought, *made light and full of puffs of air for the young master's festival.*

Remembering the fancy Easter breads of her Italian childhood rather than the thin-crusted pastries that were actually baking at that moment in the citadel ovens, Safiye sometimes daydreamed, sometimes dozed, sometimes drifted fully asleep and dreamed true dreams of delight throughout the long, hot afternoon. It would leave her fresh and wide awake for the exertions of the night.

⚜

AS THE MASSEUSE'S firm hands caressed the soft, pink skin, Safiye began to work her hips in an ardent response to that kneading, unconscious of what she was doing. A climax came in a smart slap across her buttocks.

"Save that for my brother!" Esmikhan teased.

Having just come from bathing herself, Selim's daughter found that the wet end of her towel was more useful as a whip for bare backsides than as a cover.

"Why, you little——!" Safiye cried and, throwing aside the masseuse's hands, she dashed off in hot pursuit, armed also with a towel she paused to dip in the bath as she passed. Safiye made up for a slow start with her long legs and limberness compared to the other girl's plumper docility. Neither would cry halt and the battle raged on all about the pool.

The two girls' screams of laughter and of pain echoed off the marble walls and brought Nur Banu in from the latticed corridor where she'd been watching for the men. Her anger and concern were infectious and immediately brought the two dripping, panting, naked girls to bay.

Nur Banu wasted little time in either scolding or apologies, for the marks of Esmikhan's towel on Safiye's skin needed instant attention with oil and aloe lest they turn to welts that would last until the morrow. Nonetheless, a quiet smile crept to Nur Banu's lips to see her young charge in such lively spirits. Safiye could tell that if the older woman was cautious, it was only to make sure that those spirits would not all be spent before nightfall.

"The men are returning from the mosque," Nur Banu announced when the emergency had passed. "You can hear and see them from out there in the corridor. Make haste, make haste!"

XXXIII

"AUNTIE, MAY WE bring Safiye out there in the corridor so we can see, too?" Esmikhan begged. "Her hair will dry so much faster there in the sun."

Nur Banu gave her permission and now the toilet began with an earnestness that all but stifled any carefree chatter.

"The sheep are being led into the courtyard," Nur Banu reported, her voice crosshatched against the carved wood of the grille.

Safiye raised herself off Esmikhan's knee, where she had been resting while the other girl brushed and combed her hair. By shifting her head from side to side, first to one diamond-shaped opening, then the next, she found it possible to see most of the courtyard below.

"Hold still!" Esmikhan begged. "I shall mess your hair."

But Safiye couldn't resist. The large company in the yard were all men, of course. They were differentiated, however, into dusty peasants on the perimeter, dumbly watching the motions of their betters under banners and poles dangling horsetails at the center. *This might be a costume play at home, in the theater of the Foscaris.* Safiye felt herself grow warm and was grateful no one else here remembered the occasion. Not just actors but all men dressed in such costumes in this land, these long robes that blinded with their richness when the sun hit them just right.

"Which is your brother?" she asked, surprised at her own breathlessness.

"There." Esmikhan pointed with the end of the comb. "Standing next to my father. Murad is the one with the brown pheasant's feathers in the ruby aigrette pinned to his blue-and-gold-striped turban."

Safiye felt her heart race at the announcement, but the lanky young man had little to recommend him at this distance beyond a certain disinterest and lassitude in his stance. His father, Selim the Sultan's heir, certainly upstaged him, as did a trio of shepherds who had their hands full trying to control the flock.

"Are the animals bleeding?" Safiye had quite forgotten where her attention ought to be.

"No."

"Not yet," Fatima added.

"They are marked for the holy sacrifice with splotches of red on their white wool," Esmikhan explained.

"I see."

There is nothing to fear out there, Safiye told herself as she leaned back to let Esmikhan anoint her hair with fragrant oil, then comb again. *A few hot, impatient men and dirty sheep.*

"Ah, your hair gleams as gold chains in a jeweler's shop would under the same treatment," the princess declared.

Meanwhile, other oils mixed with perfumes were applied to Safiye's skin, along with a cream of henna to check perspiration.

"The pit for the sacrifice is now dug," Nur Banu announced.

Safiye leaned forward and looked again. She saw Selim, assisted by a shepherd, struggling with the first of the sheep.

"One sheep for each member of the household," Esmikhan explained. "Male sheep of a certain age."

"Male sheep? Even for the females here?"

"Yes. Without blemish."

Safiye forced herself to look at the pheasant's feathers. It was difficult to imagine that through this unremarkable figure lay the path to everything of which she'd ever dreamed. Well, the unremarkable doors were always the easiest to turn. She remembered Andrea Barbarigo and young Veniero, but neither with regret. They were behind her; in time, so would this Murad be.

Actually Safiye found herself more interested in which sheep might be hers. Or did slaves not warrant one? *Next year at this time I shall certainly have one of the finest,* she was convinced.

Now Nur Banu's personal slaves brought out the garments that she had chosen for her daughter-in-law-to-be. First, of course, came the great *shalvar* of finest crimson silk and the diaphanous undershirt that had a trimming of lace from faraway Flanders, as delicate as spiders' webs. The *yelek,* or floor-length jacket, was the color of lilac blossom and worked all over the bodice with threads of a deeper purple and of gold into a pattern of full-blown roses, each with a cluster of three tiny pearls as stamens in the center.

The jacket buttoned to below the hip so the curve in from the bosom and out again could be followed without distraction. Then a girdle of crimson velvet was tied about Safiye's hips in such a way that the golden fringe of its ends would bounce against her left knee when she walked. The girdle was set with five amethysts the size of almonds. Amethysts, too, were the stones in the earrings Nur Banu fastened in Safiye's ears and let cascade down to her shoulders. But there was no such coordination in the other jewelry she put on, all of which was lent for the occasion by all the members of the harem, all deeply concerned in the evening's outcome.

Because it was not hers to keep, Safiye soon lost interest in examining each piece. She leaned over the weight at her neck to look into the yard once more.

"Our master Selim strokes the sheep's throat, oh, so gently," she said. "He is speaking, too. What does he say to it?"

"He offers a prayer," Esmikhan's voice came from where she was struggling with a clasp behind her. "As it says in the Koran: 'Mention Allah's Name over them.' "

Bracelets of every description were forced up to the elbow so there was hardly room for them to jangle against one another on either forearm. Necklaces, rings, and anklets, too, were added until Safiye exclaimed, "Please! I can hardly move."

Nur Banu conceded after a moment's thought and, while

the older woman gave her next orders, Safiye escaped to the
grille once more. This time she gasped in horror. Five sheep
lay twitching in death and the sixth was jerking its life's blood
into the pit over the white of entrails.

"Why—why he is killing them!"

"Of course," Esmikhan replied. "You have never eaten
meat before?"

"How quickly he draws the knife!" Nur Banu leaned over
Safiye's shoulder to catch a glimpse. "The beasts hardly struggle."

Safiye's hair was sprinkled with gold dust. *Like the baker
dredges his pastries with sugar.* But it was a desperate thought.
The first thing that had come to her mind was the roast and
its salt.

"The gold is redundant," Esmikhan chatted happily.

Nur Banu kept the phial of gold dust carefully in her own
possession and spoke with earnest precaution. "Nonetheless—"

The hair was formed into four thick plaits, but given
enough freedom at the ends to show the willfulness of its curl.

"My son, Allah shield him, never looked more handsome."
Nur Banu said with pride looking out the window yet again.

Safiye looked and saw only how a shepherd thrust a tube
up a dead sheep's leg.

"A few good puffs of air and the retainer can remove the
fleece all at once," Nur Banu said.

Safiye saw nothing but white light and clung to the grille
to keep her feet.

A small red cap studded with pearls served as an anchor
for the great lengths of fine, transparent veil. Red embroi-
dered calfskin slippers went upon her feet. Then finally her
face was painted: her eyes into almonds, her brows into
"Frankish bows," her cheeks into peonies, and her mouth into

a full-blown rose which, with its natural pearly teeth, rivaled the glory of those worked into the *yelek*.

"The meat is divided, as the holy Koran says: 'when their flanks collapse . . . feed the beggar and the suppliant.' How the poor praise the generosity of our master!

"But come," Nur Banu said, breaking her own report. "Come, girls. The cook is taking his portion into the kitchen right now. There's not a moment to lose!"

Now the harem scurried out of the bath and into the main part of the house, for there was hardly time for a proper evening prayer before the door to Murad's apartment would be opened.

Away from the grille, and shown her own reflection, Safiye's courage returned. The beauty that stared back at her from the mirror could not be crushed by any slavery, to fashion or otherwise. And it was clearly destined for only the greatest of things.

That evening at prayers, Safiye looked upon these foreign prostrations in much the same light as she looked upon the Turkish dances and songs she had learned. Though there was haste in the movements that evening and Safiye was weighted down with many ornaments, still she managed to include between the lines of Arabic a little prayer to Saint Catherine that her aunt had taught her. Just such a prayer would have been uttered on her wedding day, if she had married that lowly Corfiot. *Rather too much favor with heaven,* she thought, *than too little.*

In the confusion that followed as the menial slaves hurriedly rolled up the prayer rugs, Nur Banu called Safiye to her. Surveying her handiwork at arm's length, she nodded with satisfaction.

"If my son will not have you," she said, "may he never become Sultan at all—as Allah wills."

Then she kissed Safiye fondly on both cheeks and, as she did, she pressed a pair of small silver cases into her hand. Safiye opened and examined one after the other. Each contained perhaps two dozen objects the shape and size of fingers—black in one case, yellow in the other—that released a medicinal smell.

"What are they?"

Nur Banu replied with the word *farazikh,* which Safiye had never heard and wouldn't have known in Italian either, had someone been around to give it to her. "Pessary" was not in the vocabulary of a convent girl.

"No, do not touch them," Nur Banu warned, and Safiye obediently withdrew her curious fingers. "Body heat will make them melt. You are to place them inside yourself, the yellow one before the act, the black ones after."

"What are they made of?"

Nur Banu raised the perfect crescents of her brows so her eyes could pierce deeper. Did this girl plan to make *farazikh* on her own? The idea was so startling—so unthinkable—that the older woman told her anyway.

"The yellow is the pulp taken from between the pips of a pomegranate mixed with alum, rue, myrrh, hellebore, and ox-gall, kneaded with the tail-fat of a sheep so it will melt. The black is colocynth pulp, bryony, sulfur, and cabbage seed in a base of tar."

"Are these formulas of which the Quince approves?"

Nur Banu's brows went higher still. "Yes," she snapped.

Safiye laughed lightly, realizing she had, for the moment, pressed for too much control of her own enslaved body. "Then I know they'll work."

The lightness, the girlishness in her voice served as an apology, and the older woman's brows settled down to their usual arcs.

"May you remain childless many blissful nights."

XXXIV

THE AIR WAS different in the *mabein,* that strange half-world
between the world of men and that of women. It seemed
darker, heavier. The dust of disuse a day of airing had been
unable to remove lingered in this room of the young Murad,
for he rarely cared to make contact with the world of shadows that stood always at his back while he went about in the
male, sunshiny world of everyday. Here in this space between, opposites met. Things as unlike as oil and vinegar
mingled either, like that dressing, quickly and bitterly to
separate or, like the opposites of flame and powder, to mix
and explode into one.

Nur Banu had time to enter and arrange things to her liking before her son came. This she did with the precision and
display of a man of the theater. Lamps were lit and set in all
the niches. Bowls and trays of nuts and sweets were loaded
on a low table until it groaned. The cushions on the divan
were plumped up in four places, one for Nur Banu, two,
close together, for Esmikhan and Fatima, the sisters, who
would also join in this party, and the fourth for the young
prince himself.

A row of beautiful slaves, Aziza and Belqis still nursing
hopes among them, was lined up against one wall, arms
crossed upon their breasts, heads bowed, to await their mistress' further orders. But as for the actual performance, for
which the Prince's arrival in the room would be the cue,
Safiye could not be a witness to that. As soon as the excited

whisper ran, "He comes! He comes!" the door to the harem was quietly but hurriedly shut, and Safiye had to remain on the women's side of it.

Of the initiatory salaams and embraces, Safiye heard nothing at all. The first thing she did hear was a voice rather thin and weak for a man's (but that might only be from tedium, she thought) saying, "Dear Mother, send your silly girls away."

Now the harem door opened and the row of girls filed in. Upon their faces Safiye read all she could of what had transpired. Upon those who had cherished hopes, in spite of every previous reason to abandon them, the disappointment was as clear as if seen through glass, and threatened to spill immediately into tears. The others could greet Safiye with smiles and murmurs of "Allah bless *you*"—for, so far, all was going according to Nur Banu's script.

Now they must be seated, now Nur Banu must offer him the dainties on the table. The meat of the sacrifice must be brought in. Murad must eat of that, of the accompanying rice, pulse, and yogurt with cucumber. He must finish with a nibble on a favorite pastry out of politeness. A sherbet. Then rose water and incense must be offered for cleansing. And then, finally, his mother must suggest the water pipes. . . .

Safiye counted the entrances of the serving eunuchs and ran the scenario over and over in her mind so many times that her heart began to race with the idea that something must have gone amiss. But to actually play a scene takes much more time than to rehearse it in one's mind and Murad really had found but brief diversion in anything up to the mention of "pipe."

The three sharp claps came soon enough. Safiye took the pipe from Aziza who stood behind her—the stem and mouthpiece lightly in her right hand, the small silver tray in her left as she had been carefully taught. Then Aziza opened the door for her and she stepped into the close and dusty air of the *mabein* alone.

Slow, measured steps had been rehearsed and came naturally as she felt, not only the burden of the pipe, but that of four pairs of eyes upon her.

"Four," she told herself. "I know it is four and he is not just looking at the pipe," though she did not dare to raise her eyes to confirm this feeling.

She brought the pipe down to the smoker's level and carefully worked the mouthpiece through her fingers toward him, all without so much as a glance to affirm that it was indeed the man in the room that she approached. A hand of white, skeletal fingers relieved her of that lightest part of her burden and assured her that so far she had done well. But as she set the main body of the pipe down upon its little tray, Nur Banu spoke to her.

"O my fair one, I shall have a pipe, too." That was a cue that things were not progressing as rapidly as hoped; it was necessary to draw the meeting out.

Now Safiye found her performance interminable. She returned for the second pipe and, offering it to her mistress, felt Nur Banu killed the time all too obviously before she took the mouthpiece in her hand and Safiye could set it down on the table. Then she had to return to the harem—slowly, slowly—get the brass brazier from Aziza, return, and, kneeling before each smoker, place a glowing coal in each one's bowl with a little pair of tongs. She paused there on her knees until assured that each pipe bubbled well. The smokers drew and the sweet aroma filled the room. Then, and only then, could Safiye retreat to the corner where, the brazier nursed beside her feet, she stood with each hand upon its opposite shoulder, head slightly bowed, waiting for a further order.

The nervous energy created by being the center of attention now slowly drained from her. It had made her want to skip in with the pipes and say aloud, "Here you are, you drugged excuse for a man. But wouldn't you really rather have me instead?" just to get it over with. Glad she had not succumbed to this temptation, Safiye could now afford to be aware of other things besides her every knotted muscle, and she began to follow the conversation taking place there in the room with her. It was no more than pleasantries and it was immediately clear that Nur Banu was in a rising panic—or, at least as close to panic as such a controlled woman would ever allow herself to come.

Esmikhan said nothing. Fatima did sometimes try to help out with a giggle, but the young man did not even chuckle. Though from time to time he did say a word or two, they were as weak and as bored as ever.

Nur Banu had prepared some patter for herself, but she had always stopped not two minutes into the rehearsal to say, "Well, by now he surely will have noticed you and said something. After that—it is Allah's will."

Now it was clear she was out of script and, though never one to be at a loss for words and always easily capable of filling any hour with pleasantries, Nur Banu was leaving great gaps of silence, which she kept desperately hoping her son would fill with the question. The question—it mattered not what question it was. All that mattered was that it asked something about the new slave girl—her age, how long she'd been in the harem, where she'd come from, her name perhaps. The question would not be answered, but the girl would be called forth to kiss her master's hem, then left to answer all questions on her own in the best way nature could teach her.

The bittersweet smell of opium filled the room, but Safiye

knew it came from her mistress' pipe, not the master's. She had watched with care as they were loaded. Into Nur Banu's pipe had gone a sliver of the brown, sticky stuff, but into the young man's had gone only cinnamon bark and gum of mastica mixed with a little bran to make it burn. This was not a concoction that would fool any smoker, but it was hoped that politeness and the aroma from his mother's pipe would keep him from complaining about it.

Safiye had seen both wads of fuel in place, packed neither too tightly nor too loosely, but as the interview dragged on, she could not resist a glance up to make certain she had given the right pipe to the right person. Yes, the glint of silver was in Murad's hand while Nur Banu's mouthpiece was of green jade.

She quickly dropped her eyes again, for they had met head-on with the young man's. Two or three more glances at minute intervals were enough to assure Safiye, "Well, at least he isn't ignoring me." They also gave grist to the millstones of her mind.

They were not dull eyes that met hers from the sunken ash-pits of their sockets. They glinted with life and intellect. One could even go so far as to say interest and humor. But that these features suffered difficulties breaking through clouds of boredom, inactivity, irresponsibility, studied disinterest, and the drug was also easy to see. (Yet to place these principles in clear genealogies of cause and effect would not be such a simple task.)

A few more glances satisfied Safiye that the eyes alone betrayed the young man's complexity. As to his further features, they were quickly discerned and with but little excitement. He had a thin, sunken face framed by a sparse beard that only appeared such an inflamed and infectious red because the flesh it grew from was so pale. The color of his beard would actually come closer to the natural glow present in the flesh of a much healthier man. Khurrem Sultan, his grandmother, had come from Russia. Safiye had heard her hair described as being the color of paprika, so Murad came by his shade legitimately.

Beyond that, he was of medium height—perhaps shorter than Safiye herself—with thin limbs that ennui and a stronger taste for the drug had kept from ever gaining flesh once their height had been attained. That his clothes were masculine was the only thing that made them interesting to her after five months shut up with women and eunuchs. A pale yellow silk summer caftan revealed the boniness of his elbows and knees, and brown and blue stripes on his sash echoed the turban. Apart from the ruby and the feathers in the aigrette, nothing had been chosen with any interest or desire for effect.

Even in the presence of his mother and his sisters, the young man sprawled across the cushions and the divan, one hand making the effort to hold the mouthpiece to his lips but the other lifeless at his side, as if he hoped at any moment to escape the scene into sleep. One thing only—the eyes—continued to disturb the somnolence of his person.

If one must be more precise, it was upon her hair that he trained his eyes, her hair that spilled in golden vapor from her braids. Safiye fancied that he was undertaking experiments upon that hair as an alchemist may do to test the veracity of his metal. Both eyes would close, then first one would peek and then the other in turns, squint, stare, roll around, open wide, then close again. If Nur Banu noticed this peculiar behavior (and they were *her* eyes the young man had inherited), she despaired of it as just one more sign that her son was hopelessly lost to a world of visions and dreams.

Sofia

I wish Nur Banu Kadin had given me a little part in this farce not connected with the water pipe, Safiye thought. *Something unpredictable and lively to show this young man the difference between waking and sleeping. Well, if she is too much mother to wish cold water thrown on her son, then I must do it on my own. Something— but what? I cannot very well interrupt their talk with singing and dancing.*

Shortly Safiye had devised her plot. Never moving her hands from their positions on her shoulders, she slowly, slowly worked the ring off one of her fingers. Then with a twist of the wrist more subtle than was needed to manipulate a narghile's mouthpiece into position, she let the jewel drop to the floor. Its landing on the carpets at her feet was silent and unnoticed by either Nur Banu or the princesses, who were too busy wondering what they could possibly say or giggle next.

But Murad saw. She knew he saw, for both eyes opened at once and forgot their flirtation with sleep. Still, he said nothing, not even, "Mother, why do you waste money on slave girls who are so careless with their jewelry?" which would have been all the question needed.

It was not long after this that Nur Banu admitted defeat. She did not say so aloud, nor did she lose the tone of graciousness in her voice. But she began to make her farewells, and that was exactly the same thing. With a sinking heart, Safiye picked up the brazier, carried it out, and returned for the jade-mouthpieced pipe for which her mistress had long ago lost the taste. An impatient wave of dismissal from the bangled hand told her that the young man was to be left with his smoke, mock though it was—to choke on it, if Allah were so merciful. Safiye held the door open for mother and sisters, followed them into the harem, then closed the door behind her.

XXXV

THE STONY SILENCE with which Nur Banu greeted the anxious subjects of her domain told them immediately to stifle their questions. They did not want to share the fair Venetian girl's awful punishment—two weeks, maybe three, of being ignored, talked of only in the most defaming of terms behind her back. In the closed world of the harem, death was preferable.

Nur Banu swept to the retreat of her own room and every other woman was dragged along by her draft. Every other woman except Safiye, who remained at the *mabein* door, the site of her defeat.

"At least he has not touched me," Safiye tried to combat her misery even when it had hardly had time to begin. "He is not Sultan—yet—so I may still be given to another man when—if—I win Nur Banu's favor again and she has in some way forgiven what truly wasn't my fault at all."

Yet, as she stood deserted there by the door, Safiye clung to one last hope: the ring still lay where she had dropped it on the rug in the *mabein*. Surely none could blame her if she returned to get it.

"Now, what do you expect to gain by this?" Safiye scolded herself even as she did it. "Do you expect Murad to be on his feet, hunting for the ring himself, and to be obliged at least to say, 'I found it!'?"

No, of course not. She entered the room, made the deep bow she had been taught to do, retrieved the ring, and returned to the door again without reaction. Indeed, it occurred to her that the room might well be deserted. Just to make sure she had not bowed to empty space, she ventured one last look up to the spot where the young man lay. He hadn't so much as changed the hand holding his mouthpiece and his eyes were now half-shut in a sort of self-satisfied drowse.

The indolence! she almost cried aloud. *Who would want you anyway, you lethargic, useless bag of bones? I shall become great without you, just you wait and see!* And she did not hesitate to give the young man a glare that would relay this message to him, even if it were not in words.

Halfway into her good, vindictive glare, Safiye stopped quite short. Something about the young man was moving. Ever so slightly, but it was. Had it been his chest, she would have credited him with breathe which at the moment was otherwise doubtful. Had it been his knee, she would have passed it off as a nervous twitch such as happens when one settles into sleep. But it was a finger. The forefinger of the long, pale hand at his side, it was crooking ever so slowly but definitely. Definitely, yes, it was beckoning her to approach him.

Safiye had half a mind to refuse so weak and slovenly a gesture. But ambition got the better of her spite and she approached until she stood directly before him, just to one side of the table covered with untouched festive dainties. The young man continued to scrutinize her with his half-closed eyes until finally these squinted into a dry, soundless laugh which contorted his face and shook his flimsy body.

At last he spoke, not to her, but to himself aloud. "Well, guess you fooled her this time, Murad, my old friend. She thought she could take your vision with her when she went, the old sorceress, your mother. But see, we have just proved her wrong. Here the vision is, and *she* is gone. But it would not obey your commands and mental summons while she was here as other visions do. It is a very curious vision, this one, which probably explains why it is so lifelike. I think, Murad, you may look upon this day as a day you reached a new level of experience with the Milk of Paradise."

Safiye knelt now beside the divan in an attempt to prove to the young prince that he did not control her actions. That did not work, however, and so she decided she must speak.

"I am not a vision," she declared. "I am not a figment in your mind. I am as real as you are."

Murad laughed and shook his head, "All my visions say that. They do that to teach me that my life is nothing, not that they are something. No, I will not let you fool me, you least of all."

His laughter made him shut his eyes now, but they immediately reopened.

"Curious," he said. "Though all my dreams tell me they are real, you are the first that has vanished when I shut my eyes."

"That is because I am real," Safiye declared. "Your mother put no opium in your pipe—only mastic and cinnamon. See, I will show you."

And, against the protests that it disturbed his smoke, she sifted through the ashes in the bowl and insisted that he look and see that there was little left but charred bran and gummy mastic.

"I knew that," the prince sulked. "You think I didn't know that? I knew that from the first. Yet, you came with the pipe. I knew there must be something extraordinary in it. Tell me what it was so I can get some for myself next time."

"You cannot control me like that," Safiye cried. "Yes, I am

a slave and you are my master, but I am Sofia Baffo, daughter of the Governor of Corfu. You did not will me from the harem and, just to prove it, I shall now return there. You can't stop me."

Safiye returned her hands to their place upon her breasts, but it was with a sort of contemptuous dare. With the same attitude, she gave a little nod of farewell and began to get to her feet.

Murad watched this whole performance without other response than to smile as if the antics of his unpredictable vision were highly diverting. Unseen by Safiye, however, he was fumbling in his sash for his dagger and while her head was bowed, he used it to make a lunge at her.

XXXVI

IT WAS NOT a deep wound, for Murad had not bothered to remove the sheath and besides, since it was never used, its sharpness had never been of any concern to him. He had fully expected, however, to stab at the nothingness of vision through which his hand should pass unhindered to the table behind her. Such was not the case, as he discovered, and the rough edges of the sheath's encrustation caught upon her very real flesh in such a way that he was jolted awake.

For her part, Safiye gasped aloud at the pain and, fully chastised for the presumption of her last speech, remained humbly bowed, her hands where they belonged across her breast, though the right one where the knife had hit shook with pain. Tears began to curl from her eyes and blood from her hand.

With these proofs, Murad was forced to admit, "Well! May I never be my father's first-born son! It is real!"

"May I return to the harem, then, good master," Safiye murmured, "and never bother you any more?"

She was, for all her ambition, a child of but fourteen after all, and the pressure of all this very real playacting suddenly crushed her.

Before he could give her a reply, however, the harem came to them. Nur Banu flung open the door and stood there with a barrage of abuse for her willful slave girl on the tip of her tongue. The scene that met her eyes—her son bent over the kneeling girl with more concern than he had shown for anything short of Indian poppies in over a year—took her aback for just a moment and, in that moment, Murad spoke instead.

"Mother, if you please."

Just that much, and Nur Banu closed first her mouth and then the door. Murad got to his feet and locked the door behind her. As he turned to the room again, he chuckled with ill ease.

"Now what am I to do with you?" he asked, himself more than her. "If I send you back tonight, Mother will eat you alive. So you must stay here, I suppose. Here's the key. Leave only when you're sure it's safe. As for me—no, I shall demand no more blood of you. There are plenty of other rooms in this citadel where I can sleep, indeed, with much more comfort than in here—

"Oh, for the sake of the All-Merciful, do something with your hand before it drips all over your dress."

He sat down on the divan next to her again and offered a napkin from among the platters on the table. "Here, here," he waved it at her. "Take it."

Safiye did at last and slowly, hampered by quivers that shook her whole body, she began to wrap the wound. As she took her hand from her shoulder Murad bent over and replaced it by his own. He took the end of her braid and weighed it in his hand. Then he let the plait fall and looked at the residue it left on his skin.

"Ah," he nodded. "Just as I thought. Gold dust. My mother is a sorceress."

But his skepticism did not keep him from handling the braid again, undoing it, and slowly working its kinks loose with his fingers. He gently removed the pearl-set cap and its veil as he asked again, "Now what am I to do with you?" and shook his head as if to dispel the thoughts that crossed her mind or his.

The other braids came down one by one and Murad filled his lap with the luxury. "Now what am I to do with you?" he murmured once again.

Safiye began, "You might——"

"Might love you?" he covered for her hesitation and, taking a great mass of golden curls in each hand, he gently brought her face to his, "Yes, I might. And if Allah grants me mercy, I shall. I shall indeed."

XXXVII

IT WAS ALMOST three days later before the door to the *mabein* opened and Safiye returned triumphant to the harem. The key to the *mabein* door had become a toy for the lovers. They had played hide-and-seek with it, first the slave hiding it from the master, who pretended he wanted to escape, and then the roles were reversed. Murad had hidden it last—under the cushions he sat on—and when Safiye had tried to reach under him to get it, he had drawn her into yet another long and lazy bout of love.

Afterward he slept, a long, thin body sprawled among the cushions, careless of his helpless nakedness. She had gently withdrawn the key, gathered up what clothes she could carry on one arm, and slipped out, leaving the key behind on the table.

"By Allah, I am famished!" were her first words to the harem's inmates who met her dumbfounded as if she were someone raised from the dead.

During the three days, the lovers had fed upon the festival dainties, being too jealous of the world they were creating between themselves to allow it to be peopled by even so much as a deaf mute with a water jug. They had scrapped like kittens over the last of the crumbs, then come to love again two or three times more, their hunger for food only adding to their hunger for one another. Though she could have claimed any dainty she wanted from the harem kitchen, after three days of nothing but dates, pastries, leftover lamb, and the heady sweetness of love, plain water and last night's pilaf sounded better than anything.

While she washed her hands and helped herself, the inmates crowded around to wonder and to hear the tale. The death of a pride of lions or fifty men in battle are the only feats a *selamlik* could ever find to compare to this in the harem.

"But what gift did he give you for such a long time?"

"Allah forbid, we thought he might have killed you."

"Yes! We were about to send the eunuchs to see."

"Three days, by the Merciful One! I tell you, it would have killed me."

"He must have given you something fine."

"Come on. Tell us. What did he give you?"

Finally Safiye managed to fit the word "Nothing" into this barrage.

"Nothing?"

"I don't believe it. She must be hiding it."

"But I would have thought it too big to hide."

"Is it a slave, perhaps?"

"A fine fat eunuch of your very own?"

"A villa on the Black Sea? Surely he could give nothing less."

"I tell you, by my life," Safiye said with a careless wave of her pilaf-greased hand, "he gave me nothing." She helped herself to another mouthful and then said, "Except, perhaps— Allah willing—a son."

She shot a glance particularly at Nur Banu as she said this. The older woman had lost enough of her pride that she would not hear the news secondhand and crowded around with the others. Besides, she had healed most of her wounds with the thought that it was her plan after all, even if it had worked out in spite of her.

Still, a touch of bitterness caught in Nur Banu's throat as

she said, "He gave you nothing? Well, you cannot have been such a success as all that if for nearly three days' toil you have earned nothing."

"Toil, lady? You call it toil?" Safiye met the woman's eyes with a self-assured, almost taunting smile. "Well, for those who call it toil, let them charge a fee. I myself am quite content. Quite content," she repeated, giving it the cushioned sigh it had had, no doubt, when murmured in the *mabein*.

"Do not blame your son," Safiye continued. "Perhaps he would have given me a little something, but he was asleep when I left."

"He was——? You mean you left while he was asleep? Without his permission? You left the room before he did?"

"Yes. Yes, yes, and yes."

"Well, it simply is not done. Safiye, I insist that you return to the *mabein* at once and do not leave until my son says you may, gift or no gift."

"Esmikhan Sultan." Safiye ignored this demand and turned to the girl instead. "Esmikhan, will you come to the bath with me? I cannot tell you how good the water will feel! My skin is crusted with dried-on sweat."

The young girl took the hand Safiye offered her without a moment's glance at Nur Banu. There was a new power to be reckoned with in the harem and everyone knew it. Safiye, of course, could never displace the mother of the heir. But now she had won a claim upon the outside for herself. The mother of the heir no longer held her reins directly and this greatly weakened their force.

"And, lady," Safiye called over her shoulder as she and Esmikhan walked off hand in hand towards the bath. "Lady, if your son should send for me—as I suppose he might—refuse him. Yes, tell him I am indisposed and to send again—oh, let us say next Friday. Certainly not before."

Esmikhan could not smother a giggle at the wonderful

brashness of the girl—woman, now—who held her hand. Safiye joined the giggle and the two scampered off as if there were years of virginity left in both of them.

Safiye and Esmikhan were still in the bath when, indeed, Murad did send.

"Tell him I am indisposed," Safiye said and returned to her scrubbing.

The messenger was back just minutes later with a much more urgent appeal.

"I am indisposed," she said again with fierce insistence and Esmikhan, giggling, joined her in splashing the messenger from the room for the safety of her silk robes.

Then the presents began to arrive.

Those who had clicked their tongues in pity were now put to dumb silence. At first they were only simple gifts: a basket of perfect peaches, a small inlaid box which, though very pretty, had seen some heavy use. Murad had not concerned himself with women before and had never bothered to lay in a store of appropriate trinkets as other men do, nor had he even thought what "appropriate" might be.

Soon, however, it was clear that he had sought out tutors, that his scouts were going farther and farther afield, with ever more money in their pouches. The silks that came, the jewels! Kutahiya had never seen the like before.

With these gifts, Safiye herself made gifts, binding carefully chosen women to her as only an unpaid debt can. Had Murad seen how little attachment his love fixed upon his lavish tokens, the despair would have devastated him.

Some few gifts only did Safiye keep and guard most jealously. These were the half dozen or so rather badly written poems that the prince had scribbled in his own hand. Safiye, of course, could not read them herself, but she was hard pressed to hide from Esmikhan—the only one she trusted to act as her reader—the emotion they brought. Oh, yes, they were terribly bad. Even in just a few months, Safiye had been exposed to enough good Turkish love poetry at the frequent harem recitals to know bad copies when she heard them. She had always had a quick ear and discerning taste for her native Italian poets. But it was the very clumsy triteness of Murad's attempts that made them so dear to her.

"Tell me what this word is," she would ask of her friend who could read. And, "Where does it say that again?", trying, often succeeding, to find echoes of the way his hand had moved across her own flesh in the lines drawn out upon the paper.

"Thank you, Esmikhan." She would excuse the girl when the latter, not Safiye herself, was obviously weary of the repetition.

Then Safiye would carefully fold the letter and push it into her bodice so as to keep it close to her heart and to prevent jealous hands from obtaining the wherewithal to work love-destroying spells. Still, neither bribes nor pleading turned Safiye from her resolve not to see him, no matter how flippant and impulsive her first enactment of it had seemed.

At the end of the week, Nur Banu could bear this unholy disruption of the peace and decorum of the harem no longer. She called the girl to her room with no one besides the Kislar Aga in attendance. The great white eunuch represented the physical hand of Nur Banu's might. It was completely within her power to have him take any girl out and whip her—on the feet until she was lame forever or, less drastically, on her back or buttocks until she could neither sit, sleep, nor wear her fine silks for a month. Safiye imagined the temptation had more than once occurred to Nur Banu, but the older woman had so far resisted calling down such punishment. If her son, frustrated as he was, heard of it, she might lose all influence over him permanently. The eunuch, Safiye knew, was only there to lend silent force to the words her mistress would say.

Safiye was Nur Banu's protégé, after all—her private property owned, body and soul, indeed, her creation from the very dust. Should the girl be surprised that Nur Banu could hardly control her rage when she was brought to her? But no matter how hard she tried to stand properly, her hands crossed on her breast, it was with a humility that was nothing but mockery.

"You thought you were so clever, my pretty little miss," Nur Banu began with deepest sarcasm. "Toying with my son as if he were some scabby craftsman and you nothing but a cheap overnight whore. Well, you should know what I have just learned this morning. Murad has sent away his lovesick poets and his jewelers and called for his smoking companions once more. You played him one day too long, my girl, and within the week I shall sell you to the whoremonger who best deserves such sluttishness."

Safiye fell to her knees as if she'd been struck and ignored the look of delight that crossed Nur Banu's face as she did so. Catching the gold-stitched hem of the older woman's robe, she pleaded, "Please, believe me, lady, I thought only of his good. I meant only to help cure him. Please, please, believe me. Let me go to him at once. I will satisfy him, if Allah may find favor with such a miserable creature as I am."

Nur Banu smiled quietly, then told her eunuch to go tell the prince that, thanks to the persuasion of his ever-careful mother, the girl was coming.

Safiye was not deterred when she entered the *mabein* and saw that the danger had been grossly exaggerated. The prince had smoked a pipeful, that was all, to combat a gloomy depression, and he still found Safiye herself a much more welcome cure.

Nur Banu knew she was not the sole victor in this struggle. She knew her son loved the fair Italian in a way he could never love her. That would be a sin unthinkable. But it was more than just the laws of incest that were against it. Nur Banu had to admit, even if only to herself, that the girl understood her son better than she did. Safiye seemed to know with a sixth sense just what Murad needed and when. For, after her first withholding in the harem, the girl was not cured of that trick, but only learned to use it with more and more skill.

"It is only the roll and thrust of the act itself played out on a much grander bed with a proportionately greater time incorporated in the rhythm." So did Nur Banu brush the game aside. "Any girl has the instinct to move and curl beneath her lover."

And yet she never ceased to be amazed at the precision of this girl's instinct and the throes of passion into which it threw her son. (Sometimes she heard his groans and animallike yelps responding to the girl's staccatic little purrs—they echoed into the harem from the *mabein* and she could not escape them.) If this was instinct, it was one she, Nur Banu, had been born without.

Nur Banu liked to flatter herself that she had known such passion and devotion in her life. But in the still, quiet times, she had to admit that it was only by chance that she was the first of Selim's many early loves to bring forth a son and heir. He, the only man she would ever love—and he would never love her again—had only turned to her in the anonymity of a drunken bluster one night. Every time she remembered his putrid, bloated flesh and wine-soaked breath upon her, she was repulsed. Indeed, she had thought her morning sickness only an acute revulsion for many days. She had never known either her master's passion nor her own. If Nur Banu enjoyed anyone's passion at all, it was that of her All-Merciful God who had smiled with favorable stars upon her fate that night.

Yet how could she complain? The remarkable blond-haired girl had accomplished all she had been purchased for and more. Murad still enjoyed his drug from time to time, but who did not? There was not even the complaint that he had given up one addiction for another, because with Safiye's encouragement, he began to take an interest in the other activities a young man should enjoy at court.

As an appreciative patron of both painting and music, her Murad soon made a name for himself throughout the district. He collected a small circle of favorites who loved him not only for his generosity but for his willingness to learn and for taste that was not merely the ability to buy it. He would bring miniatures for Safiye to see before he bought them and, often desiring her presence for a concert, would demand that the musicians be blindfolded so that she could sit by his side and receive his caresses that were the music made physical.

Murad also began to take an interest in the more mundane affairs of state and often attended when his father held court. Returning to the *mabein* afterward, pent up with frustrations at the insidiously formal and self-seeking ones who frequented the place, he would sink gratefully into his lover's arms to let her loosen the tensions with her gentle caresses and finally press them from him completely between her long white thighs. It was, incidently, with loving croons and caresses, that Safiye gained from him a working knowledge of the government of Kutahiya and of the greater Empire beyond.

And it happened more than once that a problem which had stumped Selim and all his counselors for weeks found solution in her quick mind. For, in the harem, a mind had the luxury to remain unfettered from the pressures of narrow and particular interests.

When Murad would carry the solution to his father the next day, the young prince would shrug off the praise and say, "Allah smiled on me—I had only to sleep upon it."

Part III

Abdullah

XXXVIII

IT WAS A night in autumn with a touch of winter already in the air when I was shown to my bed in the citadel of Kutahiya and then left on my own. A trip to wash the dust of my journey from my face and feet revealed that a long, wide hall marked the barrier between *haremlik* and *selamlik* in this prince's house. On one side were the various rooms of the harem, on the other side opened the doors to the eunuchs' quarters and the two chambers of the *mabein* where the governor and his son could enjoy their women. This hall was paved in rough stone and also opened in a long, high clerestory to the sky above.

I got the definite and purposeful feeling of having gone out of doors and passed from one building to another as I went from the world to the harem. There could be no mistaking the transition, even for the stranger.

That night, the windows had caught a brilliant moonlight in just such a way that it was channeled like sparkling water in a cascade down the walls and into a beautiful dappled pattern—like little waves—on the flagstones below. The beauty of the scene struck me as I'd been too numb to be struck by anything in a long, long time. I paused, all alone, to contemplate it and let my mind follow those waves back to days that were gone. To ships and sea I should never again enjoy.

As I did so, the door from one of the rooms of the *mabein* opened furtively and a figure joined me in the hall, walking upon the water.

She wore nothing more than a thin sheet caught haphazardly about her tall, slender body, leaving her neck and soft shoulders bare, over which her golden hair tumbled without constraint. Her light, naked feet scampered across the cold stone with a sound like walking in melting snow. There was in her step the haste and warmth of caresses in foreplay.

I knew at once who she was. It was as if all my dreams and nightmares of the past six months had suddenly taken on material form.

"Hello, Sofia." I said it in Italian, and with surprising calmness.

She started, having heard neither her native tongue nor her Christian name for half a year. Still, Sofia Baffo was never one to let anyone think he had bested her in any situation. She regained her composure with remarkable speed, and even let the sheet drop more loosely over one shoulder to indicate her nonchalance as she said, "Veniero! Well, this is a surprise! Still as foolish and daredevilish as ever. Still climbing convent walls."

"I am here in Kutahiya at my master's bidding, not yours this time."

"A slave, are you? So am I."

"Well, there are slaves and there are slaves, as my old friend Husayn might say."

Delusions are the greater part of any infatuation, and removal of my physical reaction to her taught me what a flimsy thing my love had been. I closed my eyes against the pain of my loss, but afterward my speech grew steadier and I spoke in my most flowery Turkish.

"My master is Sokolli Pasha, soon to take Esmikhan Sultan to wife. I am to see his bride safely to Constantinople."

Baffo's daughter seemed at a loss for something else to say, as the mighty often are when faced with unwanted, unlooked-for suits. So I drew a paper from my bosom. I

knew it from the other two there by its finer Turkish grade.
It was an announcement I had picked up in the bazaars of
Constantinople as I ran my errands and had kept out of curiosity, never imagining when and where I might use it.
Posted by the Venetian embassy to the Porte, in Turkish,
Latin, and Italian, it offered in the name of Governor Baffo
of Corfu a ransom of five hundred *ghrush* for the return of
his daughter, who, he had reason to suspect, was being held
captive somewhere in the harems of Turkey.

I placed the paper in Sofia's hand saying, this time in Italian, "You might find this interesting as well."

I had successfully broken down her defenses. To unfold
the paper, which her curiosity could not resist, she had to jug-
gle the corners of her sheet most precariously. But a few rapid
blinks of her eyes against some tender memory were the
only other signs of weakness she would give me, even after
she'd read the announcement.

Quickly, firmly, she tore the paper into a hundred
fingertip-sized pieces. "My father," she said, meeting me
firmly in the eye, "underbid by a whole sack of *ghrush*. To
people here I am now worth six hundred."

At that moment, the door to the *mabein* cracked open and
the voice of a young man whispered, "Safiye? Safiye? Are you
there? My love, you promised you'd be gone only a moment,
and I am dying of desire."

"You see, Veniero," Safiye said. "I can't stand here gos-
siping with you all night long."

"Safiye? My love?" the young man said again.

"No," I agreed in rather brazen, mocking Italian. "Your re-
sponsibilities are most onerous indeed."

I made no attempt to muffle my words and they must have
carried quite far. I could usually, with concentration, hold
my voice down in a man's registers and the next thing I
knew, a very wiry pair of hands was about my throat. The

bubble of my voice escaped and drifted higher, ending in a squeak. I managed to keep my balance during the onslaught, for though he was a few years my senior, my attacker was neither as large nor as strong as I, all bones and angles. But I was forced against the wall by his energy, nonetheless.

Not since Husayn have I heard such abuse in Turkish as I heard then. Subsequent to leaving my Syrian merchant friend, my training had all been geared to courtliness and manners. I did not know the meaning of half the words that were spat into my face by that furious young man. Clear enough, however, was the accusation that I had greatly wronged the honor of his women and that the only satisfaction he could take was my immediate death.

Safiye's Turkish stumbled as she tried halfheartedly to intervene, "My love! My love!"

I was so busy trying to fend off my unknown attacker's frenzied blows that I hardly realized when other women entered the hallway. They were drawn by the yells, the thud of his flesh on mine, and my scuffles trying to defend myself. In various stages of undress, the women came to see what the matter was.

I heard the voice I already recognized as that of my new young mistress, Esmikhan Sultan, cry: "Murad! Brother, stop!"

This told me the man was a prince of the blood and I must go easy on him. But months of unexpressed anger were seething within me and, between blows, I grew reckless. By God, what could they do to me that hadn't already been done? Even if I killed this milksop, all they could do would be a blessing compared to what they'd already done.

Esmikhan cried again: "Murad! A eunuch! Only a eunuch!"

The young prince misunderstood her. He thought she meant to say that he was nothing but a useless eunuch compared to me (he could not help but be aware of the difference in our sizes) and it made him absolutely senseless with hurt and fury. Fortunately, my strength prevailed even against such passion.

"It is just as I said," exclaimed one of the unseen ladies of the harem.

"Yes," replied another. "Whatever can Sokolli Pasha have been thinking? To buy such a one for Esmikhan!"

More harem talk came in snatches through the ringing of blows to my head.

"Surely he cannot have been thinking at all."

"It is even as I was told. The Pasha is too caught up in his work to have any clear thoughts of marriage."

"Really! Such a young servant! Does he know his duties at all?"

"It is not a question of duties," another voice chimed in, brimming with delight. "Such a young one, of such handsome face and features! I wonder if he is to guard Esmikhan or to woo her!"

"In my father's harem," fussed a stern old hag, "we were given no guard until he was clearly passed his prime or had been well disfigured by the pox. There is a tradition of the Prophet to support such caution. I know. My father was . . ."

"Sokolli Pasha is so old," said yet another, nearly hiccoughing with giggles, "that he has sent another man to be groom for him in his place."

Now the whole hall shrieked with laughter and the sweet young voice of my mistress cried out above them all, "Silence, for the love of Allah." But they laughed more all the same.

"Where are your eunuchs, ladies?" I managed to gasp. "Is a fistfight such a novelty to you that you can only stand and stare?"

I sparred to the right, but caught the wall behind my opponent instead. "For the love of Allah"——I took a blow to the face and felt the blood swelling at the base of my nose that made my voice sound nasally—"call your eunuchs." Then I got in a pair of good ones, cleverly fending off a jab to the kidneys. "Tell them to pull him off me"—next I got a hold on the prince's arm, which he only escaped by ripping the fine damask of his caftan's sleeve—"or I will do him harm."

"Do me harm, will you?" The young prince choked with rage and hit me such a blow to the jaw that I was speechless after that. "We'll see who does the most harm."

"Ah, Veniero, Veniero!" Safiye's Italian rose above all the rest. She stood, wringing the corner of her flimsy costume which was, for her, earnest concern. "This isn't a convent, my dear Veniero. This is a harem. Don't you know by now that to be found in another man's harem is death?"

The mortification that she had known me in my former strength (which was, in fact, a weakness, groveling at her feet) was enough to envigorate me to get the prince by the shoulders in a strong hold and keep him there. This same emotion pushed into my throat and could be heard in my next words.

"And don't you, my beautiful Sofia, know how to tell a eunuch from a man?" I forgot all Italian then and said it in Turkish so there'd be no mistake. "Even now, you look for secret lovers in castrati such as myself? Sofia Baffo, I am a eunuch. Thanks to you—" I turned to the prince. "Master, I have no designs on your women. I am a *khadim*."

XXXIX

"COME HERE TO the light and let me have a look at what you've done to yourself."

In her own room, Esmikhan Sultan led me by the hand as gently as a child to the lamp that swung on a chain from a low beam.

"That eye will not be good." She set me on the divan and leaned over to inspect. Attar of roses escaped her bosom as she did so with a scent that was noticeable even through the clots of blood forming in my nose. "And your lip is already swelling."

With a few quick orders, she sent her maid scurrying off for the equipment that shortly allowed her to sponge my wounds with warm water smelling of steeped comfrey and myrrh. The odor of disinfectant brought back a nightmare of events I had to push from my mind with a physical gesture as if I were struggling with the prince once again. Esmikhan Sultan sat back and waited for the pain to pass me. She said nothing, but the sympathy in her eyes brought me more quickly into control.

"You know, *ustadh,* I haven't named you yet."

As if I were a puppy; I stiffened at the thought.

"I'm sorry," my lady said. "I meant to warn you it might sting. I'll try to be more gentle."

I couldn't tell her that it wasn't her ministrations that made me flinch. I tried to relax my hand back into hers as she dabbed at my knuckles that had missed her brother's face and hit the stone wall behind him instead.

"Lulu," she announced. "I've always wanted to name my first *khadim* Lulu. Lulu if he was white, Sandal if he was black."

"For the love of Allah!" The words escaped me. "Not Lulu."

My lady blinked in surprise, as she would have if a puppy—or even an infant—had protested at his naming. I closed my eyes with renewed horror at my situation. These pampered women considered their eunuchs at the mercy of their wills no less than they did infants and puppies. I could not endure it.

"You don't like Lulu?"

I was incapable of answering such unfeigned astonishment.

"It means a pearl and I thought—Pearl for a white, Sandal, the sweet-smelling wood, for a black. We always name our eunuchs such names. Don't you know? Hyacinth, Narcissus. For precious metals or perfumes.

"You don't like Lulu." She repeated the idea in an attempt to convince herself. "You looked so much like a beautiful, rare pearl when I first saw you this afternoon." She laughed a little as she gently daubed at my blackening eye. "I must admit you don't look much like one now. More like blotchy marble. Or a carbuncle. Shall you go through life with the name Carbuncle?"

"My name is Giorgio Veniero." I hissed at the sting of pronouncing a dead patronym.

My lady rocked back on her heels and blinked at the sounds in incomprehension. That eunuchs should have names—or lives, even—beyond what their mistresses gave them was clearly novel to her.

"Giorgio Veniero," I repeated. "Veniero."

She made a couple of attempts at the foreign syllables,

making them sound like the sort of disease my uncle once caught from whores. By San Marco, she was simple, protected so unnaturally in that simplicity. And I was to spend the rest of my life with no company but such women? Why had my reflexes of self-preservation taken over once again? I should have let Prince Murad kill me.

Finally, I realized it was hopeless. She would continue to mangle my name that way day in and day out.

"But what shall I call you then?"

"Just call me a man——"

"A man?" There was no insult in her voice. Just surprise.

"No, I cannot be called even that any more. Just call me a soul whom God—Allah—has seen fit to curse beyond any other. Adam got off lightly compared to me."

Perhaps my struggle with the Turkish failed to convey all the bitterness I meant with it.

"You are Allah's servant," she stated.

"His slave, his *khadim*."

"So are we all, Abdullah. So are we all when we have the humility to know it. Some are more blessed because Allah helps them to learn it more readily than others. Yes, so are we all." Was she merely reciting something Turks learned by rote? Or was this her own intelligence? "So. I will call you Abdullah—Allah's servant."

"Abdullah." At least it was male. "That was the name my friend Husayn always teased he'd give me if I came to play Turk in his homeland. Like I called him Enrico."

"Do you mind?"

What did it matter? What did anything matter any more? I shrugged my acquiescence.

"Abdullah it is then." She wrung her cloth out in its bowl with renewed determination. "Yes, I do think it suits you. Much better than Lulu. You are different from other *khuddam*. Perhaps you are newer at it than others?"

"Perhaps."

"Is this your first post?"

"Yes."

"Perhaps that explains it."

"Perhaps."

"Well, I shall do my best to see it is the only one you ever have. It isn't easy, so I understand, for *khuddam* to change mistresses once they've become attached, like family."

Attachment to anything seemed impossible, but I said, "At your service, my lady."

For the first time, I felt some gratitude for the patience Salah ad-Din's fat, sloppy wife had had in trying to teach me the stiff formalities of my new station. She insisted on teaching me when becoming a more marketable commodity was the last thing I wanted to do, when I was too consumed with rage to breathe evenly for days on end. There was some purpose in these forms. They were an escape.

"Is there truth in what the others were saying?" Esmikhan began again.

"What others?"

My lady bit her lip, flattening its usual roundness, until it was more like an average mouth. "Sokolli Pasha—my betrothed—perhaps he made a mistake in sending you, one so young and inexperienced."

"I think he hasn't much experience with eunuchs, lady, that is true."

With a sigh, she turned more merry. "Well, I see nothing wrong with you. The way you stood up to my brother— I'd trust you on my side against anyone."

"It's only when I knew he was your brother that I let him get off so easily. Anyone else—"

"I appreciate that, *ustadh*. Anyone else would need more help than Safiye can offer him tonight."

She finished with the water. It was getting cold in any case.

She tossed the cloth into the bowl with a little splash and gestured for the maidservant to remove it.

When the girl was gone, she said: "You know Safiye, don't you?"

"Safiye? Is that what you call her?" Not she-demon? Not bitch?

"You know her? From before?"

"From before."

"She is Italian, too. Is it such a very small country? You Italians certainly give my grandfather the Sultan trouble enough in battle and on the high seas."

"Italy was a long, long time ago." Couldn't we finish with the subject?

"I see." I think she did make an attempt to change the topic, though it wasn't far enough for me. "Well, Safiye has certainly brought life to this harem. Life to my brother, too, which you tried to knock from him again tonight. I have never had such a dear, dear friend as Safiye is."

"What pleases my lady pleases me." Another one of those good, noncommittal phrases.

"I do hope Sokolli Pasha will allow me to continue to see her."

"I am sure that what pleases my lady will also please my master."

Selim's daughter chuckled.

What was so humorous about the way I ran through a eunuch's dialogue? "My lady?"

"Nothing. Just—wasn't it funny when my brother finally discovered that he, not you, was the intruder here in the *haremlik*? How he soon skulked back into the *mabein* with his seriously wounded pride? He is such a blustering bag of hot air. You mustn't mind him."

"I shouldn't mind him so much if my eye wasn't throbbing like it is."

My lady laughed again, louder. "And Safiye, how she turned so indignantly from you and quickly followed her lover. Nobody ever brought her to heel before like that."

"She would follow her lover."

"Oh, not Murad. She only does what Murad says when it pleases her. You, Abdullah. You, with your put-down. 'Looking for lovers among the *khuddam*?' I wonder who'll recover sooner, Murad from his black eyes or Safiye from your words."

My lady and I had met only briefly before, just long enough for me to register her plump, healthy youthfulness in my mind. I had weighed it sadly against the sharp middle age of my master, who was to be her husband—and even more sadly, equated it with a younger form of Salah ad-Din's wife. But now, I saw how truly pleasant she was to look at. Not overwhelmingly beautiful, perhaps, with her round face and round, dark eyes, black curls and round mouth dimpling with her laughter over a round chin. A prominant mole marred the left side of her nose. But she was good-natured and pleasanter still when her personality bubbled unhampered to the surface.

I laughed in spite of myself and she laughed back.

Then, with sudden and inexplicable unity, Esmikhan and I laughed together. It was infectious, a fever of laughter. We laughed and laughed until the tears flowed, until our sides ached. We couldn't look at one another without falling into another fit. Finally, first she and then I collapsed to the cushions of the divan and rolled and laughed and cried until we were spent.

"GOOD NIGHT, MY lady."

How long had we lain thus side by side until a chill brought me to myself? Selim's daughter had laughed herself into an immobile exhaustion. She didn't reply. Perhaps she even slept. I shivered again in the autumn chill that had crept into the room. I found a quilt and tossed it over her sleeping form. Her little hennaed feet curled up under it in gratitude, but her breath came deeply now. She slept.

It was good for Esmikhan Sultan to laugh. As a bride, she must have been under a lot of tension, and would come under more.

But it was also good for me. I hadn't allowed myself to laugh since I'd slept in Husayn's guest room so very long ago.

I'd been afraid it might hurt my mutilation. I found now that it did not.

XL

WE MOVED THROUGH the autumn hills that were thick with the acrid smell of asphodel like smoke to the flame-orange turn of the leaves. The bridal train was more glorious than I had dared to hope. The master had meant to send only his old black retainer, Ali, and myself. He was too busy with duties of state at the moment, though he promised he would travel a day's journey out of Constantinople to meet us.

At the last minute, some word of conscience, perhaps from the Sultan himself, had reminded Sokolli Pasha that this was a princess of the blood he was marrying, not just any old peasant. For duty's sake, he had increased our numbers to thirty out of the capital. Our escort, however, was not composed of musicians, mimes, acrobats, and other merrymakers common to wedding parties, but a squadron of janissaries. It was as if our charge were a chest of taxes in pure gold traveling through a land of barbarians rather than a bride crossing the very bosom of the Turkish homeland.

Now, on our return, Prince Murad himself was in the company. The most trustworthy harem gossip told me this was Safiye's doing. Nur Banu and most of her suite were retreating from the mountains for the winter, as they always did. A skeletal harem only would be left to see to the needs of Selim during these cold months, and Safiye had no desire to be part of the powerless dregs. Yet now she could not be permitted to leave Murad's side. Her only alternative was to convince the young prince to convince the *sandjak* and his father that he should winter in Constantinople, too. This Safiye accomplished in ways known not to the daylight disputations of the divan, but only to the secret nights of lovers.

Whatever the gossips said, I could not help but think that part of Murad's purpose in making this journey was that he did not really trust me with the honor of his women. I could feel his suspicion like whiplash on my back every time I approached one of the curtained sedans. I did notice, however, that he was rather careless of my dealings with his sister, so I suspect he was more jealous of the curt Italian Safiye and I exchanged and the tension of a past he could feel between us than he was of Esmikhan's virginity.

For her own purposes, Safiye handled this very well. Though my mistress barraged her with messages and tidbits of gossip all day long, sent on my feet and through my tongue, Safiye initiated nothing in response. All of her attention went elsewhere—via other eunuchs to the prince, who rode on his horse at the head of the column.

On our third noonday halt, I returned once again empty-handed to Esmikhan.

"What says Safiye?" my lady rose to ask.

"She said nothing, only took the message through her grille in silence."

"She will not come and join me. Again."

The hurt in Esmikhan's voice was deep. She sat down once more, but found no comfort on the cushions her maids had fluffed up for her under an oak gone crimson and making the ground rough with its dropping fruit. Her maids tried to tempt her with dainties from the kerchiefs full of lunch, but they made the mistake of offering a little Turkish bonnet first.

"Safiye's favorite," Esmikhan sighed, and pleaded no appetite after that.

"Lady, Safiye is busy with her love," one of the maids coaxed. "Soon you'll have enough love of your own to keep you as busy as she is. Think of that. Think forward to your husband-to-be and do not be sad."

The other girls murmured their agreement with these sentiments, but Esmikhan avoided their words and, while trying to avoid their circle of eyes as well, her gaze fell on me. I had not been dismissed and stood clumsily by, wondering if I should dismiss myself. The sudden excitement that beamed through the clouds of tears in her velvet brown eyes momentarily increased my apprehension. But when she saw me, Esmikhan suddenly let out a little laugh. Forced though it was, it was nonetheless an echo of our laughter three nights ago in her room in Kutahiya.

"Abdullah," she said.

"Lady, I am at your service."

She held out her hand and insisted I take it in mine. Her hand was soft and warm. "You shall come and sit here on the cushions, Abdullah, right by me, and tell me everything there is to tell."

"Lady?"

"Tell me all you can about Sokolli Pasha, who is to be my husband."

"My lady, I'm afraid I do not know much at all."

"Surely you have met him?"

"Yes," I replied. "But only once."

"See? That is once more than anyone else I know. All these silly women mean either to terrify me or to placate me with their false rumors. But they have never even seen him and I refuse to believe them. I will believe only you, Abdullah, so you must tell the truth. They say Sokolli Pasha is old. Is he so terribly old?"

The maids left off their protests of Esmikhan's breach of etiquette to listen, for they were almost as curious as she was.

"He is not young," I confessed. Then, to still the murmurs of disappointment this brought forth, I continued, "But, lady, this is said only because you yourself are in the bloom of your youth, Allah protect you, and would prove his better were comparison made between you on this count. You know well no man can bear defeat in any matter from his bride. He is the one who is supposed to defeat her."

The disappointment turned to titters of delight at this statement.

But, "No, don't you tease me, Abdullah," Esmikhan said. "The others tease me; you must not. I understand Sokolli Pasha has been in my grandfather's service for almost thirty years. I can do sums. He must be forty at least."

"May Allah double his years," I said. "My master is fifty-four."

"No! Do not pray to double those years! Fifty-four! That is three times—almost four times my age! My father is younger than that!" Esmikhan wailed.

"Sokolli Pasha is a man of strong, fit body and keen mind. He is a soldier who will endure, Allah willing, at least two more decades of warfare, diplomacy—and love."

"But I am just a child, with my whole life ahead of me. Allah, I am to be married to a grandfather!"

"If it is any comfort, lady, rumor has it, and my meeting with him did nothing to dispel it: Sokolli Pasha is as much a stranger to the ways of love as you are."

"If he's a healthy man, as you say, how is that possible?"

"Do not forget, lady. Sokolli Pasha was raised from his youth in the Enclosed School."

"He is one of the tribute boys, then?"

Had Esmikhan been a Christian girl, with centuries of crusade in her upbringing, there might have been a tremor of horror in her voice. That, or at least deep pity to think that her betrothed had been one of the thousands of lads taken as a tribute from the Empire's Christian communities every five years. These lads became the Sultan's personal slaves, forcibly converted to Islam, never to see their families and homes again.

But Esmikhan knew only the Turkish side of the story in spite of the fact that in her seclusion she had never actually seen a tribute boy. She knew that Christian parents were as often as not glad to give up their sons and would try to cover up their defects in an attempt to get them chosen for the levy. To be taken away from the misery of poor, war-ridden lands on the border to the glittering capital with every chance for education and advancement usually outweighed any considerations of religion and family togetherness. It was not unheard of for Muslim families to put off circumcision and pay the local priest to pass their sons off as Christians, too, for even True Believers rarely knew such a good life as the most favored of the Sultan's favored slaves.

Neither did Esmikhan turn up her little round nose to think that her husband would be a slave. Although the first lesson boys learned in the Enclosed School was absolute obedience to no master but the Shadow of Allah, the Sultan, they learned plenty of other things, too. Those with brains were taught to read and write, those with brawn to fight; most were as handy with the pen as with the sword. There, in the barracks that became their home, nothing counted but individual ability, neither family's prestige, wealth, nor the prejudice of acquaintances. Some became gardeners, some cooks, some men of religion and study. The greater part of them filled the ranks of the janissaries, where their fierce devotion to the Sultan made them fight as one man and put even life a lowly second place. If one showed his devotion particularly well, he joined the Sultan's private bodyguard.

But some very few, like Sokolli Muhammed Pasha, whose superior abilities had come to Suleiman's notice before he was twenty, were set on the path toward becoming governors and pashas. They made up the very backbone of the Turkish government, for the Sultan trusted them explicitly in a way he could trust no free-born Turk. They were his creations, after all. They were his slaves, even as pashas and viziers. All they managed to amass of worldly goods reverted to the imperial coffers upon their deaths, and the Sultan always maintained the right to send them to that death at a moment's notice. No trial, apology, or explanation was possible. And their own muster mates pulled the bowstring if the lord but waved his hand.

I told Esmikhan all I had managed to learn of Sokolli Pasha's career from the day at nineteen or twenty, when, fresh from the hinterland of Europe, this young recruit had caught the Sultan's eye and been set apart for better things. It was a simple tale, as all tales of unremitted success must be. He rose from post to post until now he sat among the pashas and viziers in the Great Divan itself and was followed in the Friday morning procession by a standard bearing three long horsetails.

"Sokolli Pasha's elevation demands some outward display of extravagance lest diplomats and politicians refuse to believe he holds such power as his title declares," I said. "He therefore purchased a large park in the City just across from the Aya Sophia Mosque."

"I am not familiar with much of Constantinople outside the palace harem," Esmikhan said. "But I have heard of that park. It is not far from the new palace, is it?"

"Not far at all. And I think that was the master's first consideration in the purchase. He can answer the Sultan's summons within half an hour from deep sleep at home to full command in the Great Divan. Of only minor consideration to him are the land's lovely waters and plantings and the gentle rise that was the perfect spot to build a palace of his own. The palace has been built, too, by the loving hand of Sinan."

"My grandfather's own royal architect?"

"Yes. And it is a building very worthy of his famous skill. But always Sokolli Pasha remembers that on his death, it will all revert to the throne. What is the use of building a small private kingdom, of marrying, of begetting sons, when all his efforts will only leave them paupers at his death? So he never has peopled this palace with wives and children. Besides, the Enclosed School taught its prize pupil well. None of the things that give other men pleasure are a temptation to Sokolli's discipline. More than fine clothes, music, or women, he loves duty. In fact, compared to a day spent enforcing the Sultan's will upon distant provinces, foreign ambassadors, and whining tax collectors, any other pastime drives him to impatience with its frivolity.

"There is one way a high-ranking slave of the Sultan might leave a permanent name for himself on the earth, and Sokolli Pasha has taken full opportunity of this," I explained to Esmikhan.

"He can build *medresses* and endow *awqaf,*" she suggested.

"Yes, there is hardly a province that does not boast a brand-new religious school, mosque, or dervish *tekke* bearing the master's patronym. But where other men hoard behind them, in their harems, Sokolli Pasha has remained a Spartan indeed.

"Now, at last, in his fifty-fourth year, private pleasure is offered to him. Not only offered, but presented to him in a way he cannot possibly refuse—in the person of the Sultan's own granddaughter as a solemn duty to guard with life and honor. Because of your royal Ottoman blood, he need not worry on his own death for the care of either you or the children we pray Allah may grant to you. The state will see to that. I suspect Sokolli Pasha has yet to get over the shock of this honor, and he will certainly never overcome the burden of it.

"I'll wager," I said finally, daring to meet her eye and wink, "he will be shy in your presence, and you are the one who will have to do some coaxing."

Esmikhan blushed prettily at my words, then said, "But tell me, is he handsome? Is the pasha handsome? That is the most important. It shall all be easier if he is handsome."

I smiled gently and chose my words carefully. "I'm afraid, lady, that I cannot answer that."

"Oh, but you must," Esmikhan said, tears rising quickly in her eyes again, though this time they were tears of frustration rather than grief.

"Please, lady, you must understand that a man, even if he

is a eunuch, does not look at another man the way a woman
would. Understand, too, that I am but new to this calling and
have but little practice in being—shall I say?—a woman's
eyes."

"Poor, poor Abdullah!" Esmikhan interjected briefly, simply to give me encouragement.

"Please understand, lady, that the first—and only—time
I ever laid eyes on Sokolli Pasha, it was to view him as my
new master, and not as your new husband."

"But tell me what your impression was. Surely a wife is
often no better than her husband's slave." Esmikhan reached
out a hand to my shoulder and fixed me with her clear brown
eyes.

This look and those words struck me deeply and forged
within me a bond with this young woman I sensed at once
would never be broken. Indeed, I have sometimes felt that
Esmikhan and I were married with those words, sworn into
a marriage much closer than she would ever enjoy with the
pasha and one more real, for it was made between our spirits. Bodies did not enter into the question at all.

I spoke quietly now, and from the heart, wishing there
were not so many ears to overhear us. "Lady, you bade me
speak the truth, and so I shall. Sokolli Pasha is not what you
would call handsome. But do not fret. Hear me. What
women call 'handsome' I have often found to be closer to my
definition of 'delicate'—a quality one would rather find in
one's infant sons than in one's husband. For example, I have
often been told that I am handsome—and the reaction when
I walked into the harem at Kutahiya convinces me that my
recent pain has not so greatly altered it. But I wouldn't do
you much good as a husband, would I?" I said this, and she
nodded, but our eyes avoided contact, as if my words were
a formal lie covering a truth we knew was deeper.

"There is nothing of the cuddly little boy in Sokolli Pasha.

He is of a single and firm mind, and his features reflect this. He is tall—perhaps a hand taller than I am. He has a thin, sharp nose and rigid, cleanly formed brows and jaw. They tell me his surname 'Sokolli' means 'falcon' in his native Serbian language, and if he has his ancestor's looks, they were aptly named indeed. He has the regality of that bird, but also the impatience with frivolity and with fancy looks of a wild predator.

"Nonetheless, I felt great relief come into my slave's heart when I saw him. 'Thanks be to Allah,' I said, 'here is a master I can trust.' He may not be handsome. He may not love to sit and listen for hours on end to poetry or music as I do. But he is a man who knows and loves his duty and would rather die than not fulfill it. I know that if I am ever beaten or mistreated at his hands, it will only be because I strongly deserve it. If I do my duty to him, he will do his to me and never be intentionally unkind. He will feed me and clothe me and see that my needs are met and that I am not unhappy, as far as it is in his power and Allah's will. As a slave, I rejoiced greatly in that."

"And as a bride," Esmikhan said, lying back against her pillows with a great sigh of relief, "I rejoice, too."

Unfortunately, there was little time for her relief to be exploited in true relaxation there under the oak tree. The call went up that it was time to be moving if we were to reach our night's lodgings. Esmikhan allowed me to take her hand and help her to her feet. I packed her into her sedan, then closed the lattice behind her with tenderness, like closing the lid on a jewelry case. I gave signal to the bearers that they might at last approach and heave the burden to their shoulders. I walked along side for a few hundred paces with my hand still on the grille as if for further security. But my thoughts were far away.

My first and, to date, my only meeting with Sokolli Pasha

still played through my mind, and it was not in the hopes that I might glean further details from it to lighten Esmikhan's fears. The strength of our union made me remember some part of that meeting I had ignored until then.

There I had sat, among bolts of fabric and packets of spices purchased against the wedding. I was one gift among many, and that fact did little to make me feel proud of my role. It chafed my humanity to be treated like just so many dry goods and I had, so far, been unable to form the words "my master" on my lips in the dreadful fear of how bitter they would taste.

Then Sokolli Pasha had entered the room. Black Ali, who had made the purchases—more with the gaudy eye of an old spoiled slave than with any sense of a delicate young lady's taste—had to call the master's attention to the pile, reminding him that they needed his perusal to make the purchases final.

Sokolli Pasha obviously had other things on his mind and wanted to return to them instantly. "Fine, fine, Ali," he said quickly, cutting explanations, apologies, and little marketplace triumphs short.

Then his falcon's eye fell on me. I bowed, as I had been taught, but I did it stiffly, hoping to express in that one movement how I thought a government, his government, that would allow such things happen to honest men, stank to high heaven.

"The *khadim* you ordered, master," Ali said, grinning.

"So I see."

"A fine *khadim*. And I got a good deal on him besides."

"Good, Ali. Very good."

Sokolli Pasha spoke the words, but had to clear his throat on them, and he blanched noticeably until I dropped my eyes before his obvious discomfort. He did not ask my name or whether I knew my business—which I truly did not. He simply stared at me for a moment or two as if struggling with a memory he thought he had long ago dispelled. When he gained control of that memory and was his usual man of severe restraint again, he laid his hand ever so briefly on my shoulder, then quickly turned and left the room. At the moment, I had been too relieved that he did not decide to reject me and send me back to that slave market again.

But now I found, with my hand similarly on Esmikhan's grille, that the moment still haunted me. I said nothing to my lady, of course, for what was I to make of it, even to myself?

XLI

"HIS MOTHER? OH, Abdullah, Sokolli Pasha has a mother? Why didn't you let me know before this?"

The grief and fear in her voice could not have been greater had Esmikhan just learned that the Empire of Islam had collapsed. And I knew I was to blame.

At our halt in Inönü, I had learned that this town on the edge of the high plateau was the recipient of one of Sokolli Pasha's minor pious endowments. It was only the corner of a shopfront that dispensed bread and a goats' milk gruel to the poor twice a day. But Esmikhan had insisted that I visit it, take a silver necklace of her own as a donation so that vegetables and perhaps some meat might be added to the fare, and then report back on all I had seen and heard in every detail.

At first this task had seemed simpleminded, but by the time I returned to give my report, I'd been brought up short several times by the massiveness of the task, if I were to do it honestly and thoroughly. How to describe the apricot light of late afternoon filling a small town's bazaar in undiluted strength to someone who has never seen light without its being strained through the confines of a harem garden? How to describe the faces of poverty to one whose lowliest slave eats far too much and wears cast-off brocades?

It was in fumbling desperately for words she might understand to describe one of the endowment's patrons that I accidentally said, "Well, she had the same sun-worn face as the master's mother."

I meant nothing malicious by neglecting to mention earlier that greatest bane of a new bride—her mother-in-law. The simple fact of the matter was that Sokolli's harem's sole occupant was such a shadowy figure that she slipped my mind when we were on related subjects. My good intentions to bring it up as soon as possible were always renewed when either I or the conversation seemed too far away to do so gracefully. All thought of the endowment was now forgotten in my lady's mind and I must say I had to fight her feelings of betrayal boldly. I tried my best to explain that it was the old woman's very lack of threat that had made me put off mention of her existence.

"She is a small, mousy woman, my master's mother, and her feet will no longer carry her weight. So she never moves, day or night, from the divan in the largest room of the *harem-lik*. Her eyes and her fingers are as keen as ever, though, and she spends her days at needlework from sunrise until the colors blur into one another at dusk. Her work is delightful, intricate, colorful patterns of flowers and birds such as I have never seen before."

"It sounds rather idolatrous," Esmikhan attempted.

"Anathema to pious Muslims, perhaps, but I suspect such designs are native to Bosnia where the master was born. Clearly her religious education has been lacking, but I could not speak to her of that. I couldn't speak to her of her work—I could speak to her of nothing, for in the twenty years since her son brought her to share his fortune, she has learned not a single word of Turkish. Visits from her son—which he performs not because he especially likes his mother, but because they, too, are a duty—they are the only dialogues she ever has. I suspect the babble with which she greeted me was incomprehensible as much from senility as it was from foreignness. Though I smiled and nodded in reply, I was convinced life in Sokolli's harem would be as lonely as its great halls were empty and full of echoes.

" 'Don't fret,' old Ali's wife, who cleans and cooks for the woman, said when she read my thoughts. 'The bride will soon fill this place with life.' I see it is Allah's will that her words become reality."

Esmikhan tried to take comfort from what I said, first because she knew I wanted her to desperately and secondly because I was still her only friend in this strange new harem that was now peopled by a mother-in-law. I have only just begun to realize what a truly remarkable, powerful thing it is to wink in the face of what anyone else would call an unforgivable betrayal, to wink and come back with more unfeigned grace and desire for friendship than before.

At the time, I thought it was either fate or something of my own virtue that made sharing our lives so easy, even after such a mistake on my part. I see now that it was effort, great effort, like an army of slaves straining to raise a stone the size of a small hill, their veins and muscles popping, their skin ashower with sweat. This effort was all Esmikhan's, the strength of her little hands, soft brown eyes, and boundless heart. After all, there was very little of a previous life she had to barter with me for mine. Sheltered as she was in her father's harem and but fourteen years old, her life, as she said, was "more like a poem than a story," and she recited these verses from the poet:

Think, in this battered caravanserai
Whose portals are alternate night and day,
How Sultan after Sultan with his pomp
Abode his destined hour, and went his way.

But she had that divine skill of listening whereby the speaker is made to feel not as if he has won a bargain with his words, but that his words are more precious than gems in the ears of his hearer. It was remarkable how she turned from her fears of Sokolli Pasha's mother and made my fears overshadow them.

There, alone in the night rooms of Inönü's governor's harem, with my lady tucked under strange quilts for bedtime, I told her of my childhood and of my adventures at sea. That was easy enough; I could hide behind the voice of a market storyteller and delight us both with how exotic it was to our present lives.

But with the skillful fingers of a blood-letter, Esmikhan also drew from me scenes from my more recent past. I did not give her details of what happened to me in the close, dark house beyond Pera, the real poison festering my core. That I avoided like a hot stove. But she prodded closely, as close as I thought I should ever let anyone venture. She gleaned and I gave, enough, I thought, in a couple of brief events that happened to me in the bazaar while I was making the purchases for her nuptials.

"Given plenty of coin," I told her, "and the name 'Sokolli Pasha' to throw around, the task was easy and also quite pleasant."

I did not say, but I prided myself that my taste was more to a woman's liking than Ali's had been. At first I had hoped for praise from the master, but I knew enough now not to hope for that. Still, I found I wanted praise for a job done well and with sensitivity. It was all I could do to keep from spoiling the surprises to get praise from Esmikhan before we got home.

"While in the market," I hurried on with the story to resist the temptation, "I saw two men of my native land. In their feathers and hose, they stood out as if they had been silly peacocks in a crowd of sensible, domestic hens. Now I was thankful for my somber clothes—the long robes I had feared at first would surely trip me—and I hoped to avoid their notice, for I was suddenly burning with shame. Still, I was as exotic for them as they were for me and, as they took no care to guard their speech, I heard one say to the other, 'By Jesù, there's another one!'

" 'Poor devil. He's a young one, too.'

" 'And very fair-skinned. I'll bet he's a Christian lad the damned Turks have stolen and lopped. Say, try some of your Christian tongue on him, Brother Angelo.'

"With this encouragement, the second Venetian began to babble mass-Latin at me which anyone born from Ireland to the shores of Crete should have stopped for. I ignored it studiously, however, by pretending to take an interest in some pink satin in one of the shops. Actually, I had found much nicer stuff at a better price not half an hour before, and it was a difficult pretense to maintain in the face of a pushy shopkeeper. But, I felt, worth the trouble.

" 'Leave him, Angelo,' the first of my countrymen said at last. 'He doesn't understand. Must be a Christ-killing Jew, a Protestant heretic, or some other such soul, already damned before the Turks got to him.'

"I mused about my reaction to this meeting for some time. How I had screamed out during the long, awful summer of my pain for just such people to hear and rescue me. I had used the very same words of the mass, ready to let my savior be a Spaniard or a Pole, anything, so long as he was Christian. But he was a Christian who butchered me, at least he had been once, and for long enough to make a mockery of the liturgy I had hoped would save me. And he was Italian, too.

"Lest I make the mistake of condemning all my race, that very same day fate sent another young Italian into the market. When first I saw him, I wanted to turn and run, to avoid another scene like the one I had just escaped. But this young man approached graciously and addressed me in a stilted but polite Turkish. I couldn't very well pretend not to understand that—indeed, it became my sudden concern to speak my Turkish flawlessly and without an accent so as to maintain my anonymity. When the young man actually used the word *'ustadh'* to call me, I could not refuse, and met him in the eye."

"Why should he not call you *ustadh?*" Esmikhan asked. "It means 'teacher, master.' "

"Of course."

"It is a term of great respect."

"Of course."

"And *khadim* are often addressed so."

"I knew that, of course, but it was the first time I had been called that, and I was flattered. From one of my own country!"

"I shall always call you *ustadh,* if it pleases you, Abdullah."

"If Allah wills, I may always deserve it from your tongue, lady. But you must try and imagine the shock it was to hear it from one of my own country.

"When I met his eye, I saw clearly that he meant no mockery, although he still struggled with the depths of a void he saw in something he could treat neither as a man nor as a woman. I did not blame him. I face the same struggle myself.

" '*Ustadh,* please. Will you come and join me in a sherbet?'

"A lemon-flavored glass of his own sat on a small table under the sherbet seller's grape arbor, where it had obviously been for some time. The snow had melted to water, and the flavors had separated. I was not the first to decline him. I even refused a seat, which made his face grow hot and his Turkish stiffer and more confused, but I did agree to hear him out."

"So what did he have to say?" Esmikhan asked.

"He introduced himself as Andrea Barbarigo, aide to the present Venetian ambassador to the Porte. Well, I needed to hear no more."

"You knew him?"

"I knew him at once—as the youngest of that proud and ancient family. I smiled ironically to myself, for Sofia Baffo—Safiye—had once told me she intended to make a match with the Barbarigos, perhaps with this very young man." I didn't think it was necessary to speak of elopement.

"Safiye?" Esmikhan interrupted here. "Safiye knew this young man, too?"

"Yes. Long ago and far away."

"Knew him so well she wanted to arrange a marriage with him?"

"If that name was any more to her than the very symbol of Venetian power and wealth."

Esmikhan stared off into the night in the direction she imagined even now Safiye to be working a woman's mysteries on her brother. Perhaps it was also the direction she imagined her future husband to lie and she wondered about her ability to work those same mysteries. Her eyes and voice were filled with that wonder as she said, "Such a strange land you and Safiye come from. Where a girl may think of choosing her own husband. No wonder Safiye is so—so much the way she is."

I suppose I should have explained to her that all Venetian girls were not like that. Only Safiye, and she would be an anomaly in whatever land she found herself. Instead, I referred back to the young Italian nobleman, and told how in my heart I had thought, "There, but for the wrath of God, am I."

It was from Andrea Barbarigo's hands, of course, that I had received the notice of Governor Baffo's offer of ransom for his daughter. I told Esmikhan about that, and again she wondered at the ways of a land that would foster such a lack of devotion in a daughter. Selim was not much of a father actually, and Esmikhan had probably never sat upon his knee or even received so much as a kiss of affection from him, but she could not believe that any daughter would tear up such a message from her sire instead of treating it with reverence. Again, I could have said, but did not, that this was only Safiye we were talking about, and not Venice as a whole.

At last, as the lamp burned very low, I made a confession to this saint of naive but deep and perfect understanding. "There is yet one more person I met in the bazaar."

This was pushing time back, back closer to the horrors of Pera. *Close, close enough,* I thought, this occasion when I was on my first training errands for Salah ad-Din's wife. But then I looked into my lady's face and decided, *not too close.*

"And I must say he was the very last person on earth I wanted to face in this, my new condition. Only my father and my uncle could have made me wish more that I had never been born rather than to see the hurt in their eyes when they learned that their line and their hopes in me were extinguished. I had nightmares, actually, when the delirium was on me, of just those eyes. . . .

"It was in Pera. That was all the further I was allowed to wander in my training as yet, so he must have crossed over the Golden Horn specially."

"Looking for you."

"Perhaps. In the bazaar in Pera I saw my friend Husayn talking business with some fellow merchant, and though I had longed and cried out for him so during my time of pain, now I immediately turned and fled. The priest in my old parish church in Venice would have liked the image—the sinner flees from the face of God and His final judgment, and cries out for the very mountains to fall on him and hide his shame.

"But it was too late. Husayn had seen me, and he called out my name. The catch of emotion in his voice tripped up my feet. I turned clumsily, helplessly, and, when the little round man flung himself at me like a ball shot from a cannon, he forced the breath from me in a sob.

"At first Husayn wanted me to come home with him. He said that he would find my captor and pay any price, call down the law, petition the Sublime Porte itself for redress.

"I said, 'I can't spare the time.'

" 'You are content with your life? The young lady—that was one thing. But you, my friend, content with such a life—?'

" 'What life is left to me? My time is no longer my own.'

"He said, I noticed, no word of Venetian glass."

"Venetian glass?" My lady asked, but I didn't answer her directly.

"He gave no apology but settled for a pair of seats under the nearest grape arbor. He paid for our sampling of the strong black brew called coffee."

"Coffee? I have not heard of such a drink."

"No. It is new in Constantinople. Very popular among some circles, but frowned upon by the most pious. Let me tell you, lady, it is not worth the trouble in my opinion. And that day it curdled my stomach.

"Anyway, over this coffee, Husayn's friendliness and joy was matched only by his delicacy. 'How I worried for you,' he said. 'I went to the slave market the very next morning, and they pretended never to have heard of you. It was then that I assumed something like this must have happened. Our laws forbid it, and raids are made almost monthly, but the practice cannot be stopped, to our great shame. It is too profitable.'

"Husayn would have been willing to stop all mention of my condition here, and speak on as man and man. But I found myself unable to do so. It was I who persisted, weeping, 'My friend, O my friend. Why didn't you seek me out? Why didn't you come to find me? You can't imagine the pain I have suffered.'

" 'I knew I would find you sooner or later,' Husayn replied. 'If Allah were willing.'

" 'What about me? Your Allah showed no mercy to me at all.'

" 'True, it may not seem so. But when your apprenticeship is over, you may be purchased by a great man, a great master. Who can say what doors may be open for you if you please him in your service? Allah willing, you will become a greater man with him than you could ever become with me.'

"I choked with sobs on his word 'man,' but I said no more. What was the use? Husayn had not changed at all since I'd seen him last, whereas I myself had stepped from a world of light into utter darkness and was groping, helplessly trying to find my way."

As if heaven itself suddenly took a hand in the telling, the lamp over our heads now sputtered itself out, and I finished my tale in darkness. "I cut our meeting short and left feeling it would be the last I ever wanted. Husayn might seek me out again, but I would have difficulty trusting that friendship. No doubt he will only bother if he thinks my position in Sokolli Pasha's household could win him some favor."

"You are being hard on your friend," Esmikhan said. "A friend who was more than a father to you? How can you value him so cheaply?"

In the dark she was disembodied, like a voice of the spirits. But I ignored her optimism and finished the tale in two short, hard lines. " 'Do you realize,' Husayn said as a parting offering, 'You have been speaking Turkish all this time? You have learned it remarkably well.'

" 'I am forced to,' I replied, and walked on toward my master's house."

XLII

BAFFO'S DAUGHTER THRUST out her lower lip in a luscious, round pout. Had we been in the company of men, its effect would have been devastating. All resolve, will, and concentration would vanish before the passion of slaking their appetites upon that fruit. One would gladly give one's throat to the ax just to have the sweet, cool juice trickle down it.

The effect of that lip on women, too, was not negligible. Esmikhan stammered in confusion at the sight and could only repeat lamely, "But I gave that necklace to charity, O sweetest Safiye." She knew before she said them that her words would not be accepted but, by her life, in her simplicity, she was incapable of understanding why not.

"Then you must go back to Inönü and get it." Again the words curled like fruit syrup over that pout.

"I can't do that."

"Of course you can. If charity really means so much to you, you can give them some other trinket, but that silver chain goes too well with my blue jacket for me to allow you to throw it away on peasants. As I've said, I mean to wear the blue tonight—for your brother, Esmikhan. I've all but promised him. You must go back and get it."

"How . . . how can I do that?" Esmikhan asked. She had to ask, for the very thought was unthinkable to her. But she said it as if apologizing for her stupidity. She knew no way around the matter which to Safiye, with her superhuman powers, seemed so easy.

"You simply open your mouth and tell your *khadim* where you want to go. A fine pasha's wife you'll make if you can't bid eunuchs."

Now I was caught in a vise between those two looks, the devastating seduction of Baffo's daughter's eyes, and the doe-like pleading of Esmikhan's. Was my lady really going to ask me to do such a thing? Yes, she was. She could not resist. But at a deeper level, I read her plea, "Take care of me, Abdullah. Think for me. I am in over my head and must depend on your strength."

It was not my place to speak until spoken to, but I decided something had to be said before Esmikhan did bring the request forth from the confusion of her mind and then any-

thing I said could only be interpreted as insubordination.
"It is curious," I murmured, as if to myself, like no more
than Esmikhan's conscience. "For all these days, your over-
tures to your friend have been soundly ignored. And now,
suddenly, Safiye makes such demands of your friendship that
she expects you to put it above the charity of Allah."

The almond glance Baffo's daughter sent me was coated
with poison. She sank back into the roominess of her sedan,
a cabin which, at Murad's insistence, would carry two in a
snug embrace. It was borne between two horses who would
not blush or blink if their burden rocked vigorously on route.
I took her withdrawal as a retreat, but I should have known
better. Before I knew quite what was happening, Safiye had
enticed Esmikhan in after her and given orders to her eunuchs.

"See?" I heard from the muffled interior as the door
snapped shut. "I will go back to Inönü with you, Esmikhan."

My hand went instinctively to the great curved dagger that
is as much a eunuch's uniform as his fur-lined robe. But was
I to use it against another woman and her eunuchs? That
seemed ridiculous. Foolhardy, in fact, in the face of those particular eunuchs. Murad had hand-picked a trio of monstrous
hulks, thinking, no doubt, that a brute physical siege would
be the greatest threat to his favorite. They hadn't the brains
among them to ward off the simplest stratagem. They were
as obedient as lapdogs to their mistress; their remarkable
musculature must have kept them men enough to be affected
by her eyes and her pouts.

So I could do little more than run alongside the sedan saying, "But what about His Royal Highness Prince Murad and
the rest of the party?"

I waved my hand in the direction of the next hillock where
the people in question had halted. The thirty janissaries in
their road-dusty red stood out against the throbbing blue of

a clear autumn sky, their division banners limp in the breathless air. Every one had the rump of his horse and the white featureless wedge of the back of his headdress to us with the discipline of the Sultan's Friday parade to prayers. If the prince allowed his mistress to indulge in her present fancy and go back to the rear to speak with his sister, why would they gainsay him? The greater discipline they demonstrated now, the more likely they were in time to earn a harem of their own to indulge.

"What will they think? What will they do?" I panted.

To this I received the careless reply, "We'll be back with them before noon. They will hardly miss us."

The echo of the hills around, the pleating of my desperate footfalls into the folds of the dried, brown grassland were of more response than our guard.

"The march will be halted no more than a few hours," Safiye continued to chant cheerily while I had lost my breath to running. "Tonight, when Murad has rested a little, stirred by concern—unnecessary but delightful. . . .Tonight, with me in that silver necklace. . . I swear by Allah, all shall be forgiven—tonight."

I stumbled along after the sedan, its drivers and its eunuchs, over the steps we had just covered that morning—up a fair-sized hillock and down into the dry stream bed beyond it. The bed could not always be dry, for its banks threw up a thick growth of oaks and shrubbery. Though a good number of leaves had already been lost and crunched to pinkish powder beneath our feet, the dry, gray branches had the screening effect of harem lattices. The rest of the party could not fathom what was afoot within this sanctuary until it was all but over.

The copse also hid the horses and dusty turbans of a band of brigands.

XLIII

THE BRIGANDS WERE a ragged lot, as bristling with irregular knives and pikes and bows as their homespun woolen shalvars must have felt on their legs. I would learn later that they had, in fact, been following us for days, but the heady threat of the thirty-janissary escort had kept them invisible. A lone sedan guarded by four eunuchs, however, they could swallow as easily as one does a gulp of water on a hot summer's day.

Two of Safiye's eunuchs were dispatched at once, and the third incapacitated by an arrow to his right shoulder. I suppose their fearsome size and demeanor made them necessary targets.

Personally, I skidded for cover under the belly of the sedan, pressing up against one *khadim* as the death whistle left him.

The horses bearing the sedan were gentle beasts; they'd had no training at all for the battlefield, and the smell of blood sent them rearing at once. The sedan rocked dangerously, and the occupants, who were still ignorant of the precise nature of their predicament, knocked against the sides like a pair of beans in a rattle, and shrieked in fear.

My first reaction, like that of the other eunuchs, had been to go for my dagger, in spite of its futility against ten men armed to the teeth. But soon I realized the best thing for Esmikhan's immediate safety was to calm the horses, which I proceeded to do. The brigands appreciated the gesture; at least they relaxed the tension on their bows. And probably I presented such a harmless figure that they felt easy ignoring me. Their greatest concern now became not to risk any unnecessary injury to prime horseflesh.

As soon as the sedan was steady enough, Safiye opened the door, oblivious of her unveiled face, and seeing no one at first but me, began to rail in a mixture of Turkish and Venetian that I should stop being prudish and let them continue on their innocent road.

Her shrill tones prickled the horses' ears. The beasts' eyes rolled and their feet skidded off the ground again. This time Safiye would have suffered more serious injury, for there was no upholstered wall between her and the ground. Fortunately, the leader of the brigands saw the danger, too. He urged his horse as if it had been a glove on his hand, and brought it alongside the sedan in a moment. When she tumbled, Safiye tumbled into his arms. The fellow dragged her up onto the horse in front of him and fought her long limbs and her shrill lungs into obedience with skill, with a length of rope, a kerchief, and also with a grin that declared he had not had so much fun since the adventures of his youth.

His comrades, too, took what enjoyment they could at his antics. But they did not let it interfere with their haste to cut loose the horses, unpack Safiye's caskets of jewels and clothing, pry off the sedan's brass fixtures and in general do the work of locusts in half the time.

Soon there was nothing left to unpack but the little princess still cowering in the rear of the sedan, clinging to the handles for dear life, her veils muffling her from head to toe. It fell to a fat brigand to bend in through the narrow doorway and try to extract her. He was so big, he found it difficult to maneuver in the cramped quarters women call home for hours at a stretch. More than once he had to come up for air, red faced and basted with sweat. He looked sheepish about his tactics, which were those of a child trying to get a kitten down from a tree.

"Here, let me at her," said the dashing young man whom I would learn was the lead brigand's son. He drew his sword as he shoved the big man out of the way.

"Come out of there," the young man bellowed, "or I'll cut your throat."

Esmikhan whimpered, but she did not obey him, either. That show of force would have brought any man around, but a well-bred young lady, though she may be vague about the details, knows there are worse fates than dying by the sword.

Her whimper brought me to action. "Excuse me, sir." I hardly flinched when the young man turned his sword on me instead. "If you will allow me one of the horses, sir, I will bring the young lady wherever you wish, and in safety."

The young man snorted in anger, but he stepped out of the way. He was not stupid. The sword was not making its usual swift progress, and time was running short.

I bent into the sedan and gently took Esmikhan's hands in mine. Then I carefully helped her up and out. I readjusted a corner of her veils, which were really in no danger of revealing anything, but the gesture helped to reassure her and steadied her feet upon the ground. Then I led her to the horse and lifted her up.

"Oh, Abdullah! I've never ridden before."

She thrashed her slippers in fear. They kicked me in the face and the horse skittered. She tumbled back into my arms.

"It's been years for me, too," I confessed. "At least since I've been bareback." I didn't say, but the thought brought my stomach to my throat: *Who knew but what riding a horse would cause me pain I could not endure?*

The young brigand clopped his horse up behind me and tickled my ribs with the point of his blade. "You need some help here, eunuch?"

"We will manage," I assured him. I kept my face so only my lady could read my terror. She nodded, ready to try again, for my sake.

Sidesaddle clearly wasn't going to work. But then I remembered that this was no European woman who would expect such niceties. My lady was even supplied with *shalvar* to make parting her legs easier. And I noticed, besides, that the horse was a gelding.

"It's you and me together, fellow," I calmed him, and got Esmikhan up astride.

Then, hitching my robes and getting a good hold of the mane, I took a deep breath and swung up in front of her. The bony ridges of the beast's withers met my pelvis with a jar. I waited for the pain; there was none.

The young brigand shrugged his amazement, sneered under the vanity of a shaggy moustache at my rumpled robes, but waited no longer to herd us on after the others.

I heard a loud crack followed by a groan behind me and turned to look, nearly losing grip as the horse lurched the opposite direction under me. Our janissaries were now in view, driving to the attack, and the fat brigand had taken a musket ball in the jugular which spurted like a fountain. Esmikhan clung to me tighter and buried her face between my shoulder blades. The firearms with which the sultan's men were armed could not be fired while riding, but I knew I must concentrate on working the horse and keeping our balance or we ran the risk of getting in the way of a bullet as well.

The young brigand got off our tail long enough not to aid his fallen comrade but to claim the dying brigand's horse and tie its reins to the rear of his own saddle. He fired one taunting arrow at the janissaries, but we were already out of range. The shrubbery closed behind us like a veil, often close enough to whip my legs. Along with it closed our hopes of rescue.

Within minutes we had come to another stream bed, this

one ankle-deep in water. We crossed it, again, again, and again. Then we doubled back and crossed a very treacherous expanse of sheer stone. Within half an hour I would have defied even a hawk to follow us.

For Murad and his party, I'm sure it must have seemed as if we'd vanished from the face of the earth.

XLIV

BY EVENING, WE had ridden far up on the plateau in an area where the gray-white rock folded with the ruggedness of gathers in sackcloth. Tucked into one of these folds, approached only by the narrowest of defiles, was the brigands' hold. Like a needle lost by a careless seamstress, it could there prick the wearer repeatedly, but finding and extracting the thing would prove no easy business.

I also noticed that these folds of rocks, like folds in a garment, held dampness even when all around them was bone dry. By the time we arrived at our destination, we'd been rained on more than once with enough respite between only to catch a chill in our damp clothes. Dank wet odored the horses and spiked their hair in places like that of a hedgehog.

Yet another foggy drizzle was obscuring all but the horses immediately in front and in back when I realized we would finally be allowed to halt.

I'd tried to judge direction by the sun when I could see it, but clouds and then an early sunset brought on by high peaks left me now at a total loss. Distance was a factor, too. Many things could make me misjudge, but every jarring ache in my body as I eased off the horse convinced me. We'd covered more terrain since our capture than the sedan chairs had allowed us in the past four days.

The milling of the horses set loose a soup of mud that dragged at my feet. No food or rest since midmorning: my head reeled. If I'd been relieved that my mutilation hadn't hurt at first, that was no consolation now. My hips and knees would not unbend and between them pulsed a pain that caused periodic spasms I could not control.

But when I was no longer there for her to cling to, Esmikhan tumbled with exhaustion from the horse. At the last moment, I managed to open my arms to catch her. Dragging my breath in between my teeth with a hiss, I broke the barrier of my own pain and straightened up. Then I carried my lady gently over the muddy yard and into the shelter offered by a small hut before our captors could order me to do so.

The hut was actually quite a bit bigger than it appeared from the outside, else there would hardly have been room for us and all the brigands, too. The miserable heap of human-laid stone surrounding the low doorway served only as a front room to further rooms let naturally into the mountainside as caves.

Two people waited by the fire in the main room for the brigand's return. The first was the leader's wife. A very thin woman, she fearlessly faced all those men without a veil and struck even the largest of them away from her soup pot with her spoon. This fierce manner caused Esmikhan to shrink even closer into her veils and my arms. To my lady, such a woman was as unnatural an apparition as a eunuch is to the Occidental.

The second occupant disquieted me more. He wore the plain brimless woolen cap of a mendicant holy man and rags that left his hairy arms bare. He did seem a little too-well fleshed for the role, but what disconcerted me most was the way he looked at me—as if he recognized me, and I should recognize him in return. Mystics always unnerved me. They seemed the same among Muslims as among Christians: their every look and stance threatened my soul with similar entrapment.

I had enough to worry about at that moment with the entrapment of my body. I was almost glad when the brigands commanded me and my burden out of their cramped common room. I trudged through the low doorway where they pointed me and into one of the back rooms. Even though it was away from the fire and populated already by half a dozen goats, it was as close to escape as I could hope for under the circumstances.

Safiye was likewise ordered into the room with us, but she was not so ready to make it her home. Her first priority toward comfort was to stretch all the kinks of the ride out of her long limbs. She did so with the grace and movements of a dancer at a feast, but restlessly.

Esmikhan could not have stood if she had to. One particularly inquisitive nanny made my charge whimper with fear by coming up for a trial nibble of lady's veils. Esmikhan had only seen goats roasted whole and docile on beds of saffron rice before, and the sharp odor of their life was enough to send her into shivers.

I shooed the creature off and then did my best to make my lady comfortable on a heap of dried grass—which is what I suppose the goats thought she was in my arms. Fortunately, my lady was exhausted enough that once she'd gotten used to the burn of goat in her nostrils, she fell sound asleep within moments. I gently opened her wrapper and veils somewhat and was pleased to find that they had kept her other garments from getting too damp to sleep in.

Sounds of someone entering the room made me hastily draw the veils again, but it was only the brigand's wife bearing soup—green and fragrant with mint—flat bread, and cheese. She returned moments later with a pair of musty but warm blankets, and only sniffed skeptically when I thanked her as if she wanted to say, "Yes, well, you can thank me if we come out of this alive."

I remarked to myself that in spite of the haul of riches her menfolk had brought home with them, the labor of that single peasant woman had provided us with the things that were most important: this good goat cheese, the bread, the rough woven blankets, and kilims brightly dyed with red madder.

"At least it does not appear that they mean to let us starve to death."

I meant my tone to deliver a comment on Safiye's nonchalance. The brigand's wife wasn't even out of the room before Baffo's daughter sat down on the floor and began to eat with great appetite.

"Of course not," Safiye said between thick bites of bread. "What good are dead hostages?"

"We're to be held as hostages then? For what?"

"Ransom. And revenge." Safiye's appetite for those words was obviously no less than for the soup and cheese.

The quick ride out of Murad's earshot was all that Safiye needed, so it seemed, to take stock of the new situation and to plot her future accordingly. Not too much further on, she had gotten the brigand leader to ungag her, then untie her, and then her probing into the situation began in earnest.

"Surely you noticed Crazy Orhan" (by this familiarity she meant our captor) "is missing his right eye."

As a matter of fact, I had not noticed this detail during the heat of our capture. Later examination showed me that his face served to strike terror rather than compassion in the observer. The black, burned-out socket was camouflaged to the casual glance by a sagging lid and the shadow of simian brows. Black, too, were his boar-bristle beard, mustachios that could be knotted thrice behind his neck, and a rudely shaved forehead from which the hair appeared to have been torn out in clumps. A saggy felt cap and a rag of red turban too small for a bestial breadth of face completed the picture.

"You know how he lost it?" Safiye asked.

I did not.

"Your Sokolli Pasha did it. With a red-hot iron."

I gave an expression of disbelief.

"Yes, it's true. Oh, years ago, of course. You wouldn't expect a pasha to dirty his hands with such business. But years ago, when he was a janissary in his first service. The man who was Grand Vizier then, Ibrahim Pasha, under the shadow of the Sultan Suleiman's good graces, began to confiscate the holdings of honest, faithful Turks such as Orhan for his own purposes. A certain dervish came preaching to the men to stand up for their age-old rights, which they finally had no choice but to do."

I shivered a little at the thought of that dervish in the next room with double meaning in his eyes.

"Well, they were no match for Ibrahim and his Christian-boy janissaries. Those who were not slaughtered on the battlefield were blinded or incapacitated in other brutal ways so they would not rise again."

"I'm sure Sokolli Pasha was only fulfilling his duty," I said in defense.

"Yes. The duty of a lackey to fulfill the wishes of a greedy master."

"Still Orhan is missing only one eye, not both."

"It seems the mercy of Allah called Sokolli away for a moment in the midst of his deed. When he returned, Orhan, in all his unspeakable pain, had managed to escape by hiding among the dead, by crawling over thorns and stones with the fluid of his eye running down his face all the while. But of course he never got his land back, so one eye is little consolation."

"I am sure Sokolli Pasha did only what was necessary," I found myself coming to my master's defense again. "He is a good man. His pious foundations exist from one end of the empire to the other."

"Yes. And who lines up for bread at those places? Men his hand blinded or lamed so they cannot dig for their own bread. Women his hand made widows. Children—not heathen children, but the children of Turks—children his hand left fatherless and without inheritance."

I looked uneasily over at Esmikhan and was glad to find her still asleep. I did not want her hearing this.

"Do not worry for Esmikhan," Safiye said, watching my eyes. "She has been saved from a much worse fate. Now she will never have to marry that pasha."

"Surely you can't believe Orhan will succeed in his plans for us."

"Why should he not?"

"He is one man. One half-blind man with a handful of followers against an empire. You cannot believe, Ibrahim Pasha or no Ibrahim Pasha, that Sultan Suleiman—he the West calls Magnificent—will let this happen to his own granddaughter in his own backyard. And what about your precious Murad, eh?"

Safiye shrugged the name off as if it were only water. "Orhan has the hand of Allah behind him in the secrets of these mountain passes."

"And in the inspiration of mad dervishes. The time for such fanatic leadership is passed, here in Islam as in our native Italy where Savonarola met his heretic's doom in our father's time."

"Veniero, it is not like you to be such a cold realist. You were always full of such dreamy idealism before. You were going to save me from the Turkish pirates. You were going to climb walls to save me." She fluttered her eyelids at me and dropped into a sultry Italian.

I refused to let such gestures have their desired effect. I spat in anger. "Thanks to you, I have since had done to me something that cured me of such idealism."

"Now, now, are we bitter?"

"By God, I have a right to be. And you, Baffo's daughter. Just look at you. One moment you want to traipse halfway across Anatolia for a silly necklace to entice one man, the next you are willing to throw your lot with a total stranger. By God, you are like a pat of butter; you pick up the taste and smell of whatever garlicky, oniony man handles you."

Safiye tossed her hair—in the half light it did have the rich color butter gets in spring—as if I'd given her a compliment. "It will not do to underestimate the power of Crazy Orhan," she said simply. "He is a man seethed in a lust for vengeance these twenty years. And we are his captives. Murad is *farsakh* upon *farsakh*'s ride from here."

"Yes," I said, and the weight of this knowledge pried me up from the food and led me to Esmikhan's side. Something fearful in my lady's dreams made her call out and thrash away her veils as if at invisible demons.

XLV

"THE BOY HAS gone where? You let him go all the way to Constantinople on his own—with this kidnapping on his head, by Allah!"

"He is not a boy any longer, woman. He is a man." Crazy Orhan tried to appease his wife's wrath, and he quoted to her a familiar proverb, " 'If you do not give a man a man's business, he will take it for himself.' He asked to be the one to take our demands to Sokolli—may Allah take both of his eyes—and to the Sultan."

"They will kill him as soon as they look at him!" The woman wrung her hands.

"I gave him some of the trappings off the litter, and if that's not enough I should hope he has sense to steal until he gets all he needs to buy himself an envoy into the Porte. If he hasn't the sense to take such simple precautions, well, he's no son of mine, and I blame his manhood—if you can call it that—all on your womanish upbringing."

"Oh, and I looked to this horrible risk of yours to at least bring the boy a bride. Until now, your blood's been too hot with revenge to see to that simple father's duty toward his son. 'No girl but one worthy of the noble blood in his veins,' you said. Very well. And I prayed it would slake your awful thirst for Sokolli's blood at last, after all these years, that we might have some peace and live like normal mortals for a change. Snatch Sokolli's bride from under his nose. Defile that Christian fiend's honor and the girl at once and, incidentally, give your son the granddaughter of the Sultan to wife. After all, that is no less than he deserves. But now I see, I see. You are determined to go to your grave without progeny and I must resign myself to Allah's will."

In such shrewish words, Safiye first learned the brigand's designs for Esmikhan. But she never bothered to tell us, who clung in the back as to the safety of our native harem, fighting off goats, fleas, and bedbugs alike. Safiye could not remain confined like that. She had to be out and about and our captors gave her quite free rein for they had no fear that she could possibly escape the fastness of their hideout. Indeed, escape was, at present, the last thing on her mind. This was not because she feared the wilds about us, but because she relished too much the wilds in the midst of which we found ourselves.

The head brigand saw Safiye's almond eyes watching this exchange between him and his wife, and it threw him into a rage. Only the three of them were in the room. There was no threat to the wife's pride in a young captive girl, but there was to the brigand's.

"I, Crazy Orhan, bring the rulers of this world to their knees!" he cried, punctuating his words by hurling the closest thing to hand—a wooden truncheon—in his wife's direction. It fell harmlessly but with a greatly satisfying crash among her pots and milking pails. "Can I not have some respect in my own home?"

The wife set about to clean up the mess as if after the tantrum of a young child. Her silence was hardly one of deep impression.

Safiye, however, ventured into that silence with as much awe and respect as any words could bring forth. "Oh, my master. Is it true that Allah has favored you with but a single son in which you place all your hopes for the future? By my life, such a great man as yourself should not rest so content.

If one wife cannot give his heart's desire to him, what prevents him from taking another?"

The wife laughed scornfully, partly at Safiye's accent, which sounded silly and pretentious on her ears, and partly at the notion that any other woman in the world would be such a fool as to let herself fall into the drudgery that was the life of brigand's wife.

Orhan was rendered more thoughtful. The word "master" from those carefully pouting lips soothed his rage in a way no other sound ever had, and her courtly tones put in his mind a higher, more worthy life than that to which fate had condemned him. He tried to revive his anger and stormed out of the hut, feigning the emotion. But the way he rubbed his burned-out eyelid—a tender spot on his soul, if no longer on his body—destroyed the camouflage.

"Yes, get outside and cool off," the wife snorted in contempt.

Crazy Orhan turned back to the room now in a high state of agitation that, had he not been given his nickname for other reasons, would have given it to him then. Yet another day had gone by with no word from his son, yet another day with the nervous sensation of the Sultan's women beneath his roof, and his wife would treat these things like child's play.

"Another word from you," he said dangerously, "and I will have your shrewish gizzard." The woman opened her mouth and he stopped her. "No. I don't even want to hear your whining apologies."

His wife smiled knowingly and pretended to be afraid until her man's back was gone from the room. Then she turned her violence onto Safiye instead. "Look at those eyes," she sneered. "A slut's eyes, squandering what the labor of honest women has bought for her. Whore! I see those eyes, like dice, risking all on a single roll. Whore, I see."

Safiye could have escaped to the back room, but she did not. She sat taking the abuse calmly, almost with delight, for its vicarious effect on the brigand, just outside the door, was not lost on her. She had asked for and received, however grudgingly, the loan of the woman's broken wood comb to substitute for her jewel-studded one that had gone with the brigand's son to Constantinople. She made certain the brigand was in the hut when she cleaned its teeth of the black and gray strands as if of years of accumulated dust. Then she sat, for hours it seemed, combing out her yards of gold. She combed with the thoughtlessness that in reality bespeaks a deep self-absorption. Such an absorption only workers of spells lapse into over their amulets and piles of golden, fruitful grain in the back recesses of the marketplace.

"Here," the wife said, reaching the end of all patience. "Here, girl. You grow pink-cheeked and fair on the toil and sweat of my hands. Why don't you make yourself useful for a change instead of cluttering my kitchen with your demon-colored hair?" And she thrust a spindle at her.

Safiye took it, trying to oblige. "But what is it?" she asked.

"A spindle, stupid girl," the woman sneered in triumph. Orhan was in the doorway, within earshot, and he could see how stupid this baggage of his was.

"A spindle?" Safiye did not know the word, and held the tool gently but clumsily so that all the previous work on it was in danger of being lost.

"Of all the simpleminded . . . !" The woman snorted, snatching the spindle back to save her last weeks' efforts.

Safiye cried out—in affected alarm; there is no chance that she was really wounded.

"And who is so simpleminded but you, peasant!" The brigand shoved his wife away from Safiye with a snarl. "Can't you imagine that there are women in this world who have never roughened their hands upon a spindle?"

"Useless leaches, dressed in the sweat of others," the woman snapped back, "as you, Orhan, have said yourself so many times."

"There are words in the Turkish language this girl knows that would send your simple head spinning, woman. As Allah is my witness, they would set you head spinning with their luxury, though she is but a newcomer to this country and this language."

"And you are so fluent in the language of luxury," the woman mocked, in the fury of the moment quite careless of her gizzard. " 'Bath,' for instance. Now there's a luxury you're a stranger to, and I'm sure the fact hasn't missed the girl. 'Bath, bath, bath.' Now whose head is spinning? I dare say you are even afraid of water, for Allah knows, I've never seen you come near it."

The brigand rubbed his missing eye, but only for a moment. In the next moment he had snatched Safiye to her feet, sending the comb flying from her hand. It broke in two upon the floor, but Safiye, who had cried out in alarm at a violent movement not minutes before, said nothing.

"I shall show you who's a peasant," the brigand said.

"I bet you're afraid of water, like a cat," his wife retorted.

"I'll show you!" the brigand said again. "I'm every bit as good as a Sultan's son, and can bathe whenever I damn well feel like it. Not only that, but I can bathe with Murad's very own attendant—whenever I feel like it. A pox on you, woman."

And with that he dragged Safiye from the hut.

After the year's first bout of stormy weather, it had turned balmy again. But this false return to summer and the warm colors of the leaves could not make up for the fact that the little mountain stream, running a hand deep over iron-cold slabs of stone, was kept from turning to ice overnight only by its movement. Even then, with a morning of sun on its back, it was a far, far cry from the blood-heat in which Murad liked to soak. However, Orhan was nothing if not immune to physical discomfort, especially when his pride was at stake. His clothes were off and he was in that water in a moment.

But it was not his wife, long out of earshot, almost out of memory, against whom he railed in that state. "Prince Murad, you're a woman compared to Orhan, the Crazy One. By Allah, yes, you are."

Safiye was left standing alone on the banks and I dare say that, braggart though he was, Orhan would have left her there. A mountain stream was his element; with a woman of courtly manners he was a stranger and quite honestly afraid of her. He even avoided her almond eyes as he fumed against her lover, and would have done so till the bath was over, had not a soft noise and movement in that direction wrested his attention. Safiye had removed her robe and stood there in underblouse and shalwars.

"I thought it best," she said. "There are pearls on it, and surely, master, you would not want to risk having them wash away downstream."

The brigand saw how the breath of a wind through the sheer underblouse tickled her nipples into tight little peaks and his heart pounded in an emotion to which he was a stranger. He called the emotion fear or shame, and clambered out of the water and onto a sun-warmed stone on the other bank to escape it. More disconcerting still was the state of his manhood, that thing he had boasted of all his life for the great control he held over its virility and it over womankind in general. He sought to hide it from her, but in a moment she had crossed the stream to him.

Even mystics relishing martyrdom will ease into impalement. But Safiye delved coaxingly on, once or twice, before she took him in completely. With her little white knobs of breast bouncing before his face, she whispered hoarsely, "Taste the pearls you've stolen from Prince Murad."

Orhan caught one as a gasp escaped his lips, and his nails clawed against the stone in a tarantella of gratification.

The dervish, his meditation among the trees disturbed, moved silently away, thoughtfully smoothing his scraggly moustache into his scraggly beard. But I myself, who could not escape, heard through cracks in the cavern walls, many another time over the next few days when Orhan reveled in the spoils of Murad.

XLVI

ESMIKHAN, BLESS HER heart, was of such a nature that she found it impossible to believe that any woman, Safiye in particular, would ever stay long of her own free will in a place where her honor was even threatened, let alone compromised. Safiye stayed away from us for hours at a time. Well, she was braver than Esmikhan herself, but she wasn't wanton. I thought it best not to disillusion my mistress; to protect her even from defilement of the mind seemed to be my duty. But, although we were as yet unaware of what it meant for our personal futures, the day did soon come when the young brigand, Orhan's son, returned from Constantinople.

"But where's my father?" he asked, growing impatient with the tears and thanksgiving of his mother's welcome.

His words threw the woman back into the dark gray mood she'd been laboring under for days now. "Villainy!" she spat into the back of the hut. "Your son is here."

"Coming, coming." Orhan muttered, impatient, sheepish, and came out of a small side room still struggling with the wide bands of his sash.

The young man looked quizzically at his father, but did not comment as he dove headlong into an account of the success of his mission. He had received no firm confirmation of the Porte's willingness to negotiate. Indeed, Sokolli Pasha, at the head of a small army, had left the city in the same hour with the intention of taking the brigands as one takes a castle or a town.

"But we know that is impossible," Orhan said, smiling as he imagined the fastness of his fortress.

"It is indeed," the son replied. "I left them in Inönü. Beyond that town, they have no clue as to where to go, no more than the prince does who has been sitting there a week."

"Good. Yes, they will soon be ready to talk. I give them till midwinter—at the latest."

His deadline grew so much closer that very night; it began to snow.

THE BRIGANDS WERE up late that night. The young man had brought wine from the forbidden Christian vats of Constantinople, and success tasted sweeter, closer than it ever had before. Safiye sat up, too, wishing she could be in front there with our captors, watching the warm glow flared from time to time by raucous laughter in consolation. Esmikhan herself fell into a fitful sleep, scratching, even in her dreams, at the rawness raised by the bedbugs that had snuggled closer for warmth.

I think I must have dozed as well, at least the grasp on my shoulder in the dark came as a surprise. The empty hand I put up to defend myself suddenly found itself fumbling around the hilt of a dagger.

It was a strange voice, yet a voice strange in its almost-familiarity, that assured me in the darkness, "It's not your own dagger. I'm sorry. They guard that too well, because of the jewels in the hilt. But I think you will find this more serviceable than that eunuch's weapon time and form have atrophied to little more than show."

I realized by this time it was the dervish. He cautioned against unnecessary speech and then spoke on hastily in his hoarse yet mystical whisper. "They mean to give your young lady to Orhan's son. This very night. You must fight out of it. There is no other way. For the sake of her virtue and your life, I pray Allah may side with you in this."

I weighed the weapon in my hand and found it heavy and good. It sparked in me feelings of strength and sudden wholeness which I see now were returns to the foolhardiness of youth. But at the time they were gratifying.

I turned to thank my benefactor, but he had disappeared. Surely I would have seen him against the light if he'd gone out the door and back into the main room. But it was too dark to see in the other direction, and even after a few low calls, "*Ya shahim, ya shahim?*", I failed to hear him as distinguished from the stirring of the goats behind me. So I shrugged and went to the brightly lit doorway to observe the situation for myself.

A silence had fallen over the drinking men, and at first I hoped they might have retired for the night or sunken into a stupor over their cups. But it was a silence of heavy anticipation which Crazy Orhan broke with the loud announcement, "Bring in the girl!"

Thus did I learn that the triumphal dishonoring of Sokolli Pasha was to be public, not private. And I realized as two brigands shoved their way past me armed with torches that, dagger or no, against such odds I might not even exist. I could only kill one or at the most two before they finished me off and Esmikhan was left not only honorless, but friendless as well.

"Up, Princess, up!" The men leered with demon faces in the torchlight over her pile of hay. "It's your wedding night."

Esmikhan did not yet comprehend their cruel jest as she stumbled past me. Her feet were still heavy with sleep, yet she was conscious enough to weep over the fact that they had discovered her unveiled. That she had clumsily managed to replace her coverings by the time she was hauled by the elbows into the center of the main room's blinding light was little consolation. Nor could I meet her eyes through those veils to offer comfort, though they pleaded with me to do so. I was as helpless as she.

Directly across the room from me was the door to freedom, and next to it sat Safiye. She had obviously been there quite a while, bare-faced and unashamed in the company of all those men. I guessed she had tasted some of the forbidden wine, too, from the pretty pink glow in her cheeks and the moist sparkle in her eye. Would that they were tears and discomfort for the fate of her friend! But I saw clearly that they were not.

Next to her sat Crazy Orhan, who had given up the place of honor to his son that night. But he had not quite given up control of the assembly with that seat, for he called the next move. "So, my son. To your business! And the best of luck!"

Safiye did not smile at these words as the rest of the company laughed and cheered. But she also did not squirm or look away.

The young man got to his feet and strode up to Esmikhan, vainly trying to huddle in the middle of the room. She was surrounded on all sides, no wall to put her back to, so although she remained on her feet, I could tell she wanted to shrink into the straw mats and rugs on the floor. She looked more tiny and helpless next to that strapping figure of a brigand than I would ever have imagined possible.

The drink and attention made him graceful, that son of Orhan, something of a dancer with a strong bent toward showmanship. He removed Esmikhan's wrapper and veils with a flourish that even her weak struggles and protests could not detract from.

"Take that, you swine-eating Sokolli!" Orhan cried, and his men echoed him.

Esmikhan hid her face in her hands as if she'd been lashed with a whip. The young brigand forced these hands apart and, with her chin caught tight in a vise of thumb and finger, he lifted her pretty round face to the light, and turned it full circuit around the room. Esmikhan kept her large dark eyes— I've often thought them her best feature—tightly closed as if against blinding light, but this did not detract from the company's loud and lusty appreciation of the display.

"O Sokolli, may it burn you as the iron did my eye!" cried the voice of revenge.

Awash with sweat, my hand slipped almost uselessly on the handle of my dagger. But what was I to do? Take this horror as the will of Allah, and simply stand and stare in awe at it? The only other option seemed to be to instantly jump into the center of the room and plunge a knife of mercy into Esmikhan's heart. I might have time then to turn it on myself. If I did not, a dozen brigand hands would very shortly finish the task for me. It would take a great deal of courage, strength I was not sure I could muster. But there seemed no other way. I closed my eyes and silently called on heaven for the attempt, committing myself to Its hands.

Meanwhile, the ruttish dance went on in the center of the room.

Whimpering like a puppy wounded quite to death, Esmikhan managed to break away for a moment. But two or three pairs of even coarser hands handled her until Orhan's son came to reclaim her. This time he was careful to hold her much tighter about the waist. And she did not struggle so much except involuntarily and settled to her fate as does a lamb to the slaughter.

The son of Orhan forced his mouth upon hers as he fumbled with the row of pearls on her bodice. One pearl broke off in the process, and there was a scramble for it among the onlookers. But that business had resolved itself in time for all to appreciate the real prize of this activity. Orhan's son produced it as a conjurer produces an alabaster egg from a basket we thought empty: a round, white breast. That breast could not help but hold itself up in the firmness of youth, though obviously its owner would have made it wither and sag with shame if she could.

The heady atmosphere was sending Orhan to mimic his son on the person of Safiye. Her breasts, too, were exposed and he was already at the drawstring of her shalvars.

Only Crazy Orhan had had a woman in months, perhaps years, and as the audience groaned and shouted its pleasure, I realized that when the son had spent himself at last—he was young and strong and four or five entries were easily within his reach—no power on earth could keep the others from making the revenge their own as well. It would kill my lady, of that I was certain. Yes, better to kill her mercifully now with one blow and what came later to me was of small matter. My life had ended in the dark little house in Pera months ago, anyway. Encouraged by these thoughts, I began to move into position.

"Hey, eunuch! Out of the way! What need have you for a better view, capon?"

The words threw me for a moment into self-doubt, and before I could recover, we were all overcome by a commotion at the other side of the room.

"Daughter of a wanton!" the brigand's wife shrieked.

Her next words were drowned in a shattering of crockery, but those following were more in the same tenor, "Heathen, Allah-cursed and defiled! I'll teach you to go stealing men from honest women!"

More broken crockery, and heavy thuds of things that could not break against the stone walls. Safiye, the target of this attack, was now shrieking in horror and in pain as some of the missiles hit her and drew blood from the arms she raised to shield herself. Somehow she managed to reach the door and find safety in the snow outside.

"Good," the wife said triumphantly. "May you freeze to death."

But her anger was far from spent, and now it was Orhan's turn to be battered. He swore, roared his wife to the devil and his men to his aid. It was in this confusion that I ran to the center of the room, and made use of the dagger. I caught my victim in the ribs under the left arm. Orhan's son's lungs had been exploding upward in laughter. That air now found another, more immediate outlet, and spurted froth mixed thickly with blood.

"Now, lady," I shouted over the din. "We must run."

Alas, even pulled by the hand, Esmikhan refused to budge until she had recovered her precious veils. That gave at least one man time to realize what we were about. He was the one by the door to the goats' room, and, as fate would have it, the one best skilled with the bow. I saw him nock an arrow and lift his weapon to his sights.

We're done for now, I thought, and shoved Esmikhan toward the door in front of me. In a moment, one of us would be transfixed by a deadly shaft. God give me the courage to allow myself to be the one!

I heard the arrow fly and felt something like a lash on my arm that as yet gave no pain, but would very shortly. Imagine my surprise when I saw that arrow continue beyond me without a lag in force. It caught Crazy Orhan himself full in the chest.

Surely the bowman must have drunk more than his share to shoot so badly, I thought as I shoved Esmikhan outside. And I could not resist even the threat of a second arrow flying truer to take a glance as I turned to slam the door shut behind me. I saw the dervish, having likewise armed himself with a dagger, move quickly away from the bowman's side. I saw the bowman slump to the floor—with a slashed throat. The next brigand was too occupied with the sight of the brawl in front of him to turn and look behind; the mendicant stepped into that blind spot and raised his blade.

"By God," I could not help exclaiming. "The man moves like the Angel of Death himself!"

But there was no more time to think about the matter then. I hustled Esmikhan and, since she was there, Safiye, too, across the yard and onto Orhan's stallion. His son's horse I took for myself, but could not begin to race them because I had to lead the girls' by the bridle. At least I was depriving our pursuers of their best horseflesh if I could not use it to full advantage myself.

And snow was falling, lightly, but in thick, wet flakes that quickly filled in our prints. After an hour or so I began to think, except for the fact that I had no idea where we were going, we might just have a chance to escape. Behind me, the girls began to think so, too. Safiye, at least, began to let out her tension in a string of abuse aimed primarily at me.

"Why did you bring us away from the warm safety of Orhan's house?" she fumed. "You are an idealistic fool. We shall be lost here in the mountains. No one will ever find us."

I replied nothing because at the moment I feared she might be right. The snow that covered our tracks also served to hide what primitive sort of trail there might be and moreover prevented me from taking a sailor's bearings from the night sky. All I could do was to make certain each step was lower than the last one, taking us farther and farther down the gorge.

"Veniero, I am likely to freeze to death. My fingers and nose are quite numb. Surely, being by Orhan's nice warm fire, even if we were prisoners, is a better fate than this."

"You should have kept your wrapper and veils with you like a good girl, like Esmikhan Sultan," I could not resist saying. "She seems warm enough. At least she is not moaning to return."

The truth was that the air held that curious sort of warmth it sometimes does in early snowstorms, and exercise and nervous energy made me doubt that even in our unprotected condition we had too much to fear from exposure for a while. The lower we came down the gorge, too, the warmer it became. The precipitation turned first to sleet, and then to rain in heavy, messy droplets. Unfortunately, in this form, it soon soaked us to the skin and that, I had to admit, was unhealthy. Besides, the mud was a more permanent medium for our tracks and a less stable footing for the horses.

Safiye continued. She would not believe Orhan was dead. Could not believe that I, a lone and foolish eunuch, could orchestrate a successful escape. Nor would she heed my entreaties for silence lest our position be betrayed to any pursuers.

"By God, I hope they find us," she said, and shouted once or twice, making the walls of the gorge echo shrilly.

The brigand had the right idea when he bound and gagged her, I thought. *She will surely betray us.* But though I'd killed a man, I didn't know how to go about controlling this woman.

In any case, Safiye's complaints soon became so repetitious that it was easy to turn a deaf ear to them. It was so easy, in fact, that before another hour had passed, Esmikhan was asleep to their singsong. Safiye was too busy thinking of new things to complain about and ways to try and flirt me into listening to them. She did not realize that the head resting against her back was growing heavier and heavier.

But she did notice—and scream—when that head dropped away altogether.

XLVII

ESMIKHAN SCREAMED, TOO, because she landed none too gently in the mud in the stallion's wake. I hastened to pick her up, but could find nothing seriously wrong with her. Nonetheless, she continued to sob bitterly, and to shake in my arms as if death were at her shoulder. Dreams of her recent scrape with dishonor must have haunted her sleep, I decided. In the end, only a promise that I would seek the very first shelter, and hide there until light, seemed to calm her.

"You've hurt your arm," she was able to choke through sobs then, and tentatively touched the spot.

"Just a scratch," I assured her. "The arrow that killed Crazy Orhan."

I took the time to wrap it with a strip of my light under-caftan, although it had long ago stopped bleeding. That comforted her, and she was at last willing to brave the horse's back once more. Much against my better judgment, I kept my promise and when, in the first light of a false dawn I saw an outcropping in the rock above our heads, I led the way to it.

"At least we are out of the gorge," I said.

I did not admit that, it would, in fact, be safer to wait until sunrise so I could judge better which way we should go.

"Can't we have a fire?" Safiye complained.

"By God, now you're really asking to go back to the brigands again. Nothing could give us away more. The smoke from this wet wood. . . ."

But the damp of our clothes was settling in hard now. I could hear Esmikhan's teeth chattering even through her veils. So I sighed and gave in, thinking the activity of gathering wood would keep us warm at least. And since there was very little chance I could get a spark going in such dampness, it would be time to move on before the dream of a fire ever became a reality.

Some dry leaves, twigs, and pine needles blown into the back of the overhang were a help, and I did in fact manage to get some smoke going. Even I was so cold by then that I was glad to see it come. But before my exultation quite carried me away, I heard a noise in the gorge below us. I smothered the smoke with my damp fur cloak. The girls moaned in disbelief and horror, but I motioned them in no uncertain terms to be silent.

Our horses nickered. Old friends of theirs were approaching. Then we heard voices. Soon, although the speakers remained invisible, their words were quite plain.

"There. Up under that overhang. Smoke. Smell it?"

"Yes, by Allah!"

A few moments passed while they climbed closer. In the predawn light, I saw two shadows, possibly three. They were close enough to hit with a stone, and I actually did pick one up, assuming that was what I would have to defend us with.

"No. Look. It's just the girls and the eunuch."

"I told you so. The dervish would not leave a trail like that. A trail like an elephant."

"He left no trail, that dervish."

"Are you sure he isn't with them? The dervish?"

"No, I don't think so."

"He left no trail, I tell you."

"If you ask my opinion, the dervish isn't a man at all. Iblis, a devil, a jinni."

The two other men spoke words to protect themselves from such an eventuality.

"I told you it was foolish to start after him in the first place."

"But the blood of our slain comrades demands it. That was my brother he killed."

"And six others, all our true companions."

"By Allah, he moved like the very Angel of Death. No, no human could have done that—against fully armed men."

"And then to just disappear. . . . No, it is beyond us, comrades, as I said from the start. Let us admit the will of Allah when we see it and seek no more vengeance against devils."

There was agreement and the shadows began to retreat.

"Well, here, let's take the horses at least. The girls and the eunuch—they'll die of the cold in any case. No use letting good horseflesh go with them."

"No, no use at all," the other agreed.

In a moment, our mounts were gone, but along with them, our foes.

"They didn't come and get us," Esmikhan exclaimed, amazed and thanking heaven.

"They didn't even care." Safiye stamped her foot. "How is that possible? Do you know what ransom they were asking? Two thousand *ghrush*! How is it possible that they could just turn their back on us so?"

Then she went to the edge of the outcropping and shouted to the drizzle, "Fools! Damnable fools!"

"Well, you heard what they said." I was trying to explain our miraculous delivery to her as well as to myself. "Seven of their number must be dead, including Orhan and his son. It was Orhan who was really the driving force behind our kidnapping. His eye—it's been burning in his head all these years and now Allah has finally given him peace. The others—I don't suppose they had any personal grudge against Sokolli Pasha or the royal house. I think we may say that the bandits of Crazy Orhan are now effectively disbanded and will not bother the Porte again. Allah be praised."

"Fool!" Safiye said to me.

"Can you think of a better explanation?"

"Fool!" she said again, this time shouting it out over the countryside. "You praise Allah," she returned to me once more. "But now we don't even have any horses. The man was right. We are bound to die out here."

"But we can at least light a fire now without fear," I said, beginning to gather kindling in earnest.

Esmikhan bent to help me, and even tore off a bit of the hem of her veil to get things started.

"Patience, dear Safiye," she begged of her friend. "Really, we have much to thank Allah for."

"Yes," I agreed as a tiny flame leaped to life. "Allah, in the person of that mysterious holy man."

By the time the sun rose, I'd finally gotten the girls comfortable enough to sleep. I slept, too, although somewhat fitfully. Once I started wide awake. I'd dreamed a re-enactment of our escape from the brigands, but this time there was no mistaking the face on the dervish as he whirled from victim to victim. It was my old friend, Husayn.

By God, I thought. *The things men dream!* But even waking did not replace that face with any other.

For want of another face with which to fill my thoughts, I let my mind linger over the sight of the two girls sleeping in a slant of early morning sunlight and in each other's arms. As she slept, Esmikhan lost the pinch of worry and cold, and her features sank back into their pleasant, blooming, almost infantile roundness which even now she only half unveiled. And Sofia Baffo—she took all the sun to herself, veilless, and remained as cool as alabaster. Sofia Baffo was still beautiful, still as chillingly beautiful as moonlight, still, after all—

I shook my head and stood up. I've heard it said that men who've lost an arm or leg are sometimes tormented by an itch in the missing limb, an itch they cannot scratch. My discomfort was like that. But more a need to empty my bladder. The mutilation tended to confuse sensations in that area. I walked past the fire, adding the last of our gathered wood to it as I did, and then out and on to a copse of oak.

Luminescent, hard-shelled beetles rattled across stone and gravel about their autumn business. White snails buttoned up every blade of grass and twig of bush. When I raised my eyes above these creatures, the copse offered a grand view of the countryside. No habitation or sign of humanity interrupted the wildness of the place, but below, a ribbon of water spangled like new-polished sequins on a woman's scarf and promised to lead the way. The aching brilliance and clarity of the world after a storm collapsed distances. And as the mist rose before the rising sweep of the sun, I found it strange that I could not hear the plash of the stream over the silence when I saw every ripple.

The vista remained rocky and steep in places. What herbage there was clung to the cracks of precipices and stunted in clumps: goat country, though so far I'd seen none. The rocks, for all their daunting untamed faces, were fragrant when the sun hit their soaked skins, the pools their pockmarks caught, and set them steaming.

Two birds soared high above through the gorge gap—a bar of sapphire—wing to wing. In my mind I called them hawks, although I knew only too well that hawks rarely hunted in pairs. I didn't like to think of them as vultures. A swift cloud of smaller birds skirted the threat. South, I thought, watching where they disappeared over the mountain behind me. I confirmed that observation by the angle of the sun.

Then I saw that the low, scrubby part of the copse was mulberry. Many of the bushes' leaves had blown away in the storm, but numerous berries still hung among the tangled branches. They were overripe and black, but a handful in my mouth brought all the sweetness of those last autumn days on the Brenta River lands when I was a lad. My mother, my nurse, the maids, would all be busy packing for the return to Venice for the winter and I was left to wander, find mulberries and eat to my heart's content until they called for me. They called all together, at once, and frantically at sunset, like a chorus of maenads. "Birichino! Birichino!" My pet name.

When I felt my heart grow discontent with its loss, I comforted it with another handful. At least I can still know the pleasure of mulberries, I thought, and set my mind instead on how the girls could eat these when they awoke. Then we could walk all afternoon. We could make good time in such brisk weather, downhill, even on foot. Certainly nightfall would find us among some humanity.

With such thoughts, I shifted my stance a bit so as not to splatter on breakfast and reached up into my turban for my catheter.

"Abdullah!"

In my start, the catheter dropped from my hand.

"Oh, there you are."

"My lady."

"I sensed, even in my sleep, that you had gone, and I was afraid. I—I dreamed that awful brigand was—"

"Yes, lady. I had a nightmare, too."

"Did you?"

"It's all right. The brigands are dead and can't hurt you any more. And I am just here."

"Answering nature."

"Yes."

"As any man must from time to time." She smiled, reassured.

"Yes, lady." The safety of formalities again.

"Excuse me."

"Go on back to the fire." My breath smoked like the damp stones. The dampness of the whole world around me was agony on my bladder. "I'll be back soon."

The instant she was gone, I dropped to my hands and knees, shuffling wildly through the damp oak leaves, staining my fingers, making them sticky and clumsy with crushed mulberry. The rain showering down on me from the oak twigs seemed to send my brain into my bladder and my pelvis was ready to burst with the strain. I couldn't find the damned catheter.

"Abdullah? What's wrong?"

"Nothing. Go back to the fire."

"But what are you looking for?"

I blurted it: "My catheter. I dropped it—here—some-where."

"I don't know what that is. A catheter."

"And may you never have to know, lady."

"But how can I help you look if I don't know what we're looking for?"

"I don't want your—"

Esmikhan Sultan reeled back from my words as from a physical blow and I regretted my tone as much as I was able to regret anything beyond my own need.

With a deep breath, I said: "It's a thin brass tube about so long." I was so full of urgency and dread that my forefingers and thumb shook as I expressed the size between them.

Esmikhan dropped to her hands and knees beside me. "*Us-tadh, ustadh,* slowly, slowly. You move so wildly you're bound to knock it away from us. Let's go calmly and slowly and we'll find it."

Her plump little hand found mine under the leaves and pressed it until it stopped shaking.

"I . . . I might have a fever," I suggested rashly. "The damp and all."

"No, I don't think so." She swept my slipped turban back up out of my eyes with her other hand. What she saw in my face breached reserve with concern. "You mean to say you cannot relieve yourself without this little tube?"

I meant to be noncommittal while I searched under other leaves with my free hand. The truth was I could see better with the turban up where it belonged. I guess she could, too.

"Is this the case with all *khuddam*?"

"Not all are as . . . as radically served as I was. If one is younger . . ."

She pressed my hand again when I couldn't go on. "Ab-dullah, we will find it."

Desperate to change the subject, I asked: "Do you know

the wooden Tower of Leander?" When I spoke slowly and deliberately, my hands searched that way, too.

Esmikhan shook her head. She had looped the ends of her veil up and under her cap to keep them out of her face. Her cheeks were flushed with the open air. Her black eyes sparkled with the wind like the last of the rain clinging to the grasses.

"It is in Constantinople. It sits on a lone rock right in the center of the bay where the waters of the Golden Horn, the Sea of Marmara, and the Bosphorus all meet together, over against the Asian side. I am certain you can see it from your grandfather's palace and have passed it in your caïque many times. Your grandfather the Sultan likes to draw a chain from this tower across the entire bay and keep either untaxed trade or entire navies out. But there is a story to the tower, above and beyond its practical uses. My uncle told it to me."

"Tell me the story."

"It is said that the fair Hero of ancient times lived in that tower and every night her lover Leander, of whom her family disapproved, would swim out across the water to be with her. Just before dawn, he would swim back again."

"How could he see his way?"

"Hero would light a lamp for him and set it in her window."

"That's a sweet story."

"Not so sweet. One night, a storm blew out the lamp. As the brave Leander floundered without guide, the high waves overcame him and he was drowned."

"Oh, no."

"When Hero looked out of her lonely tower with the morning light, she saw her lover's body washed up on her rock. For grief, she flung herself down from the tower and died."

"How awful! I liked the story better when it ended earlier."

"But this way is more like real life—it never ends soon enough."

"Ah, say not so, Abdullah. Not the day after you have rescued me from a fate worse than death."

"Look for the tower when you cross back into Constantinople. You cannot miss it. I could see it even from Pera, from the high little window, through its bars and over the red-tiled roofs while I suffered my end. And there was nobody to save me from a fate worse than death."

I meant to stop right there. That was already more than enough to say, in fact. But I found myself speaking with an urgency suddenly more desperate than my physical need.

XLVIII

I TOLD ESMIKHAN Sultan all about that dark little house beyond Pera, how it was set in the midst of gnarled old olive trees.

"That must have been nice," my lady exclaimed.

"So no one could hear my screams," I quickly disabused her. "So no one would come to my rescue."

I continued. I couldn't stop myself. "The trees were in bloom and the pollen swelled my eyes shut while I slept. Sometimes sheep wandered through the orchard, shifting boulders in the springtime mist."

"It was in spring?"

"Yes."

"A hard time for such a fate."

"Ramadhan came."

"Yes, I remember. Most of my life, the holy fast has been in the summer and we haven't been allowed a sip of water in the heat until after sundown."

"You know, the first time I heard the cannon from the walls——"

"The cannon that announces the end of the fast every night at sundown?"

"Yes. The first couple times I heard that, I thought, 'It's my countrymen. They've turned their big guns on Serai Point. They've come to rescue me.'"

"But they hadn't. They wouldn't. And once I thought about it, I decided I didn't want them to. Not like this. There can be no recue from this fallen state."

I took a breath and continued: "Then there was the Night of Power, just when I was starting to feel——well, not myself again. I shall never be myself. But——better. A little better. The Night of Power, what irony! When Muhammed was translated to the moon on his fabulous steed——"

"Blessings on Allah's Prophet."

"And all the minarets are lit with lamps."

"Like Hero's tower. I will always think of that from now on."

"There was such a minaret just over the tops of the olive trees, a low one, a little neighborhood mosque with moss on its tiled roof. Five times a day, the call came, measuring out the time of my torture. I found it a most melancholic sound."

"Did you?"

"Void of all hope."

"It must just have been that muezzin."

"Perhaps. But the birds in the orchard——to torment me,

there were lots of birds about their spring rites. And a nightingale, even. I heard a nightingale, just returned from the south. He sang every evening.

"And when the mist cleared, I could see all the way to the water, to Leander's Tower, from the tiny barred window of my second-story cell. The view was like a painting. The festival, and all that came after it. A painting. Captured. Artificial. Cropped. A painting your religion believes it is presumptuous of mere mortals to make in tortured imitation of Allah's creation. That painted world, that world of happy, bustling people had nothing to do with me. No more. I would never enter it again."

Yes, slowly and deliberately was easier.

"They gave me nothing but plain water for a day after my arrival—like a pullet is starved, or a sacrificial goat. To make the cleaning easier. And on the morning of the second day, they brought me a warm posset and I was so hungry that I drank it right off without considering its contents. Only later, with the cramps, the diarrhea, and the terrible unquenchable thirst, did I realize it must have been a special brew. To purge me."

"Aloe? Autumn crocus? Mandrake? Mustard?"

"All of those, any of those, more besides. Yes, I remember the smell of mustard and garlic, but that may have been to cover the other things and make me think the mess was edible. Anyway, while I was in agonies in the privy, I overheard Salah ad-Din and another man with a high, whiny voice discussing my case. I'd had to stand before them—in my sickness—like Michelangelo's *David*."

"I don't know what that is," Esmikhan reminded me.

I had seen the famous Florentine statue in small plaster copies, but of course my lady had not. I began to try to explain it to her, but the notion of nakedness was too offensive to her sensibilities to even imagine trying to capture it in art.

"Well, I certainly didn't feel as beautiful, as nonchalant as young David," was the best assurance I finally found for her.

" 'What beautiful lines! What physique!' said Salah ad-Din, just as if I had been a masterpiece. Heedless of what I felt, he poked and prodded with his bony fingers." I closed my eyes at the memory. "He poked until I rose in spite of myself. The two of them had a laugh at this and commented how that would be the last time I enjoyed that sensation. This was Allah's will for me. I don't think they realized I spoke Turkish this well. I didn't realize it myself, until I became a subject and it seemed a matter of life and death.

" 'We must drag and crush him so he can still function,' Salah ad-Din said. Drag and crush. Those were words a client might use when he complained of what had happened to his cargo in transit.

"Salah ad-Din was not complaining. 'Such reflexes! There's many a high-born lady will pay top price for a certified eunuch with such looks, such youth, if he can satisfy her without the ill effects.'

" 'But look,' said the whiner. 'He's already got a bit of fuzz. He's too old. To drag and crush when they are this old is too dangerous.'

" 'You are a skilled artist, my friend.'

" 'There is art and there is foolishness. To drag and crush will kill him.'

" 'Try it.'

" 'I daren't.'

" 'He's a strong, sturdy lad.'

" 'I can see that.'

" 'There's nothing builds them ruggeder than a sailor's life.'

" 'I appreciate that.'

" 'He'll survive—*inshallah*.'

" '*Inshallah,* perhaps, but I can't guarantee it. Maybe one chance in ten.'

" 'It's a risk I'm willing to take.'

" 'Not I.'

" 'You'll have your price, by my life, whether he lives or dies.'

" 'What guarantee have I of that?'

" 'My word.'

" 'No, old man. I've dealt with Salah ad-Din the Cutter before.'

" 'I'll give it to you up front.'

" 'Still, the death on my hands—'

" 'What are you squeamish for? You who spent twenty years in the cutting huts of Upper Egypt? You who'd do twenty or thirty little black lads a day? With the heat and the flies to exacerbate things?'

" 'I'm not so young any more.'

" 'Can't keep down your old man's gruel?'

" 'I've got the hereafter to think about.'

" 'Well, suppose we drag and crush him first and, after a day or two, if it doesn't look good, we quickly stop the spread of infection with the knives.'

" 'Do it to him twice in other words?'

" 'Only if it's necessary. To save his life.'

" 'And you'll pay me up front?'

" 'I'll give you the purse right now.'

I told Esmikhan how Salah ad-Din went then and made his wife give up the coins she was saving for a new sash. The only girdle she had to her name strained so thin in places you could see the color of her dress through the threads.

"They spoke idly after that, of market gossip. The next soul I saw was Salah ad-Din's wife, she with the wide girth and thinning sash. She brought me a cup of wine. But because it had a strange smell and because I could tell she hadn't forgiven me the loss of her coins yet, I decided to dump it out the window. I was asleep when they came for me—sheer boredom, I guess. But I was wide awake and struggling by the time they tried to strap me, naked and splayed, to the table in a windowless hut. The leather straps were black and stiff with blood.

"The second time I broke free of his grasp and managed to kick him, if not in the groin, at least close enough to count, Old Whiny said, 'Salah, you fool. This fellow's not drugged.'

" 'Of course he is. He's strong and resilient, that's all.'

"Another good kick.

" 'Oooh—! He's not drugged.'

" 'I had my wife—'

" 'Maybe she drank it herself. Instead of getting her sash. Quick, have her brew more or he'll break your corroded old straps while we work on him.'

" 'I told you he was strong. *Mashallah,* what a fighter!' Salah ad-Din said, full of pride, as he hurried off to comply.

" 'Pfah! When I was in Egypt, we got new straps every six weeks or we didn't work. The desert dryness and all.' Old Whiny whined this to himself as consolation, for I managed to keep him at bay with only my legs free.

"But when Salah ad-Din returned, the two of them together got at least some of the opium wine past my teeth. They hadn't the patience, however, to let it take full effect. As soon as they managed to get my stupefying legs bound, I suffered the pulling, yanking, then crushing of my very nature between two ribbed stones while yet half awake.

"Then, thankfully, oblivion set in."

Next I told Esmikhan how, when at length I came to, I heard Old Whiny say, " 'Doesn't look good. Not good at all.' "

"And Salah ad-Din: "Very well, old man. You win. Take it all off and see if you can save his blaspheming Christian hide.'

"This time when they returned me to the table, they lowered two of the legs on hinges so that my reeling head was lower than my torso, the blood throbbing in my brain. This time they wanted me awake."

I told her how they bound me tight about the abdomen with linen bands till the circulation pulsed to a stop. I told her how they made the cut, quick, clean, and close to the belly, with a piece of new-chipped obsidian as this was less likely than forged knives to fester. How they cauterized the wound with iron, red-hot from the fire. And how both cutting and burning caused pain enough to wipe heaven and earth from existence.

"And for this they wanted you awake, poor Abdullah?" my lady asked.

"They wanted me awake because for two hours after they have swabbed you with comfrey and myrrh—and I can't bear the smell of these simples to this day, even at your hands, lady—after this, and after they have made a pack of clean desert sand to take the place of what you've lost—"

" 'In the desert,' Old Whiny said, 'we used to bury them up to their necks in sand. Well, we had the sand for it there. We hardly lost a one.'

"—After this, and while you vomit where there is nothing left to vomit, and faint as the pain rips down your legs and kills them, your torturers must keep you on your feet. They must walk you back and forth and back and forth in the tiny hut, the scene of your very death throes. Back and forth to keep the blood going to heal what you can never be healed of. And all the while, there in a bucket, gathering voracious spring flies, is all that's left of your manhood."

"Nur Banu—" Esmikhan gulped. "Nur Banu once had a eunuch that came to us all the way from China. He kept his—

his parts with him always, preserved in honey, in a jar on a chain about his neck. He believed he would see no life in the hereafter if they weren't buried with him."

I felt a flush of fear. What if the heathen beliefs of a single man from the edge of the map might prove true after all? My own beliefs were so disturbed by what had happened to me that I gave this fear some moment's dreadful credence.

Then I moved the scene quickly on to three days later, three days of which I have very little recollection, and that recollection is crucified with pain.

"I will gloss over those tortures except to remark that all those three days, I was unable to relieve myself. Though they refused even water for my parched tongue, the pressure on my bladder swelled up into the ghastly amputation.

"On the third day, they came to remove the bandages. They seemed to expect something, but nothing happened.

"Old Whiny whined: 'A plug of pus. He cannot pass his urine. It's death for certain, and in the most horrible way. I'm sorry, old man. We did our best—'

"Anger clenched my inflamed flesh and, when the easiest way would have been to avoid the pain—a pain greater than any I had known—anger pushed against it. Anger pushed out the hard, yellow plug, and a fountain of putrid, scalding urine followed. Old Whiny got all soiled and stinking, but he didn't care. 'You'll have to give him a catheter, Salah, old man. But the *khadim* will live.'

"He could not have given me a harsher sentence. Life," I concluded. I shook now from head to toe and vomited up the mulberries.

☙

WHEN MY BELLY was empty, Esmikhan Sultan opened her palm. In it lay the catheter. She had found it earlier, much earlier, and tried to give it to me then. But I had been so caught up in the spilling of this horrible tale that no muscle left to me could sphincter off, I hadn't taken it. I took it now.

"When we get home, Allah willing, I will have a jeweler make you a new one, Abdullah, a silver one," she said.

I laughed harshly. That was a ridiculous substitute. But I did remember when I'd thought to buy a coral for old Piero's ear. Where was he now, sleeping with fishes? I had lost my chance, for that as for so many things.

I took the catheter from her hand and turned my back. The brass was warm from her touch.

XLIX

Esmikhan Sultan couldn't sleep.

"You expect me to go back to sleep after what you've told me?" she asked. "How can I sleep?"

She was having no trouble eating, however. She popped mulberries into her mouth like a nervous tic and, between whiles, scraped the leaflets off stem after stem of a patch of wild thyme our scrambles had uncovered by its thick scent.

"I eat when I'm distressed," she apologized.

"Lady, all your life you've slept under the watchful eye of creatures who've undergone torments similar to mine." Personally, I was exhausted, suddenly more exhausted than I'd ever been in my life. The reliving of the past six months had turned my joints to a stiff, achy gel.

"But I never knew," she protested. "People don't talk about things like that."

"You assumed the sexless ones were born that way."

"Perhaps. Yes. Why not?"

"Well, they're not."

"Don't be angry with me. You can't be angry with me for ignorance."

"No. I'm not angry. Just tired. Let's go to sleep."

Her neat little mother-of-pearl teeth worked on another stalk with nervous precision. It must be distress that moved her. What else could make a person eat so much thyme straight without intervening pulse or meat stew?

"But I just can't think how to make it better," she fretted.

"Sleep would help—for a while, anyway."

"All these years I've reaped the benefit. . . ."

"Yes, and the benefit of little slave girls torn from the bosom of their families."

"I don't feel so badly about that. I don't know a single girl—once she gets used to it—who isn't better off in our harem than she was starving and shivering at home."

"Maybe they are careful to move the malcontents from your ladyship's view."

"We are kind to them; their fathers used to beat them. Why, look, even Safiye—"

"Yes, let's look at Sofia Baffo for an example."

"Some day she—*inshallah*—will be the mother of a Sultan. She couldn't have done that in Italy."

"No, indeed."

"And I think in many cases, eventually, it must be so with most of the *khuddam,* or more would be complaining, don't you think?"

"Lady, at the moment, I am complaining for lack of sleep."

"But I'm trying to sort out what I can do about your suffering."

"I would admire the tenacity of your empathetic feelings, lady, if they weren't interfering with sleep—yours and mine—and the good amount of walking we must do this afternoon if we are ever to get back to civilization."

"All of this, slaves and castration, is Allah's will."

"That's what Salah ad-Din and his cohort agreed upon."

"What can I, one little princess, do against Allah's will?"

"Yes. A whole system based on Allah's will."

"It's sinful even to contemplate thwarting Him."

"So let's not thwart the divinely given need for sleep one moment longer."

"You go back to the cave, Abdullah. You sleep. I can't."

I took a step or two in the direction of compliance, but then turned quickly toward her once more. Perhaps it was just exhaustion, but in those two steps I had had a vision of some vague threat. Beast or brigand, what did it matter? Heedless of how tired I was, I couldn't sleep as long as she was out here, exposed to God knows what.

"Look here, my lady. A man can suffer no greater defilement than what I have suffered. Death is preferable. There is nothing more to be said on the subject."

"But what if he were to suffer the defilement of all his harem?"

"Pfah, that is nothing. I hate to disillusion you, but as long as he's got his balls, a man can hope to return tit for tat and rape the other guy's harem. You don't know how many times I imagined Salah ad-Din's sloppy fat wife wriggling and screaming under me—"

It wasn't until I saw the ashen color Esmikhan's face took on that I realized just how cruel my words had been.

"That was what Crazy Orhan's son was about, wasn't it?" she asked.

"I guess so."

Her voice had grown very faint. "I think what you have suffered must be like rape is for a woman."

"Oh, no, lady. There is no comparison. After a rape, a woman gets up and goes on."

"Do you think so?"

"There is no going on for the likes of a—a creature like me."

"No, Abdullah. I am not at all certain I could have gone on if . . . if you hadn't . . . stopped it last night."

"Yes, well, look at Sofia."

"Safiye is something else again, Abdullah."

"A truer word was never said."

"I don't think you can say that what is true for Safiye is true for all other women or even many of them."

"I've no doubt you're right, lady."

"Sometimes I think Allah put her by accident on the wrong side of the harem curtain—if it weren't blasphemous to say so, for Allah makes no mistakes."

"Well put."

"She is difficult to rape and impossible to castrate."

"A remarkable, dangerous combination."

"But Safiye is not the normal case of the world. All I can say is, had you not saved me last night, my life would now be worthless. I would have wanted to die—even as you did after your mutilation."

"As I still do."

"No, Abdullah. Say not so! If you had died, so must have I. For certainly no other *khadim* in the whole world could have saved me as you did."

"Once a man is castrated, they can do nothing worse to him," I recited my litany. "An arrow through the brain—it would have been much, much easier."

"But only consider, Abdullah, what it is to us womenfolk.

Even if rape did not mean, as it very often does, rejection by our menfolk and eternal shame. Even if that were not the case, having known the fate worse than death, to live with the knowledge that it can happen again and again, any and every day of our lives until death. And having come so close and been rescued, that is still no release from the sentence of this curse. The realization of how vulnerable we are—it's made only so much more vivid. Perhaps some of the bodies—male bodies—to whom this violation can only happen once must suffer it to spare females, in as far as it is possible, the horror of the potential for repetition. Isn't our vulnerability worse than to know it can only happen once? You—you are free."

"Freedom, you call it?"

"Free, in Allah's hands. To know that now the worst is over and, Allah willing, you are free from any threat of any man."

"But there are scars. By Allah, the scars, the crippling of muscle for even the simplest of functions—"

"And how do you know we don't suffer scars, on the inside, where you can't see. Scars just as vicious and debilitating."

Esmikhan turned her face from me and I saw only the wind-whipped tail of her veil against the gentle roundness of her little shoulders.

"Perhaps you cannot think so, Abdullah, and if not, I am sorry if I've hurt you." She turned to me again, her eyes sparking with the wind. "The fact of the matter is, I can only be grateful that by your suffering once, you were in a position to save me similar suffering last night."

I grunted, even formulas failing me.

"I, at least, must say if Allah's will was that it had to happen—what happened to you in Pera—I can at least show some gratitude for His Almighty will."

"Gratitude! A curse on any God who could sit passively

by and let such a thing happen to a dog. You can apologize and say 'We are a civilized people, a pious people' and 'We have laws against such a thing.' You still encourage it to happen if not clandestinely in Pera, then openly in Egypt. 'They are pagan there. It doesn't matter.' By Allah, not a dog or a sheep or a steer should suffer so, much less a man, pagan or no. A curse on the God of all such creatures."

My burst of blasphemy silenced her babble for a while and pressed her lips together, thin and white. In exhaustion, I slumped to the ground beside her, arms over my head and my head between my knees.

"No, Abdullah," she said eventually, very quietly so perhaps she only thought it and, in the stillness, I was able to read her thoughts. "No, even now, try as I might, I cannot wish this thing undone against Allah's will. You may think this very selfish of me, or cruel, but I can't help it. For if Allah had never willed it done, I never would have known you and that—even after so brief a time, I can tell—that would be the greatest loss of my life."

Over the high, distant midmorning call of birds, I heard her front teeth working vigorously on bits of thyme. No mouthful was ever enough to send back to the molars; her incisors just made quick little rhythmic, nervous chops. Sleep thrummed up from the earth like the night's evaporating storm, like the hum of bees on a last-minute raid to the mulberries.

After a long, drowsy while, Esmikhan murmured as if in her sleep. "And Safiye has something to do with this, doesn't she?"

I felt myself floating on the warmth of the sun and could reply with no more than a grunt.

"I've seen you watching her, heard how you speak her name. Did Safiye bring you to this pass, Abdullah?"

This time my grunt attained no more than a deep sigh.

"Never mind. Perhaps, *inshallah,* you will tell me that story another time." Her voice drowsed into unburdened breath.

THE RECURRING DREAM of dervish and death brought me suddenly wide awake. Perhaps I groaned or even screamed. My lady, sleeping nearby with her veils all awry, and pillowed on the tuffet of thyme, stirred, too.

"Abdullah? What is it?" she murmured.

"It makes sense. Finally, it makes sense."

"What makes sense?"

I doubted she could make much sense of anything, still half-asleep as she was. "Just a mystery that's been preying on my mind for a while."

"What mystery?"

"Nothing. Go back to sleep, lady. I'm sorry I disturbed you."

"I'm awake now. Besides, it seems late."

"The sun is past its zenith. We should be on our way soon. Rest until then, to build your strength. It was only something I dreamed."

"Now you must tell me. A dream untold brings misfortune. It must be told and analyzed."

"Is that a Turkish custom?"

"Custom? It is only common sense."

"Oh, I see."

"It will help me lose the drowsiness. Of what mystery did you dream?"

"Just something having to do with Salah ad-Din's death."

She sat straight up now without a hint of sluggishness. "Salah ad-Din is dead?"

"Yes."

"The man who made you a slave and mutilated you is dead?"

"Yes."

"*Mashallah!* You never said that."

"I didn't?"

"*Mashallah!* How?"

"Murder."

"Abdullah——? Not you——?"

I gave a brief laugh at the horror in her face. "No, lady. Calm yourself."

"Well, I have seen what you did to the brigands. I know you're fully capable."

"Certainly I wished his death, wished it at my hands, every waking moment."

"*Mashallah.* Allah turn the evil of that thought from you."

"At first, of course, I was too weak to consider it. Later, as I mended in spite of myself, I began to look for opportunities. But he was wily, that Salah ad-Din, very wily. Mostly he had his wife see to me and kept his distance."

I continued: "Coward! Damnable coward, hiding behind his woman. I was allowed no knife. My food was heavy on the sweets and dairy foods they say make tractable eunuchs. Once in awhile a little veal, but not often, because of the cost and then always prepared in bite-sized pieces."

"It's a wonder you healed so well without flesh to eat," Esmikhan commented.

"And the other knife with which I would have taken my revenge on the wife, they'd done away with that as well."

"You never tried to escape?"

I had to smile at my lady's explicit faith in the proportions of my heroism. "I thought of it, yes. But you know Pera. I was kept in the center of Pera."

"It is the home of your countrymen."

"Exactly."

"But you could have escaped to them."

"Could I? And what sort of life was there for me back in Venice? Now?" I couldn't keep the cry of anguish from my voice.

"Your women have no *khuddam*?" Her voice was full of sympathy—for Venetian women more than for me.

"Of course not," I snapped. *We are not barbarians,* I almost continued. Then I thought better of it and sought to ease any hurt my curtness might have caused with: "Unless they can sing."

"With you they make *khuddam* just to sing?"

"Now, that is odd, isn't it? Well, I can't sing. I've never had a voice. In any case, I couldn't bear the shame. I've already told you about those two countrymen of mine I overheard in the bazaar, how mortified I was for them to see me. The more I thought about it, the more I realized what an effective fence Salah ad-Din had created in his location. What other life had he left for me to return to?"

"I see. But the murder, Abdullah. Get to the murder."

"I'm coming to it. As I was saying, I had about decided just to kill myself and at least deprive the bastard of the profit of his deed. I had even fashioned a rope from old sheeting that

I hoped could bear my weight. I had it hidden under my pallet for the hour I should get my courage up. I was about to do it, too."

"Speak not of that, Abdullah, only to thank Allah your hand did not succeed against yourself. But the *murder*—"

"I actually had the rope swung over a dubiously rotten rafter when they brought the body home."

"From where?"

"Salah ad-Din had gone across to the City that day to see to his shop in the bazaar. Most days, actually, this was his custom. He often slept across in Constantinople, to save himself the trip. Whatever there was between him and his wife—and a mismatched pair they were, too, he so thin and she so fat—it was nothing the Greek prostitutes—or his own merchandise, for that matter—couldn't see to just as well. They had no children. In this he resembled his merchandise.

"So usually, it was just the wife and me in the little house, she with the keys to the door hung safely about her waist. She was trying to train me in a eunuch's social graces: how to serve at table, how to run errands, how to shop in the bazaar with a woman's eye, how to lard my Turkish with elegant phrases as opposed to sailor's talk, how to hold the curtains as she got in and out of a carriage, all of that.

"And she tried to make a Muslim of me. 'That you were uncircumcised when you came here is no longer an issue, is it?' she told me. 'That is the biggest fear most men face for conversion—unless they're Jews to begin with. You know, there is honor for your kind among us. Only *khuddam* are allowed to be attendants in the holy cities of Mecca and Medina. Didn't you know that? Female pilgrims need guides as well as male, of course. And *khuddam* stand guard at the boundaries between sacred and profane as well as between men and women, that other boundary Allah in His All-Knowing wisdom ordained. Perhaps, if you embrace the Faith with your whole heart, *inshallah,* this could some day be your calling.' "

Esmikhan asked with some concern: "She didn't make a Muslim of you, Abdullah?"

"One who is neither male nor female can stand at the boundary between Christian, Jew, Muslim, and pagan, can he not?"

"I suppose."

"She was a nice enough woman, I guess, in her own sloppy way, though my thirst for revenge found it difficult to see her as anything but vengeance's object. She did favor capers in her cooking—even a eunuch's food—entirely too much. A Turkish woman married to an Italian turncoat who gave her no children, not an enviable fate. She might have been more apologetic for the way in which her husband earned his living at my expense. I suppose she would have been, too, if the fact that he usually couldn't afford to provide her with a eunuch—just a little Armenian girl in the kitchen—didn't tempt her into taking full advantage of one when she had him.

"In any case, I did my best to learn as little as possible— of everything."

"Oh, Abdullah, you are too modest."

"Salah ad-Din came from time to time to have a home-cooked meal and see how we were coming along, how soon the profit could be turned on his investment. His wife had a vested interest in this. Her sash frayed right in two while I was dawdling along."

"But the last time this man came home?"

"Dead. Throat cut. In the bazaar. The men who found him—other slavers—ferried him over and brought him up to the house, laying him out on a low wooden couch covered with a white sheet in the courtyard. It was summer, hot, and the flies had already found and followed him. He stank. The new widow was beside herself. It was, in fact, her screams, that made me leave my purpose with the sheet just tossed over the rafters. Oh, she could wail! Keening until the rest of us would fain lose our wits as well."

"Poor woman."

"Anyway, I was sent down to the local mosque for the imam at once and I had to help with the washing of the corpse."

"Yes?"

I shrugged. "I was sent for sheeting and I pulled the stuff down from my rafter and used that to wash him with."

"Yes?"

"It was then that I saw what the men who brought him had been careful to conceal from his wife. The man who'd cut his throat had also castrated him, leaving a gaping red-black hole alive with blue bottles. It was impossible to say whether he'd bled to death from the neck or the groin first."

"So it must have been someone with revenge on his mind. Someone who knew—"

"Revenge. For me? Or others? I didn't know. It didn't matter. It was enough that he went to his grave without his manhood, without children and that hope of eternity—if he has the faith of your Chinese. Same as he condemned me to do."

"Allah balances all, they say."

"In any case, very shortly thereafter—within two days— the widow learned that her husband had vast outstanding debts, never mind her sash money. With him gone, so was his credit. She had to sell it all—including me—to save a pittance to take back home to her brother's house. That was when I went to market, cheap. When Ali, unable to resist a bargain, even with a master the likes of Sokolli Pasha, bought me. Since then, there have been so many new things on my mind, I haven't thought about Salah ad-Din's end—except with brief feelings of warm justification—since then."

"So you don't know who did it?"

"I didn't. I didn't care. Some angel. So I was content to think until this morning."

"What happened this morning? Your dream?"

"Yes, partly. I also remembered the mutterings of the men who brought the body home."

"They had seen the murderer?"

"Someone had. 'A dervish,' they kept saying over and over again. 'A dervish. A crazy dervish.' That such a madman could never be found or put to death for his crime was clear to them."

"Dervishes have that ability to vanish in thin air."

"We saw that last night, didn't we?"

"A coincidence."

"More than a coincidence."

"So they never did find him?"

"I suppose not. But I have."

"You? How?"

"It was the same dervish that helped our escape last night. As I said, more than a coincidence."

"How can you be so certain? There are hundreds of dervishes. Thousands. And this one wasn't so crazy. More like a guardian angel."

"Exactly."

"You can't know it wasn't just the coincidence of two dervishes—two dervishes and a dream."

"But I know."

"How, Abdullah?"

"Because if your added gold teeth to that man's gap-toothed grin, a month's good eating to his skinny waist, trimmed his beard and hair, gave him a bath and the clothes of an Aleppo merchant, you'd have an old friend of mine. Husayn."

"He seemed familiar to you?"

"At first, familiar yet strange. But now, in the dream, I am certain of it. In some miraculous way I cannot say—"

"But that it was the will of Allah."

"Yes. In this case, I'll join you, lady, in saying it was Allah's will. By Allah's merciful will, my dear friend Husayn has given up his luxurious life of trade and become a homeless mendicant."

"It sounds to me as if his home is your constant aid. Abdullah, you are blessed indeed to have a friend like that."

"Yes. Yes, I am."

Truth to tell, at that moment, I had forgotten completely that there was ever any such thing as the secrets of Venetian glass.

I got to my feet and looked through the brilliant clarity of the afternoon wilderness about us, sensing I should be able to discover this dervish, my friend, Husayn, if only I looked hard enough. Like the mantle of Allah's will. But this was only the hope of a swelling gratitude with no place to put itself. Because there was nothing left for us to do to find our way back to safety but set one foot in front of the other, I knew perfectly well that no dervish would be found.

LI

FOR THE FIRST time in my life, I truly appreciated the Turks'
addiction to baths, the hotter the better. I came to stand before my master and Prince Murad, clean, warm, fed, rested,
and my arm doctored—yes, with comfrey and myrrh—to
kill the heaviness of infection. I felt like a new man, quite lit-
erally.

At the end of one afternoon of miserable wandering, we
had found a goatherd who'd given us directions, a bed, and
cheese in return for a single pearl torn from Esmikhan's
dress. We got the better of that deal. At the end of two
miserable days, his directions brought us to a scouting party
of janissaries who, in turn, brought us to their leaders in
Inönü.

But a bath washed all that misery away to no more than
the cozy memory of thick, warm quilts, and crackling, warm
braziers. I had the feeling of having been reborn, an exultation of immortality.

I felt so good that it was quite a shock to see how grim the
faces of Sokolli Pasha and the prince were.

The girls had been given time to recover, too: baths, new
clothes, sweet salves smelling of aloe and myrrh for their flea
bites. Esmikhan wore her veils. They had been washed, but
the hem of one was fraying: gone to our fire under the outcropping. Safiye had had to borrow veils to make herself
presentable. Anyone who knew her could see that these
drapes were of an older, more provincial style than she was

used to. The prince could not raise his eyes to meet hers through them.

Safiye and I flanked the princess like an honor guard at this first and irregular meeting with her betrothed. But there was something even more irregular about the men we faced across Inönü's divan. They were flanked by two others, big, burly creatures. Anyone in the palace knew enough to side-step these monsters, not so much because of their size, though that was awesome enough, but because of the fact that they had no tongues. They committed private executions—and were trusted to tell no tales afterward.

As if he, too, showed only a tongueless cavern of a mouth when he yawned, Sokolli Pasha silently placed three instruments on the low table in front of him with his long, talon-like fingers. His face was firm with duty. Just such a mask he must have worn as he came upon Orhan with a burning poker before the man went crazy.

Two of the weapons were daggers. The third, the one in the middle exactly opposite Esmikhan, was a bowstring made of silk. Ottoman blood may never be spilt, whatever the crime. It must be strangled.

A long silence followed. Perhaps we were meant to defend ourselves in it. But Esmikhan simply bowed her head humbly under the silent weight. She was ashamed in front of her betrothed. And now she was quite convinced that what had happened to her in the brigand's hut deserved death.

I, too, could think of nothing to say. My lady was innocent, but death would be easier to bear than the guilt she felt. As for Safiye, nothing could be said in her defense, but to blame her would be to condemn myself.

Safiye didn't speak, either. At the time I thought it was because her very true guilt had caught up with her, and shamed her, for once, into holding her tongue. I know now it was because she didn't realize any defense was required of her.

Sokolli Pasha swallowed and shifted his firm, thin face under the firmer, more pinched mask of his duty. He raised a hand and the mutes rocked with anticipation on their heels.

And then a groan escaped from Murad's lips. One pale, pasty hand crossed over his eyes and smeared tears down across his cheeks. They seemed to wash away the little layer of healthy tan he had only recently acquired.

"Ten days," he moaned. "Ten days we searched these hills for you, my angel, my most fair one, and knew not where to find you. What I have been through," he choked, then recovered, "in those ten days."

Safiye spoke lowly and her voice seemed to build the privacy of a bed between them. "But I am back with you now, my prince, my charm and my strength. Let us thank Allah and rejoice."

"Rejoice! I shall go to my grave," the prince choked again, "without you, my love. My death shall follow so quickly upon yours, my beautiful, beautiful, faithless one. My faithfulness shall pursue your faithlessness across all the vaults of eternity."

"My death. . . ." Safiye began to realize.

"Yes, yes!" Murad said, and rose to flee the room. "Kill her!" he cried to the mutes. "Kill her first of all. I cannot endure her faithless presence in this world one moment longer."

"I am condemned, then, on suspicion. Mere suspicion of. . ." She swallowed and picked up her defense as a reckless young soldier does his shield when he prepares to dive into battle. "Is not the vow of my eternal faithfulness enough for you, my love?"

Murad looked at her for the first time, seeing through the veils as a lover can see through any garment. He wavered on his fleeing feet. His head raised itself to nod in violent emotion. But then he tore his eyes away and shook his head instead.

"But all ten days," Safiye said. "All ten days when I thought the world would end without you, Esmikhan and I were under the most careful protection of Veniero—Abdullah, the *khadim* here."

I hadn't the slightest desire to say anything in defense of Baffo's daughter. But she had shifted the blame to me and I refused to take it, particularly not at the verge of death. I had to say something, with five pairs of mute eyes on me and only heaven to prove my innocence against the devilish enticement of her beauty, leaking even through veils.

"I have enjoyed the baths of Inönü," I said, "and this puts me in memory of a way Allah may be called in to try the proof of guilt in this case. It is customarily reported that an innocent woman may walk through a bath full of men with no ill effect while the guilty—"

I looked at Sofia Baffo and she parted her veils ever so slightly to meet my stare. Her eyes over the film of silk were as hard as almond shells. I had to look away first.

"—The guilty have their shame exposed."

Well, Baffo's daughter's galliard to the tune of "Come to the Budding Grove" just might bring a wind into a men's bath strong enough to blow her skirts over her brazen head.

I felt rather than saw a shift of hope under Esmikhan's veils beside me. She believed in the custom and would be willing to try it. A pain in my belly—above my scars—suddenly prayed she could. I cared not for my life, not for Baffo's daughter. But all at once, I was fighting for my lady's honor—and for her life. I urged: "My lords have heard of the custom, perhaps?"

I read my master's face. He didn't particularly believe in

this superstition, but he was a man of violent justice. He did believe in allowing victims to prove their innocence when possible, and was willing to fight for that possibility when not readily granted. I also read a glance of gratitude in my direction. He appreciated that my quick thinking was helping him out of an unpleasant duty.

"That is an old wives' tale!" Murad suddenly exploded. "Only foolish women and eunuchs would believe such prattle."

I'd missed what had passed between Sofia Baffo and her prince. Perhaps Baffo's daughter believed just a little too much in the wind of a man's bath. I liked to think so, but liking didn't help us around the fact that this proof of innocence was now rejected.

"I do not trust that eunuch," Murad bit the words off fiercely. "I haven't from the start. I should have killed him that first evening in the *mabein* at Kutahiya."

I saw my master struggle to gain control from the brief flinch that lashing caused him. I was, after all, his responsibility. He touched the dagger that pointed at my heart.

Murad went on: "Besides. One eunuch against a dozen brigands. For ten full days. Brigands with no honor, with axes of their own revenge to grind. Even were he a giant of a man, I cannot, I cannot believe this Abdullah could defend you."

Yes, kill us all, I thought, bowing my head. I've wanted to die for six months and now—well, better late than never. Now is as good a time as any, than to face such continued insults from such as calls himself a man.

Beneath her borrowed veils, Safiye moistened her lips. It was an invisible gesture, but one that bound the magic of shared quilts even tighter between the two.

"My vows are of no use," she said (and one could hear the delicious moistness of her pouting lips in those words). "Neither are the tokens of my body because, as Allah is my judge, you know I gave them all to you—gladly, joyfully—on the night of Id al-Adha."

Murad turned from the memory with a moan as if it had struck him a physical blow.

"Save in that it yearns to return to yours as a pigeon to its roost, in my body there are no proofs," Safiye reiterated. "And yet in Esmikhan's there are." She paused to let the meaning of her words sink in.

Then she continued: "My prince, your sister and I shared this trial together. And, by the mercy of Allah, we also share in the deliverance—unscathed, by my life. Prove my faithfulness by hers. Please. Marry her to the honorable Pasha as planned. Look for the tokens of virginity. I swear by my honor and hers, you will find them. Then you will know for certain that what I say is true.

"If the marriage bed is not stained, then, yes, you will have every right to kill us, all three of us, and with perfect conscience. If, however, you find the tokens present, you will know that our guardian, Abdullah, did not receive the wound on his arm in vain as he put his body between us and those who would have defiled us. You will know that by his diligence, and by the mercy of the All-Knowing One, we were spared the fate you imagine for us. You will know that you may reclaim us without shame or dishonor, but with twice the joy that was all our sorrow during that nightmare of ten days."

Murad stood intoxicated by her words and by their promise. Color flushed his cheeks and even his beard seemed to grow ruddy with health and hope. I think he would have rushed across the room, and taken Safiye in his arms then and there. But he remembered, suddenly, that there were others present, and he turned to Sokolli Pasha instead.

My master had been looking steadily at me ever since the

middle of Safiye's speech had called attention to my feat—
what it had been, if indeed it had been. My master's eyes
seemed to wonder if even the best of his janissaries could have
fulfilled such a dangerous assignment with such success. And
under his gaze, I began to feel a little remarkable, too. He
made me almost proud to hold that post of such great trust,
proud to have traded manhood for that trust.

But quickly I humbled myself and dropped my eyes from
Sokolli's gaze. Of course he looked at me because, in all de-
cency, and even though she was veiled, he could not look at
Esmikhan, not until ritual—and duty—demanded it.

As soon as my eyes were gone from him, Sokolli Pasha
spoke. "Very well," he said. "I am content with this test—as
it also clearly pleases my master, Prince Murad."

Then he dismissed the mutes with a wave of his hand.

LII

I HAVE SINCE heard lavish descriptions of how Sultan Suleiman gave his granddaughter away out of the palace in Constantinople. I've heard of the festivities that accompanied
the occasion, how the viziers vied with one another for the
honor of walking—not riding as is their usual right—before
the pavilion draped in blinding cloth-of-gold that covered her
horse from mundane view. These marketplace historians

confuse the occasion—in their nostalgia for the empire's past glories, perhaps—with another princess's bridal day.

I, who was in Inönü on the day, don't bother to correct them. Their memories comfort me that the our efforts to conceal the true irregularities of the case have worked completely.

The worthies of Inönü did their best, but even helped lavishly from Sokolli's purse, their resources were but pitiful compared to those with which the Sultan would have feted his granddaughter and Pasha in the capital. Half a day's warning was insignificant against the months of planning for weeks of celebration Constantinople would have provided. The governor's home in that small provincial town was like a closet when one thought of the Imperial palace, Sokolli's palace, and the arena of the hippodrome between them in which the guests, spectators, and entertainments could spread.

Nonetheless, it was thought better this way. If things did not work out, the shame could be quickly buried in the provinces, and the capital never the wiser.

Of course, there was little here that conjured the idea of "wedding" to my mind. There were no silk- and flower-draped gondolas on the Grand Canal, no high mass in St. Mark's with the formal procession of bride and maids. Nothing I had always imagined along with the words "happily ever after."

Esmikhan didn't even put in an appearance. If a woman is without male guardian, she may send a eunuch to the ceremony in her stead. But my lady had her brother and, while the legal documents were drawn up, Murad stood in his best brocades, brown and blue silk turban with the phesant-feather aigrette, facing the imam opposite Sokolli Pasha.

Even as a eunuch I had little notion what the women did all the while in the harem. I stood guard, arms crossed in defensive stance over a new ceremonial dagger, at the stairs to the forbidden area. Only once in a while was I sent: "Out for more henna!" "*Khadim,* more scarves to drape the bed!" "What? Have all the *taratir at-turkman* gone to the men? The Fair One will not have it. Fetch us a tray at once, *ustadh.*"

But like Venice there was music. The folk of Inönü managed to foot an orchestra, aided by musicians from Sokolli's squadron of janissaries. The instrumentation relied heavily on the drums and played only haphazardly on any beat but the martial. This, however, they set to with a good will and vigor until the seams of the old stone house where the formalities were reaching their climax seemed ready to split with trying to contain them. Nowhere in the building—or in the neighboring ones, either, I dare say—could one go without the rhythm coming in pursuit, sending jolts up and down the skeleton. To this rhythm the local singers did their best to fit the traditional wedding songs, but the tunes had the thrust of war. Clearly the ease of bride, or, more particularly, of groom, could hardly be hoped for against such odds.

Old dust and drying herbs thumped down on our heads, as the beat rocked from the heavy center of the drum skin to the rattling rim and back again. There was no help for it: my attention was continually drawn up through the rafters and the floor boards where fate rested on a marriage bed in Sokolli Pasha's hands. In Allah's hands, my lady might have corrected me.

Prince Murad's mother, sisters, and retainers had continued on to Constantinople from the moment of the brigand's raid so as to be out of harm's way. Without their calming influence, the prince was anxious. Perhaps something I was missing made him contain his anxiety worse than I did, standing still at my post.

Murad paced back and forth like rude gusts of winter wind

among the strangers he should have been entertaining. The drums openly rattled his heart like a dried gourd. He seemed close to bursting, and the local men, not fully comprehending the reasons, thinking their prince had only a sister's honor at stake here, stood in awe of the sensitivity of royal blood.

One reverend gentleman with age to protect him ventured to suggest, "Patience, young prince. Who of us has not had a sister marry? Ninety-nine times out of a hundred, all is well, thanks be to Allah. And Allah, who smiles with favor on the house of the Ottomans on the battlefields of Asia, Africa, and Europe, surely He will not frown now on so small a field as the marriage bed."

"But why is he taking so damned long?" Murad exploded.

"Now, majesty, love does not come so fast after a certain age as it does in youth."

"That Sokolli Pasha will drive me to my grave! My grandfather adores him, but I say it is because they are both so old and doddering. . . ."

"Fie, son!" the old man said, and hastened to add words to protect the souls of his rulers from evil spirits. "The Pasha is an excellent man. He has not the haste of youth, perhaps, but certainly it has been replaced by firmness and good, solid sense, not senility. If he moves slowly, it is because he knows she is a virgin. No one spills Ottoman blood unadvisedly."

The little old eyes glittered mischievously between age-weighted lids, but Murad passed them by with impatience. Two strides brought him to the foot of the stairs that led to the wedding chamber, ten strides and he had escaped that sight to hide at the other end of the hall, nine strides and he was back again. He cocked his head and listened, his brassy beard suggesting a wild beast that remembered the freedom of a jungle through which it had once roamed. Murad listened as if anyone could hear anything over the throb of those drums. As if he could hear not only the rain that was falling outside on the already-saturated road to Constantinople, but every breath taken in the room upstairs.

Suddenly something was heard over the janissaries' drums: women's trills of joy from the infinity of the harem above and behind us. Murad shoved others out of his way to see: an old, old woman, whose task it was to be judge of such things, was making her way down the stairs in full state. She was reciting from the Koran. Murad waited only to hear that they were verses from the Sura in which evil men sought to disparage the honor of the Prophet's favorite wife. After a night spent lost in the desert in the company of a strange young man, Heaven vindicated her: " 'Did not the faithful of both sexes . . . say, "This is a manifest lie" . . . ?' "

Murad stayed long enough for only half a glance at what the old woman held stretched out between her fingers like a tent between its gnarled stakes: the fabric of his sister's *shalvar*, stained with blood. Murad nearly ran into me in his haste, and stopped long enough to meet my eyes. He said nothing, but dropped his lids for one brief second—as close as a son of Othman may ever come to a bow acknowledging indebtedness to anyone. Then he was gone, up the stairs three at a time and into the *mabein* where he'd told Safiye to wait.

The drums struck up a triumphal march and the old woman and her burden were paraded around and around as if it were the personal victory of every man there. I got out of their way by taking the stairs. I stood and watched the festivities from the balcony for a while, a window open for the cool night air at my back. Then I turned to retire. Imagine how startled I was to find, in the shadows at my elbow, my master, watching likewise.

I bowed, clumsy in my surprise. "Felicitations, master," I managed to say.

"Thank you, Abdullah." Something struggled under his

rich bridegroom's robes. "Excuse me a moment," he said.

I looked away, embarrassed, as he turned to the window. The dark night air possessed just the quality it had had over the Grand Canal from the Foscari's chamber so many lives and deaths ago. A dark cloud of jealous grief swept over me for what he had that I didn't.

But then the most absurb squawk made me turn back to him with a start. I was just in time to see a paroxysm of black feathers disappear into the night. In a moment, the capon my master had loosed crowed prematurely and ineptly to set his ruffled dignity to rights under cover of darkness.

"My master," I couldn't help but laugh. "What on earth was that?"

Over the hawk's beak of his nose, his right eye almost winked. "I took him to your lady's chamber with me. In case things hadn't—worked out."

"You would have killed him?"

"Cut his throat and used his blood instead of hers."

"You would have done that? To cover for me?"

"I never doubted you, Abdullah. Nor your lady. Only Murad's fair one. But what can one do with the favorites of princes? They make life difficult for the rest of us, don't they?" He took a deep sigh. "It was myself I needed to cover for—in case—There is no reason either of you should suffer for my deficiencies."

I wasn't sure what he meant but didn't feel it was my place to pry. "So the bird flies free, master. Congratulations I say again."

"But more congratulations are due to you, I believe. A group of my men went up into the gorge, according to the directions you gave them, and found the brigands' hut today. They've just returned with nothing but an old woman, half mad, whom I suppose we shall have to release onto charity.

More pious donations are due, I suppose, out of my purse to commemorate the event."

"Allah's will," I murmured. He sounded nothing like a groom on his wedding night.

"Yes, but it is more than that. My men reported the scene in the hut; seven burly, hard-bitten criminals dead these three or four days and unburied. Abdullah. . . ."

I blushed under his gaze. "Believe me, sir, I'm not responsible for a half of those deaths. There was another, a dervish. . . ."

"A dervish?"

"Yes. He killed most of them. While I merely acted as diversion."

"What sort of dervish? What did he look like?"

"To tell you the truth, sir, he resembled an old friend . . . but maybe I only dreamed. No, I cannot say."

"No. It is hard to say with dervishes. Most of them look alike. It is the anonymity of being lost in Allah."

"Yes, master."

"And, as they're all elusive as shadows, I think you must not hesitate to take most of the credit for this in his stead. Abdullah, I thank you. I could not have faced my master, the Sultan, again with the dishonor of his granddaughter on my head. From the bottom of my heart, thank you."

He touched my arm then as if he, my master, were half afraid of its strength. "I thank Allah my trust in you was not misplaced."

His words moved both of us unaccountably. I was glad to be able to bow now and escape something in his eyes that asked—or offered, I could not tell which—so much more.

I turned to move away without dismissal, a breach of form which Sokolli Pasha quickly spoke to cover for me. "Yes, Abdullah. Get your sleep. You have earned it well indeed."

"Good night, master."

"Good night, Abdullah."

As I turned, I noticed a smear of red-brown on the back of his neck. More blood? Or was it henna that had not had time to soak into my lady's hands properly in just one hurried half a day?

But I left him standing there over the celebration of his victory which he took little notice of, and certainly no credit for. Nor did he return to the marriage chamber that night to take his victory again.

For a complimentary copy of the Ann Chamberlin newsletter, please send your name and address to:

Ann Chamberlin Newsletter
c/o Forge Books
175 Fifth Avenue
New York, NY 10010